Dodie
Hamilton

Fragile
Blossoms

Thanks, as always, to John and Josie Lewin, founders of Spirit Knights Paranormal Investigation; to Pat and Poppa Jay in Spain for their endless generosity; to Ingka Charters, the Artist, and Julie Whitton Dexter whom I love most dearly, and to Simon Richard Woodward, the Magic-Man.

This story, a glance into Edwardian English life, is dedicated with love and respect to my sister, Audrey Little Night Hawk, and her Family and her People.

Other books by Dodie Hamilton

Letters to Sophie
The Sequel to A Second Chance

The Spark
Prequel to The Lighthouse Keepers

A Second Chance

Perfidia

Silent Music

Dodie Hamilton, The Spiritual Midwife, is known throughout the world for her work in psychic counselling and Healing, her particular interest being the Near Death and the Out-of-Body experience. Over thirty years she's given countless private consultations and appeared at the Mind, Body & Spirit Festivals. All her books and writings, no matter how real, how flesh and blood, as in say, A Second Chance, the first in the Gabriel Books, are borne of years of study and personal exploration, the late Robert A Monroe, of the Monroe Institute, Virginia, author of Journeys Out of Body, Far Journeys, and The Ultimate Journey, her mentor.

Thank you, Robert for All That Is..

http://www.chillwithabook.com/2017/08/
perfidia-by-dodie-hamilton.html

Three of my novels have one Reader's Awards:

A Second Chance won The Chill Reader's Award

Fragile Blossoms also won A Chill Award

Perfidia, the sequel to A Second Chance won a Chill Award and A Diamond Award.

Reluctant Angels, the Prequel to A Second Chance, and Dodie's latest novel has received The Readers Chill Award.

Kill or Cure

A dainty little china cup was the first to go - a pretty thing, so fragile and fine one could see candle light shining through.

She ran to the shed and finding the biggest, heaviest hammer, went back to the cottage. A sun-beaten arm across the door, he tried barring the way.

'What are you going to do?'

Scornful, she ducked under his arm. 'I'm going to rid myself of a problem. I've borne the damned things long enough.' She set the cup on the table and swung the hammer. Always a good shot - Daddy used to say she could've played Hurling for Ireland - the cup exploded, sending costly porcelain flying.

Next to go was a triple cake-stand, a delicious thing, rose-sprigged with gilt edging. Plate, hammer, and table, she weighed up distance.

'Oh don't, madam!' the maid wailed. 'You surely can't mean to do that!'

'I surely can, and will, so, if you don't want to watch I suggest you leave!'

The maid ran weeping, her apron over her head.

One blow and the cake-stand disintegrated, gold metal pegs used to support the plates lethal bullets flying every which way.

Eyes as green as the seas he travels, he leant against the door-jamb, so handsome and so perfidious. 'You should cover your eyes. What you're doing is dangerous as well as foolish.'

'And you shouldn't be here!' she said. 'The cottage may be on yours, yet I am in possession therefore you trespass.'

'It's not my cottage.'

'Whose is it then?'

'Yours! I willed it to you this morning.'

'Why would you do that?'

He shrugged. 'I am a sailor, madam, my life in the hands of a ship's crew and Lord God Almighty - I thought to make your life more secure.'

'Am I supposed to thank you?'

Again he shrugged. 'It wasn't done with gratitude in mind.'

'Good because I'm not grateful. I don't want the cottage and I don't want you. You are here at your own invitation. Please leave! In staying you take advantage of your position.'

'And what is my position?'

'Where I am concerned it is nothing and nowhere.'

It's warm and the evening sultry. What they need is a storm to clear the air. She is aware of another watcher, a girl, a would-be woman who brought the village screaming to this door, and now unable to do worse peers through a spy-glass. I'll give them a storm, she thought. I mean mercy's sake, why waste time taking items down one-by-one when every shelf on the dresser is full.

Lace tearing, she pushed back the sleeves of her gown. 'If as you say this is dangerous you'd better stand back. I wouldn't want to hurt you.'

'Wouldn't want to hurt me?' He laughed. 'You hurt me every second of every minute of the day. You stab me through the heart and then you stab me again. Go ahead! Do your damndest! Kill the Meissen as you are killing me.'

She gazed at him. Unshaven and great coat travel-stained, he looked weary. Back from the farthest reaches of the earth, ship duly docked in Southampton, it's likely he's travelled all day, the horses sweating out in the yard.

'You called here first?' she said. 'You didn't climb the Rise?'

'I always call here first, don't you know,' he said his mouth tight. 'It's the rules of the game - the beloved first and the family second. I thought you knew that. Indeed, I thought it was what you wanted.'

It was too much. That bitter tone and seeing of himself the injured party was the last straw. How dared he blame her for this? How dared he!

Screaming, she ran at the dresser, the hammer a lot heavier than thought, she mistimed the shot, catching the middle shelf. It leapt up in the air, tipped and struck the top shelf, which began to slide - plates falling and smashing on the stone floor like a deck of brilliantly painted playing cards.

Weeping at such destruction, she struck again and again, until there was nothing but razor sharp porcelain, and the knowledge that, even as she struck, the shards would pierce her heart throughout this lifetime and the next.

Book One

Daisies

Needed and Necessary

March 1897, Bakers End, Norfolk.

'Mr Simpkin?' Julia gazed about. 'Why is the cottage known as the N and N?'

August Simpkin, of Simpkin & Simpkin, Solicitors of Law, laughed. 'That was the writer chap Charley Dickens! The Newman sisters who lived here called it Pleasant Cottage. And it was pleasant. You could get a decent cup of tea and the odd knickknack. Then Mr Dickens wrote them into a book calling the cottage the Needed and Necessary Tea-Shop - next thing the world is heading this way, rich and poor knocking on the door. Over time needed and necessary a bit a mouthful, it became the N and N, and that's how you find it today.'

'Fascinating.'

'It was. You could see why he wrote about them. They weren't what you'd call every day. Miss Justine and Miss Clarinda were society people. It makes you wonder why they'd want a tea-shop, can't have been lack of brass.'

'They didn't marry?'

'Not that I know of. There were rumours but when aren't there.' He sighed. 'I see it now, fluted parasols, the scent of cinnamon in the air and Miss Clarinda's green Macaw squawking. I was a lad then with my life before me. I thought it a magical place. I daresay every child in Bakers End thought the same.'

Julia smiled. 'I do like the name.'

'Everybody does. It's why it's stuck.' He gestured. 'The front bay windows were the tea room and the middle room a trading place for whatever those dear gentlewomen could find. Silk thread, pills and potions and plants from their garden, if they couldn't get it, it couldn't be got. Autumn '76 Miss Clarinda collapsed among her beloved roses. Miss Justine died in '81 more or less a recluse. This is how things were left. Had I known it such a mess I'd have tried clearing it though in terms of the Will cottage *and* contents are yours and not to be meddled with.'

'How did the Will come to light?'

'Hand of God I'd say. There was a fire, a gas mantle left on and a row of shops and Geddes Law Firm in Surrey Street burnt to the ground. Thanks to a constable on watch some of the papers were saved, the last Will and Testament of your mother's great-aunt among them.'

'So this house has been empty for almost twenty years?'

'It has and this,' he passed his hand over a table, 'the dust of another age.'

* * *

Two hours they trudged about the house, the lawyer apologetic and Julia weary. It's as well she didn't bring Matty. Mildew and mess mean nothing to him. Three years old, he would only see the beauty of the place, the tissue-paper leaves of the copper beech glowing in the evening sun.

When the letter arrived telling of the bequest so soon after Owen's death - a home of their own and no one hammering on the door demanding payment - it felt like a miracle; now having seen it the miracle appears a little tarnished.

'If the house were on the market, d'you think anyone likely to buy?'

Mr Simpkin fingered his hat. 'Well as I said before, should you decide to sell, a clause in the Will gives first refusal to a named party. '

'And the name of the party?'

'Geddes has that *if* they can find it. The place was gutted. It will take years to sift through. It's why it came to me.' He sniffed. 'As they say it's an ill wind that blows no one any luck. I shouldn't worry. The clause is valid only if you sell.'

'I believe the cottage once belonged to the Lansdowne family.'

'Aye, a gate-house to the estate. Mr Edgar Lansdowne, a cousin to the family, lived there with his wife and children. Then the railway came and a chunk of the land was sold off. The House and the Park all are that remain.'

'And is the cottage still entailed to the Lansdowne Estate?'

'It was gifted outright to Miss Justine. It's a pretty place and good location for a tea-shop, the road to Cambridge close by, though...' he glanced sideways, 'you being a delicate lady, I wouldn't have thought a cafe quite your style.'

Julia smiled wryly. 'Delicate or not, Mr Simpkin, one must survive.'

'Indeed so.' He stared, and then colouring, tapped on the window. 'Good glass this, ma'm, even when crusted with dirt.'

The windows are beautiful, the sun low in the sky turning the double bays of bottle-glass into a dozen miniature sunsets. Julia would have liked to ask more of the previous owners but hadn't time; Mrs Roberts, the proprietor of the Lord Nelson Inn where they are lodged, minding Matty.

'Do you know what plans the interested party has for the house?'

'I imagine it would be returned to its original state.'

'Wouldn't that mean rerouting the avenue?'

The lawyer smoothed his hat. 'Possibly.' The possibly and smoothing of a hat told Julia more is planned for the N and N than Mr Simpkin is willing to tell.

* * *

They toured the gardens, the lawyer poking the borders with his cane. 'I reckon you've trouble with moles.'

'If there is trouble I doubt it's moles,' said Julia. 'They don't usually carry a trowel and leave surrounding plants undamaged.'

'You think it a thief! Nay, that's not likely. Why would anyone steal plants?'

'It happens. Botanists have been known to travel the world to do just that.'

'You mean down south, Cornwall and the like?'

'I was thinking more China and the Upper Reaches of the Congo.'

'What? Go all that way for flowers and be paid to do it?'

'Some look for financial gain, others for the joy of the quest. My Uncle William was a keen botanist. He travelled the world in search of orchids.'

'Chasing a flower?' Mr Simpkin shook his head. 'I'd sooner stay home and grow a nice chrysanthemum. But these are good gardens. The ladies were keen gardeners. I understand your mother was the same.'

'She was. How do you know that?'

'It's mentioned in the Will, *the passing of a garden to a gardener*. It seems your mother used to visit as a girl. It's all in the Will. Did you not read it?'

'Not all of it. My husband died in September. My time has been very much taken up with other matters.'

He nodded. 'I imagined something of the kind, the sadness in your eyes. Was the poor gentleman ill awhile?'

'Mr Passmore was knocked down by a bullock cart.'

'A bullock cart?'

'Yes, in Cairo.'

'Cairo? Not one of the flowering gentlemen was he?'

Julia smiled sadly. 'Doctor Passmore hunted Egyptian arte-facts, a treasure equally rare but not nearly as sweet smelling.'

* * *

Chilled to the bone, Julia was glad to return to the inn. The Lord Nelson is a Coaching House in the centre of the Market Square. A prosperous establishment with decent rooms and a fine kitch-en, it is a frequent stopover for people on route to Cambridge. A hand-painted sign of HMS Victory over the door declares the proprietor as Albert Roberts Esquire and Sons. Another sign invites the onlooker to attest the skills of *A Roberts and Sons, Master Builders and Property Renovation.* Mrs Nanette Roberts is the true captain of the ship. Skirts crackling and cap ribbons flying, she sails through the corridors, guests and boot-boys alike scattering. A canvas in the parlour shows an angel breathing life into a drowned kitten, the motto '*So Shines a Good Deed in a Weary World.*' In caring for her visitors Nan Roberts takes the motto to heart.

Sunday evening she tapped on the door. 'It's none too warm up here. I'll get the maid to bring more coal. Such a beautiful child!' Mrs Roberts leaned over Matty as he slept. 'He's been ill hasn't he, poor lamb.'

'Yes but he's better now.'

'I see our Tabby cat found him. Shake her off if she's a bother.'

'Let her stay. Matty loves animals. Thank you for taking care of him.'

'Not at all! It was a pleasure having the lad…not that I saw much of him. He spent the afternoon at the Forge with my son, Luke, helping shoe a pony.'

'So Matty told me.'

'You understand your lad then when he makes them sounds?'

'He talks in his own way.'

'Luke says he's bright.'

'Matty is bright. It's not lack of intelligence that hampers. Throat surgery left him with problems. He can make himself understood. It's about people being patient. Not everyone is as patient as your son.'

'Phuf!' Mrs Roberts blew out her lips. 'I can't think of our Luke as patient, more a thunderstorm waiting to break. He rooms above the Forge and it's as well he does! I couldn't stand his moody ways. Albert is a placid man. There's nothing placid about Luke. His temper is as black as his eyes.'

'And yet he is gentle with my son.'

'Ah well, he likes children well enough. It's everyone else he doesn't like. God help the lass that gets him, I say. She'll rue the day.'

Chilled, a draught blowing, Julia drew her shawl close about her shoulders.

'Come down to my sitting room,' said Nan, 'and I'll make us a warm drink.'

* * *

Lamps lit and coal glowing it is cosy in the parlour. Nan Roberts took up the patching of linen. 'How did you get on with Gussie Simpkin?'

'Oh, you know about the cottage.'

Nan sniffed. 'Bakers End needs no Town Crier, a pint of ale in the bar and tongues start clacking. We heard you'd been left the N and N. It's not just idle curiosity that gets folk going. The Big House has been empty too long. Carriages coming and going we want to know who's moving in.'

'I'm afraid I can't help. Oh, I've a hole in my skirt!' Julia grimaced. 'It must have caught on brambles coming through the lane.'

'That lane! I've been on the council but they say it's not their responsibility. But should you have been on foot, Mrs Dryden? It's a fair distance to the cottage and you a slip of a thing, August Simpkin should've brought you back.'

'He offered but I preferred to walk.'

Mrs Roberts snorted. 'I bet he was relieved. Squashed up in that old growler with a beautiful widow-woman is more than his nerves could take. I was only thinking with your hair you'd best wear a bonnet indoors as well as out. It'll give the lassies here a fighting chance. There's a shortage of good men as it is without you setting them in a coil.'

'You believe in straight talking, Mrs Roberts.'

'I'm from Yorkshire. I believe in honesty. You've secrets, my dear, I can tell, but they're your secrets and as long as they don't trouble me and mine they will stay yours. So shall you stay or sell?'

'I don't know.'

'Don't be hasty. It's as good a house as you'll get anywhere. A dab of whitewash and it'll be good as new. My Luke will sort it. He'll put his shoulder to the wheel and unlike some round here not charge for what he doesn't do.'

'There are mice.'

'We're on the edge of the Wash. If we were to quit on account of mice the village will be empty. Get a dog and cat. A dog will scare off the rogues and a good mouser'll clear you of everything *and* offer the odd rabbit for the pot.'

'Matty would like a dog. He was fond of the college dog.'

'You lived in Cambridge.'

'My husband taught there.'

'A clever man then?'

'He was.'

'And your boy will take after him.' Nan sighed. 'Luke's teacher wanted him to go to college but we weren't as we are now and needed him. He resented us, thought he could do better and to be fair he is clever. Give him a problem and he'll figure it out. It's him that keeps the wall bottom of your garden.'

The Wall! If the gardens are a blessing then the wall back of the property is a curse. Julia did ask Mr Simpkin if she should be alarmed, was there something on the other side that needed to stay so.

'There's nothing sinister that I know of,' was his reply.

'Then why build a wall? It casts a gloom over the whole house.'

'I don't know why it was built. I only know if you accept the property you accept the wall. It's in the Will: *'Not to come down until the stars fall.'*

Julia enquired of Mrs Roberts. 'Why is there a wall?'

Nan shrugged. 'People are always asking. I tell them what I'm telling you, only Miss Justine knew and she took the answer to her grave.'

'Who were the Newman sisters?'

'They were gentry from County Clare in Ireland. There was talk of them dining with Her Majesty. I wouldn't be surprised. I met Miss Justine when we had the Beehive Inn at Coddleston. She was in a barouche, a coat of arms on the door. A trace on the lead horse snapped. When Luke fixed it she gave him sixpence and whispered in his ear. He gave me the sixpence but wouldn't say what she said. That was twenty years ago. He still won't say.'

Julia sighed. 'I do like the cottage. It is a pretty place and the gardens are well stocked. As for repairs, I do have a little set aside.'

'There you are then! Settle and be happy!'

'Are you happy here?'

'I'm not unhappy. The business thrives and we are well. I don't look beyond that. Luke can't abide Bakers. He reckons folk here are small minded with small minded ways. He's right.' Nan jabbed the needle into the cloth. 'I don't like nodding to Fussy Gussy's shrew of a wife but in business, as in life, you can't be choosy. I go to church two Sunday mornings a month. I pay my dues and I follow Cromwell's advice, keeping my head down and my powder dry. I advise you to do the same.'

'Do you?'

'I do.' Nan's glance was steady. 'You are young and lovely and a widow. There'll be those wanting to help and those to hinder and for a time you won't know who's who. Until you do there's a place here with me and mine.'

'You are very kind.'

'No, not kind! It is our duty in this world to help one another. If you leave that skirt with me I'll see it mended. You have beautiful clothes. That shawl you're wearing is so soft. You wouldn't want a thing like that spoiled.'

'Do you like it?' Julia laid it about Nan's shoulders. 'It's yours.'

'Oh, I couldn't!' Nan passed it back. 'I was admiring it, that's all.'

'You have been kind to Matty. Please take it!'

'Well then if you say so but things like this are costly. You have to work to earn them. They don't fall from the skies.'

'Sometimes they do.'

'What?' Nan took a closer look at her guest. Three days she's been watching this young woman. Heavy silken hair and amber eyes, young Mrs Dryden is a rare beauty and her clothes costly in style and make. Take that blouse with the pin-tucks? There's a similar garment in Bentalls priced at five shillings. And the skirt and the snakeskin boots! You won't see boots like that in Norfolk. And why room here? Has she no relatives to take care of her and the boy?

Nan is proud of the Nelson. They don't rent the Inn as do most victuallers. It's paid for, lock, stock, and barrel, and not a farthing owing. She's proud of her husband and her son and the work they do as builders - a reputation as the best in the business. That a lady should choose to bide here is no surprise, many gentlefolk stopping over on the way to Sandringham - but wouldn't you think a person of such elegant manner would be accompanied by a maid?

Six months a widow and not in black! Now, she's giving shawls away and talking of them falling from the skies? And why when she said that did her lovely face strike fear in Nan's heart as though realising the kitten she nursed at her bosom was in fact a wild cat with yellow eyes and claws.

* * *

Later, Julia lamented a foolish tongue. The shawl was gifted along with a travel coat and moleskin furs, Lady Evelyn Carrington of Russell Square, London, the benevolent giver. It's what was meant by falling from the sky. So foolish! Her remark brought Bloomsbury to Bakers End and yet another wall between her and the villagers.

Julia pondered the wall? Why is it there? What does it repel? Walls can't make a house safe no matter how high. A window left open and rain will get in, a door unlocked and a thief will rob you of all you cherish. No one person can decide your fate. Only God's good grace can give you safety.

It's years since she felt safe. January 11, 1890, at three minutes past seven Abigail Dryden climbed a stool to take down a jar of pickles. She fell and never got up again. Sixteen-year-old Julia fell with her and has not stopped falling. With Mother gone the heart of the family was pinched out and all safety invested in Father, Rector Philip Dryden. Sisters Charlotte and May were married with children and living in Cowper. It fell to Julia to care for Father. It wasn't long before he began to fail. She tried shoring him up, every day a fresh egg in a Willow-patterned cup for breakfast and a walk in the garden to see the hedgehog under a flower pot, and in the evening a chapter of *Oliver Twist*.

Two years she struggled to keep him alive. He hid in books, escaping the bleak 19th century for Homer and Ancient Greece. Thursday evening choir practice was his one joy, Julia at the harmonium thumping out choruses from Handel's *Messiah*, Father unable to resist the declamation, '*Wonderful! Councillor!*' It was to no avail. The Rectory passed to a new incumbent, Julia must marry and who better and more at hand than second cousin Owen Passmore. Julia begged another way but her sister Charlotte - five years senior and strong of temperament - would have none of it. 'Uncle William's step-son is sober, solvent, and ready to marry. What other way is there?'

A night in Owen's company and Julia knew he hadn't thought to marry, nor, though he nightly battled to create them, had he thought of children. An ugly house in the College grounds, a borrowed piano and a telescope, marriage was a means to an end. The telescope was parked in the bedroom window. Every morning Owen would say, 'I'd be obliged if you didn't touch it, my dear. I have it in the right position, a quarter inch left or right and I must start again.'

Every night in their lumpy bed suffering his apologetic fumbles, a riposte to his directive hung in her mind like a sampler: '*Show me Thy way, O Lord and make it plain.*' Owen rarely found his way to his goal. If he loved Julia he never said, the words, like the deed, too worrying. Egypt was his love, Egypt and gazing through a telescope at Venus. A new bride was unsettling - though she did bring a body that nightly drove him crazy.

Owen surely loved Matty. In early months he'd sit by the cot gazing at his son as if doubting the fruit of his endeavour. Then Matty fell ill. As a baby he made the usual gurgling sounds, after surgery gurgling sounds were all he made.

Owen was shocked. 'I don't know why he's like this. The surgeon is an awfully good fellow. I knew him at Caius.'

'Damn your awfully good fellow!' Julia had raged. 'Look at the mess he made of your son's throat!' Owen didn't want to look. He went to Egypt seeking comfort in a sunken city. What he didn't want to see he wouldn't.

He was like that with the annuity. St Mary's, Bentham, is a small church with a small congregation. When Father died he'd nothing to leave but a blessing. Another blessing came when Aunt Eleanor bequeathed an annuity of one hundred pounds per annum to each of Philip Dryden's daughters. Nan Roberts says Julia has secrets; a second annuity and how it came about is a secret known only to Julia and an artist in Bloomsbury - and is best kept so.

* * *

Matty stirred. Opening his eyes and finding her watching he smiled.

'Why you not asleep, Ju-ju?'

'I am asleep, dear heart,' she whispered.

Strange how in the warmth of sleep his speech is less constrained; Julia understands his every word. Owen tried signing for a time. 'He's not deaf,' she would say. 'It's no good waving your hands about.'

'I know,' he replied. 'I was hoping he might sign love to his Papa.'

That was the last time they were together. Now Owen is dead and will never hear his son say anything.

Julia was woken by rain coming through the window. It was bitterly cold.

Shivering, she got out of bed and leaned into the rain to close the window. In the yard below a man took shelter under the eaves, a piece of sacking over his head. As she reached out to close the window he looked up. Brow furrowed and unsmiling, he stared, rain from a broken guttering dripping on his face.

Such eyes, dark and unfathomable they held Julia transfixed. Rain blew in soaking her nightgown. Still she stared until he, with impatient gesture, slapped the wall: 'Go in why don't you, woman, and close the window!'

She did.

CHAPTER TWO

Owt for Nowt

The document is signed. As of this day, Monday 10th of April, in the Year of Our Lord 1897, the N and N, mice, mould, and wall, is theirs. Matty has given his approval. Saturday afternoon, a fur cap on his head and sturdy boots on his feet, he came to view. 'Mumma, look!' he cried. 'It's smiling.' Preoccupied with mice and mould Julia missed what a child would never miss: thatch over an attic window creating a winking eye.

Work needed, it was a while before they moved in, renovation undertaken by Albert Roberts & Sons. So far Julia is only aware of one son, Luke Roberts, the grim-faced individual who sheltered under eaves and whose imperious hand commanded her retreat. The Roberts' soon proved worthy of hire, the son tackling the heavy work, the father more inclined to chat. Even with a biting wind coming off the Wash Julia keeps to the garden. Muffled in furs, hands and feet developing chilblains, she pulls weeds, hoes borders and shivers.

With only an estimate to go by and a diminishing purse she worries about costs. 'Is this really necessary?' she asked Monday morning through a haze of dust, the upper rooms gutted and pipes laid bare. Luke Roberts paused in hammering. 'It is if you want a decent plumbing system.'

'I do want such things but am conscious of escalating costs. Last night looking at the new bathroom I wondered if we were exceeding the original intention.'

'Did you not like what you saw?'

'I thought it exceptional work.'

'And do you know what we need to do to make it exceptional?'

'Well...no.'

'Then rest easy. It's right to worry about cost but spare a thought for future peace of mind. We're on the brink of a new century. The modern and fashionable lady must move with the times.'

'That's all very well, Mr Luke, but after this will I be able to afford to be either modern or fashionable?'

He shrugged. 'Can you afford not to be?'

Julia is perplexed by the man's manner. He rarely speaks and when he does it is to challenge. 'What were you thinking for the walls?' She passed a scrap of wallpaper. 'This William Morris damask would look well in the sitting-room.'

He shook his head. 'I'm not putting that on the walls.'

Taken aback by the blank refusal Julia stared.

'It's heavy stuff,' he said. 'It'll drag on the size.'

'Then perhaps a lighter paper? He does a lovely Japanese print.'

'English or Japanese I'm not hanging William Morris on any of your walls.'

'Then perhaps you'll suggest someone who will!'

'I can hang wallpaper. I won't hang William Morris. The paper has arsenic in the patterning. In time it would make me sick to hang it and you to watch it.'

'Good heavens! Is that true?'

'It is. Find me paper that isn't Morris and I'll hang it.' A blood-blistered thumb caressed the paper. 'Do you usually carry scraps of wallpaper in your pocket?'

A memory too intimate to be picked over by strangers Julia took back the sample. Freddie Carrington did this, tore a strip of wallpaper from his sister's dining room. 'For heaven's sake!' she'd whispered. 'What are you doing?'

'You like it and might need it to match the pattern.'

'I do like it but not for you to do this!'

'Evie won't mind,' he'd waved a long strip. 'I took it from behind the dresser. She'll never know it's gone.' Leaving that day Julia offered apologies. Evelyn had raised her big blue eyes. 'Don't worry, Ju-ju. I'll not hold you to blame.'

'I'm sure he meant no harm.'

'I'm sure he did. It's what angry children do to gain attention of the one they admire. They shout or slap. At least he didn't slap.'

* * *

Julia is getting to know the cottage. Walking the gardens she learns of the sisters and the animals they loved by headstones scattered about. There are dogs, Marlow and Meribone, behind the herb garden, and cats, Samson and Saraband, opposite. She's had good moments and bad, happy finds and tragic losses. A double tragedy was found in the wash-house, tea-chests filled with broken china. She covered her mouth in horror. 'That's too dreadful.'

A mindless jigsaw of razor edges, the chests were full of precious, worthless, Meissen china. 'There's something sick about it,' said Albert Roberts. 'Hidden away year-after-year, why would you keep such ruin?'

'It's a reminder,' said Luke Roberts.

'Of what?' said Julia.

'Of how it felt when he or she took a hammer to them.'

Luke buried the china as one would bury the dead. For a time then nothing in the cottage gave pleasure - nothing until the piano.

It was discovered in a back closet. Hearing of the find Julia hurried along.

Albert was in the kitchen supping from a mug. 'Mornin, ma'm.'

She shook her umbrella. 'Mr Luke not here yet?'

'Aye, he's up in the attics and none too happy about it.'

'Forgive me for asking but is he ever happy?'

'He's not the cheeriest of men, I grant, but here today since early light he's got cause. Last night's storm shifted tiles on the roof. You've rain coming in.'

'And he's been here since early light?'

'He has. He heard the rain and couldn't sleep.'

'And I called him miserable!' Julia was mortified. 'Ungrateful wretch that I am! Luke must do as he wants. He wasn't hired to smile and play the fool, only to prove worthy of hire and that he has most assuredly done.'

'Don't fret, lass,' said Albert. 'He is a moody chap. Nobody knows that better than me. He's never been what you might call a smiler. That was his brother. Our Jacky smiled for Queen and Country.'

'Jacky?'

'My youngest lad that was drowned in the quarry.'

'Drowned? Oh, Albert! I am so sorry!'

'As are we all.' He stood contemplating the piano. 'You'll be alright with this. It was stored with lovin' care as the china wasn't. We've an upright in the public bar a chap plays of a weekend. You play piano, do you?'

'I do.' Afraid of speaking amiss she patted the keys. 'And you're right, this has been lovingly preserved and speaks well of the cottage.'

'Speaks well of the cottage?' Hair plastered to his head and shirt wringing wet Luke stood on the stairs. That he'd overheard their conversation was evident. 'I'd say it speaks well of the ladies that took care of it.'

'I'm sure,' said Julia. 'I meant only that the condition of the piano might have been helped by thick walls and an ambient temperature.'

'I get what you meant. Next time I'm up at two in the morning, rain dripping down my back, I'll think on ambient temperatures and take comfort.' He strode into the kitchen pulling his shirt over his head as he went. 'You never know if the mood takes me, miserable man that I am, I might jig about a bit.'

* * *

The day continued as heavy and unrelenting as the rain. Albert took the labourers to another job. 'We were to whiten ceilings but not wi' muck flying about.' He hooked his thumb. 'Why don't you pop over to the Nelson for a cup of tea! Hangin' about won't help. Not wi' misery guts in charge.'

Misery Guts was clearing the attics. Arms braced and head down he swept all before him, sodden rugs and bird's nests, tangled messes of mice and moth thrown through the window. News spread of a house clearing. A queue formed by the wall. All was going well until a man snatched another's bedspring.

Black hair peppered with dust, Luke leapt to the window. 'Get you gone, Nate Sherwood!' he roared. 'You've thieved your bit of junk now clear off! And don't let me see your ugly mug within a mile of this place!'

The man ran, the bedspring a portcullis over his head.

'Who was that?' said Julia.

'Nobody worth knowing.'

'I gathered that by your tone.'

'And what's wrong with my tone? Is this another aspect of me you'd see different? Should I have danced a two-step with him?'

'I don't know what you should've done! I only wonder why it need be so violent. After all, it was a bedspring he took not the crown jewels.'

'It was your bedspring and you don't want him sleeping on it!'

'It wasn't my bedspring!' Julia was sick of his testy ways. 'It wasn't anybody's bedspring! It was junk as you said so why couldn't he have it?'

'Because he's a bad 'un and you don't want him near anything of yours!'

'Such a fuss!'

'There was no fuss until he came. Owt for nowt, if you'd nothing against folk taking stuff no more had I! But oughtn't it be decent folk that benefit from cast-offs not one that spends half his life hurting those that can't defend themselves and the other half ripping the shirt off an honest man's back!'

Recalling Luke pulling his shirt over his head and the breadth of his shoulders compared with that of the man with the bedspring Julie smiled. 'You've had a shirt ripped from your back by such a man?'

He saw her smile, heard the scorn in her voice, and colouring left the room.

* * *

Julia worked in the terrace garden, the Mole here again and foot-prints in the soil. She returned to empty attics and the parlour ceiling in process of being whitened. Maggie Jeffers, a maid on loan from the Nelson mopped floors.

'Everything gone, Maggie?'

'Looks like it, ma'm.'

'Did I see you out there earlier?'

'You did.'

'And did you find anything nice?'

'I wanted the blue ribbons you flung but a parlour maid from the Big House got 'em. Shame! Blue ribbons mean a wedding in the family.'

'They were terribly tarnished.'

'They might've washed.'

'I suppose.' A trunk from the attic stood by the door. 'I wonder if there are ribbons in here.' Julia knelt at a chest and the maid with her. The smell of camphor rose from folds of linen and a not so pleasant smell from Maggie.

Julia held up a lace collar. 'This is pretty.'

A bone to a starving pup the maid snatched the collar and ran.

'Is that wise?' Luke Roberts splashed paint on the ceiling. 'Get too close to Maggie Jeffers and she'll have you spitting over your shoulder when the moon is full and counting your children through apple seeds.'

'Maggie can say and do as she likes. I believe we make our own luck.'

'Do you?' He wiped his face on his sleeve, white chalk on his cheek making his eyes sapphire blue. 'Then God knows I must be doing something wrong.'

* * *

It was cold in church. Julia wished she'd worn a fur cloak as well as a muff but heeding Nan's advice came clad in plain bonnet and cloak. Two minutes and she knew she may have gone the whole hog since people stare anyway.

The vicar conducted Julia to an ornately carved pew. 'As mistress of the former Lansdowne gatehouse you are entitled to worship here.'

'I suppose I must sit here.'

The vicar smiled. 'Indeed you must. St Bedes is a small church. Every member of the congregation has his or her own spot. The occupying of another even when the church is half empty is a dark sin - as I am sure you understand.'

Julia took her seat. 'I am a parson's daughter. I understand only too well.'

A solitary figure in a wooden box she knelt to her prayers. Matthew attended chapel in Cambridge. His absence today is noted by members of the congregation. A newcomer, her household is under assessment, however the issue today is not the whereabouts of a child - or why he croaks like that, poor lad

- it is why a widow of six months wears brown instead of black.

Owen didn't want it. 'If anything should happen promise me you'll not wear widow's weeds. I do like glossy shades of black but only on bird or bear.'

The keeping of this promise hasn't been easy. Even on campus where the modern scholar disowns God in favour of Charles Darwin's theories, the absence of black raises eyebrows. The day they were due to leave the Bursar's wife offered a parcel. 'Here you are my dear, a black alpaca skirt and a half-crown. The skirt may serve until you purchase your own.'

* * *

A fortnight passed and though the parlour walls are still to be papered the cottage is habitable. Weary of trekking back and forth Julia plans to move in but asked if Matty might stay with Nan. 'Of course he must stay!' was her reply. 'Paint is caustic to the throat, Anna. He can't be inhaling that.'

Nan refers to Julianna now as Anna. At home it was always Julia, the only time she was afforded a full name was when Mother was irritated. Here in Bakers it's Matty who brings about familial shortening. Nan dotes on him and him upon her. As for Luke, he follows him everywhere aping the stride and gruff voice. This morning he sidled up. 'Mister Wolf, what big teeth you have.' Mister Wolf snatched him up, and growling, ran up and down the yard, Matty shrieking with joy. Matty does this, gives people fairy-tale names. Julia wishes he wouldn't, what is charming in a three-year-old is less so in an older child.

That night she said he was not to do it. 'But he is a wolf!'

Matty pointed to a picture-book. 'Huff, puff, and blow the house down.' Julia thinks Luke is to blame. Were he to smile instead of snarl he would be a handsome prince, instead he's a nursery rhyme villain and the terror of Three Little Pigs.

'I'd rather you didn't encourage Matty,' she said. 'He'll get used to saying it.'

'The lad's alright.' Luke shrugged it away. 'He'll stop when a real wolf comes along.' Dependent to a degree on Nan's good favour Julia didn't pursue it; with Matty in safe hands she can boost their coffers working as an artist's model.

There was a time when Julia was ashamed of sitting for the artists. A sawbones surgeon changed that. It happened in May '94. Owen forgot his class notes. Julia delivered the notes and was hurrying home when a woman climbing the College steps hailed her. 'Mrs Passmore isn't it?'

'I'm sorry,' said Julia, 'I can't stay to chat. My son is unwell.'

'Nothing serious I hope.'

'It may be. He had a tonsillectomy and his throat is badly infected.'

'Oh my dear, that is serious! Do you have a physician you trust?'

'We have someone but I wouldn't say I trust him.'

The woman produced a card. 'This is my man. If you feel in any way worried do give him a call.' Julia had scanned the address and the royal crest. 'Thank you but a physician to Her Majesty is beyond my means.' The woman pressed the card into Julia's hand. 'But no beyond mine! Take this! Tell him Evelyn Carrington says to come and he will.'

Julia pocketed the card never thinking to use it but when

Matty's condition worsened she showed it to Owen. 'Ah yes, Stefan Adelman, cousin to Karl Adelman. I attended a lecture of his on Karnack and the Valley of Kings.'

Typical, his son struggles for breath and Owen looks to the dusty treasure of yesterday. It was a modern treasure, a telephone in the Bursar's office that brought Stefan Adelman's kindly eyes smiling over steel-rimmed spectacles.

'Lady Carrington told me of your concern and being in the neighbourhood I thought to see your son.' A heavy man in a grey overcoat he flowed into the room as a calm sea. Huge hands, the hands of a farmer rather than a surgeon, he reached into the cot. 'Open your mouth to me, *mein kind.*' Ten minutes and Matty was gathered up. 'You will wear a hat and coat, *Frau* Passmore. We take your son to a good place.'

There are two people in the world beside her son for whom she would do anything, Stefan Adelman, consultant cardiologist to the Queen, and Evelyn Carrington, artist and friend. But for them Matty would not be here. No hardship then in the spring of '95 to return a favour. Freddie Carrington was in his last year at Jesus College. Evie would visit the college and then call at the Passmore house. The third visit brought a chance to repay a debt.

'Let down your hair, Rapunzel,' said Evie, 'and I will paint you.'

Julia protested. 'I couldn't do that. My husband would hate it.'

'Must your husband know?'

'Of course! How could he not with you and me here in the house.'

'I could never paint here!' Evelyn had grimaced. 'This house is too awful. My muse would quite forsake me.' The next visit she

37

pulled pins from Julia's hair. 'All this glory bundled up and you never sharing.' She'd gripped Julia's face between her hands and kissed her. 'You are cruel, Ju-ju, cruel and beautiful.'

The kiss shocked both into silence. Evie then nodded. 'I must have that look. It's exactly the look I want for a show in September. Come to my Gloucester house next Thursday. We're picnicking with the artist, John Sargent.'

That summer Julia sat for John Singer Sargent. Blue silk robe and hair undone, she sat under an apple tree, a bowl of strawberries in her lap and Matty playing with a puppy. Those sessions were peaceful. Evelyn's house in London was not - doorbells chiming, people spilling out of cabs to play cards or forfeits, while a string quartet played in the salon - it was madness.

'What is that they're playing?' Julia asked one afternoon.

'*L'apres midi d'une faune,*' said Evie. 'It is you. You are the music.'

The painting, *Faun Surprised*, hangs in the National Gallery, valued in hundreds of guineas. 'I've had many an offer but won't sell,' said Evie. 'I know it's all I'll ever have of you.' Evelyn Carrington is generous with her time and favours. 'Take these!' She'll heap furs onto Julia's lap. 'So much clutter, you would be doing me a favour.' When it came to offering fees for sitting Julia refused. 'Mr Sargent doesn't pay me, why should you?'

'With John there's no question of money,' said Evie. 'Your fee is the adulation the portrait brings.' She suggested the Grosvenor Gallery for colleagues who'd seen *Faun Surprised* and begged a sitting. 'The fees will help Matty's needs.'

'What kind of work is it? I'll not remove my clothes.'

'You might bare your shoulders. They'd settle for that and

pay by post so no one need know. How about another hundred to add to your annuity?'

When Owen died Julia reverted to the family name Dryden.

'Dryden is a good name,' said Evie. 'Shared with a poet what could be nicer.'

It is a good name taken to avoid creditors who, until they came knocking, she didn't know existed. So much owed, even for the telescope! The day she was about to hand it over Freddie appeared. 'I say there, fellow, step back from the door!' Who will ever know the true nature of the Honourable Frederick Carrington, he of the canary yellow waistcoats and affected manners, who says he has no purpose in life other than giving and knowing pleasure.

That day his eyes glinted steel. It was suggested they quit Cambridge. 'Your life is with us. No need to return to that hovel.' There was a need. The house in Russell Square is exhausting. It tires Stefan Adelman. 'Lady Carrington is a charming lady but an hour among the peacocks and I am in need of a doctor.'

That was said the morning Julia received a letter from August Simpkin telling of the bequest. She'd passed the letter to Stefan who read and passed it back. 'Fortuitous wouldn't you say, Mrs Dryden?'

She'd nodded. 'Indeed I would.'

* * *

'Go now, Maggie.' Julia lit the gas mantle. 'Your mother will be anxious.'

'She won't. She don't care for me. It's my earnings she likes.'

'I'm sure that's not true. Your money is on the table.'

39

Maggie slid the pennies into her pocket. 'I could work here.'

'You are employed by Mrs Roberts.'

'Missis has plenty maids. I could do your hair and tidy your clothes.'

'Thank you, I have a maid arriving tomorrow.'

Maud McLaughlin is Evie's suggestion. 'You can't be alone in that barren place. Mrs Mac will be with you on Thursday, bag packed and sleeves rolled.' Evie is in her middle years. Elfin figure with blue eyes and bubble of golden curls, she might have modelled the cherub in Nan's parlour and yet is forged of such will the combined strength of Samson and Hercules couldn't bend her to their want. 'Do take Mrs Mac! She's a good woman and thankfully a little too withered about the neck to attract trouble.' A grey lady with grey moods, a spinster - the Mrs a courtesy title - Julia would've preferred another but who can withstand Evie. 'You ought not to put up with my sister,' said Freddie the last time they lunched at the London House. 'She's an awful manager.'

'She is very generous.'

'No, not generous, Ju-ju, she plays with people. She arranges their lives like a bloomin' chequer board, this move one day and that the next.'

'She has a great heart.'

'She has a great appetite for interferin' in a fellow's life.'

'She interferes with yours?'

Lashes drooping, he leaned against the chaise. 'Everybody interferes with my life. It's the fashion of the day along with buttoned boots and cloth caps. I hear 'em snippin' and snatterin', "let's set Freddie on the right path."'

'Are you on a wrong path?'

The question that day ignited a fire in his eyes. He grabbed her hand. 'I could walk the right road with you.'

'Freddie!'

'No listen! If you were with me I would walk the straightest, sharpest road there is. I need help. I can't keep turnin' temptation away. There's only so much darkness a soul can deflect before the glass cracks.'

She'd eased her hand away. 'I must be going. Matty is restless.'

'Yes,' he'd shrugged, 'off you go to Cambridge and the Doleful Don.'

Doleful Don? It's not the first time she's heard Owen described so. She understands the expression, a look in his eyes, the wrong place at the wrong time. Dear Owen, Julia never understood him and had thought he didn't understand her, but words and memories pieced together, she now realises he knew her very well. The day he left he took her hand. 'Tomorrow I join the expedition, and though I know what I do has little meaning for you, I want to say how grateful I am for the opportunity. I wasn't born into wealth like your London friends. All my life I have had to cut my coat according to my cloth. It is my dream to be present at the opening of a great tomb, to stare through the dust of today into the morning of yesterday. Who knows, dear wife, this may turn out to be the day I find my shabby coat is lined with velvet.'

* * *

A new bed, and no Matty to snuggle, Julia slept only fitfully. She was woken around midnight by a noise under the window. Fearful, she crept from the bed and peering down once again looked down at Luke Roberts.

She went to open the window but finger pressed to his lips he shook his head. A moment later she saw why, a shadowy figure creeping over the wall. The finger remained pressed against the lips and the eyes warning silence until Luke sprang forward, slapping the intruder to the ground.

'Did I not tell you, Nate Sherwood, to stay away?' A boot planted on his backside, the man went sprawling. 'This is your last chance. If you're seen anywhere near this house I swear to God you'll not walk again.'

The shape crawled away to slither over the wall into darkness.

A bird in a hedgerow squawked.

The beginning of another day.

Trembling, Julia looked down.

For a long time Luke held her gaze. Then he nodded. 'Go in,' he said.

And again she did.

CHAPTER THREE

Grudge

Julia opened the window and tossed the breadcrumbs.

'Birds!' Matty clapped his hands and the sparrows scattered.

'Don't do that, Matthew! You're scaring them! And don't kick the door! Doctor Adelman comes tomorrow. Be a good boy and tidy your room.'

Pulling faces and making ugly sounds Matty stomped back upstairs.

Julia closed the window. Maud McLaughlin hovered at her shoulder. 'I am sorry, Mrs McLaughlin,' she said, exasperated. 'If you're unhappy it's best you seek another position. I'm sure Lady Carrington would welcome your return.'

'No, madam, I couldn't go back. I was never comfortable there.'

'I could suggest you to Mrs Roberts?'

'A public house? Oh, no, I couldn't work there, not where strong liquor is sold. I'm Temperance. It would be against my principles.'

'Then I don't know what to suggest. Not familiar with Bakers End I don't know the employment situation. It's best you ask Maggie.'

Mrs McLaughlin shuddered. 'I couldn't ask her. She's the problem. I've nothing against working here. I like my room and the way you treat me kindly. I'd be happy here but for her and her ways.'

'What way in particular?'

'She's slovenly, madam! She doesn't wash as she should, she won't listen when I bid her, and she will sit with me of an evening.'

'Why should she not sit with you?'

'Not in my sitting room!'

'But is it your sitting room? I thought it for all of you.'

'I shouldn't have to share. I never shared in Russell Square.'

'Perhaps not but I understood you to say life there was less than agreeable.'

'It was anything but. I spent all my time keeping out the way. You don't know who's who in that house. Dodging in-and-out of folk's bedrooms! There was no privacy for anyone, and I'm talking below stairs as well as above.'

'Mrs McLaughlin! Please stick to the subject at hand. You have your own room. Maggie has hers. Surely you can share a sitting room.'

'I like the sitting room, madam. It looks out on the parkland. I wouldn't want not to sit there. I have my bird in there, Joey, my cockatiel.'

Julia had sympathy for the woman. She may complain but she is decent and Maggie is not the cleanest of beings. 'I'll have a word.'

* * *

'Gracious!' She made for the yard. Matty difficult, the help bickering and plants stolen, life was less of a problem in Cambridge. Joseph Carmody, the gardener, was already at the wall. She knelt to look. 'What has gone?'

'Daisies.'

'Daisies? Why when they're ten a penny?'

'This is nowt to do wi' plants,' said Joe. 'You've upset some-body and this is meant to make you feel bad. I tell you, I catch the beggar messing with them Persian roses I put along the back wall and I'll skin him alive.'

'Trouble again, Joe?' Luke Roberts joined them.

'Looks like it.'

'Good morning, Luke.'

'Morning, ma'm.' He knelt alongside. 'What's he taken this time?'

'Daisies. Joseph thinks it is a person with a grudge.'

'That's plain enough, though I doubt it a real grudge. He takes without damaging anything else. If it were real malice he wouldn't care.'

'Then why do it?'

'Maybe he thinks it a joke not really hurting anyone.'

'He's hurting me.'

'Is he?' Luke turned to stare. 'Aye, maybe he is.'

Tears in her eyes, she hurried away. Six weeks she's been here and though Luke is often here it's the first time she's heard caring in his voice. Tough and sharp as blackthorn he is to be avoided wherever possible, his work, however, is excellent. As Nan said he is clever, his use of space to accommodate twists and turns of the cottage and still maintain the rustic charm is exceptional. An example is the attic bathroom, where once a closet there's a bath, a wash-pedestal and WC that flushes. Friday morning she was trapped in the linen cupboard trying not to laugh as on the land-ing Albert extolled the virtues of the Whispering Falls water-closet to Joe Carmody: '*We have 'em in the Nelson. You wouldn't catch me going back to china piss-pots, too cold on your arse in tmiddle of night.*' Julia had scurried away to the herb-beds to giggle unseen, it was then she saw plants had been taken and laughter ceased.

Julia sighed. 'Should I tell the constable?'

'If you like, though heck of a fuss over a clump of daisies.'

Luke Roberts was behind her. 'Sorry. I thought you were Joe.'

'No, it's only me, big bad wolf, miserable as ever.'

Julia ignored that. 'You don't think it was the Sherwood person?'

'No! He's more like to steal the breath from your lungs.'

'He is a rogue then?'

'He is, and a nasty streak where women are concerned. He's been up before the Beak more than once.'

'Then thank you for scaring him away.'

'I did nothing. I merely let him know how it stands.'

'You had our welfare at heart and I was less than grateful.' She offered her hand. 'Might we shake hands and be better friends?'

'Friends?' Brow furrowed, he questioned the word, and then, polishing his hand on his shirt, took her hand. 'We'll be friends, Julianna Dryden,' he said, his clasp strong and accent even stronger. 'It's better than nowt.'

* * *

The following day Julia walked to the Nelson to tell Nan of a proposed visit to London. By the time she arrived she was soaked, the heavens opening.

'You must get a conveyance, Anna,' said Nan. 'You can't keep splashing through mud. It's not seemly.'

Julia scraped her boots. She hadn't the money to waste on cabs.

Nan nodded. 'Bit strapped for cash are you?'

'I had to tell the cook I wouldn't need her while in London.'

'She was lucky to have you at all. From what I've heard she's a plain cook and you a generous employer. Room and board and an afternoon off a week, there aren't many doing that hereabouts.'

'You don't approve.'

'You must run your house according to your likes. Just make sure you're not making a rod for your own back with Maggie Jeffers.'

'She and Mrs Mac don't get along.'

'They're pushing for elbow-room seeing who can control the young widow-woman. Keep 'em in check! Too much leeway and they run amuck.'

* * *

Julia wrote Evie of the domestic feud. She said much the same as Nan. *Let them go if they're not doing right. As for being none too clean I suggest a little reverse psychology. Praise your Maggie, make her think cleanliness is next to godliness. I'll pop a parcel over, a couple of bits for you, my dear.*

A parcel arrived the next day, a velvet jacket for Julia, an ink-carrying pen for Mrs Mac, and dresses for Maggie. The note was in Evie's spidery hand: *The frocks were for my maid but she is preggers with a village lad! I hope your Maggie is more a Plain Jane. Breaking in new maids is such a bore.*

Navy-blue dresses with pin-tucks and aprons like sugar

frosting, Maggie was dazzled. 'Take them and be mindful of Mrs McLaughlin, who is older than you, and wiser, and who I would *not* be without.' The hint taken, Maggie scuttled away. When Julia returned to the sitting room Stefan Adelman was smiling.

'You are amused, Doctor Adelman.'

'I am thinking the maintaining of a modern household requires the strength of Hercules and the diplomacy of Mr Gladstone.'

'As I am learning, though in the battle of Maggie versus Maud I believe even Mr Gladstone would quail. Sit and tell what you think of Matty.'

Bulk squashed into a chair Stefan sat. 'He is a dear young soul. I'm sure he had a good papa. I'm told students at the University enjoyed your husband's classes. They thought him a dry stick with a ready wit.'

Julia grimaced. 'Did they indeed?'

Stefan frowned. 'It is not a good remark?'

'It has a touch of irony.'

'Ah, so I misunderstood. My English is not so good. I mistake the sardonic nuance of British humour for statement of fact.'

'English humour is not easy to understand. Basically we mock the things we like, though I must say I wasn't aware of Owen's wit.'

'A wife cannot know all of a man. He has another life that is not home.'

'As do we all, Stefan.'

'Ah-hah!' Stefan clapped his hands. 'At last my Christian name! Does this mean I may now refer to you as Julianna?'

'If you so wish.'

'Thank you, Julianna.' He folded his arms. 'And so to Matthew. His health gains from being here but his impediment continues.'

'I know, and yet waking from sleep it is not so noticeable.'

'That suggests an unwillingness to talk.'

'But why that? I am his mother, the one person he can talk to!'

'Or the one person he cannot! A child's greatest fear is loss of his mother. It might be that having lost his papa he is afraid of losing you.'

* * *

Julia is unable to settle. Matty left alone in the world is her greatest fear. Owen's death was unexpected. Though slight of build he was rarely unwell. When he left for Cairo no one doubted his return. Even now her ear is tuned to his key in the lock. News of the accident came via the British Embassy. The Chancellor said the house was hers for a month but then she must make way for the new tutor and his wife. In the last month in Cambridge she was in receipt of several proposals - one was for marriage.

'You can marry me,' said Freddie. 'Other than pride what's to stop you?'

'It's not a question of pride,' Julia had retorted. 'It's about respect.'

'Respect for whom?'

'For Owen and for me and my son!'

'I do respect you and given the opportunity would adore your son.'

'Freddie, this is wrong,' she'd protested. 'You ought not to talk this way.'

'I dare not do otherwise. It's time and opportunity.'

'But why now? Do you think it right to declare your feelings with my husband not cold in his grave?'

'Owen Passmore is alongside his beloved Pharaohs. The sun will shine on his bones forever and a day. Neither he nor his grave shall ever be cold again. The same cannot be said of me, Julianna, or my grave should you not save me.'

* * *

Last night Matty dreamt of Mister Punch. One summer the Punch and Judy man came to Cambridge, a gaudy striped tent set up in a field. 'Let's go and see the puppets,' said Owen. Matty returned screaming. 'No Mister Punch!' Since then if he has a nightmare hook-nosed Punch is the bugaboo. Last night Julia heard him crying. 'Mumma, Mister Punch is here!' Newly painted, the door to his bedroom stuck. Matty's screaming stopped. The silence worse than any shriek she pushed the door. It opened. He was asleep.

At breakfast she said Punch was a puppet and couldn't hurt anyone. Matty was serene. 'He's gone,' was all he said. To the Wolf he said more.

'I hear Punch came to your lad last night,' said Luke.

'Yes, he had a nightmare.'

'Well, he won't be having another, leastways not wi' Mister Punch. The nasty brute was eaten up by a crocodile.'

'A crocodile?'

'Aye, the Seed Lady brought it in a basket.'

'And did the Seed Lady leave an address so I might thank her?'

'No, but Matty says he's seen her putting seeds in the ground.'

Seeds have been found in the loft and good linen bed-sheets and a Georgian silver tea-service. There was a diary too with notes on sowing and planting. This morning Julia shook seeds into her hand, a strange feeling, as though touching the one that had placed them in the trunk.

* * *

Half-past nine and Matty is still awake. 'Go to sleep! It's late.' Julia closed the door and went downstairs. 'We don't want a repeat of last night!'

He spends too much time at the Nelson. Feted as Nan's little man and entertained by guests at the Inn, he finds life at the cottage dull and the cooking not to his taste. Yesterday he spat his porridge out. 'Bumpy,' he said. It was lumpy but that is no way to behave. Unfortunately, until she's back from London there's nothing she can do.

Knowing he is to visit the Nelson tomorrow Matty is happy and talks of seeing Tabby Cat. Dear Matty, unable to converse with the outer world he creates an inner world. It would take too long to list the joys and fears inherent to that world. His greatest fear is of being stifled; lean too close and he'll cover his eyes with his hands. Now at one with the night he sings of whiskers and paws and his love of Luke Roberts. The day Owen died Matty sang to the stars. It was a warm summer evening in England, a lamp-man lighting the quad. Silver and sweet, Matty's humming had rose through the evening air.

'What are you doing, Dear Heart?' she'd asked.

'Singing to the stars.'

51

'And do the stars hear you?'

Matty's eyes were great pools of knowing. 'Papa hears me.'

* * *

Julia sits at the piano. From song-sheets found in a piano stool one imagines the Newman sisters were fond of Stephen Foster. Julia was weaned on Schubert. Owen preferred early music, Gluck's *Orpheus and Eurydice* a favourite. He once asked what she thought of the aria, *Che faro*. 'For like Orpheus,' he said, 'I would go to the Gates of Hell should you need me.'

A clattering of hooves brought her from her reverie - Luke Roberts leads a pony and trap into the yard. 'Mister Wolf!' The bedroom door slammed. Night-shirt billowing, Matty rushes down and out through the front door.

'Hang on, lad!' Luke caught him. 'Don't go throwing yourself at animals like that!' Highly strung and frustrated, words trapped in his head, Luke sees himself in Matty. 'Animals don't like sudden moves. They're like to bolt.'

Hair untied and face glowing Julianna appears at the door and straightway he's in a tangle. Resentment locks up heart and head the minute she comes into view. She's been nothing but polite, even so the sight of her or mention of her name and his tongue grows in size and he splutters like an angry fool.

'Don't swing on Mr Roberts like that, Matty,' she says. 'It's not polite.'

'He's alright. He means no harm.'

'He shouldn't do it. It's presumptuous.'

Luke swung the boy up in his arms. 'Do you hear what your

mother says? You're presumptuous. Now what does that word mean?'

Matty laughed and shook his head.

'No, me neither. We're both a couple of ignorant clods. You stay here and learn and I'll go back to my lonely room, dredge out a dictionary and try to understand what she might mean.'

The boy laughed again. Then he took hold of Luke's ears and pulling him forward delivered a smacking kiss. 'Huff 'n puff, Mister Wolf.'

Luke smiled, out of the mouth of babes! 'Go to your mother. It's time you was abed.' Remembering the point of the journey he turned. 'I brought Matty a present. I thought it might keep him company and help you be less afraid of plant-stealers.' He opened the box and the dog peered out. 'This is Kaiser, so the chap in the bar said. Poor brute, ribs like a harp, maybe when he's fattened up he'll be more an English dog and you can re-name him.'

'I'll keep the name.' Julia stroked the dog and it licked her hand. 'He looks like he could be a king.'

'He's a good watchdog. The slightest noise and he's on it.'

She touched Luke's hand. 'This is so kind.'

He couldn't stop the fire burning in his cheeks. He opened a bag and two kittens peeped out. 'He didn't come alone. These little dears were with him. I don't know if you want them. I couldn't leave them. I wasn't sure what the chap would do if I didn't take them. Most likely end up in the cut. Do you want them?' he said diffidently. 'It's alright. I can take them if you don't.'

'I'll take them all, dog and kittens.' Hair cascading streams of silken gold over sooty fur she gathered them up. 'Thank you,

Luke,' she whispered, 'You could not have given me and my boy a nicer gift.'

Huff and Puff! God smote Luke Roberts. Swallowed up in her eyes Mister Wolf fell from a great height. Lord, she is lovely. Of an evening he comes to stand by the wall to hear her play. The Forge is the other end of town. If he can't come she's still there, back straight and hands poised, the tinkling sound rising in the evening air. It's as he said to Matty, you ought not to make a sudden move on a wild creature. They're apt to bolt. This, the peony red of her lips and her hand on his, is a sudden move. Now, a maddened creature, Luke is bolting headlong in love with Julianna Dryden and nothing on earth will haul him back.

CHAPTER FOUR

A Corset

Julia is staying at Langora, the house in Russell Square. Seven am Friday morning she woke to find Evie crawling into bed beside her. 'A hug, please, Ju-ju,' she groaned, her face lined with pain. 'I have a headache.'

'Why do you get such headaches? The way they knock you out suggests more than the everyday complaint.'

'I am a sinner. One gets according to one's lights.'

'No really, Evie, why do you?'

'My sycophant doctor says it's due to extreme sensitivity. My honest Stefan says it's a neurological disorder.'

'Did he suggest medication?'

'He said I should join the Suffrage movement.'

'What!'

'No, he didn't, though the amount of spirit imbibed this quarter points to one thing, either Jamieson or me is on the way to being an alcoholic.'

'So what do you plan to do about it?'

'Sack Jamieson!'

'You wouldn't dare.'

Evie laughed and winced. 'I would not. I am terrified of the man.'

'He is rather fearsome looking. What exactly does he do?'

'He's my butler and chucker-outer.'

'Do you need to chuck out?'

'Not so far but there's always a first. Oh hush! I didn't leave the warmth of my bed to talk of Jamieson. I came to be comforted and to say I want you to leave that miserable croft in Norfolk and live here in Russell Square.'

'I can't do that.'

'Why not? From what I hear they don't deserve you.'

Julia put her arm about Evie, a headache is a headache and the needs of a forty-year-old not so different to a three-year-old. Arm under Evie's head, she gazed up at mirrored glass that is the bed canopy. It reflects the luxury of the room: heavy bed hangings and lace pillows, pale blue silk-covered chaise by the bay window and elegant French dressing table. Here, the floors are covered with Aubusson rugs. Back home Julia steps out of bed onto floor-boards. Even on the warmest day she rushes from bed to bath snatching clothes as she runs. It's not as Spartan as it used to be, Luke Roberts having worked his magic. It has hot and cold running water and other amenities but compared to the opulence of Langora - and the excess - servants ever on hand to light the way through the many rooms with tens of candles that glitter throughout the house, the cottage is as Evelyn says, a croft.

'You don't use oil-lamps here.'

'I can't bear the smell,' Evie replied. 'I have them in Gloucestershire, my man there an expert trimmer it saves a deal of mess.'

'And electricity? I've been reading about that.'

'What, harsh light exposing me and my bones to the world! Thank you I'll cleave to candlelight. It helps me look less of a wizened old woman.'

'You could never look like a wizened old woman.'

'If I don't it's because of the fancy creams I buy at fancy prices.'

Evie talked of cosmetics. Julia fears she must stop coming here. In Norfolk she wakes knowing she must do her best for those dependent upon her. An hour here and she's yearning for silly things like crushed pearls to lighten the complexion. This house is not restful. Evie is not restful! She's either laughing or in deep depression, 'the Black Dog barking,' she calls it. Freddie says wealth makes one dangerous - one must be careful not to be gifted into ruin. Julia is increasingly wary, Evie one minute giving and the next taking back.

'I say!' Evie nudged her. 'Come back from wherever you are.'

'I was thinking of Matty.'

'You should have brought him with you then you wouldn't have to think. He makes me laugh. Do you know he calls me Mary-Mary as in quite contrary?'

'He shouldn't! And you mustn't let him. He does such things at home.'

Evie leant on her elbow twining Julia's hair about her fingers. 'You see that place as home do you? I see the appeal. Windswept moors and foggy dales chime with the romantic in you, Bronte and unquiet spirits.'

'This is Norfolk we're talking about not Yorkshire.'

'No but your Nanette is from Yorkshire as is her son, the dark-eyed blacksmith who breaks ice on the pump of a morning and defends his lady's honour by banishing ruffians from the castle walls.'

'You know a great deal about my life.'

'I don't know enough! Who is he that he should defend you so?'

'Luke and his father work on the cottage making improve-ments.'

'What kind of improvements?'

'They knock down walls.'

'Ah bully-boys! How delicious!' Evie kissed Julia's shoulder. 'And are they good at what they do? Are they strong but sensitive, warm but in control?'

'They are reliable.'

'Lord, how boring!'

'No, not boring, honest and able.'

'Not too honest I hope. That would make them hesitant. I don't like hesitance. We should all rush at life waving a big cudgel. Do you think your Heathcliffe might rush at me waving a big cudgel?'

'Evelyn!'

'Well, why not? Why should you have all the fun? I must have my bit even if only a bit. Invite them over and bring your Nan with you.'

'I don't think she'd leave the Lord Nelson.'

'The Lord Nelson?' Evie shrieked. 'What-ho, Lady Hamilton, yet another woman tied to a man's lanyard!'

'Nan's her own person. Owen would've liked her.'

'And that's why you like her. You judge everything through your late husband's eyes.'

'Is that a bad thing?'

'It impedes rather. Owen was a silent man. He rarely offered opinion on anything yet I suspect he knew more about life than anyone living. He saw through veils.' Evie yawned. 'He certainly saw through mine.'

'Do you wear a veil?'

'Certainly I do, every minute of every day, and not so much a veil as a suit of armour. It's the only way to get by.'

'Why do you wear it?'

'Why does any warrior wear armour but to protect himself?'

'And from what do you protect yourself?'

'You.'

'Me?' Julia laughed. 'Why protect yourself from me? What possible harm can I do you?'

'You can break my heart.'

'Break your heart...?' It came then, that tight feeling in the chest and sense of being drawn into a situation she can't manage. She knew what Evelyn was saying and understood the implication and that it had always been there.

Blue-veined and paper thin, Evie's hand lies on Julia's breast. During the day the fingers are heavy with rings and the wrist covered by a knitted bracelet. This morning fresh from slumber the hand is free exposing a pattern of scars. Evie's right wrist bears similar marks. Julia doesn't enquire - the wounds too deep and too recent for anyone to ask.

Such a tiny hand, it opens and closes as though clutching air. There is such need in that hand, such fierce hunger, it terrifies Julia. She sat up. 'It must be late. People will be wondering where you are.'

'This is my house,' said Evie. 'None question my whereabouts. None asks of my intention. I am mistress here. Servant and guest alike wait upon me.'

'Even so, I think I should get up.'

Evie shrugged. 'Then get up. No one is stopping you.'

Oh, she should've stayed silent, should have bitten back the words, but unable to lie the denial burst from Julia's lips. 'I can't do this.'

'Can't do what?'

'I can't do whatever it is you want of me. I can't give in that way.'

Evie leaned away. 'I don't know that I have asked anything of you.'

Julia was silent.

'Have I asked anything of you?'

Still Julia was silent.

'Tell me!' Face tight, Evie sat up. 'Have I ever asked anything of you?' When still there was no reply she got out of the bed and left the bedroom.

* * *

Julia didn't see Evie again until mid-afternoon. Time ticked away and silence descended over the house. Then around three Evie poked her head round the library door. 'Can you give me a moment? I need to finish the portrait.'

They walked through to where the easel was set up. There might have been a wall between them. 'How is your head?' Julia ventured a question.

'Monstrous. I can't think beyond it. In that you might do me a service. I have a box this evening. It's not a big party, John Sargent, his *bon ami* Paul Hellue and the news chappie, Masson. There's Stefan, of course, Freddie, and Robert and Mamie Scholtz. Robert is on the board of the Museum of Fine Arts. He's been here scooping up hotels. Tomorrow they leave for Boston. I promised Puccini while they're here and Puccini I'd like them to have.'

'I'd be glad to help.'

'Glad to help!' Evie mimicked. 'You are so mealy-mouthed.'

'I've never been to the opera.'

Evie wiped the brushes. 'You'll like it. People in their best togs, everyone looking to see who's there and who's not - it is a bit of a circus.'

'So it's not only about music.'

'Lord no! It's Cats looking at Kings! Most could care less what happens on stage. They've come to gape at their betters. As I said, a circus, a Grandstand view of the day's flesh-market, and tonight, you being the new and most beautiful face, you're the main dish.'

'If you really mean me to go, Evie, I suggest you stop there.'

'God's sake don't pet! As usual you're flapping at the thought of being seen, though why I don't know since you're every day on display at the National. A woman should have her portrait painted when she's young and beautiful. It's to look back on when old and furious. And none of your chocolate box *Lady of Shallot* either, a John Sargent beauty, silent and silky.'

She rang the bell. 'I'll have Bella fish out the blue *Poiret* gown.'

'As this is a very public place don't you think a darker colour?'

'I do not. This is Covent Garden not Hackney Town Hall. You go glorious or not at all. I don't believe in mourning. Why should a woman shut herself away when a man dies? It's one step from burning on the bier. Only a man would think of it. Sidney died and I was sorry, but that don't mean I need put a pistol to my head. The dead are not sad. Why weep when they do not.'

* * *

Two hours into the sitting and Julia is weary. Usually Evie chatters, today she works in silence, Julia appearing as an angel astride a Unicorn.

'Why a Unicorn?'

'It is a mythical being.'

'And the angel?'

'Is also a mythical being. Now ask me who and what you are, Ju-ju!'

'You're angry with me. I hurt you. I'm sorry. It wasn't meant.'

Evie shook her head. 'I don't want apologies.'

'What do you want?'

'I want not to be used.'

'Do I use you?'

'Not you particularly but someone always wants something! And please keep still! This was meant as a gift for Freddie. Twitch and all he'll get is a bare canvas.' She laid down the brush. 'That's it. I had thought to have you kneeling at a manger but see you now a Pagan goddess or that other bovine creature Freddie's always waffling about, the one minus arms.'

'The Venus de Milo? Yes, Owen always found her amusing.'

Julia left and Evelyn sat gazing at the painting and then dipping the brush into scarlet paint streaked the angel's wings with blood. 'You and your Owen!' she muttered. 'I dare say he did find Venus amusing. Naked and minus paws and claws is how most men see the ideal.'

* * *

Julia is desperate to leave. It's not only Evie being difficult. Freddie was at the station yesterday to meet her. He'd doffed his hat. 'Close your eyes, Ju-ju!' he said. 'You've a smut on your cheek.' She closed her eyes and what did he do but kiss her lips. 'I've been an age kicking my heels in this hell-hole,' he whispered against her mouth. 'I deserve a reward.'

They travelled then to Russell Square in silence, Julia's lips afire and Freddie pale and troubled. Widow of the Rhode Island railroad man, Sidney Bevington-Smythe, Evie is fabulously wealthy. The Honourable Freddie is heir to a name but that's all. When his parents Lord and Lady Baines Carrington sent him out into the world it was not to return with the hand of an impoverished widow. Evie says he's meant for the American market. 'These girls have the very best calling cards. They are the hope for impecunious children like Freddie who only has a pedigree to recommend him.'

Nan is another keen to point out the dangers of fortune-hunters. Last week they stood in the terraced garden watching carriages arrive at Lansdowne House, or Greenfields as it is now known. 'Why Greenfields?'

'I don't know,' said Nan, 'but whoever they are they're not gentry.'

'Is that not promising for Bakers End?'

'Newly rich don't know how to spend. And they won't use local trade, they pay over the odds at the Army and Navy thinking it makes 'em gentry.'

Julia was not inclined to judge. 'People must survive the best way they can.'

'Aye, and there's plenty men as likes a bit of fun while surviving, so mind you keep your treasure under lock and key.'

'I doubt I'm in danger.'

'You think not?' Nan had smiled grimly. 'Greenfields leans against your property. One look at you and they'll come runnin'. Keep the doors locked. You don't want a fly-by-night playing fast-and-loose with your heart.'

Now, Julia stands before the cheval-mirror in a satin corset while butterflies play fast and loose with her nerves. Scarlet with black satin ribbons, the corset is Evie's rebuttal to a plea for a sober gown.

'You're tired.' Julia regarded the maid. 'Sit while I do my hair?'

'I couldn't, madam. Milady wouldn't like it.' Yet Bella perched, her stomach swollen. 'You're quick with your hair, madam. How do you get it to stay?'

'I curve it round my hand. There's a trick to it. I'll show you if you like and then you can do the same for Lady Carrington.'

'I don't do Milady's hair now. My hands won't let me.'

'They do look rather swollen.'

Bella hid her hands behind her back. 'It's the baby.'

Julia's heart went out to the girl. This is a large household and she but a child bearing another child. 'How old are you, Bella?

'Sixteen come August.'

'That's young for a lady's maid.'

'I was learnin' to be a dresser. I hate this baby. It's ruined my life.'

'You mustn't say that. You must look to the future. See how I loop my hair back of my neck? You could do it next time I'm here.'

'I'll not bother, thank you, madam. I go tomorrow.

'Will you go to your mother's?'

'I can't. She wouldn't want me this way.'

'She doesn't know about the baby?'

'I daresn't tell her.'

'Forgive me for asking but the father, can he help?'

'No.'

'So where will you go?'

A tear slid down Bella's cheek. 'Where girls like me go.'

Julia snapped the last pin in her hair. 'I leave for Norfolk on Sunday. Would you like to come with me? You'd have to share and I couldn't pay much, probably only food and board at first. Best you think about it.'

'Must I think?' said the girl wearily. 'Can't I just come?'

'Let me speak with Lady Carrington first.'

'Do you think Milady will mind?'

'I'm sure she'll be pleased for you.'

* * *

Julia called the Nelson enquiring of Matty. Nan answered, or rather shouted. '**Hello then, Anna, can you hear me**!'

'Yes I can hear you.'

'**Are you sure? It's a long way**!'

'It is a long way, even so I can hear you. How is Matthew?'

'**Oh don't worry 'bout him! He's been out with Luke fishin'.**'

'Did they have fun?'

'**I don't know about fun! They didn't catch anythin' but judging' the racket they made comin' in they had a grand old time.**'

'That is so kind of your son.'

65

'**Luke loves the lad as do we all**.' There was silence then as though Nan were meditating on her comment. Then she was back and shouting even louder. '**I'm off! I've things to do! Be careful! London is a big place. I'm goin'. Did you hear what I said... Anna? I am puttin' the thing down now...!**'

Julia went from the phone to the conservatory to look at the Lovebirds. Owen would say fine feathers make fine birds. Blue silk overlaid with a skim of darker tulle, bodice low across the bosom, the only touch of light the diamond clip in her hair, Julia wears fine feathers indeed, and yet the atmosphere in the house so sharp she feels stripped naked.

'I say, Ju-ju, remind me to consult you next time I mix my colour palette!'

A fairy between two giants, Evie is coming through the loggia. She strips paint-splashed cuffs away while talking in a lisping drawl that accompanies too much wine. 'John, you remember your strawberry milkmaid? Today she is a River Maiden, soul wrapped in ice. Beware all who fall under her spell.'

John Singer Sargent bowed. 'Good evening, Mrs Dryden.'

'Good evening, Mr Sargent.'

'Ju-ju was keen to proclaim her widow status tonight and wear black but was persuaded otherwise.' Evie gestured. 'And, as you two connoisseurs of beauty do now bear witness, blue works well with such glorious hair.'

John Sargent smiled. 'I believe this lady would be beautiful whatever the colour of her gown. Mrs Dryden, may I present my friend, Daniel Masson?'

'How do you do, Mr Masson?'

'Your servant, ma'm.'

'What kind of introduction is that?' Evie dragged Daniel forward as though producing a gorgeous buck-rabbit from a top hat. 'This is Daniel Greville Masson, American cousin to the Warwicks. No doubt you've heard of him, Ju-ju. Prize-winning writer and journalist, hero and fighter of wars, he is a man in the mould of Livingstone and Stanley!'

Daniel Masson winced. 'I am a news man and writer but beyond that a complete nobody.'

'Oh you're too modest and a deal too throwaway of your life!' Evie patted his arm. 'I envy you, happy male that you are, free to travel the globe without needing to put down roots. It must be so exciting.'

'Don't envy me, Lady Carrington. A news-man's life can be exciting but more often is downright tedious. As for putting down roots I've long wished to do so but always found the present incumbent preferring his.'

Evie laughed. 'We do like to hold onto our own, be it ee'r so humble, as the dear Queen would have it. Are you drawn to one particular country?'

'I'm drawn to many but lethargic by nature I'd sooner it not beset by war.'

'That limits your choices somewhat, Daniel,' said John Sargent.

'Yes, John, as I have found.'

'And your stay here?' Evie took his arm. 'It is of peaceful intent?'

He bowed. 'Peace, Puccini, and the pleasure and privilege of an hour in Mrs Dryden's company.'

Julia looked up. 'I beg your pardon?'

'Ah *mia culpa!*' Evie bit her thumb. 'In all the rushing about I forgot to say it was Daniel who asked you to sit. Do you mind terribly, Julianna?'

'Not if it has been arranged.'

'Excuse me, ma'am, but that's not right.' Red faced, Daniel Masson stepped forward. 'Pushed at you like this it is an imposition.'

'I am happy to sit for you.'

'Are you sure? I wouldn't want you uncomfortable.'

'But Ju-ju can't be uncomfortable.' Evie put her arm about Julia's waist. 'She is a statue, cool and quiet as alabaster and thus never at odds with the world.'

The silence was broken by a shout. Freddie has arrived.

CHAPTER FIVE

The Opera

Charles Dickens says every house has secrets, London houses especially: '*an ancient city in an ancient land every footfall rattles somebody's bones.*'

Friday evening the bones in Russell Square were rattling, and Evelyn Carrington a tipsy butterfly flitting from one guest to another leaving them dazzled. Everyone was ill at ease, the most obvious tension between Freddie and Daniel Masson. Tall, fair, and with natural grace, both men were alike in looks. Tail-coats and white weskits, both wore similar apparel, the difference in boutonnières, Freddie sporting a pink rose and Daniel white frangipani.

That they had met before was apparent, clipping hands and stepping back with such cold disdain one might've thought Evie's drawing room a forest glade at dawn and a Second drawing attention to a brace of pistols.

Julia retreated to the Hall and a mural of the Last Supper where the Lord Jesus is depicted as a lion and apostles grouped about other animals.

Daniel Masson joined her. 'What do you think of this, Mrs Dryden?'

'A lion seems right for the Lord as does St John envisioned as a deer.'

'And Judas as a Billy-goat?'

'I'm not sure about that. My father had another view of

Judas. The congregation of St Mary's Bentham is small and very conservative. If aired, his views on many things would have sent him, and us, packing.'

'My father was a business man. He saw everything through the mighty dollar. He reckoned he knew one animal from another. In Judas he would have seen a snake. Can I ask what your father saw that set his view apart?'

'He saw a man more loyal to the Lord than we are taught to believe.'

'Ah well, I do see how that opinion might raise eyebrows.'

Julia smiled. 'Phillip Dryden had many such thoughts along that line. He would say as with the bible truth is open to debate - one must search for it.'

'Well then, with truth in mind I need to talk with you in private.'

'I say!' Freddie was at Julia's elbow. 'What are you two discussin' so closely?'

'The mural.'

'And did you come to any conclusion?'

'Not really,' said Daniel. 'Mrs Dryden and I were just playing with ideas.'

'Playing with ideas?' Freddie took Julia's arm. 'Aren't we all?'

* * *

Clearly angry, he bundled her into the first carriage and then flung into the opposite seat. 'You oughtn't to waste your time discussin' tosh, Ju-ju,' he said chewing the top of his cane. 'It don't get you anywhere.'

The carriage was pulling away when Daniel climbed aboard. 'I'll share with you, Carrington. The cab back there is awful tight for us tall guys.'

They rolled away. Twenty minutes later, the road heavy with traffic, they'd hardly progressed. Freddie rapped the roof. 'What's taking so long?'

The driver shouted back. 'There's a horse down in Cambridge Street, sir.'

'Well cut along the back! Much longer and we'll miss the first half.'

'If the road's blocked and people affected won't the house delay start?' said Daniel. 'They do in Philly when the weather's bad, though having said that a minute late in Bayreuth and you're locked out.'

'Been to Bayreuth have you?' said Freddie.

'I caught a couple of performances last year.'

'What did you see?'

'*Gotterdammerung*. I thought the music swell.'

'Swell?' Freddie sneered. 'Wagner requires discipline and commitment. In '87 Evie and I sat through the whole of the Ring Cycle here in London.'

Daniel Masson smiled. 'And you just a lad in short pants.'

'Old enough to appreciate genius when heard!'

'And what are your thoughts on Senor Giacomo Puccini?'

'I have no thoughts. It would be like comparing the ballet to Burlesque.'

'I have a liking for the Burlesque.' Daniel yawned. 'It's good to laugh. John and I are fans of Stephen Foster. We sing his songs all the time.'

Freddie curled his lip. 'You don't say.'

'My father liked Stephen Foster's music.' Julia tried easing tension. 'So did the ladies before me, copies of *Oh Susanna* in their piano stool.'

'What do you know?' Daniel Masson grinned. 'The parallels are stacking up. Little more of that, Mrs Dryden – nothing too heretical, of course - and our meeting will be what I'd call fortune and my mother fate.'

* * *

The curtain came down. 'Don't bother applauding!' Freddie grabbed Julia's arm. 'We've a booth reserved in the upper bar. If we scoot along now we'll have time for a bottle of fizz *and* a bite.'

'Thank you, I prefer to stay here.'

'Oh come on, Julianna! Any second the orchestra will be on the run and we'll be lucky to get a glass of beer.'

'You go, Freddie. I prefer to stay.'

'I can't go and leave you here alone.'

'Mrs Dryden won't be alone,' said Stefan Adelman. 'I too prefer not to plough through the scrimmage.'

House lights were brightening. People were heading toward the bars and refreshment areas. Freddie shrugged. 'Suit yourself. Coming, John?'

John Sargent hesitated as did Daniel Masson.

'Please don't wait for me,' said Julia. 'I am perfectly comfortable.'

She turned back to the stage, her head filled with glorious sights and sounds how could she sit and chatter about nothing.

Stefan was smiling. 'You feel it?'

'How could I not?'

'There are those who do not as I'm sure you're aware.'

'It's not just the music! It's everything, the audience and the giddy moving to-and-fro! I didn't know such a world existed.'

Julia talked of her father, who could translate Latin and Greek and converse in Italian and French, but whose world, he once said, had shrunk to the size of a pea. She said how in the evening he would sit, one candle alight, transcribing *Messiah* so the church choir might be able to rehearse.

'Would your father have liked *Madama Butterfly*?' said Stefan.

'He would've loved it, as he would've loved Evie who brought you to me, Stefan. You saved my boy's life.'

He was silent.

'I'm sorry. All this chattering? I'm doing the very thing I didn't want to do.'

'Not at all! Your delight is a gift! Through your eyes I see again what I have lost.' He shook his head. 'But I'll not dampen the day talking sadness.'

'Stefan, please! What is it?'

'My beloved wife, my Karoline, cannot appreciate music as she did. A terrible disease strips her of all joy in life.'

'I'm sorry, poor lady!'

'*Ja*, poor indeed, her mind bedevilled with many anxieties.'

'Can nothing be done?'

'Nothing.'

'Might one visit?'

Stefan shrugged. 'You could and she might smile. She doesn't know me. My only consolation is the care given at the sanatorium.

The day I met your boy I had just visited. I left the bedside of one suffering child to find another.'

'How long has she been ill? I mean, when did this start?'

'Soon after the birth of our son.'

'You have a son?'

Stefan shook his head. 'He died before drawing breath.'

'Oh my dear!' Julia took his hand. 'I am so very sorry.'

'It is I who am sorry to have given you pain.' He squeezed her hand, his fingers iron bars. 'It is my pain to bear and not to share.'

They sat in silence, Daniel Masson coming through saw the chairs pushed together and turned to go. 'Excuse me!'

'No!' Stefan stood up. 'Do not go, *Herr* Masson!'

'Forgive the intrusion. I was bringing Mrs Dryden a glass of wine.'

'Sir, your appearance is timely. I am making a burden of sorrow. It ought not to be. Give my apologies to the rest of the party. Say I am called away.' He kissed Julia's hand. '*Gute nacht, gnadige Frau.*'

Daniel Masson hung back. 'I guess I barged in on something.'

'Doctor Adelman is a friend. He has been a great help to my son.'

'Your boy is ill?'

Julia couldn't speak of Matty, not after learning of Stefan's life. 'He is better now, thank you.'

'May I sit?' Daniel offered the glass. 'I came to bring refreshment but also to say how frustrated I am with the way the sitting was thrust on you.'

'Don't be. Evelyn suffered a headache most of the day. It's

likely she forgot to tell me.' She sipped the wine. 'Are you in London long?'

'When I came it was only for a month or two but an issue with property holds me. My mother likes England. She is looking to buy.'

'And you? Do you like England?'

'I don't care for your grey skies. I have a ranch in California where the sun always shines. My mother hails from Philadelphia. A Greville among the first settlers she is genetically inclined toward the British climate.'

'Your mother returns to family roots and you to advise her in her quest.'

'Hah!' Amused, he laughed. 'Callista Greville Masson doesn't take advice. She lives and breathes by her own deliberations. A creature no bigger than my thumb and yet she has more energy than the whole of the South African Company and their war-mongering shysters clubbed together.'

When Julia stared he spread his hands. 'Excuse me, I'm lately back from the Transvaal and saw too much. Mrs Dryden?' He leaned forward. 'I must speak with you. It concerns Norfolk and where you live.'

'The cottage?'

'Yes, the cottage.'

'Ah there you are?' The door to the Box opened. 'Beautiful Julianna, bird of Paradise, you haven't flown away yet?' Freddie was back with the rest of the party and conversation ceased.

* * *

With the last curtain call echoing they fought to get out. It was madness out in the square, people surging up and down looking for transport.

'Bit of a scrum here, John,' said Daniel Masson.

'It's always the same after a concert, good manners down the plug-hole.'

'Freddie!' Mr and Mrs Scholtz were first to leave. 'We can take you and Mrs Dryden! We've room and it wouldn't be out of our way.'

'We're fine, thanks,' Freddie grasped Julia's elbow. 'We'll take a motor cab.'

Having suffered his fidgets throughout the opera Julia was determined not to be alone with him. 'I will go with Mr and Mrs Scholtz.'

'I don't think so.' Freddie pushed toward the kerb. 'Sugar frosting outside and hot spice beneath, you're delicious candy, Ju-ju. I must open you up.'

A cab pulled alongside. 'See Mrs Dryden back to the Square, will you, Paul?' Daniel Masson lifted her inside. 'John and I will shuffle Carrington along.'

Paul Hellue climbed in, Daniel tapped the door and the cab chugged away.

* * *

A foot inside and Evie came running and with a grasp not unlike Freddie's, hotly proprietary. 'How dared you to do it!'

'What?'

'How dared you lure Bella to your home?'

Julia stared. 'The maid?'

'Yes the maid! How dared you interfere in the running of my house?'

'I didn't think I'd interfered. I offered a place to stay, that's all.'

'Well you'd no right to without talking to me.'

'Yes, I'm sorry, I should've spoken but I didn't think you'd mind.'

'That shows how little you know of me and the workings of my house. I do mind and can't think of any of my connections that wouldn't feel the same. You have undermined my authority and exposed me to ridicule.'

'How have I?'

'Bella was my maid. She was intimate to me. She knew my ways and was privy to situations personal to me. How could I or any other sensitive woman be comfortable knowing her in the employ of an acquaintance?'

'I see. Well, put like that I understand your concern, though I assure you I'd never enquire of your doings as I'm sure Bella would never tell.'

'How do you know she wouldn't? These girls have eyes and ears. They see and hear things and for a price can be induced to reveal all.'

'Not Bella! She seems a nice girl.'

'Pregnant at sixteen? Yes that is nice! Of course she'd tell. A personal maid to Lady Evelyn Carrington, she'd spill the beans to anyone willing to listen.'

'I don't know what to say to you other than I wouldn't pry into your life.'

'Don't be naive, Julianna! You must see how awkward you've made things.'

Julia stared. Who is this? Where is the real Evelyn Carrington, has some white-faced fury stolen her soul? 'She had nowhere to go.'

'Then she should've come to me instead of tattling behind my back! And why would you want her? She'll be popping soon and you saddled with a squalling brat. What would you do then?'

'Keep her and the baby.'

'You shall not keep that baby just as you shall not keep her!'

'I don't understand. You dislike me taking Bella and yet were happy to recommend Mrs McLaughlin. Where was your shared intimacy then?'

Evie laughed. 'There was none. I couldn't have borne that woman's hands on my flesh. Bella's young and fresh. She smells of flowers not pissy drawers. The closest McLaughlin came to a secret of mine was via backstairs gossip.'

'Then perhaps it's as well she is with me.'

'You say so?' Evie's eyes narrowed. 'In point of interest, how do you plan to support all these waifs and strays when you can barely support yourself? Another mouth to feed, and the baby when it comes, I doubt anything earned sitting will plug a hole that size in the housekeeping.'

'You think not?'

'I do and I think the same of any of my dispensations. They're done. You've cooked the Golden Goose, Ju-ju! Nothing left now but the bones.'

'I had better withdraw for the night and catch an early train tomorrow. Will you allow me to apologise to you for hurt caused, and to Mr Masson for a broken engagement, and to Bella for disappointment incurred.'

'I may pass on your regret to Daniel but will say nothing to

Bella. She and her tears left via the back door hours ago.'

'Oh Evelyn!

'Don't you Evelyn me!' Evie's eyes flashed. 'This morning you questioned my feelings for you suggesting I sought a gift you were not willing to give. You hurt me when you said that. What have I ever asked of you other than friendship? It's all I ever asked. I've given so much to you. What did you give in return, Julianna Dryden, other than middle-class suspicion and ingratitude?'

Julia fled. Once inside the room she locked the door, an image burned into her brain, a shell cracked open and another face peering through. More distress waited in the bedroom. The closet had been stripped of the rest of her belongings, the clothes she had on and a railway ticket all that was left.

* * *

Three in the morning the bedroom door was tried. Julia heard the first fumble and saw the doorknob swivel. A brief cessation of movement and then the knob was turned again and furiously worked back and forth.

The twisting ceased, footsteps padding away.

'Oh!' She leapt from the bed and dashing through the dressing room locked the outer door. A moment later that door was tried and with the same fury.

Horrible! The key heavy and cold in her hand she stood gazing at the door. She had never before thought to lock it. Maids needing access she always left the key in the lock. There were no maids tonight, Evelyn denying aid.

The rattling ceased. There was an odd hush and then a mouth was pressed to the outer lock and breath blown against the metal. No words, none that she could understand, only a soughing hiss. 'Ju-ju......!'

All night she sat watching the hands of the clock crawl toward dawn. Eventually floorboards began to creak, the maids going about their business.

Taking her bag she unlocked the door. Jamieson, the butler, the chucker-outer, was at the bottom of the stairs. Face impassive he stepped forward. 'Good morning, Madam.'

'Good morning.' She handed him the fur cape.

'Pardon me.' He hung it back about her shoulders. 'It's chilly outdoors first thing in the morning. Best you keep it.'

She didn't argue. She could hardly walk the streets with bare shoulders.

'Might I call you a cab?'

'Thank you, I can walk. It's not far to the station.'

She turned down the path and had walked about twenty paces when Jamieson came after her. 'Your handkerchief, madam!'

'My handkerchief?'

'Yes.'

A handkerchief was proffered, a scrap of paper visible through the cloth.

She took it. 'Thank you, Jamieson.'

He bowed. 'No, madam, thank you.'

CHAPTER SIX

Too Late

Julia didn't read the note until she was inside the Cottage. Throughout her journey home - early morning travellers trying not to stare - the handkerchief remained clenched in her fist along with tears she could not shed. Once indoors, and having waded through Mrs Mac's grievances, she went to her bedroom and unfolded the cloth. Scrawled on the back of a laundry list was an address in London and the words '*she's here.*'

One person would help. She changed and then went to the post-office, wiring Stefan, saying she needed help and would he call at his earliest convenience. It seemed wrong to involve another but what else could she do.

On the way back she called at the Lord Nelson. 'Is Matty well?'

'He's fine!' Nan bundled her in, 'which is more than can be said for you!'

A lock grated in Julia's ears. 'I didn't sleep last night. It was rather noisy.'

Nan questioned the trip, how was the opera. Julia described the gowns and the jewels but after a while ran out of words.

'That don't seem like much,' said Nan. 'I reckon I'd get more satisfaction from a brass band playin' in the park. Will you be going again?'

'I don't think so.'

'Well that's no bad thing. If you're runnin' about with your posh friends you're not with your lad. You need to find a way to maintain yourself, Anna. Don't want to lean on others, especially if they're going to let you down.'

Days passed and Julia wondered if offering Bella a home was a mistake. Evie feels things deeply. She loves to give and make others happy. Then she drinks and takes pills and flies into a rage, beating her brother about the head while threatening servants who displease with dismissal. So many souls under one skin, one wonders who is uppermost when breathing through keyholes.

Julia wrote to thank Evie for her many kindnesses. She then resolved to put thoughts of Russell Square aside. As Nan said, she must make her own way.

Sunday was a long day made longer by peevish servants. Julia could hear them, nothing specific, a general moaning long enough and loud enough to be one moan too many. She rang the bell. There was scuffling outside who should enter first, and then, caps askew, they pushed through the door.

'I am rethinking my domestic arrangements,' said Julia. 'As yet my plans are unclear but since any change I make affects you I thought to warn you.'

'*Warn you*!' The words hung in the air. Neither woman spoke. Whatever they planned to say - a long list of petty annoyances - shrivelled to nought.

Mrs Mac was silent, Maggie was less knowing. 'Would madam like Master Matthew's boots polished? And did madam know Maggie takes Kaiser for his evening walk to do his business.' After a while Mrs Mac joined the clamour. 'Had madam noticed the arranging of the sitting-room, all getting along famously?' Three or four similar visits were attempted until they grew weary. Julia doubts she'll keep either, Bella, if found, to be given first choice.

* * *

Six am the bedroom door bursts open, in bounced Matty and the dog.

'Kaiser talks Mumma.'

'Get him off the bed, dear heart. His paws are muddy.'

'But he talks to me and I talk back to him!'

'I'm sure you do. Now remember he is to be your dog! You must take care of him and feed him and not let him dig the flower boarders.'

Matty ran off. 'I'm going for my bath with Mother Hubbard.'

Mrs Mac is a seasoned warrior. Espying an opportunity, she prepares Matty's bath every morning while supervising his dressing. Matty likes it. Oldie Hubbard, as he calls her, reads him a fairy story. Maggie also begins to mend her ways; breakfast is calm, a boiled egg and clean fingers of toast served with a napkin – Maggie's cap a starched sunflower about her face.

Julia was in the garden pulling broad beans when Luke came by.

'Good day to you, Mrs Dryden.'

'Good day to you.'

'A grand day.'

'Yes.'

'Though it promises rain.'

'So I believe.'

Arms folded, he stood watching. Julia carried on picking. 'Everything alright?' he said at length, 'nothing wrong with Matty?'

'He's with Mrs McLaughlin. I believe she intends giving him lessons.'

'Does she? That'll be good for him. He needs to be kept busy. There's a decent school in Lower Bakers but I expect you'll be thinking a private tutor.'

'The thought had crossed my mind.'

'I suppose one-to-one is better if the man is right.'

'Yes, he'd have to be right.'

Luke was silent. 'I finished the front parlour,' then he said. 'It needs to dry out then it will look better, stolen wallpaper and all.'

'I have seen it.' Julia knew he attempted to make her smile and was sorry she couldn't oblige. 'I am pleased with your work. I would recommend you to anyone. Perhaps you will let me have a final reckoning.'

'There's no rush.' Again there was a long silence. 'You'll let me know if there is anything you want doing no matter how small.'

'Thank you.'

Still he looked and still he frowned. Then he gestured. 'Pick from the top or you'll be left with leathery beans.' He was gone striding away.

* * *

Julia goes through the closet removing items given by Evie. It would be churlish to return them but neither in good conscience can they be worn. By midday the closet was thinned to Cambridge days. Fine feathers depleted, she was revealed as a modest house sparrow.

Item after costly item consigned to the loft, many items familiar to her time in Russell Square, Mrs Mac wondered why. 'Are they all to go, madam?'

'More or less.'

'Summer stuff as well and us just coming into it?'

'I'm afraid so.'

'What about the furs? You're surely not bunging them up there.'

'I am.'

'But they'll get the moth! Why don't you put them into cold storage? Lady Carrington does with hers.'

'That costs money.'

'It does but you must do something. If not airtight you'll lose them.

'Then I shall have to lose them.'

Mrs Mac eyed Julia's apron and worn frock and made a decision. 'Perhaps we could do what others do and wrap them in oilskin and box clear of the rest.'

'That's a thought.'

Crouched together under beams in a confined space, Julia with bare arms and soot-marked cheeks, Mrs Mac became chatty. 'It's a bit cramped in here, isn't it? We'd have more room if I shifted those wicker tables.'

'They could go. We shan't need them.'

'What are they exactly?'

'I suspect they were used when the cottage was a tea-shop.'

'A tea-shop? You mean this used to be like a Lyons Corner House?'

'A more humble version I imagine.'

'Well I never! You know it's in all the newspapers, Joe Lyons opening those places. They have waitresses in dark frocks and white aprons. I did wonder back in Russell Square whether I might apply.'

'It's a thought. Can we put the shoes in that rack?'

'…though thinking about it, waitressing I mean, it's young women they're after and I'm not as young as I was.'

'None of us are! Oh, Mrs Mac! I think I hear the doorbell!'

* * *

Stefan arrived, red-faced and perspiring, it was obvious he'd rushed to get here. Julia offered brief details of Bella's difficulties; that he didn't enquire further suggested he knew of the situation. 'Can you help?'

'What do you want for this girl when I find her?'

'I thought she might come here.'

'In what capacity?'

'None particularly, just to be here, I suppose, with the rest of us misfits.'

'Misfits? Is that how you see yourself?'

'Today I do.'

'You are not happy. Something other than this has made you sad.'

'I have offended Lady Carrington. I offered Bella a place without consulting her and now as I speak I see I was wrong to involve you. You are friends. I've drawn you into a situation where you too may possibly offend.'

Stefan shrugged, a Gallic gesture that sat strangely on stiff Germanic shoulders. 'One must value friends but one must value honesty above all. I know this area.' He perused the address. 'I shall bring you your Bella. However, being aware of your somewhat straightened circumstances you'll forgive my asking how you propose to support the new misfits.'

'I don't know.' Julia gazed out of the window. Matty was playing with the dog. As she watched he fell, Mrs Mac swooping to kiss his tears away. 'I suppose I could do as the Newman sisters did, make the cottage into a tea-shop and serve my patrons all that is needed and necessary.'

'*Bitte?*' Stefan frowned. 'Needed and necessary?'

'The ladies used this as a tea-room. I could expand a little making the cottage a miniature Lyons Corner House, where as well as doling out sugar buns, we offer tea and sympathy - a hug for a headache and a kiss for a bruised knee. In short everything needed and necessary to make a person feel better.'

'Do that and you'd soon be opening a chain of tea-shops! Yesterday I paid sixpence for a helping of apple strudel. In offering love and kindness as the dish of the day I imagine you'd need a very different tariff.ow would you di it'

Julia smiled. 'I'd make it up as I went along. Maybe introduce a swapping system, say, a portion of strudel for an unblocked chimney?'

'Ah yes, payment in kind. It is how people used to live.'

'It was certainly how my father lived.'

Stefan nodded. 'You must do this and you must make your tea-shop a loving thing. Times change, we grow old and yet the need is ever with us.' His smile faded. 'One thing I wish to know, Julianna. What price for a broken heart?'

* * *

Julia didn't mean it to happen. Now sitting at the window staring out into the warm night, she can't believe she kissed Stefan. Truly, she couldn't help it. His face so bewildered and sad, she couldn't bear to see it. She kissed him, and he, gently and beseechingly, kissed her back. Does she regret the kiss? No, though she might regret accepting financial backing for the tea-shop.

'Let me do this for you,' he'd begged. 'I have no one for whom I can care! *Bitte*, Julianna, let me help you and Matthew. It would give me such pleasure.'

How could she deny him? How does one look into suffering eyes and say, 'sorry. Today I put away box-upon-box of obligation in the loft. I don't believe I should ever attach my soul in that way again.' That kiss broke the rules. It's too late to shut the door. The horse might not have bolted but the stable door is open and he cuts the air with flashing hooves.

Midnight she was woken by stones clicking against glass. She pushed the window wide and once again looked down at Luke Roberts.

He beckoned. 'Come down, Julia.'

She shook her head.

'Do come down,' he said urgently. 'I need to speak to you.'

Heart beating madly she clutched at the windowsill.

The night was still and quiet. Nothing moved, not trees rustling, nor birds shifting under eaves, not even the cloud back of the sky. All hung motionless and on tiptoe waiting to see what she would do.

'You sent a telegram. You said it was an emergency. You said you needed help.' He shrugged. 'You can't keep anything private in this place. Everyone knows you sent it. Now I know and want to hear what help you need so please come down and tell me.'

Knuckles white, she clung to the sill.

'If you're in trouble I can help, dearest dear,' he said. 'There's nothing in the world I wouldn't do for you. I love you, Anna. I love you like crazy! My heart beats for you and you alone. Please come down.'

Oh and she wanted to! She wanted to leap over the sill and fall down onto his arms! But she couldn't. It is too late. He is too late!

'Anna!'

'Why?' Shoulders naked and satiny breast resting on green laurel she leaned down. 'Why now?' she begged, the words hurting her mouth. 'A little earlier, a minute or a second, and it would've been alright. Now it's too late.'

'What do you mean too late? What happened to make it so?' He pushed his fingers through his hair. 'Anna! Julianna please!'

'No,' she shook her head. 'You must go away. You're too late.'

She closed the window.

CHAPTER SEVEN

Gifts from the Dead

Bella, or rather Susan Dudley, as she turned out to be, arrived Friday evening. A hansom cab and a cart drove into the yard. All eyes and bump, she stepped down from the hansom. Julia motioned her in. 'Are these your boxes?'

Susan shook her head. 'They belongs to him as fetched me.'

Stefan coughed. 'It's a few things to help you settle. No doubt Mrs Dryden will give all she deems necessary.' Overawed, Susan blinked at him and he, overweight Angel doling out blessings, blinked back. 'There's more,' he said, porters heaving trunks from the cart. 'I'll wait and then be on my way.'

'Won't you wait awhile?'

'You have things to do. I shall not presume.'

She touched his hand. 'You could never presume.'

'I must go.' He made a sad moue. 'I am needed in Bradbury.'

They talked briefly of Karoline, how it is soon to be her birthday, and of Stefan's plans. Julia kissed his cheek. 'Give her my love and tell her I shall visit.' He stepped into the hansom and was gone. He left a letter. *This is Susan Dudley, Lady Carrington preferring body maids to be known by the one name Bella. I brought Susan in the hush of the evening to save unnecessary neighbourly interest. Small towns have codes of conduct that are not to be breached. As a man now happily claims the status of friend I will try not to overstep the boundaries of good manners and create for you difficulties.*

I am always your most humble servant, Stefan Willem Adelman.

Along with the letter were details of a monthly sum to be transferred in her name to a local bank. Having seen the statement, and blanched at the generosity, Julia is resolved to draw as little as possible.

The following morning she called at the bank and then went to the Nelson.

Nan seemed rather cool. 'You left your back door unlocked last night. Luke found it so and not for the first time. '

'Please thank him and tell him I shall take greater care.'

'Aye do! You don't want anyone stealin' from your fancy tea shop.'

'You've heard of our intention?'

'Everyone's heard.'

'And you don't think it a good idea?'

'I do not. You've no experience runnin' a place like that. Caterin' is hard graft, twenty-four hours a day non-stop. Take it from one who knows.'

'If the Newman sisters can do it why not me?'

'There were two of them. You've none but yourself.'

'I can manage. You forget I looked after my father. A man whose wits are wandering needs a great deal of care.'

'Yes and your father's the reason you shouldn't be doin' it! You're a vicar's daughter not a person in trade!'

'Nanette Roberts!' Julia smiled. 'You are a snob.'

'I'm no snob. I like things to be in a correct order, every man in his rightful sphere, a "rich man in his castle and a poor man at his gate," so to speak. You dishin' tea and scones to every Tom Tiddler and his wife, it's not seemly.'

'Seemly or not I'm going to do it. I've Mrs Mac to help, and

Maggie Jeffers and our new young lady.'

'Maggie Jeffers is a hindrance not a help. As for your young lady she might be young but from what I hear she's no lady.'

Nan is cross with Julianna. What does she know of business? Elderly spinsters pursuing a fancy is one thing, an English rose pursuing the same - a wilting rose at that - quite another. Smiling and promising to bring back an opera programme she caught the London train. She brought back more than a programme, shoulders naked and hair loose she brought a reputation.

The whole of Bakers, Upper, Middle, and Lower is agog. Seven in the morning looking like that! And see her now! What happened to her clothes? She's gone from giving away costly scarves to sending begging telegrams to London.

And what about Luke! He's over his head dizzy on the girl and has been from the start. Nan asked yesterday why he was getting involved. His reply was more a snarl than an answer: 'I'm involved in nothing.'

'You should stop workin' there,' says Nan. 'Better to step back from a tangle than be drawn in.'

'Don't talk rubbish! I'm not drawn into anything.'

'Rubbish is it? Everything's rubbish to you nowadays! No one can get a kindly word from you, not even the little lad you profess to love.'

Face moody and lips bitten to pieces, he'd shrugged. 'You said it, Mother, best not to get drawn in. As for letting go of business you're piping a new tune.'

'This is different.'

'How is it? One man's brass is as good as the next. Why turn it down?'

'Because money isn't the payment you seek. You're after somethin' more precious. You're after her heart.'

Slam! A closed door on a locked room is Luke Roberts. He never yells, the more enraged he becomes the more silent. He doesn't visit the Nelson. It's as Nan said to Albert: 'But for the odd rabbit on the table and logs chopped you wouldn't know he was alive.' Albert said leave him alone, he doesn't need his ma pokin' her nose. Nan wasn't poking her nose. She is afraid for him.

Every mother thinks her son handsome. Luke is real handsome. Muscles of iron and body of an athlete, he takes after his father. And he has brains too, a mathematician able to count the stars in the sky. Young Matty calls Luke Mister Wolf. The child will never know how right he is. Luke has the heart and soul of a wolf, an Italian wolf hunting the mountains fierce and dangerous.

Albert Roberts is not Luke's father. It was Albert who years ago took Nan in when she was two months gone with another man's child. Back in '68, Letty Morris, a seven-year-old mule-gatherer used for scavenging weave under cotton gins, fell into the canal. Luke's pa went in after her but both he and Letty got caught up in the suck. Apart from a mangy cat bedded under the sink, the child left none to grieve. Luke's dad, Lucca Claudio Aldaro, left his lover a peppercorn ring on her finger and a child in her belly.

Lucca Aldaro was born in the Apennine Mountains: '*Where the light streams over snow caps, mio caro, Nanette, and where the grey wolf runs free.*'

As a boy he and his mother left the sunshine of Italy for the soot of Manchester. A shuttle-maker, he worked for Murrays Mills, Ancoats in Little Italy as they call it. Nannette Ramsden, as she was then, met him by the canal. '*Buon giorno, bella signorina,*'

93

he said, dark eyes smiling. Instant love and misplaced passion she was then. Now that passion is alive in her son.

He knows nothing of his real father but from the start treated Albert with the kindness you offer a child. Albert is the only one he does treat kindly. As far as Luke is concerned compassion died alongside his brother Jacky.

Nan blames herself for the tragedy. Firstborn conceived out of wedlock, she sees Jacky's death as punishment. Luke blames himself. 'I shouldn't have left him.' Pointless saying you can't watch everything, as Nan mortifies the flesh, so does Luke. His passion then was for his brother. His passion now is Anna Dryden and as with Jacky will endure forever. No matter what he will hold true until he does as his father did - jump in the deep end and drown.

* * * * *

Nose out of joint, Maggie Jeffers knocks on Julia's door. 'Is Susan to share the work? Only with that bump I can't see her bendin' over a stove.'

'Never mind that, just carry on with your own work.'

'But what will Susan do?'

'Like you, she'll do as she's bid!'

Julia settled it with Mrs Mac. 'If you are willing to take on the post of nanny and help in Matty's general welfare then Susan can be parlour maid.' Mrs Mac's face lengthened until Julia continued. 'If the tea-shop is to happen I must manage my own makings. Early to bed and earlier to rise, I shall need a right-hand man not a personal maid. I shall need you, Maud.'

Mrs Mac was elated. 'I'll do it, madam! I'll be nanny to Master

Matthew *and* I'll cook. I never said before but I am a good cook. My almond tarts have been called melt-in-mouth. I'll make a batch and you can taste.'

Maud went to bed wreathed in smiles. Julia allowed herself a smile. Kitchen politics be damned! Stefan would be proud of me, as would Owen, and for that matter Luke Roberts. But no! A sturdy bolt is shot across her heart. She mustn't think of him, it hurts too much. But it is difficult to forget his impassioned plea and the effect it had, the cutting of a honey-coated knife.

He's made no attempt to repeat his vow even so it's awkward having him about the house. With the refurbishment complete, she's no need to employ anyone...but the kitchen is in need of extra shelves and the Roberts men being better than most...she'll keep Luke.

* * ** * *

Julia plans to make table cloths from linen sheets found in the attic. 'I can get four cloths per sheet, napkins, *and* use the lace edging for cake stands.'

Mrs Mac frowned. 'Won't paper frills be better? Linen gets sticky.'

'I know but starched they will look so much nicer.'

'It's extra work, madam.'

'Yet we will do it. If we are to gain the right reputation it has be right, good food, excellent service and the best silver. Have you seen the Georgian tea service? Maggie's made an excellent job of polishing it.'

'She has her uses.'

'How does she get along with Susan?'

'She tried swanking about a bit but Susan soon put a stop to that.'

'Susan will need to be strong. It's a harsh world for a mother alone.'

'Do you know anything about her, madam, how she came to be in trouble?'

'No, and I won't ask…and neither shall you! You have been so helpful to me, Maud. I would hate us not to agree on the need for kindliness.'

The truth is Mrs Mac is fast becoming a jewel in the projected crown. She has a keen business mind and espies possibilities where Julia does not.

'Joe Lyons must buy in. They can't feed everyone from food cooked on the premises. They haven't time. We could make our own *and* buy from local wives. Good for business and sure to get them rallying round.'

'I was hoping local wives would be our customers.'

Mrs Mac shook her head. 'There'll be a few that likes the occasional outing but big trade is what we must aim for, them that like to sit and spend.'

'And where will we find those?'

'Out there!' Mrs Mac pointed to a stream of carriages winding up the Rise.

'Oh my word!' Julia rushed to the window. So wrapped in her own concerns she hadn't considered the Lansdowne place. Judging the activity, footmen and other attendants bustling in and out, the house was At Home to the world.

Mrs Mac was popping with excitement. 'Who do you suppose

lives there?

'I don't know. Rags to riches it could be anybody. But don't worry. Bakers End has its own telegraph system. Give it a day and we'll know.'

* * *

The next day Nan tapped on the window. 'Yankees have moved in!'

'Yankees?'

'Aye, Americans with bags of money! The difference this will make to Bakers. I'm so cheered with the news! This is no newly minted English Lord who doesn't know how to be happy, this is a mining millionaire, or rather his widow, with a dozen carriages and servants all over the shop!'

'That sounds like good news for the Nelson.'

'And for you, Anna! There'll be those for the Big House and others on the way to Sandringham, and they'll all have dusty throats! The gents will want beer and a nice steak pie, which the Nelson will supply, and the ladies will be lookin' for a quaint old English town to drink quaint old English tea.'

'You think so?'

'I know so. It's a certainty some will stay at the Nelson. When they do come I'll tell them of the N and N and their hostess, the beautiful Mrs Dryden.'

* * *

Julia sews squares. The back parlour is comfortable, the copper silhouettes flickering in the light. There were four silhouettes found in a bureau, three females in left profile and a male in right. Luke Roberts said two were of the Newman Sisters. 'That's Miss Justine,' he said, 'and that's her sister.'

'What of the other two?'

'The chap's navy,' said Luke of the male. 'See the epaulettes!'

This was last week, when, every sense screaming, she'd breathed him in. But that was last week. She can't serve two masters.

The house is quiet, Mrs Mac gone with Matty to post a letter. A prolific letter writer Maud puts Julia to shame. It's a week since she wrote to her sisters. Charlotte and May married and with children there's rarely word from Bentham. When it does come it is brief and to the point. *I said to James it's a pity there are no Charlottes in his ancestry, a name carries weight. So Dear Julianna, if you marry again oblige your impoverished sisters and try for a man with a May or Charlotte in tow, then we'll all benefit.*

Charlotte is the kindest of women. Wives to busy farmers, their lives are never their own. Julia has a roof over her head and a chance to make it safe. As for obligation she was in debt to Stefan long before the tea-shop. Yesterday she wrote to him saying she plans to visit Karoline. It was but a few lines yet seemed to take an age, pen pressing into vellum, the nib scratching and the ink sliding down to fill the letters. There was satisfaction in writing that note - Julia leaning into candlelight to read it and a shadow leaning with her.

* * *

Conspirators, they kneel, the lid of the first trunk is lifted and a layer of wool folded back. Gold-leaf flashed in Mrs Mac's eyes.

'Oh, madam!'

The trunk is filled with china. Julia picked up a tea-cup, so delicate and fragile, lamplight shining through, she might be touching a dead woman's bones.

'I can't do it!' She closed the lid, whispering as though louder would shatter the precious cargo. 'I don't trust my hands to do it right. Let's leave it for the morning. We'll be fresher then.'

Mrs Mac nodded. 'Yes, madam, I think so too.'

Alone, Julia read the accompanying letter.

I swore I would never give these away. I promised to keep her trousseau safe as I have kept her safe. Lately Karoline speaks of letting go of the past but not to me - never to me – always to some sympathetic soul only she can see.

Before she was taken by this vile illness my wife was the wisest of women. I believe that beneath the pain her wisdom continues, and so, with the idea of letting go of the past, I have begun dismantling our Dresden home. The Meissen has been packed away for these many years. I believe Karo wishes them to see the light again and learning of your broken china I knew you were meant to have this. Karoline would want it! Accept them with our love gifted to you as Karo was gifted to me. Do not be afraid to use them. If they fall and break it is of no consequence. We must all fall and all break.

* * *

Maggie scratched on the bedroom door. 'Susan's cryin'.'

Susan was huddled at the end of the bed. 'Are you ill?'

'No, madam.'

'Then why are you crying?'

99

'I miss my feller.' She pulled a book mark from under her pillow. 'He gave me this. Said it belonged to his mother.'

'Maggie has gone down to make a drink. Would you like one?

'I'm not thirsty. I just wanted to talk about him.'

'Now you have talked do you think you can sleep?'

'Yes.' Susan pushed under the covers. 'I can sleep and dream of him.'

It was a while before Julia could sleep. Ear tuned to the scattering of stones on glass – and the man standing beneath, moonlight making raven wings of his hair – she kept going to the window, but there was only ever moonlight and an echo: *Come down, Anna, my heart beats for you.*

CHAPTER EIGHT

The Nuance

Maggie hurled around the kitchen door. 'Madam, come quick!'

'What is it?' Julia set the saucepan aside. Is that it, she thought, looking into the depth of pink goo? Does raspberry conserve look like this?

'Come quick, madam!' Maggie jumped up and down. 'There's such a to-do in the garden, people crowdin' round and Joe Carmody shoutin' the odds.'

'Why is he shouting?'

'There's somethin' come over the wall.'

Julia untied her apron. 'I'll go see what's going on.' There was a huddle by the wall, people talking, and the stone three-headed Cerberus dogs either side of the gate world-weary. 'What is it Joe? What's been taken this time?'

'That's just it. They've *left* somethin'! But none of my pinks and other dainty dears they're forever thievin'.' Joe kicked the tray. 'Foreign muck! Moss and other bits of stuff I've never seen afore and wouldn't want to see again.'

'It's not all muck. That's a clump of Iris. And that's campanula.'

Joe was grudging. 'I suppose there's somethin'. There's lily-of-the-valley and a couple of tasty lookin' rose cuttin's, but why do it, the cheeky buggers. Excuse me, ma'm! Why sneak about in't middle of the night? Why not walk up to the house and knock on the door like honest folk?'

'I wish I knew.' Julia returned to the kitchen, yawning. A restless night, she woke this morning with Schubert's Quintet in her head; why she should think of the *Trout* she'd no idea but hummed as she worked.

'Mrs Dryden?' Luke Roberts was at the door - his voice is as cold and remote as a star. 'That's a weighty dinner-service you want putting up. You'll need stronger brackets if you don't want it crashing down.'

'Indeed no! I did think the rose tea-service for decorative purpose.'

'As you say.' He turned to go and then checked. 'And while I'm here if you don't plan on using the pony and trap I'll be taking it back.'

'Oh, don't do that!'

'You're not using it as you should.'

'But I shall! It's only that I am wary of driving into town.'

'No need. It's not gonna tip you up. Poppy's a gentle beast and that's a well-balanced trap. If it wasn't I wouldn't have brought it.'

'I was thinking of taking it to the station tomorrow for the Cambridge train but then I'll be late getting back - but I shall use it, I promise.'

'I must go.' Disinterested, he didn't shrug but might as well. 'I've left the bill for the conversion on the kitchen table. Meet it at your convenience.'

* * *

Early Friday morning she fastened the catch on her portman-teau. 'The Sweep comes today. Make sure he does all he should including de-coking the range. We can't have the house filled with smoke.'

Mrs Mac nodded. 'Should I mention it to Mr Luke?'

'No! He's busy elsewhere. If it has to be done we'll employ another. Now, the girls are to clean the kitchen and no skimping as they'll be soot everywhere! And, Maud, keep Matty away! He'll want to be in on everything.'

'I'll keep a close eye on him, madam. You can trust me on that.'

Julia picked up her bag. 'I do trust you. I am relieved to know you are here. Right then! I shouldn't be too late.'

'I'll wait up.'

'No need, I'm seeing a sick friend and then coming straight back. You'll have had a much busier day than me.'

'All that way for a couple of hours, it don't seem like fun to me.'

'Perhaps not,' Julia smoothed her gloves, 'but necessary.'

Alone in the carriage she gazed out of the window feeling as though she was leaving a part of herself behind - the anxious Julia who sat at night counting pennies into envelopes and worrying about chimney-sweeps.

The train rattled along the tracks. Mile after mile flitted by and with every mile the anxious self was suppressed, flesh overlaying flesh, layer upon layer, mind upon mind, until another woman gazed out the window, one with a greater claim to the journey and the man at the end of the journey.

Julia woke this morning aware of an overnight seeding, an idea planted in her mind that prompted a change of undergarment, a bolstering; the scarlet corset next to her skin binding body and soul together. Scenery flows by, parsley fields and cows standing motionless. A face is reflected in the glass, a woman who looks like Julia but is in fact a fusion of three: a Julia of today, a ghost of yesterday, and a woman neither living nor dead.

The assembling of this trio began with the unpacking of Meissen china. Julia had thought to leave it until the morning, but, filled with thoughts of Karoline Adelman, Stefan's wife, the lover of lace patches and white silk stockings, she returned to the sitting-room to unpack the china, the floor covered with glittering gems. Now she travels to meet Karoline, a woman she hasn't met yet who has already made her presence known.

* * *

Once through the gates they were led through a series of wards, every door in the sanatorium locked behind them. They paused outside a door. Stefan took Julia's hand. 'I am glad you're here but do not expect a happy outcome. You may find your presence will not so much as ruffle the waves.'

Karoline sits facing the wall, a clean robe and cotton slippers and her hair washed. Her nails are kept short and cleaned of any blood and faeces collected overnight through scratching. The beds are stripped and changed every morning, yet the stench of stale urine assails the nostrils. Staff here work hard but cannot avert accidents - when the wits are lost the body soon follows.

Stefan leaned down. '*Wie sieht es aus bei dir meine liebe? Schau, du hast Besucht, Frau Dryden, eine Bekannt von mir.*' His introduction of Julianna as a friend fell on deaf ears; Karoline continues to gaze at a patch of wall.

Once, out of curiosity, Stefan measured the particular patch, adjudging it by half a metre long by half a metre wide, a letter box, perhaps, or an elongated container the size of a canopic jar. As with every visit, he wipes her hands and face with a scented cloth, and then, a bib about her neck, feeds her two figs and a portion of apple-torte. She chews, opens her mouth and then disgorges the contents onto the bib.

Today being her birthday he opens a bottle of champagne pouring a measure into a cup. She sips, once, twice, and then dribbles all back into the cup.

Julianna is silent throughout. He is grateful. He couldn't bear her to question why he does it, or to say that it is a waste of time -he needs no telling.

He tells of home, of seasons changing in her garden in Dresden and the flowers on her trees. Soon, conscious of Julianna waiting, he turned to the sink to wash his hands - at that Karoline stood up and grasping Julia's hands began to speak, softly pleading, as though continuing a conversation. '... *ich muss gehen, Julianna. Dieses Leben ist mir den Meinen zu toten. Hil mir, nehmen Sie diese Last von mir, und ich werde dich fur immer segnen.*'

* * *

The iron gates clanged shut. The carriage pulled away with Stefan at the reins. After such a visit he prefers to drive, concentrating on the road and the traffic stops him from screaming. Julianna is silent, sympathy for his wife's plight pulsing through her hand on his thigh. 'I'm sorry,' was all she said. She didn't ask what was said, and he, having heard it many times before didn't explain;

after all what does Karoline ask other than to be set free? '*Help me. This life is killing me! Take this burden and I shall bless you forever.*'

Stefan knows the words, the first time of saying Karoline held a razor to her throat, the second time she stood at an open window spiked railings below; the last time she was pulled from the lake at their home, clothes dripping and pockets weighted with stones. Her words today were not for Julianna, as they are not for physicians - they are for Stefan, an invitation to join her in hell.

'Stefan?' Now Julianna turns to him. 'I think you have a house nearby.'

'Yes. I keep it should I need to stay overnight.'

'I'd like to see your house.'

Her hand is on his thigh. Stefan keeps his eyes on the horses. He doesn't want to look at her hand or acknowledge warmth seeping into his skin. If he looked she might think badly of him. 'Would you not prefer to take lunch?'

'I am not hungry.'

'So what then, Julianna?'

'I would like to visit your house.'

This time Stefan did look at her hand, he could look nowhere else, and she knowing him looking removed her glove. 'I should like to keep you company for an hour or two,' she said. 'We can be lonely together.'

* * *

It was late when they got to the station and Julia settled in a carriage. Stefan passed a magazine and box of comfits through the window. 'Is there anything else I can get for you?'

'No thank you.'

'You will write to me?' Reluctant to let her go he held the door.

'Of course. And with regard to Matty I shall look into your idea of a tutor. Mrs McLaughlin is good but as you say he needs a stronger hand.'

'Things are the same with Matthew?'

'He struggles to speak yet I believe him happier than he's ever been.'

'Why is that do you think?'

An image of Luke Roberts rose unbidden in Julia's head. 'New people, I suppose, and involvements. And the dog! He's made a difference.'

'Keep me informed of his progress. I should like to be involved.'

'You are involved. But for you we would both be in difficulties.'

'And the tea-shop? What of that?'

'I think the beginning of August might see it up and running.'

'You know you do not have to do this.'

'I need to do it. However unreal, or *ersartz*, my idea of independence, I mean to honour the terms of our partnership.'

'*Ersartz*, Julianna?' Smiling, he raised his eyebrows. '*Wollen Sie Deutsch mit mir ueben, mein liebe*? You would practice on me?'

She smiled. 'Not practice, Stefan, so much as try to please.'

'Try to please?' Hand on heart he bowed. 'I can't tell what pleasure you gave today. I do not have the words.' The train pulled away from the station, Stefan with his hat raised, a lonely figure.

* * *

The train chugged along the track. Julia looked at the magazine but could make no sense of it, other words and images requiring more understanding. Stefan's life is drear. There is more colour in this railway carriage than in that house. 'In Knightsbridge I keep a man-servant,' he was apologetic. 'I am so rarely here in Bradbury I need only daily help.' No colour and no life, but then after a visit to the sanatorium sleep is probably all he can manage.

What a strange day and what silly ideas she has! She had thought to comfort him. Comfort was not what he sought. He sought passion, the strength of his arms and depth of his kisses said so. Before today when thinking of Stefan Alderman she mentally appended the word poor; 'poor Stefan, the big man in a fur coat, the teddy bear with soft whiskers.' Coat and whiskers are real but that's where it ends. The body beneath the fur is hard, any fancy she had, any pity, quickly removed - an image reflected in a mirror a permanent reminder of this day - Julia naked, pinioned to a pristine bed, arms outstretched and body on fire, and above her, Stefan, his eyes bright with unshed tears. In that mirror she sees, and understands, this was never about her, every moment, every fiery blast was meant for '*Mein liebling!* My wife! My Karoline!'

* * *

She dozed, waking to the train lurching to a halt. Such a commotion outside, men shouting, the darkness punctured by flickering lamps.

A guard tapped on the door. 'We're delayed, madam, sheep on the line.'

'Where are we exactly?'

'Just outside of Thetford. We can't move yet. A couple of 'em got smacked about and the rest are running scared.'

The noise was dreadful, the shouting and cries of terrified animals. Men walked by the window with bloodied hands. It was cold. Shivering, she pulled her coat closer. The ribbons irritating her skin she couldn't wait to get home and remove the damned corset. Ridiculous thing! Glimpsed in the mirror of an oak chiffonier it looked exactly what it was, a tart's apparel, in this fine feathers did not make the bird, they merely disguised the shabby.

It was a while before the train started up. When it did pull away Julia was aware of alteration, of former worries settling again on her shoulders - the woman who'd looked toward Cambridge overtaken by one who believed she could lift a man's sorrow when she couldn't lift her own.

* * *

The train pulled into the station. She looked for a porter but gone midnight the platform was deserted. Her bag weighed heavy. God knows why! Nothing has been added since this morning unless it is a heavy heart.

'I've got it.' Luke Roberts came out of the shadows to take her bag.

'You came to meet me?'

'I was passing. Come! The wagon's outside.'

Hurrying after him she stumbled.

'Careful!' He took her arm. 'The steps are greasy.'

'Very good of you.'

'It's late.' He handed her aboard. 'Nobody should be out this time of night.'

'There was a hold-up at Thetford, sheep on the line.'

'I heard.' He glanced sideways. 'Shook you up some I imagine.'

She nodded. 'So much blood!'

A splash of light from a lamp hanging from a shaft, the horse trotted on.

They turned into the high street every shop and house closed. 'I imagine you find Bakers End a bit of a change after Cambridge. What subject did your husband teach?'

'Latin, Hebrew and Aramaic, but none of it reallye wash him.'

'What was he then?'

'Owen was an archaeologist at heart and a dreamer in his soul.'

'You loved him.'

'Yes.'

'I heard he was killed.'

'An accident in Cairo while on an archaeological dig.'

'Fulfilling a dream then?'

'Yes.'

'That has to be the right time to die, fulfilling a dream.'

'If one has a choice,' said Julia thinking of Karoline.

'You have choices, Julianna Dryden, and one sitting next to you. '

'I know,' she whispered, 'and I am grateful,'

'Grateful be damned!' he spat. 'It's not your gratitude I want. It's you! Body and soul, now and forever, until death us do part!'

'I can't.'

'Can't?' The horse rearing, he snatched the reins. 'What kind of word is that?' Brows thunderous, he stared. 'I don't understand *can't*. How can you say such a thing when a man is offering his heart? Won't and don't is straightforward as in I don't want you and won't love you. They make sense. But *can't* makes no sense to me. Does it make sense to you?'

Julia hunched down in the seat.

'I'm no literary man,' he continued bitterly. 'No professor of Latin. I'm a Yorkshire man. I know nothing of archaeology but I know a word when it opens a can o' worms. *Can't* implies an obstacle, something or someone stopping you from loving me. It suggests a problem, a monster in the attic no one knows about. You got a monster in the attic?'

Julia held her tongue, this weary and sad she might say anything.

Jaw working, he bit out the words. 'You're going to have to explain to me why you can't love me since until this day and this moment it never occurred to me you couldn't, only that you didn't. I was willing to settle for that. I am an everyday man with hands that graft and a heart that beats. Why would you love me? But that you *can't* changes everything.'

'Giddup!' He shook the reins, the horse trotted on.

Nothing more was said until depositing her and her bag outside the door when he leaned forward, his handsome face so close she leapt back.

'No need to be afraid, sweetheart,' he said removing a strand of sheep's wool from her hat. 'I am merely relieving you of this. I don't want you left with unpleasant dreams, no dead sheep on a railway track or monsters in the attic.'

Doffing his hat he shook back his hair. 'I'm off now to snatch

111

what sleep is left me. I bid you a good night and tell you I'm watching you now, Julianna Dryden, seeking out what it is that prevents you loving me. And when I find it,' he circled the wool about his finger, 'I shall remove it.'

CHAPTER NINE

The Right One

'Open up!' There was hammering on the Forge door. Luke lifted the bar and Albert pushed by. 'I want a word with you, my lad.'

'Make it a quick word,' said Luke. 'I'm at Wentworth's this morning fixing their pump and already behind time.'

'Aye, well, it won't take but a minute.'

Luke shucked out of his nightshirt. Ducking under the pump, he let water pound his body. Tonight he'll drop by the Nelson and take a bath. For now this'll have to do. He pulls on a clean shirt and pants - no time to shave – stuffs his feet into his boots, and grabbing a hunk of bread chews.

'What's to do, Pa?' Albert's fizzing. Ma's been on at him. Something's been said and she's nagged him, poor chap, until he can't think straight.

'Don't ask me what's to do when you know damn well!' snaps Albert. 'It's you! Where were you last night? You told your mother you'd drop by.'

'Something cropped up.'

'And we all know what! I know, your mother knows, and Pastor Meakins at the chapel knows! The whole bloody world knows.'

Luke led Betty out to harness. Late back and knowing he'd need to be away he loaded the cart last night. A drink of water and an oat bag and the horse is happy. Luke is not. Guessing where this lecture is going his skin is starting to itch. 'And what is it the whole bloody world knows?'

'As if you need tellin'!'

'I do need telling. It's why I'm here listening to you when I should be gone.'

'Then I'll be quick. I'm talkin' about you and that fancy piece.'

Luke stood still. 'Don't call her that.'

'Why when it's true? I thought she was a gentlewoman but she's nothing like.'

'Albert!' He held up a warning finger. 'Stop right there!'

'Nay, I'll not! She can go to London with her fine friends and come back lookin' like she'd been dragged through a hedge. It's a sinful city with sinful ways. You expect nothin' else. But she's not bringin' her naughty ways here to Bakers.'

'What naughty ways are those?'

'Her and that German doctor! Did you know his wife's in a lunatic asylum and your Mrs Dryden gettin' her bits and pieces? China delivered in the dead of night? Talk about steppin' into a dead woman's shoes. It's disgustin'!'

'That's nothing. He brought that to replace the broken stuff.'

Albert blustered. 'Alright then, but what's a doctor doin' bringin' that girl? Is she some other chap's leavings or dirty business of his own he squirrels away?'

'She needed help. It's why she's there.'

'Oh, you know that do you?'

'I do. I spoke to her yesterday. She told me she was saved from a nasty situation and that Anna offered a home when no one else would.'

'Listen to yoursen! You're makin' excuses for her. So wall-eyed by her pretty face you'd say black is white.'

'I would not and you know it. Anna's trying to do a good turn.'

'Acceptin' gifts from a bloke whose wife's ill is not what I call a good turn. I call that the turn of a whore!'

'Albert, please!' Luke's face was ashen. 'I'm begging you! You're my pa and I love you but another word and as God is my witness you and me are done.'

A fish on a hook, Albert squirmed. 'It's what people are sayin'!'

'I know what people are saying, and I tell you what I would tell them, whatever you think you've seen or heard about that lady there's an honest explanation if you're but willing to look.'

'And you're not bein' taken for a fool?'

'How am I taken for a fool?'

'How about unpaid taxi collectin' her from the station and makin' jobs when there ain't any? Then there's constable of the watch, checkin' her doors late at night! Christ's sake, what is that if not the actions of a love-sick fool?'

'What I do I do out of care for her safety. I do it because I *want* to and not because I'm asked, and I shall carry on doing it until she says nay. If that makes me a fool then I am a fool.'

'Well you are and it can only lead to harm.'

'Christ's sake stop!' Luke turned away. 'Stop treading muck with the herd. Be above them! Don't let them or you spoil a rare and lovely thing.'

'I'm spoilin' nothin'. I'm tellin' you what's bein' said about you and her.'

'About me?' Luke laughed bitterly. 'There's nothing to say about me and Anna Dryden. I wish to God there were! The only connection I have with her is my aching heart and her indifference to it. I tell you, if half of what was being said behind closed doors about me and that lady was true I'd be a happy man.'

'I know!' Albert shouted. 'It's why me and your mam are scared.'

'Don't be.' Luke barred the Forge door. 'I'm responsible for my doings, nobody else, and if it goes bad then put it down to bad blood.'

'What do you mean bad blood?'

'Oh come on! Don't pretend you don't know what I mean. I'm not calling you a hypocrite but earlier when you slighted Anna for taking in Susan Dudley you came close to spitting in your own beer. Another man's leavings is what you said. How can you say that when thinking of your own life?'

Albert stuck out his chin. 'I don't know what you mean.'

'It's alright. I know you're not my pa. I've always known. I'm not pointing a finger at you and Ma. You did what you had to. I'm no different. I love Anna Dryden and I'm doing what I have to.' He climbed onto the cart. 'It's said we are masters of our own fate. If that's true then I'm master of mine, she's mistress of hers, and there's nothing else to say.'

* * *

Even though he was late, Luke went the long way to Wentworth's Farm taking the route that led beside Pleasant Cottage. Justine Newman told of his real father. It happened a quarter of a century ago yet is as clear as yesterday. 'Come here, child,' she said. Though scared of the sisters - witches the kids thought them with their cooking pots and their spells - Luke went.

'You mended that rein?' she said, her voice a rusty song.

'Yes, ma'm.' Hand at his waist he'd bobbed a bow.

'And did it speedily and tightly?'

'I did, ma'm, tight as tight.'

'And how much do we owe for this service?'

'Nowt.'

'Nowt! Is that what your mama told you to say?'

'No, ma'm. She said to say sixpence.'

'I see. Come close so I might pay as your mother is owed.' A witch in glossy furs, her face a whirl of spider's webs, she whispered a spell: '*Your mother sees in pounds and pence. It's how she was bred. Your papa saw sunshine and sin and that in his stead. Take of your mother's kin but only as you need. The rest seek of your homeland, signor, and you'll be content indeed.*'

Then she kissed him and gave him a silver sixpence while talking in Italian. He didn't know it was Italian until years later. Knowledge of another heritage was leaked to him drop-by-drop, first when he was seven and then at seventeen.

It was when they had the Beehive at Coddleston. Luke was in the cellar tying off barrels. A pedlar came looking to sharpen knives. He spoke and time shifted. It was the voice. A bottle of beer and tools to sharpen and Luke relayed Miss Justine's message: '*E la tua Patria. La tua eredita!*'

The pedlar had smiled. 'You are a stranger here, signor.'

'Don't be daft!' Luke had laughed. 'I'm an Englishman born and bred.'

'You are stranger as am I,' said the pedlar. 'This not your land. You are of my country, *mia bella Italia*. I see it in your eyes and hear it in your voice.'

It was the day the Roberts moved to Bakers. In bad shape, the Nelson needed a hard-working victualler and determined spouse. You won't get more hard-working than Albert or more determination than in Nanette Roberts nee Ramsden. Nan's father was Gordon Ramsden, champion brew master. What he didn't know about beer couldn't be known; that his only child was female didn't stop him passing it on, which is fortunate, since he liked to sample as well as experiment and died falling into a vat of Piper's Best.

Drowning is this family's curse. It took Grandfather Ramsden. It took little Jacky Roberts, and, as Luke was to learn, it took his blood father, Lucca Aldaro, card-maker at Murrays Cotton Mill in Manchester.

Moved by nostalgia the pedlar talked of his own life. He said he was on his way to Manchester and that the cotton mill was an awful place, '*male, del diavolo,*' but that if Luke wanted information it was the place to go.

Then Jacky died. Luke made the trip. He soon learned the truth; a chap drowning trying to save a child - an Italian by name of Lucca, second name Claudio, who lived by the brewery and known to be sweet on the brewer's daughter - such events stay in the public memory. Luke Claude Roberts returned to Bakers with a secret. Most secrets are best left alone but as with most secrets hidden in darkness, this one grew fingers and sought the light.

* * *

'Whoah, Betty!' It's quiet on the road, most folks still abed. A light showed in the cottage top attic where the maids sleep. Maggie Jeffers is behind all the tattling, so ahead with local gossip you'd think her fey.

Fey is what Ma says about Luke. 'How do you know that?' she'll say when he offers an opinion. 'Is it something you see?' He laughs. 'It's commonsense, a thing you're lacking.' To Luke the things he sees are commonsense, like not asking sixpence of Justine Newman, who, if Mother had kept quiet would've given a shilling. Maggie Jeffers is trouble, upsetting little Matty the other day with some rubbish about crows, how if seen someone you love will die.

If anybody's fey it's Matty. The things he says have Luke wanting to screw a bolt over his mouth. Last week in his croaky pantomime voice he says, 'You are to be my next papa.' Luke nearly fell over. 'You mustn't say things like that!' Matty went quiet and he, ever hopeful in his heart, asked who or what put the idea in his head. 'My first papa,' says Matty. That damn silly wench Maggie overheard and grins, 'is that right you're to wed the mistress?'

A bad day when she wheedled her way into Julianna's employ. Ma was glad to be rid of her. She fools about with the Sweep and a potboy at the Nelson. It's Maggie who leaves the cottage door unlocked, nipping out when her mistress is not looking, and that's not good with blokes like Sherwood about.

It's said Nate Sherwood pushed Jacky into the quarry. Five minutes it took to kill the lad - five minutes of idle chat - the thought sucks the marrow from the day. 'If you must swim in the quarry,' Mother said, 'keep an eye on Jacky. You know what he's like. If someone says it can't be done he'll do it.'

'I dare you to walk through the graveyard at midnight.' That was the first big dare. Luke was ten and Jacky five. Coddleston church is right across from the Beehive, even so you don't dare

119

your baby brother to go there. They both did it. When they sneaked back, legs stinging from running through nettles, it was Luke pants that were damp round the arse not Jacky's.

How can you not love a kid who stares you in the face, swears black is blue he didn't ride Tatty Barn's goat but who's missing two front teeth from trying?

Five minutes! They were at the quarry, Luke trying his luck with the draper's daughter, who was pretty with a trilling laugh. Arm-in-arm with a friend she was coming down the lane. A flash monkey in a new neckerchief, he went to meet her. Smiling he was, though a bit set-back, because close up she wasn't pretty and her laugh like a peacock shrieking on the Squire's lawn. Nate Sherwood and his diddicoy pals stood about. Five minutes. Then somebody yells, 'Here Luke! Your Jacky's fallen into the quarry and ain't come up yet!'

* * *

Shelving that memory, Luke pulls his hat down over his eyes and drives on. It doesn't pay to dwell on the past, not when you've plans, 'cos plans cost money. Until Julianna arrived the Forge was his flophouse. A bed, a pump, and a pillow, it was enough. If comfort was needed there was pie and a soak at the Nelson. Then Julianna moved here and now nothing is good enough for a man who builds other folk's houses but with none of his own.

He is good at what he does. Give him a wreck and his mind will push the roof up and the walls out and his hands will make it happen. There's hot water on tap in the Nelson and flushing lavs. It's why folk pay top whack to lodge there. When Mother moaned about spending it was he who said, 'you're to be another Savoy HoteloyHotel, a bath with every room. No more living in the dark ages, Mrs Roberts.' Now he knows if he is to offer the name Roberts to another woman he'd best have more than a name to offer.

Saturday morning he bid for the house on Fairy Common. He'd seen a pamphlet pushed through Wentworth's door and heard it was up for sale. It took every penny he had. Ma's heard about it. It's why she sent Albert today. She's always on about him putting money aside for the future. Now she suspects that future has Anna's name carved across the lintel.

'Can't,' Julianna said last night. That shocked him and at the same time gave hope. Luke is not a boastful man, willing hands and strong back is all. There are men with more class and style. One stood by the wall the other night.

Unpaid watchman, or fool as Pa says, Luke was checking the cottage doors. It was a beautiful evening and Julianna at the piano. Luke recognised the piece, *Liebestraume* it's called. Ben Faulkner plays the piano weekends at the Nelson. He plays happy stuff, polkas and such, and as the evening moves on - folks getting rowdy - switches to gentle stuff, *Love's Dream* is a favourite.

Julianna plays soft and sad. Odd that in a village known for gossip not much is known of Owen Passmore. A Cambridge Don killed abroad is the word, now and then a gem is added, true or false none knows or cares.

'*Oh you mean Owen Passmore, Mrs Dryden's late husband, decent fellow, a Cambridge Don, tall and thin as a lath and handsome in an academic fashion.*'

That comment was heard in the Nelson recently. It came

from a party of folk destined for the Big House. Busy lunchtime trade, Luke was behind the bar helping. Whoever they were they knew of the cottage and its beautiful mistress. A member of that party stood here the other night. White tie and tails, the tip of his cigar glowing, he stood in the darkness listening to her play.

Luke wanted to shout, 'clear off! You're trespassing!' There was no trespass, the fellow was on his side of the wall and the house, Greenfields, lit up like Buckingham Palace. Whoever he was he didn't hang about. He strolled back up the Rise likely thinking spying not the act of a gentleman.

Not the act of a gentleman is Luke's opinion of his own wanderings. Pa says he's riding for a fall and it's likely he is. The German doctor, Adelman, is a successful man - you don't get Meissen china fixing washers. Right now Luke is fixing shelves for the china. Gossip says while the Cat's away in Bedlam the Mice are able to play. Sounds cruel and yet people have needs. Julianna is a widow and no doubt the Doctor is lonely.

One terrible day Luke begged a girl for a kiss. He spent five minutes spinning a tale on how he couldn't live without that kiss and while spinning, his brother died. That day Luke came of age. Years pass and the only female kissed since then is his mother. Monk or priest every night he locks the door and lays on a pallet bed staring through a chink in the roof at the stars.

A boy of twenty dove into the quarry's stinking water offering his life to God: 'Keep your kisses and sins of the flesh! Let Jacky live and I'll steer clear of girls.' A man rose to the surface, his dead brother in his arms. Maybe if he'd offered his soul to the Devil a life would've been saved, whatever, Jacky dead, and him loaded with guilt, Luke was unable to look at girls without feeling rage.

Then Julianna Dryden arrived. He's still angry but more than that he is afraid. He once offered his life for that of his brother. Now he wonders if God were feeling vengeful that offer might be accepted, only this time Julianna's life the forfeit.

CHAPTER TEN

Old Wives Tales

'Good day, ma'm.' The postman handed Julia a cake tin along with letters. 'My Missis heard you was interested in cakes and sent one to try.'

Inside the tin was a neat looking cake if a little scorched round the edges.

'It smells delicious. Thank Mrs Brocket and tell her I'll be in touch.'

Julia showed the cake to Mrs Mac, saying, they must decide how much to pay. 'Yes, if they're going to send,' said Mrs Mac. 'The other day I mentioned cakes to her as used to cook for you and she near bit my head off. Um, madam, are those letters for me?'

Julia had mail of her own; the first was from John Sargent, who wrote to invite her to a showing of his work at Sandringham. Daniel Masson also had written, sating, he was sorry they didn't get a chance to talk in London and that he hadn't forgotten her promise to sit, '*because there's not a face in the world I'd sooner set to canvas.*' The third letter was from Freddie. He writes almost every day, '*Come back, Ju-ju. I miss you, your loving friend, Freddie.*'

There is never a note from Evie and never one expected.

The wind blew the washing. Mrs Mac scuttled across the yard to gather it in. A thought crossed Julia's mind then regarding letters from Russell Square with what felt like coins inside. Why would Evie send Maud money? Is it belated wages and if so what service is being performed?

Mrs Mac works hard. Julia likes her but is put off by an air of secrecy. The girls, too, are always whispering. Maggie is the problem here. Always missing when you want her or a squirrel in winter stowing food under the bed, her influence on Susan can't be good.

* * *

Monday morning a gentleman knocked on the door. Thin-faced with cardboard in his shoes, and smell of alcohol to his clothes, Benjamin Faulkner plays piano at the Nelson, and was suggested by Albert as a possible tuner. A superb ear, he pitched the piano to perfection. Mrs Mac having prepared a delicious *tarte au gratin* - and he so undernourished - Mr Faulkner was invited to share lunch with the maids. In appreciation he played the first movement of the Tchaikovsky piano concerto, B-flat minor chords thundering through the house bringing Matty running and three choruses of *Polly-Wolly- Doodle*.

When offered a fee Ben Faulkner bowed. 'Thank you, this afternoon has been a gift to me,' he said. Matty likes to play piano. Julia has tried teaching him but thinks he'll respond better to a man. 'Do you teach piano, Mr Faulkner?'

He grimaced. 'Any musical bent of mine is purely incidental. I am, excuse me, I *was* a teacher. What I am now is a man fallen on hard times.'

Mr Faulkner, or Mr Doodle as he is now known to Matty, left agreeing to try his 'rusty tutorial skills' next Tuesday and every Tuesday following.

125

'On trial I think, Mr Faulkner,' said Julia, aware of the smell of alcohol.

He lifted his hat. 'Indeed so madam. I wouldn't have it any other way.'

* * *

Early next morning she was woken by a noise in the hall and went to investigate. The girls were out the back Maggie polishing the grate and Susan at the sink peeling carrots. 'What was that noise?'

'I dropped the coal scuttle, madam,' said Maggie.

Susan was wiping her eyes.

'Are you crying, Susan?'

'No, madam, it's the onions.'

Later, Julia took her aside. 'Have you thought of visiting your mother? I'm sure she'd be pleased to know she's to be a grandmother.'

'She's already got my sister's children. She won't want mine.'

'You have sisters? Do they know of your situation?'

'Joan, my eldest sister does.'

'Where does she live?'

'Cherry Hinton.'

'Cherry Hinton is close to where Matty and I used to live. Would you like me to write to your mother and say how you are managing?'

'My mother's not good with letters but Joan can read.'

'Alright then we'll do it this evening.'

Joe Carmody brought flowers from the garden. 'There's more if you want, ma'm. I've a whole bush of Hebe needs thinning.'

'Thank you, Joe.' She'll take them to the Nelson. It was Nan's birthday yesterday. Julia called with a gift but was told she was busy in the cellar.

The whole of Baker's is abuzz with news of the tea-shop yet no one has actually called. You'd think they would if only out of curiosity, especially the front parlour so pretty, the wicker tables and chairs glistening in the sun.

'Mr Roberts says we shouldn't bother with table linen,' said Maggie. 'We should leave the glass bare. He says it's the fashion nowadays.'

Julia frowned. 'Does he indeed?'

'I like Mr Roberts more than his missis.'

'You're speaking of *Albert* Roberts? Yes, he is an amiable man. On the subject of not so amiable did Mr Luke say when he'd finish the shelves? ...Maggie, be careful with that cake-stand! It's Meissen and fragile.'

Hands steady as a rock, Maggie stared. 'I'm not about to drop it, madam. I worked three years at the Nelson and never cracked a glass.'

Flustered, Julia hurried away. It's Luke Roberts! She hears his name and is distracted. She looks for him everywhere. If he's working here she's wishing he away, and if he's elsewhere she's wishing him here. I'll write to John Sargent accepting his invitation. Who would not want to see inside Sandringham?

* * *

Julia drove the cart to the village and was told Mrs Roberts couldn't see her. 'She's laid up in bed with a fearful head-ache.'

Julia offered the Hebe. 'Please give her these and my wishes for a speedy recovery.' She would've left but having a question returned to find the maid grinning. 'Is it something Mrs Roberts ate?' The maid shuffled her feet. 'I'm sure I couldn't say.'

Unaccustomed to traffic, Julia went to the Market Place and then, making a U-turn, took the trap back down the High Street. Nan was in the doorway talking with the maid. Julia waved, but mistress and maid darted indoors.

'I see,' she whispered, not sure what she saw only that it hurt to see it.

The rest of the day passed in a daze. Luke arrived to fit the shelves. Taking a leaf from his mother's book she pleaded a headache and left him to it. Hoping the slight imagined she waited but no one came with a message of thanks for the flowers. It had to be faced, there was no headache, nor was Nan busy yesterday in the cellar - she didn't want to see Julia.

It hurt! Her friend, the straight-talking Yorkshire woman, who dealt in honesty and warned of people who would help and people who wouldn't, had turned her back on the Needed and Necessary! Five o'clock the hurt trebled when a package containing the shawl was brought to the door. *Thank you for the flowers and loan of the shawl,* the note was cursory, *but on reflection I think the colour too bright for me*, regards, Nanette Roberts.

* * *

That night, when already abed, Susan asked Julia to write to her mother.

'I think I should, don't you, madam?'

'I see no reason not to.'

Julia penned the note, Susan dictated, it was a slow process with many stops and starts. Eventually it was done. 'Are you happy with that?' said Julie.

Eyes big and bruised, Susan nodded. 'Will it be posted today?'

'It will go first thing. You should sleep now. You look very tired.'

'I've got the bellyache.'

'Bellyache!' Julia was alarmed. Isn't it too soon for the baby?'

'It's not the baby. It's that burnt cake. Maggie said it's poison. She said if you get wet washing pots you'll marry a drunk. My sister works in a kitchen. She's always washing pots and her husband is always drunk.'

'I'm not sure it signifies.'

'I don't want a drunk. I want to marry a nice gentleman.'

Sighing, Julia got to feet. 'I'm sure we'd all like a nice gentleman.'

'I want this 'un.' Susan stroked the bookmark. 'He can sing and play the paper and comb. He sang the day the baby was born. You know?' She covered her mouth with her hand, 'when he kissed me.'

Julia could only shake her head.

'Can I sing that song to you, madam?'

'It's very late.'

'Oh go on! Just one verse!'

'Alright then.'

Susan knelt on the bed and hands clasped under her chin began to sing. '*Oh where, oh where has my little dog gone? Oh where, oh where, can he be? With ears cut short and his tail cut long, oh where, oh where is he.'*

Alone in her own bed Julia was close to weeping. It was bad enough when Susan sang, bump protruding from her nightdress, but then Maggie joined in, the two of them holding hands, the angel behind their faces so visible.

'It's so sad. Why couldn't Susan have her nice gentleman and be happy? We must we all be so sad?' On the way home from Cambridge Luke Roberts asked if Julia loved Owen. She did love him but like Susan was always looking for a nice gentleman. So blind! She had a nice gentleman all the time but didn't recognise him.

* * *

Alone in her room Maud McLaughlin pushed her box under the bed and set Milady Carrington's latest letter to the candle flame, Maggie Jeffers is not above sneaking into a person's room so it mustn't be left about.

It's late, Maud needs to finish her letter for first post tomorrow. These days she has daily bulletin to London down to a fine art leaning on details of house-cleaning rather than Mrs Dryden's private affairs, that way she hopes the letters to Russell Square will soon be considered a waste of time.

Oh, she wishes she didn't have to do it, but at forty-four, a liverish stomach, a weak bladder and only a few coins in her box she feels she has little choice.

Milady Carrington's instructions along with the ink-carrying pen were clear. *Mrs Dryden is a friend. A young widow alone and with a sick child one worries how she'll cope. You can be her guardian angel. A diary of daily events sent here to Langora will ensure my assistance long before she needs it. Do this and for your time and care I shall offer a token of appreciation.*

Pen scratching, Maud wrote of polishing silver and of making table cloths out of sheets. She told of a Gala Opening and that people in the village were sure to come, and that she, Mrs McLaughlin, (not Mrs Mac of the pissy-drawers as Milady liked to say) was in charge of the maids. She told of Ben Faulkner, the new tutor. She told how she helps Master Matty, how they play with the dog and kittens. She told of her room, how she sits with Joey, her cockatiel, and is cherished by Madam as her right-hand.

There was no avoiding Madam's trip to Cambridge to see the German doctor. Doctor Adelman is of the London circle and servants will talk. If this juicy bone is not offered, Milady will know and chew on her former servant.

Evelyn Carrington is an uncertain person, one moment kind the next stopping wages. She's the same with friends, offering the world then denying a farthing. It's a sinful house, people drinking and men in dressing-gowns tapping on bedroom doors. Milady has a thing for women as well as men. There was trouble a while back with a French lady. Rumour was Madame Dupres left early on account of illness. Truth is Patty Clarke walked in on them abed and stark naked. Below stairs lived on that piece of gossip for months. Scandal and Russell Square go hand-in-hand. If it's not Milady taking chances it's her brother and his peacock friends. Then there's Susan, footmen taking bets as to which of the Honourable Freddie's gentlemen friends was responsible.

Any nasty talk here is Maggie Jeffers doing, not enough she talks of madam and the German doctor, now she aims her poison at Luke Roberts, a nicer gentleman you couldn't wish to meet. He might only be a builder but he has such grace, and was here in the week sorting out the Sweep, chivvying everyone along and making sure things were done right.

Maud once knew another man like Luke Roberts - Tobias Lane, tutor to the Blakeleys. She was nursemaid then to Blakeley children. It was the best of times. She was young and sat in the evening talking with Toby. Then Colonel Blakeley was wounded in a war. Toby was first to go and she soon after. Now there's gossip about Mr Luke. Maud feels her share of guilt for it was she who wrote Russell Square saying he'd taken a shine to Madam. Milady thought it amusing. '*Poor Ju-ju! First Stefan now a country yokel with muscles for brains. Is it any wonder women turn to laudanum for bed-companion?*'

'I can't do it.' Maud tore up her letter. Madam trusts her. There'll be no more letters and no more half-crowns, blood money that it is.

* * *

Julia dreamt she was on the Cambridge train. Sheep were again on the line men carrying bloodied carcases. Such noise, the screams of injured animals and the hissing of a monstrous train! She tried closing the window to shield her eyes and ears but couldn't. Then in the midst of the horror the Lord Jesus appeared, a lamb on His shoulder, its delicate form slick with foetal tissue.

The lamb was bleating, calling for its mother. Julia reached down from the window. 'Don't cry, little lamb,' she whispered. 'It will soon be over.'

She woke to find Matty by the bed. Eyes wide open and face pale with fear, he was walking in his sleep. It's happened before, Matty seeming to be awake when in fact he is in a hypnotic daze. 'What is it?' she asked.

He pointed to the upper stairs. Julia ran, opening the maid's door to a dreadful sight. 'My God, Susan,' she whispered. 'What have you done?'

For the moment, she was unable to move, wondering if she was awake or still locked in the nightmare. All too soon she realised what she was seeing was only too real - Susan cradling her belly and blood seeping through her fingers.

'Mrs McLaughlin!' Julia darted along the landing, hammering on Maud's door. 'Maud, get dressed! I need you to go for help.' She ran back again to the maid's room. Maggie was hunched up in her bed. 'What happened here?'

'It's not my fault,' Maggie whined. 'I didn't tell Susan to do it.'
'Do what?'

Maggie hid under the blanket.

Julia snatched it away. 'What has she done?'

'She was doin' it all day and yesterday, climbin' to the top and leapin' down to shake the baby out. Nothin' was happenin'. She did it again a while ago and fell from the top to bottom. Now there's this red stuff comin' out!'

Susan was ashen. Blood sliding into her palm Julia took her hand. 'Hold on,' she said. 'We're getting help.'

'No,' said Susan, voice slurred, 'don't get help. Let it die.'

No point asking how long she'd been like this with neither girl sensible enough to answer. Puddles of blood in the bed and Susan gasping for air said it all. Assessing damage, Julia lifted the nightgown. Susan screamed, arched her back, and hot blood sprayed the room. 'Bring me towels Maggie!'

Snivelling, Maggie ran downstairs,

'Oh madam!' Mrs McLaughlin is at the door.

'Go to Greenfields! They have a telephone. Ask them to bring a doctor!'

'What doctor, madam, your Doctor Adelman?'

'For heaven's sake, Maud!' Julia pushed her out the door. 'A local doctor!'

Mrs McLaughlin fled.

Susan was clawing at her body, as though trying to pull the child from her womb. 'Stop that!' Julia grabbed her hands. 'You must try to be still and let me help you.' Convulsed by pain, an animal seeking deliverance deaf to all entreaties, Susan screamed again and rolling on her back pushed upward.

'Maggie!' Julia shouted out. 'Get up here this minute.'

The stupid girl was bottom of the stairs hiding.

'Maggie Jeffers! If you don't get up here this minute I shall tell the constable you were of no help and he will send you to prison.'

A galloping carthorse, up she came, her face blotched and swollen.

'You are to do as I bid, d'you hear? You are to follow all my commands and not fail me. Now hold onto Susan's hands and do not let go.'

'But she'll bite me, madam! She's already bit me.'

'No doubt you deserved it. Now, hold onto her hands!' Shoulder seams ripping, she tore the sleeves from her nightgown; what she had in mind she didn't know except that there needed to be binding. 'Where's Matty?'

'I don't know, madam,' Maggie whispered. 'Maybe's he's with Mrs Mac.'

Julia could only hope so. There was no time to look. Weak from loss of blood Susan lay panting and so very pale. 'Help me, Susan,' she said. 'Forget everything now but your little baby. Think of this life as belonging to the nice gentleman who played the paper and comb and who sang to you! Think of the baby as part of him, his child and yours to love for evermore.'

'For evermore?' Susan's voice was barely audible.

'Yes, Susan, yours to love for all time!'

* * *

Matty and Kaiser were out and running with only one thought in mind. They knew where to go, a place they both loved that smelt of horses and where stars shone through the roof. It's dark but they know the way. In dreams they go there all the time flying over bushes and chasing moonbeams but it isn't nice this time, Matty can't leap as he did before. He runs through the briars rather than over and catches his nightshirt. Perhaps they should have stayed with Oldie Hubbard but she went to get people from beyond the Wall and that's the wrong place to go. The Lady with the Seeds, who sits at night and tells of foreign lands and how she once loved a sailor, came again tonight.

'Run, Matthew Dryden,' she pulled at the bed-cover. 'Go get Mister Wolf from the Forge and take your trusty hound with you!'

Matty was late getting to sleep. He'd lit a candle and was reading a book. He can read now, Oldie showed him how. It's good. Now instead of wriggling as they used to, the letters behave nicely. His favourite line is 'the Cow Jumped Over the Moon.' When he reads it Kaiser pretends to jump and they laugh.

Mumma reads *Oliver Twist*. Papa read a book called the *Iliad*. It was about heroes and villains. Those words had funny shapes. The words in *Oliver Twist* are shaped just right. When Matty gets back he'll tell Mumma he can read. She will be pleased. He likes pleasing Mumma. He doesn't like it when she cries.

'Run,' said the Seed Lady, 'and take your Trusty Hound.'

Matty loves Kaiser and Kaiser loves him, a silver rope joins them together. It will never break. Mumma's friend, the German Bear, says Kaiser means king. Kaiser likes his name and runs faster when called.

It's taking a long time to get there. Matty is weary and Kaiser's paws are bleeding from thorns. In dreams they are at the Forge in a second. They zoom through the door. Then Kaiser sits by the fire chewing a bone and Matty and Mister Wolf play chequers. The Wolf always wins. Matty once moved a chequer in secret but the Wolf knew. 'You must never cheat.'

'Why when I can't win any other way?'

'Because it makes the winning not worthwhile.'

Last week Matty cheated on Joe Carmody, swapping bigger plant-pots for smaller. Mister Wolf is right. It's not worth it. The plants died.

Matty's legs are hurting and he wishes it wasn't so dark.

There are shadows everywhere and a big bird sits up in a tree.

It has big yellow eyes and watches and asks questions.

'To-wit-to-woo.' It says. 'And who are you?'

'I'm Matthew Dryden,' Matty began to cry. 'I live in the Nen and Nen with my Mumma and Kaiser and the kittens. Please don't let Susan die.'

Maggie Jeffers says if you see a crow a person you love will die. Matty saw two yesterday eating bread crusts. Does that mean two people will die?

It is so dark and so black Matty is no longer sure he knows the way. He thinks he is lost. And oh dear, something is coming!

'Mumma!'

A big animal, a Hippopotamus or Lion is crashing through the forest!

'Mumma!'

It's going to eat him and Kaiser up!

Matty stood still, opened his eyes, woke and screamed. 'Mumma!'

Luke swept him up in his arms. 'It's alright! I'm here.'

Book Two

Tainted Flower

CHAPTER ELEVEN

One of Those Things

Damn Bakers End and its mean spirited residents! Julia loathes the place. Left to her she'd be gone and the cottage sold to the first buyer!

Lip curled in disgust, she glanced about the empty church. Shame on the people of Bakers End! What did Susan Dudley do that they shun her so?

Events of the last few days have changed Julia forever. She can never be the same: naivety died with Susan and her baby. She'd wanted them to live and for a time Susan had wanted the same. 'I'm trying, madam,' she whispered, her lips pallid petals, 'but I don't seem able.' Even at the end, bed awash with blood and the baby sliding into desperate hands, even then there was hope.

Julia tried breathing life into the tiny rag. She tried and tried until a stranger, Callie Greville Masson, the woman sitting beside her said, 'let it go. You can do no more. Mammy and baby are safe now in the arms of Jesus.'

The coffin rests on a trestle before the altar. It was earlier in the parlour, an altar of innocence among bone china and fragrant Hebe Joe Carmody had gathered, his seamed face grimy with tears. 'It ain't right,' he'd said. 'She was only a kid herself.' She sleeps now in a bed hardly room for one sleeper. She wears Julia's best nightgown, her hair braided and tied with blue ribbon.

Maggie brought the ribbons. 'I thought she might like them.' Eyes red with weeping she lingered. 'It weren't my fault? I didn't make her fall did I?'

'No, you didn't.' Julia couldn't have hung that sin on anyone. 'It was one of those things.' Maggie wept. 'That's right, madam, one of those things.'

They are gone, Maggie to her mother and Mrs Mac to a friend in Dorset. Julia gave them time off. So much anger in her heart and they easy targets, it was best. Maggie is not innocent of Susan's death. She is as much to do with it as she is of Matty's fear of crows - a modern day oracle spinning wives' tales she should hang a sign about her neck, '*Beware the black and midnight hag.*'

As for dear Maud she's a snitch. The letters, the coins and ink-carrying pen make sense now in that she offered a diary of events to Evie Carrington. How very tedious for both! If the snitch is to continue earning her pound of flesh Julia better spice up her life, although surely this chapter in the *Adventures of Ju-ju Dryden* will keep the animals fed for years.

She should've sent them packing but Mrs Mac, ever attuned to shifting currents, said she was sorry about Susan. Maud missed her vocation. She should offer her services to the campaign for Votes for Women. Even with leaky drawers her gift for diplomacy could not fail!

* * *

The vicar is late and there's twittering at the West Door. The Good Wives enter, genuflect, and skirts lifted to avoid contamination sweep a circle round the far aisle. Good wives! Every church has such. They are the gossip-mongers and the harmonium players, the ones the vicar '*could never do without*!' Fragile and invincible they rule the land - the quilt-covered cross and nails that bind the Lord Jesus Christ. Hedgehogs, Father called them. 'Charlotte, May, Anna! Take a back seat at meetings and let a hedgehog field the day. You know how prickly they can be.' They'll be in the vestry now checking the choir-boys' cassocks for cigarette ends. No one will mention today, none rail against the vicar officiating, complaints will be muttered in the heart and head, the piffling reasons why these sinners *'should never have been brought to St Bedes.'*

The baby, the tiny sinner, is clothed in silk, a Christening robe from Evie.

Julia was appalled. 'She wants the baby wrapped in this?'

'Yes, madam,' said Mrs Mac. 'But I can't do it.'

'Leave it with me. The undertaker's not due until eleven.'

The robe was clearly a family heirloom and the instructions precise, with the baby thus wrapped Maud is to consider *'all duty to the House of Carrington fulfilled. In token of this and other commissions accept the enclosed purse.'*

Julia had to ask. 'How much was in the purse?'

Mrs Mac hung her head. 'Thirty-shillings.'

Julia undertook to dress them, the babe in the crook of his mother's arm, and the book-mark entwined about Susan's marble fingers. Such a scene, porcelain glittering in the candlelight - the Hebe sweeter and more profound than any church candle - and in the coffin a Madonna and Child remote and rare as any Renaissance icon. The babe came through the fight unmarked, the face pure and white, the Lord God saying, 'I brought this masterpiece through fire and clay but finding the world unworthy I called the life away.'

Julia begged baptism for both but none would consider it, not even Callie Masson who with Daniel appeared out of the night as rescuers. 'It can't be done,' Callie's ancient eyes were filled with compassion. 'I have none of the Cloth staying. We can't in good conscience go beyond a blessing.'

Later, when all had gone Julia remembered her dream of the slaughtered sheep and Jesus Christ with a newborn lamb on His shoulder. Then she knew they needed no blessing, He had taken mother and child into His care.

* * *

Callista Greville Masson adjusted her fur tippet. 'Sure is cold in here. Back home in Philly my church is built of wood, cool in summer and warm in winter. These stone walls chill my bones. It makes me wonder why I bought Greenfields. I'm creaking enough without adding to it.'

It was a shock seeing Daniel that night. No time for explanations, the old lady, a velvet clad frontierswoman, swept in. 'I am Callie Masson. Greenfields is my house and the man hovering on the landing is my son. I bring a doctor and my maid, Dulce, who alas is no stranger to tragedy.'

'La, Mesdames, we are too late!' A face of polished bronze, the maid, Dulce, then sank down on her knees. 'Nothing can be done.'

They were too late, Julia and her pitiful endeavours, and the doctor who, handkerchief to nose, refused to go near Susan. 'Work house girls!' he'd sniffed. 'What was it this time, a knitting needle or bottle of gin?'

Julia was outraged. Susan had suffered enough. There would be a Christian grave for her and her child. They would not be buried unsanctified.

'How dare you speak so and her lying here!' she'd said. 'Susan miscarried but not through gin or other foul object. Have a little respect for the dead.'

Callie Greville Masson agreed. 'Mother and child need a blessing not calumny to send them on their way. Do your office as doctor, sir, not a judge.'

It was in the general move that Julia saw Luke Roberts on the landing Matty asleep in his arms. A strange moment, unearthly, she looked into a source of light that quivered and shone. 'What?' her lips had formed a question. With a shake of the head he passed along the landing into Matty's bedroom and there he stayed, a watcher, his boots pushed out and face in shadow.

* * *

'Chi-chirrup!' A bird in the church tower sang.

Matty looked up from his book. 'A blackbird!'

'That's right,' said Mrs Masson. 'Do you like birds, Matthew?'

Fingers to his lips he whistled and then returned to his book.

Callie leaned close. 'He's a clever child and sensitive. When you said you were bringing him today I worried how he'd take such an occasion.'

'With the maids away I couldn't leave him alone.'

'He wouldn't have been alone.' Callie Masson hugged Matty. 'I would've come. I know a little about you, Mrs Dryden. Daniel told me how you met. I was due to come and make myself known

145

when your maid came a-knocking.'

'Thank God she did. You have been a great comfort to us all.'

Mrs Masson shrugged. 'We are neighbours. We should care for one another.'

'I've heard that said before but it wasn't meant.'

The blackbird flew singing out of the door.

'Lots of things are said but not meant,' said Callie. 'It's said in the midst of life there is death. A blackbird sings and in the midst of death there is life. It's a way of looking at things.' She twitched her hat. 'This darn hat is killing me.'

Julia glanced at the hat overtopping the wrinkled face. 'It is a notable hat.'

'I bought it in Paris with such an occasion in mind but having outlived my friends wore it today. It is a foolish hat.' She nodded toward the coffin, 'almost as foolish as that wreath.' The wreath of roses is monstrously large, so large it had to be removed to allow bearers through the lych-gate. Now like Mrs Masson's hat it hangs askew, green fern dripping like mildewed tears. 'Outrageous!' Mrs Masson snorted. 'Flowers to a maid she not many weeks before threw to the wolves? Who draws attention to such behaviour?'

The day after the tragedy Daniel came apologising, he'd wanted to tell of his mother buying Greenfields but the opportunity hadn't presented itself.

'And you left London all of a sudden.'

'I felt I had no choice.'

'I guess not. I know what happened. I saw Carrington's caddish behaviour and knew you right to leave. As for that unfortunate girl, you did your best for her. I hope you'll rest easy on that.' Then knowing her uncomfortable he switched to John

Sargent and the Art Exhibition. 'He's showing soon hereabouts.'

'He sent an invitation. I did think to take Matty but now I'm not sure.'

'Do go! I hear tell there's to be a cinematic show and Ferris wheels and all manner of fun things for children. Matthew wouldn't want to miss it.'

He offered a car should Julia decide to go to the exhibition. 'We are neighbours now. I'd like to think you regard me as a friend.'

Today her new friend sits beside Stefan Adelman. Behind them is Susan's sister to whom Julia sent news of the funeral. Apart from the vicar there is only one other villager in attendance, Luke Roberts, sober in a dark jacket. The night of the tragedy, Matty in the throes of sleep, ran to fetch him, an act of trust that touched and alarmed Julia. 'I don't know why he came,' said Luke the following day. 'I was shaken out of bed knowing he was coming.'

That there is more to the event was evident in his frown and the way he worked his fist intent on trying to keep a grip on mystery. Julia didn't enquire. No one can question her of this man, not now, not ever. That her little boy trusted enough to run through darkness to find and that Luke loved enough to be found is everything. If there is more one day one of them will tell.

* * *

'*Ashes to ashes, dust to dust, the Lord bless and keep her, the Lord make His face to Shine upon her and be Gracious unto her and give her peace.*'

The service over, Julia dropped lily-of-the-valley onto the coffin.

'Those lilies were one of my little japes,' muttered Callie Masson.

'I beg your pardon?'

'I'm your plant thief. I am the one who's been driving your good gardener crazy. I put baskets over the wall by way of compensation for odds and ends stolen from you and took plants to repay for those stolen from me.'

'Have I stolen from you?'

'Not you, Julianna, but some other person a long time ago.' When Julia stared Callie grimaced. 'Taking from your side of the wall felt like retribution. But it's a long and involved story. I shouldn't have mentioned it.'

'But you did mention it! What does it mean?'

'It means I knew the people who lived in your house.'

'The Newman sisters?'

'Justine Newman was my friend. When I stole from you I was stealing from her. At the time it amused me to creep about like a crazy person. Meeting you now I see it for what it is. Anyway, that's enough of old nonsense.' She sniffed. 'One day I'll fill you in on the details but for now I'll bite my tongue. At my age it doesn't do to stare into open graves and speak of ancient rivalry.'

Leaning heavily on a cane she moved away, Matty singing and whistling beside her. Desperate for the day to end Julia stood gazing down.

There was a cough at her elbow, Susan's sister. 'I need to be on my way.'

'Thank you for coming.'

'She was my sister. Just because others stayed away don't mean I have to.'

'No indeed. I thought Susan a sweet girl.'

'Did yer? It seems to me someone else thought the same.'

'I'll arrange for a cab to take you to the station. Do you have her things?'

'If you mean the few bits in her room I left 'em where they were.'

'Would you to take the letter? Susan meant it for your mother. It was dictated the night she died. She was anxious for it to be sent.'

'I don't know that I will take it. She was a worry to our mother from the day she was born. The times we've wept over her. A pretty girl, she'll go far they all said. Look how far she went, a hole in the ground and a bastard child with her.'

'Do take the letter! There's money in the envelope, Susan's wages.'

The woman took the envelope. 'I'll take the money. I won't say no to that. Susan was a worry but as you say a sweet girl. She was like one of them lilies you tossed down the hole, picked when fresh and then cast aside.'

* * *

Stefan is not well. Throughout the funeral he sat still and pale. At the graveside he almost fell. 'It is my own fault, the pigeon pie at luncheon too tempting. Daniel offered a bed but I have appointments next week that are pressing. If you will allow me to rest awhile, Julianna, I'll catch a later train.'

An hour later at the cottage he was no better.

Julia was anxious. 'You're quite worn out. You shouldn't have come.'

'I had to. Knowing how things were for you how could I stay away.'

'You must rest.' She took his arm and led him to the stairs. 'In this moment I am the doctor.' Stefan sat by the bed knowing he should leave before the weather worsens but is so tired. Perhaps if he lies down he'll feel better before returning home. Home? What is that? He pays lease on the house in Bradbury plus a *pied a terre* in Knightsbridge but his home is in Dresden. Every morning church bells ring and scatter the pigeons that were once the bane of Karoline's life. 'Do not feed them, Stefan,' she'd say. 'They are parasites.'

Pigeon pie is what he ate for luncheon. Indigestion, he told Julianna. She knows it is more than that. She sees what everyone sees when looking at Stefan Adelman - a heart bleeding. Saturday he was at a concert listening to the Brahms' *Eine Deutches Requiem*. In conversation afterward he said he'd like the last movement '*Blessed are they that mourn*' played at his funeral. A friend, grossly overweight, a drinker, said that since the whole of the medical profession is on borrowed time they should recall the orchestra now.

What is borrowed time? In terms of three score years and ten he has entered the last third. Rickard Adelman, Stefan's father, said we are only ever on loan. *'Mitt Gott kanst du nicht handeln... wenn deine Zeit vorueber ist, ist es vorbei.'* When your time is up it's up. There is no bargaining with God. Lying here breathing in starched linen another quote comes to mind, 'physician heal thyself.' Professor Stefan Adelman- honorary Fellow of the Royal College and consultant to the Queen - is unable to heal his heart. He has taken *Die Kur* at Wiesbaden, fasted while consulting quacks, but the clock ticks. Angina pectoris is the curse of the male Adelman line, blocked arteries is the layman's term, and good enough since blocked is what they are by hereditary trait and love of hog-roast. It's likely when he does fall that will be given as cause but his hurts are legion, devils plague his soul, Stefan made a mistake and his wife the cost, now only God and a passing drove of Gadarene swine can set him free.

Julianna is right, he shouldn't have come but he feels responsible for Susan, it was he who brought the girl from Stepney. He knows the area well and once a week repairs to a house in Beaconsfield Road where he shares another life exchanging button-boots for slippers and a stethoscope for pipe and tobacco.

Peggy Gresham lives at number 28 with her sons Jim and Tommy. To Peggy, Stefan is someone to hug when lonely - to her sons he's the foreign bloke who pays the rent. 'Hello, ducks,' she will smile, her good-natured face glowing. 'Come in and I'll make us a nice cup-of-tea.' He loathes English tea as he loathes the rice-pudding she doles out every time but he likes Peggy. As for her sons, they are pleased to see him when he comes and pleased when he leaves.

Peggy was char to his Knightsbridge house. In the spring of '94 he found her bleeding into the sink, her husband having broken her nose. That same spring the husband vanished. 'Don't worry about 'im,' said the eldest son. 'He won't be troublin' Ma again. Go fill your boots!' Permission given, and the lads out the back door, Stefan did fill his boots, the bedsprings twanging. Hairy armpits and dimpled buttocks, she is no Rhine Maiden but she is patient and once a week grips him between her knees to shake his sorrows loose.

Every visit is the last. He lies to himself, saying such visits are a comfort against the trauma of a sick wife. To say he was surprised by Julianna's advances is to understate the case. Nowadays women seek the vote. Julianna Dryden never struck him as a suffragette. He saw modesty and liked it. Then suddenly, shockingly and delightfully, modesty had her hand on his thigh!

A memory of that time is locked in the dark reaches of his mind. Foot poised on a stool she stretches to remove her stocking. He trails his hand down her a curving haunch to a shadowy cleft to warm, wet, darkness, and she shudders.

The first touch of her hand and manhood was stunned to silence. 'Forgive me!' he'd whispered, 'I am unable to give as you deserve.' She'd closed him in her arms. 'Close your eyes and let me be the one to give.' So it was in the first fumbling a door to the past opened, it was his wife he held, Karoline Kleinman of the silver hair and chipped diamond eyes, and he the young Herr Doktor, newly minted and lately wed, when they honeymooned in the bridal suite in the Hotel Vier Jahreszeitzen Kempinski. Naked but for a shift, she undid her hair. A powerful lover he was then and for an hour in Bradbury Julianna Dryden - and a second mystical being - allowed him to be that lover again.

He woke with a start, a storm rattling the window panes. Cursing, he swung his legs over the bed. Julianna is alone. He mustn't stay. Her acceptance in this village is difficult enough. He must not make things worse. The door opened, a lamp in her hand and skirts whispering she entered the room.

'Forgive me, Julianna. I slept.'

'Good,' she said closing the door. 'I meant you to.'

'*Nein*!' he said anxious. 'Do not close the door! I must not stay.'

'Stay!' She set the lamp on the table. 'It's raining and you'll be soaked.'

'Please be sensible. You are here alone.'

She smiled. 'I don't believe it possible to be alone in this house. I think the history of the world encased between these walls.' One-by-one she took combs from her hair. 'Oh, that's better.' She shook out her hair. 'At eighteen one can't wait to pin up one's hair. God knows why!'

He protested. 'Today we are speculation. Come the morning we are fact.'

She shrugged. 'They'll think ill of me no matter what I do. I wouldn't put a dog out in this never mind a man, especially a man like you, Stefan.'

He peered through the gloom. 'Julianna?' he said hesitantly. '*Bist do dass?*'

Lightning flashed, illuminating a figure of white gold. She smiled. 'It's me, Stefan. Who else would it be?'

* * *

He left just before five. Julia was stirring porridge. He stood at the kitchen door humming softly under his breath. She could feel his gaze. 'Goodbye, then, Stefan,' she said. 'I wish you a quiet journey and a calm week.'

'There is every possibility of a quiet journey but none of a calm day. I am to travel to the Cowes on Friday visiting Osborne House.'

'Ah yes Her Majesty! You move in exalted circles, Doctor Adelman.'

Suddenly young, he smiled. 'I believe I do. Certainly last night was a heavenly experience. At least,' he hesitated, 'it was for me.'

'And for me.'

With Stefan gone, the house was silent only a memory of the tune he hummed lingering, Schubert's *Die Forelle*.

'Karoline played cello. Schubert and Strauss were her favourites.' This was Stefan at two am this morning, his head on the pillow and arm across Julia's waist. 'I love Strauss's music. Brahms was not afraid to like the popular. Of the Blue Danube he wrote, "'Unfortunately not composed by Johannes Brahms.'"'

Owen would talk after making love. His talk was not of waltzes but more of the Great Pyramid. He would talk and then sleep. Stefan slept in similar sudden manner. Finding him so, Julia had crept away to her own room and to the windowsill, to cooling rain - and to Luke Roberts gazing up.

The past is repeated, rain beats down and a man shelters under the eaves. The only thing missing in the pattern is a wave of a hand telling her to go inside. There was no wave this time only a look in his eyes.

Unable to bear that look Julia rushed downstairs and out of the door. 'Don't look at me like that!' she'd shouted, rain plastering her nightgown to her body. 'Yes there's a man up there asleep in a bed, a true and honest friend whose heart is breaking! And yes he did hold me and we did cling together but not as you think! None of this is as this dirty town imagines. All is so much kinder and so sad. It is caring! It is love, and nothing but love!'

Hair bedraggled and feet thick with mud she shouted until she was hoarse. She tried saying that wanting a person to be a certain way will not make them so. Not that it mattered! There was none to hear her pleadings. Luke did as he always does on such occasions, walked away. It was in turning back to the house she realised she hadn't uttered a word, that every shout, every plea for understanding, was in her head. The rest was the wind and the rain.

CHAPTER TWELVE

Elliptical Eve

'What is the point?' Luke drove the chisel under the tile and it fell away rotten as the rest of the roof. This house! So much to do he'll be breaking his back to get it right. And what *is* the point? A robe and her hair undone and alone in the house with that chap, he must step back and leave well alone.

It's what he's been telling himself all day. But it doesn't help. To judge without knowing doesn't sit right with him. And who is he to judge! As he said to Albert their only connection is his heart and her indifference.

Early this morning Ma came to the Forge all aquiver, 'could he help out to wait on tables; they've a full house this evening and nobility coming, a Lady Eve Carrington is to visit the Art Exhibition at Sandringham and has booked three nights for her and her brother and all with dinner!'

The name Carrington is whispered hereabouts by downstairs maids as the one who kicked Susan Dudley out. Curious to put a face to a woman who could do such a thing Luke agreed to lend a hand. That she should choose to stay at the Nelson when there are grander hotels is odd, that she should visit Bakers End with Susan and the baby not a month in the ground is more so.

Word spread that she was coming. Even here in the backend of Norfolk newspapers are read, Milady's comings and goings, her paintings in London galleries and her society doings and friendship with royalty noted. Luke has another source of information in Mrs Mac. In the week following Susan's death she talked all the while of Eve Carrington, how she is temperamental and artistic and never the same two days in a row, and how her brother, the Honourable Freddie, calls her Elliptical Eve.

Luke has his own thoughts on Susan's death. Though years and circumstances apart he links it to Jacky's death. The night Susan died he was thrown out of bed. At first he thought the bed collapsed. Nothing wrong with the bed! Voice thundering, the Lord God threw him out. '**Look for young Matty! He's out with his dog and afraid**.' Luke ran and as he ran seemed to know one child would be saved but another lost. When he went to Susan's funeral Nan said people would take it amiss. 'What?' he'd scorned, 'me going to a funeral?' She'd nodded. 'They'll think you're going against them.'

Things between him and folks in Bakers are not good. Hidebound in attitude they drive him crazy. Look what they're doing now! The Good Wives of chapel that refused Susan's funeral are planning to do the same with the tea-room.

'We don't want it,' said Albert, his lip screwed up. 'Fancy people playing at business! Mrs Julianna Dryden can bake her cakes and polish her silver but we'll not sup there. This is a decent town. She must shut up shop and take herself and her fancy-men elsewhere.'

The last word rests with the Big House and the Americans, the newcomers to English shores will make or break the tea-shop. Townsfolk are waiting to see which way the wind blows, the right direction and the tearoom, and Julianna, may yet win.

* * *

Lady Evelyn and her brother arrived shortly after six. Luke helped with the baggage. A big fellow called Jamieson, more a bruiser than a valet, passed down a boxed-up painting. Luke reached up to take it. 'Whoah!' The brother, a chap in his late twenties, sprang forward. 'I'll take that, my friend,' he grinned. 'That is my life's blood. If busted I'll pop a vein and die.'

'Don't be silly, Freddie,' a voice drawled. 'No one's going to drop it, especially not this man. I have it on good authority Mr Luke Roberts has the safest hands in Norfolk. Which is why he's about to extend a hand to help me down.'

There she was, Eve Carrington, smiling through the carriage window, big blue eyes shining. 'Good day Mr Roberts! Or should I call you Mister Wolf?'

Luke laughed, he could do no other. This slender little creature, this elfin child with piquant face and cherub curls is the dreaded Elliptical Eve? It can't be so. He laughed and she laughed with him her delicate fingers caressing his palm. 'I know,' she said smiling. 'The world is absurd, don't you think.'

That evening he served wine at their table. 'Are you an artist too?' the brother queried. 'Only, you have that mean and starving, livin' in a garret look we'd all like to cultivate.'

'I'm no artist.'

'You are. I see hunger in your eyes and tell-tale damage to your hands. Mine are the same.' Freddie spread his fingers. 'It's the price of being a dauber, fingers smashed to hell and back. Why are yours so black-and-blue?'

'I'm reroofing a house.'

Freddie laughed. 'That would explain it.'

'And I do paint.' Luke pulled the cork and poured a glass.

'I paint walls and ceilings, three coats, but the brushes I wield a little hefty for your canvas.'

'Keep it that way.' Freddie emptied his glass. 'Don't even think of trying to translate the things you love through paint. It'll break your heart.'

The Carringtons ate little and drank a great deal. Come ten o'clock the Honourable Freddie was tipsy. Luke wasn't particularly sober, his heart heavy and this fellow's humour so brittle he needed some form of protection.

At the third bottle Freddie was following Luke to the cellar. 'What is that? Oh a Madeira and a good one at that! Yes, open it up. I'm lately from Paris with Johnny Sargent where they're all drinkin' that filthy Dubonnet muck.'

Luke opened the bottle and poured. Freddie smacked his lips. 'That's not bad, possibly a little on the sweet side. What do you think?'

'It's not bad. "It'll carry", as my mother would say.'

'Your mater is expert on wine?'

'My mater is expert on everything.'

Freddie waggled his head. 'My mater don't do much of anythin'. She's a kind lady but tinted grey, if you know what I mean. My pa as well as bein' a High Court Judge is an expert shot. He keeps Purdey guns like other people keep chickens. He gives displays, a Master-class in Murder. Do you shoot?'

'I trap the odd rabbit but that's all. What about you?'

'I don't see the sport in it. Now Evie's a crackin' shot. She went on Safari with her husband, don't you know, the late Sidney Bevington-Smythe, twelve gauge Purdey braced up against that little shoulder and Kerboom!'

'You're kidding me! That little lady can handle a twelve bore!'

Freddie giggled. 'That little lady can handle anythin', male or female, never mind the size. A wonderful lady is my sister if you don't mind sharin'.'

'What do you mean share?'

'Evie steals things. She sees somethin' she likes and wants it. Don't matter who it belongs to. She's always pinchin' my stuff.' Freddie pointed with the glass. 'Take you for instance? She knows Ju-ju Dryden likes you. She knows you like Ju-ju. What's the bettin' she don't pinch you?'

'What if I don't want to be pinched?'

'Won't matter! She'll still have you. It's what she does. She wasn't always into paintin'. Writing was her thing. She saw herself a new Bronte. Then I started dabblin'. Now she paints and is better than me. It's natural to her where I have to work at it. A mixed bag is Elliptical Eve. It's not her fault. It's the Black Dog.'

'Black Dog?'

'It's the family curse. Every one of the Baines Carrington is bitten by the brute. Ruinous, you can't do nothin' with him gnawing at your feet. Darkness falls over your soul. It's why she paints and it's why I can't.' Freddie emptied another glass. 'Did you know I got a showin' tomorrow at Sandringham?'

'You did mention your painting as your life's blood.'

'It is and then again it ain't. When it comes to paintin' there's only one Master, and that's the Almighty. Man can't compete with Him especially when the subject is Julianna Dryden. You ever sit for a portrait?'

'What a hammer in one hand and a brick in the other?'

'Seriously, you'd make a wonderful subject. Johnny Sargent

would pay boodles for you. So would I.' Freddie swiped the air. 'I see it now, A Wolf at Bay, people offerin' a king's ransom and me turnin' 'em down.'

'Is that the black dog talking or the Madeira?'

Freddie wagged his finger. 'My dear chap you mustn't joke about the Dog. He's a fearsome hound. He'll do for me and Evie. One day you'll see the headlines, 'heir to fortune leaps to his death, sister holdin' his hand.'

The conversation took a darker turn. Aware things said in the evening are resented in the morning, Luke emptied his glass. 'I must be getting home.'

'You don't live here?'

'I live at the Forge.'

'Who are you?' Freddie rolled his eyes. 'On the brink of a new century, trains on railways tracks, industry chewin' our ears, us in charge of a bloomin' Empire and you livin' in a Forge. It's another world!'

'Compared to yours I imagine it is.'

'Talkin' of other worlds.' Freddie hauled up on a vat and sat with his feet dangling. 'You're friends with Ju-ju.'

'I've worked on the cottage.'

'Is it a nice cottage?' Freddie closed his eyes. 'Can one wander through hosts of golden daffodils? I'd like to live here. Better than breathin' London soot. She is our muse, Evie and me, the face we both try to lay on canvas.'

'Good luck with that!'

'I know.' He grinned. 'Silly arses, we don't come close. Evie's better'n me. You should see the *Fauns* while local. Next week they'll be back in the National.'

'Fauns?'

'Yes fauns. Julianna? Do you get it?'

Luke nodded. He got it.

'Faun is a good name for her, bit different to my work. I'd show you mine but I have a thing about it not being seen until hung, superstition you know.'

'I need to get back to the bar.'

Freddie wiped his mouth. 'How is Ju-ju? I understand there was a tragedy at her place, one of her maids. I wanted to come to the funeral but Evie said no. How did Julianna manage?'

'She was unhappy.'

'I imagine so. And the girl, Bella, there was a baby.'

'There was.'

'Stillborn?'

'Yes.'

'A boy, I heard.'

The hair on Luke's head prickled. 'You knew Susan Dudley?'

'We all knew Susan and were sorry to hear of her death.' Evelyn Carrington and the bruiser valet stood at the door. 'She was a sweet girl, possibly a little wayward at times, but one mustn't speak ill of the dead.

'Hello Sister mine,' said Freddie. 'You ready to climb the wooden hill?'

'I think *you* are ready.'

Luke took the lamp. 'I'd best be going. I'm needed elsewhere.'

Evie nodded. 'Indeed you are needed and have been so this last hour.'

'I'm sorry. Freddie and I got to talking. What can I do for you?'

'You could perhaps help Jamieson guide my brother, the

Honourable Frederick Carrington, to his room.'

'Oh look out!' Freddie slid down the vat. 'Evie's ridin' her pedigree horse and you and the rest of the world mere peasants.'

'Come along!' She leaned down pulling Freddie to his feet and Luke saw then how a hand like that could pull a trigger. 'I'm not on any kind of horse. I'm getting you to your room before you embarrass the staff of this excellent establishment. We have been well served. Let's not spoil things.'

'Don't start, Evie,' Freddie protested. 'We were only chattin'.'

'And you shouldn't have been. Chatting with the hired help leads to trouble. One must keep the mind clear and not allow foolish notions of guilt to introduce an element one will later regret. Go to bed and sleep it off.' She turned to Luke. 'In the morning if you've time I'd like a word.'

'It's not likely I'll be here in the morning.'

'Where will you be?'

'Depends what you mean by morning, ma'm. I'm working on a house close by most of the day. Later in the evening you might find me at the Forge.'

Teeth like shiny pearls, she laughed. 'Of course! Where else would you be.'

* * *

She came to the Forge the following night. When she left, Luke lay looking at the stars wondering how he could have thought her little. She reminded him of Justine Newman, both women able to carry all before them, recognition of wealth and education allowing them to be at ease with King or cobbler.

Eleven thirty she tapped on the door, a carriage backed up by the willows and valet and maid whistling in the wind. He wasn't surprised to see her. Such people ignore usual communication believing that for lesser mortals. She came knowing the topic of conversation that would ensure an open door. 'Good evening, Mr Roberts. I'm here to talk of Julianna Dryden.'

Open Sesame! He dusted off a stool and she sat, her silk gown trailing in dust. 'I understand she's not doing well here, certain stories causing neighbours to cast her in an unwelcome role.'

Luke was silent.

'You do not speak?'

'I've nothing to say. The lady and her life are her own.'

'So you don't think she struggles to fit into village society?'

'Every newcomer struggles to fit into any society.'

'You think her happy here?'

'I think you should enquire of Mrs Dryden. She's in a position to know. I am not.'

'And you are not?' Glance clear, she eyed him. 'I am surprised. I was given to understand you were her staunch ally.'

'If she were to call on me I'd help. As a matter of fact…!' He hesitated and then said, '…she does need help and you're the one to give it.'

'How so?'

'The tea-shop has to succeed. You and your friends could make it so.'

'How can we?'

'By being there for the opening.'

'I see. You think success by association will bring 'em in, the twenty-four carat gilt rubbing off the ginger-bread.'

'She's worked hard.' Luke's feelings were showing. 'I've seen her sewing late into the night when all else are abed, Mrs Dryden and that maid of yours.'

'You've seen them late at night?'

Like a fool he blushed.

'You seem to care about the lady's wellbeing.'

'I more than care!' The declaration was out. 'I'd do anything for Anna Dryden. I'd lay down my life for her.'

'Good heavens, would you really?'

'I would.'

'Well I wouldn't want you to do that. Life is precious. No one should take it from you, least of all me. I'll help your Julianna.'

'You will?'

'I will. Helping a friend is the right thing to do and in this case very easily achieved. One gains a friend by being a friend. With that in mind what might I expect to receive in return?'

Luke stumbled. 'I...I beg your pardon?'

'We all struggle to find favour, me with my paintings and Ju-ju with her tea-shop. We all hold up our little hands and wave our little flags.' She removed her hat and shaking out her hair got to her feet. 'I'll be there for the opening and I'll bring friends, important friends, the kind that seal one's fate forever.'

'Thank you.'

'Don't thank me. I require payment.' Eyes bleak, she walked away. 'I'll support Julianna. I'll sit at her dainty table and smile and eat cake on the condition that you, Mister Wolf, sit and smile and eat cake with me.'

CHAPTER THIRTEEN

Cats and Kings

Sunday evening Callie Masson appeared over the Rise, a man-servant laden with picnic baskets trailing in her wake. Julia was in the herb garden talking with Joe. 'Please take note!' the call came across the wall. 'We come through the gate as civilised folk and not heathens scrambling over a wall.'

When she saw that Joe was not to be humoured she smiled. 'Good day to you, Mr Joseph Carmody. I understand you're a first class plants-man.'

That bright blast of Philadelphia air rather tipped Joe's sails but not cowed, he took off his cap and said things he'd been saving to say these last weeks.

'Yes, I do like to grow a decent plant, ma'm, when there's time and season and no interference from outside, but lately I've had nowt but trouble from your side of the wall, and while keepin' my manners, I'm bound to say a person in your establishment is causin' me and my dear madam a lot of bother, and it's not right that her garden and well-being should be interfered with.'

'And I'm here today to assure you, Joe Carmody, there'll be no such interference troubling you again...at least not from my side of the wall.'

Having said his piece Joe could think of nothing more to add other than it had been a right bother to everyone and had fair worried his arthritis.

'And for that I am sorry,' said Callie, 'and in the name of

goodwill ask if you'll accept these cuttings sent by a relative of mine who travels in search of the rare and lovely, and who, along with these cuttings, sends an invitation to join him for a pint of ale in the Dog and Duck and a tour of the Castle gardens.'

With that, dear Joe - back bent and basket heavy on his arm - took himself and his arthritis home. A picnic was then taken on the terrace and a discussion as to what Julia might wear to the Art Festival. She had given thought to the same and swallowing pride raided the attic for the apricot velvet jacket to wear over a revamped wedding gown. Brussels lace, and simple in style the gown was Charlotte's before Julia, and Charlotte's mother-in-law before both.

Callie nodded. 'The sleeves must go. Stand back!' She waved the garden shears and the sleeves were gone. 'Joseph's roses, *décolle-tage,* and you're done.' Talk turned to a hat, Dulce returning from Greenfields with a straw confection of the Nell Gwynne style. 'It's wasted on me,' said Callie. 'To wear it well a woman needs Nell's voluptuous breasts not wrinkled prunes.'

* * *

The following day the Park at Sandringham House was in carnival atmosphere, Matty was downcast. 'What's wrong with him?' said Callie.

'He's missing Nan Roberts. She doesn't visit as she did.'

'So I heard.'

'Heard?'

'It's alright, Anna. I know what's whispered in servant's hall and could care less. I choose my own company. Talking of company!' Callie read from the programme. "Exhibits 201 and 202,

Faun Surprised and *Faun Sleeping*, are the work of Lady Evelyn Carrington." Didn't you sit for these?'

'I did and had I known they were here I wouldn't have come.'

'I shouldn't worry. If they are anything like Milady's other splashy stuff you won't be recognized as a human being. Friends of mine have a gallery in Philly. They like her but I've never been tempted by the bizarre.'

'Does sitting astride a Unicorn count as bizarre?'

'Is that what you're doing?'

'Yes, while sporting a pair of wings.'

'I wouldn't worry. Who the heck is gonna recognise you doing that! Besides,' aware of heads continually turning, Callie sniffed, 'you don't need to be a painting to be seen. You naturally cause it to happen.'

'Is Daniel not coming today?'

'Yes, but later. He hates crushes.'

'And this is a crush! I didn't think the English interested in art.'

'This is nothing to do with art. See the morning coats and superior smiles? People are here because of the Prince of Wales. It's why I came to oversee your wardrobe. Poor guy, dragged from one ugly painting to another, and he particular about beauty, I thought he might like to see a true work of art.'

'You mean me in my cut down wedding dress?'

'No, me in my hat!'

Julia laughed. 'Alright then, Callie, if you say so. In the mean time let's give Matty cause to be happy. Why don't you two go to the cinematic-show and I'll look at the ugly paintings...unless you'd sooner come with me.'

'No thanks! A cinematic-show is much more our thing.'

* * *

Julia strolled through various sideshows, pausing at a marquee set up as a Japanese theatre, men in white kabuki make-up posturing.

Then John Sargent was at her elbow. 'Julianna, how are you?'

'I'm well thank you, John, and you?'

He sighed. 'To tell the truth I'm a bit at odds dashing about trying to make sure everything is as it should be. These marquees don't make life easier. You can't hang portraits on tarpaulin. You need easels and wooden floors.'

'It all sounds a bit of a bother.'

'Enough to drive you crazy.' He saw she was smiling and laughed. 'Where's Matthew? Is he not with you?'

'He's at a cinematic show with Mrs Greville Masson.'

'Sensible fellow! I am pleased to see you. I was sorry our last meeting was cut short by Freddie's fool business. Are you and Evie still at odds?'

'Freddie writes but that's all.'

'Pity. He saw you as a good influence as did everyone else. Such a child! And such a waste of talent! He's showing oils today though what I couldn't say. I wish he'd get to grips with life. I encourage him to Paris but when he comes it's to drink and doubt. No matter what is said to the contrary he thinks his work bad. The treasure burnt for firewood would break your heart.'

'Poor Freddie.'

'Yes and poor Evie.' When Julia looked he shrugged. 'I won't get into it. Suffice it to say I have known the Carringtons some time. I know and accept them as dear friends and troubled souls.

So what do you think of the exhibition?'

'It's huge.' Julia gestured across the Park. 'All the different exhibits, I had no idea. I had assumed we'd be looking at your work and only yours.'

'Art is an expanding Universe. One dare not stand still. But then I'm told competition is good for the soul so I must brace up.'

'Do you find it good for the soul?'

'It depends on the competition. Unless you want to win there's no point in fighting. Speaking of fighting, Danny says you're to open a coffee-shop.'

Julia smiled. 'You associate fisticuffs with the doling out of sugared buns?'

'It seems I do. It must be an echo of childhood, a nanny with a mean pair of sugar tongs. So you plan to serve tea and sympathy to the masses?'

'It's an idea.'

'Only an idea? I thought it well on its way.'

'So did I but changes in temperature suggest otherwise.' Unwilling to talk about that she switched topics. 'Have you seen the cinematic-show?'

'Alas no. Like you I'm committed to the doldrums. Oh, and the fellow flapping a kipper-hand over there is my cue to enlighten the Royal party on the merit of my daubs.'

'It'll be fine, John. The Prince has an eye for beauty, or so I'm told.'

'If that's the case His Highness need only glance your way! The changes in temperature you mention in no way dint your beauty. I would've liked to show *Girl Eating Strawberries* today but the owner refused public show.'

'You no longer own the work?'

'It wasn't a financial transaction, more a gift between friends.'

She pressed his hand. 'To be painted by you is a privilege whatever the case.'

'Good of you to say so. I may one day be able to elaborate on the owner of *Strawberries* but to say now would be to break a confidence. Incidentally, in the matter of who is showing today you know Evelyn brought the *Fauns*.'

'I did hear that.'

'Don't be anxious. They are capital pieces. I'd better go, the kipper is agitated.' An elegant figure in morning coat and tails John replaced his top hat. 'I understand we're to dine at Greenfields this evening, *au revoir* until then!'

Julia mingled with the crowd while thinking of the tea-shop. Recent events suggest any venture she undertakes in Bakers End doomed to failure. Yesterday she sat embroidering napkins, all thirty ice-white wads of linen now stacked in a drawer beside the new cash machine August Simpkin brought.

Red-faced and sweating, he'd dropped the machine on the table, but when Julia invited him to sit and take coffee he crept away. 'I'd like to stay but Mrs S doesn't know I'm here.' The postman was another suggesting secrecy: 'The wife says she'll make a few but under-the-counter like.' And Mrs Cross's son, 'Mum will bake but don't want her name mentioned.' There were more like that, as with the vicar of St Bedes, who said their baking produce was already allotted; 'every cook in Bakers greatly occupied this year and the next.'

Julia accepted the letter with no offence. She has anxiety enough without regretting St Bedes. Of late, there's been knocking on the door at night and glass smashed in the greenhouse. Joe suspects the work of ne'er-do-wells.

* * *

The Central Marquee is where the more illustrious painters show their work. John's work gathers a crowd - a full length portrait of an effete young man in an overcoat drawing particular attention. Julia stood among the crowd thinking that Freddie was surely the model - in that thought she was not alone.

'It's absolutely him, don't you think?'

Julia turned and Evie smiled, the pearls at her throat mirroring her eyes. 'Hello, Ju-ju. You look well.' She reached out to touch the roses at Julia's breast. 'You are as soft and dewy as these roses. Could it be you're in love?'

This is Evie! Two minutes and the brain is robbed of rational thought.

'We saw Matty in the picture-tent with Danny Masson's mother, the mining heiress.' Evie fluttered the programme. 'May I introduce Madame Eloise Dupres and Messieurs Charles Gambrel and Paul Chilcot? Such a fearful crush! I'm waiting on HRH and his blessing on my efforts. They're here, Ju-ju, both Fauns gambolling down the end of this monstrous tent.'

'You must be pleased.'

'I confess to being gratified *and* alarmed. It's not every day one gets to bare one's soul before one's future King. Royal approval or not your face will carry us through. I was hoping you'd sit again but hear you're busy with your coffee shop. Such a clever idea, Sandringham close by and all that bracing Norfolk air! And the

Lansdowne place at your heel and access to Mrs Masson!'

'Mrs Masson is a thoughtful neighbour.'

'I imagine she's Matty's friend now and Mrs Roberts forgot. When it comes to throwing toys away children can be cruel. We are staying with Nan, Freddie and I. She is as you said a person in her own right, as indeed is our host, the charming, and surprisingly resourceful, Mr Roberts.'

'Albert is a good man.'

'I'm sure he is but I was referring to the younger Mr Roberts.'

'Luke?'

'Yes, Mathew, Mark, Luke and John, bless the bed that I lay on!' Evie smiled gleeful. 'A ravishingly handsome man, I like him. Now when reading my lurid novels and the hero likened to a stallion I know to whom they refer. I am currently working my stays off pressing him to sit for me in London as is Freddie, the naughty boy. So far nothing doing but I persist. We're here another night and might pop along tomorrow to say hello.'

'Oh do! We would be delighted to see you.'

'Good, then we shall.' Evie gazed about her. 'I see Johnny is here. We don't see much of him these days. Poor John, when not being paid huge fees for immortalising ugly people he's fighting off the dogs. The Academy finally recognising his worth and the lesser talent gnaw at his heels.'

Julia nodded. 'Doctor Adelman said something along those lines.'

'Did he? See much of Stefan, do you?'

'He visits Matty and takes care of his ills.'

'Stefan is a good man with heavy professional responsibilities and carrying, as no doubt you have learned, a heavy personal burden. He is another who rarely visits, though in his case, Appointment to the Royal Household, his tardiness is forgiven. But you, Julianna, what is your excuse?'

Julia could only stare.

'Well, must away! If you plan a Gala opening of your little cafe I hope you'll invite us. We'll come and bring friends. Talking of friends we have an interesting event soon, one Madame Leonora, who locks herself in boxes and conjures spirits. She's agreed to a private sitting.' Evie closed the programme. 'Better move along. HRH is at the door. Did you see them yet, the Fauns?'

'Not yet.'

'Do try. Even though you no longer care for me I care for you. Come to the séance! I've people begging an invite but have said only the exclusive few.' She kissed Julianna. 'And who could be more exclusive than you.'

* * *

A dozen people clustered about one they came through the main entrance, John's tall figure in evidence, the rest hats and heads used to carrying coronets. Evie was among them, clothed in aquamarine lace and feathered toque she was a work of art more affecting than anything on display.

Julia brooded on the idea of old toys cast away for new. It wasn't her choice to lose Evie as a friend as it wasn't her choice to lose Nan. Last week Matty asked to see the Tabby Cat. They took the trap to the Lord Nelson where the same maid turned him away with a kiss. Furious, on return Julia took up her pen. 'I am shunned by the people of this village. Why, I don't know since I've done none harm. I give you leave, Nanette Roberts, to think what you like of me but ask you not deny a little boy who did nothing but love you and...'

She'd torn the letter to shreds. Fussing changes nothing.

Now Daniel Masson edges his way through the crowd. 'What a scrum!' he panted. 'I had to use my elbows or wouldn't have got through.'

Julia smiled. 'You took your life into your hands attempting it.'

'It felt so.' Face flushed, he mopped his brow. 'I'd love to shuck my jacket but with His Highness equally trussed thought to hold off.

'John isn't happy.'

'That's because he's thrust before the common eye. Thankfully, with neither talent nor name to my credit that will never happen to me.'

'You are a Greville Warwick. Isn't that name enough?'

'I am a Greville from the Colonial side of the family and, other than enthusiasm, have no particular talent. People like John Sargent, and of course Lady Evelyn, are the real McCoy.'

'Evie must be good to show at the National Gallery.'

'I'm not sure that's a parameter. That Evie shows at the Gallery is due to her name. That John is accepted as Associate is about the fees he can claim.'

'What about talent?'

He shrugged. 'Talent matters but money matters more.'

'You are a cynic.'

'I am a realist. It's why I don't get on with politics. Sooner than suffer red tape I'm likely to tip the whole caboodle into the Pacific Ocean.'

'I think we might've veered away from the subject of art.'

'I guess I'm still smarting on South Africa and what's happening there. Did you know they have camps in the Transvaal where women and children are holed up like cattle? But to bemoan the unfairness of life is not why I risked life and limb to get to you. Will you accompany me to the theatre one night?'

'I'd like that.'

'How about we go on a picnic tomorrow... or is that me being pushy?'

'It is you being pushy yet I'd like to. Could we make it one day next week, say Tuesday after Matty's music lesson?'

'Tuesday? Yes ma'm!' Daniel's eyes sparkled. 'We'll go on the Fens. I'm handy with a skiff and your boy would get a kick out of that.'

'You're staying with your mother?'

'Yeah, and I'm there because of you. But then I was at the Carrington place because of you, as, right now I am here, because of you. But that must wait.' He stepped aside. 'Right now it seems you're wanted elsewhere.'

'Madam?' A man stood at Julia's elbow. 'Mrs Julianna Dryden? His Royal Highness, the Prince of Wales, asks if you and Mr Greville Masson would care to join him and his party in a tour of the Gallery.'

* * *

Julia couldn't be sure who made the introduction. She remembers being glad her gloves were clean and that despite being nervous she managed to curtsey. The Prince asked if she was enjoying the exhibition and had she a favourite artist, she said she liked Ruebens and that her father had favoured Stubbs.

He nodded. 'We have a few of that gentleman about the house. His horses are good but Van Dyck's better. If you're ever in Town and care to see the work I'd be pleased to take you on a tour of the Gallery.'

The party moved on. A woman in the group she recognised as Mrs George Keppel, her picture often in newspapers, commented on Julia's gown.

'What beautiful lace! One doesn't see good lace anymore.'

Julia was tempted to mention the cut down sleeves but thought better of it.

The party halted before a painting of a dog. 'Here's a jolly little chap,' said the Prince. 'He reminds me of Caesar. Do you have a dog, Mrs Dryden?'

'My son has a dog.'

'Is it thoroughbred?'

'More of a mixture really.'

'And does the mixture have a name?'

'Yes.' Julia smiled. 'He's called Kaiser.'

'Kaiser? You named him Kaiser! '

'Not named, Sir. He came already crowned.'

'You inherited a king.' He laughed and the group laughed with him. 'And is he a good king, obedient to the cause and polite with postmen? '

'He is good and he is brave.'

'Excellent! Let the fellow be brave but let him also know his place. One can't have kings running amuck. History proves they are like to lose their heads.'

He smiled, stroked his moustache, and suddenly Julia was looking at Stefan and everything so much easier. They progressed to the alcove and the *Fauns* were set on easels. 'I know this.' He tapped *Faun Surprised* with his cane. 'My brother Arthur saw it at the National and wanted it for himself.'

Evie nodded. 'He did, Sir.'

'And if memory serves me right you wouldn't sell.'

'I believe I held true.'

'So you did despite his entreaties. And this is sister to the *Faun*?' He adjusted his monocle. 'My congratulations, Lady Carrington, and also I think my condolences. I fear you've placed yourself, and me, in jeopardy.'

'How so, Sir?'

'Quite simple.' The Prince smiled at Julia. 'My brother only wanted the one likeness. Now having seen the paintings, and the muse, I want both.'

* * *

Daniel offered his arm. 'All present and correct?'

'I am a little thrown.'

'You looked quite at ease.'

'Looks can be deceiving.'

'May I ask what you talked about? I couldn't hear being bundled to the back.'

'Dogs, His Caesar and Matty's Kaiser.'

'A Prince talking of Kings! How very droll.'

Julia laughed. 'It was.'

'You looked as if you made a connection. He seemed quite

bowled over.'

'I don't know about that. Oh, here's Freddie!'

Freddie was outside the Marquee and Callie and Matty with him. 'There you are Ju-ju!' Matty and Freddie were licking lollipops. 'We thought you'd run off with the gypsies. Is my sister in there with the Parisian people?'

'She is with the Prince of Wales. Did you enjoy the cinema, Matty?'

Matty grinned and licked the lollipop. 'It was good.'

'What about you, Callie?'

Callie scowled. 'I did not enjoy it. So many people breathing one another's air I'm sure I shall get a cold. So Daniel, I'm ready to go if you are.'

'You can't go yet!' said Freddie. 'You haven't seen my *White Lady*.' He threw the lollipop away. 'That was a mistake! My hands are all gooey.'

Daniel offered a handkerchief.

'Thanks, I have my own.' From a warm day it was suddenly cool, Daniel silent and Freddie's blue eyes glittering over white linen.

An uneasy group, they trailed to where the crowd gathered about one painting. 'Oh, Freddie!' When John Sargent said talent he understated the case. There is talent, a glittering talent that stuns the onlooker into silence.

'What do you think?'

'I don't know what to think.' Julia was looking at a creature of snow and mist. White hair, face, lips and eyes, all was white and yet so absolutely her it was wonderful and hypnotic. 'How did you achieve that with one colour?'

'Is that all you see, Ju-ju?' he said, 'one colour?'

'I see a thousand colours and all white. I see blue white, and grey white, and gold, and a millions of shades between. I see my hair, and my lashes, and the way you have my mouth, but I don't know how you did it.'

Freddie looked to Daniel. 'What do you think of it Masson?'

'I think it a master-piece.'

A man in the crowd called out. 'Pray, sir, how many brushes did you use?'

'I used whatever took my fancy! Most of the time I used my bare hands, which is why I keep 'em in my pockets, my finger ends rubbed raw.'

The man bowed. 'I congratulate you on a thing of rare beauty.'

Freddie returned the bow. 'Thank you for that. What about you, Julianna? Is this worthy of keeping, if not forever then at least while I last?'

Julia shook her head. 'I'm not sure there is a word for what you have done.'

Pleased with the reaction, Freddie rocked back and forth. 'So you like it?'

'I do. It's wild and it's lovely and it is so very clever.'

Oh dear! God knows what he wanted her to say but clever wasn't it.

'Clever?'

'Yes and unusual and so very skilful.'

Face stripped of colour, he stared. 'Unusual? Skilful? What's that?'

Daniel's hand was under her elbow. 'As I said, I don't have words for it.'

'Yes you do! You've done for it, Julianna Dryden.' He was so pale he might've been another portrait, and Julia and the others, so silent and shocked, outside the frame. 'I wanted words from the heart. Sublime would've done! As would breathtaking, which is how you are now, wide-eyed trying to understand! Beautiful, ravishing, of another world! Or even absurd, ridiculous, as ridiculous as the notion I could ever paint.'

'Freddie, please!'

He stepped back, his handkerchief settling on the ground. 'No, you're right it is clever. It's what people say when they don't understand a work. "Clever but I wouldn't have it on my wall!" So let's be clever and bung it on the furnace. Best place for it.' He kicked the easel. The portrait fell to the ground Freddie grinding his boot into the canvas. Then he walked away.

CHAPTER FOURTEEN

Telescopes

All ears and whiskers, Callie pulled Julia aside. 'You spoke with the Prince?'

'We spoke of our dogs.'

'Is that all?'

'I was one of many. Everyone else was eager to speak with him.'

'I bet they were. What a swizz!' Callie sat down. 'I thought he might ask who you are, but then Evelyn Carrington will have said you sat for the *Fauns*.'

'Or possibly John Sargent?'

'John would never spring an introduction like that on an unsuspecting friend. *She* would! Anyone who dismisses a maid without thought to her welfare and then sends roses to her funeral is able to do anything.'

'Why are we talking about the Prince of Wales?'

'Because he is a man of influence, none more so. People follow his every mood. A smile from him counts for everything.'

'And I need his smiles?'

'If you wish your tea-shop to flourish you need friends and influence and from what I've heard you've little of either! You've made your house uneasy! People are talking. I am old and can ignore talk, you can't.'

'I think the talk more outside my house than in.'

'But you are not helping! You are too open with your friendships, that absurd display of bad manners this afternoon a case in point.'

'Freddie was upset and I wasn't as tactful as I might've been.'

'Nonsense, you were perfectly reasonable! Freddie Carrington behaved badly drawing attention to himself and you! You must be more circumspect, avoiding those that by behaviour and reputation can do you harm.'

'And encouraging smiles from the Prince of Wales is being circumspect?'

'Anna, I'm trying to advise you!'

'I understand that but in this, my choice of friends, I'm not sure I want to be advised. I mind my own business. Why can't people do the same?'

'Because in the main people are evil-minded gossips, especially the people of Bakers End! They make it their business to interfere. I know. I've lived through it. Those two sisters called your cottage Pleasant. My memories of it and the people of this village are anything but.'

'Yes but they are your memories, Callie, not mine.'

'Stay for any length of time and they will be yours.'

'Is that why the wall was built, to keep the village away?'

'It was built to keep me away! Justine Newman had the wall erected, men laid the stones, but I put it there and my spleen glued it together!'

Julia was shocked. 'Why would she hide from you?'

'Because she took something of mine and wouldn't give it back. She stole love from under my nose and made my childhood strange. I arrived in this house on my fifth birthday and left on my twenty-fifth. It was Justine! I couldn't be here with her smiling beauty only a matter of yards away.'

'Justine is gone. She died a long time ago, Mr Simpkin told me.'

Callie was on her feet. 'What does he know? A person dies and people think that's an end to it. Forty-five years I stayed away from the home and the country I love, forty-five years yearning to return. Now that I am here I find it's too late. I am old and she is still young and still here!'

'You need to rest.'

'I do.' Callie sat down. 'There are pills in the work-basket. Yes those!' She put a pill under her tongue. 'Give me a moment and it will go.'

'Should I call Daniel?'

'No! He'll have me on the first boat back to Philadelphia.' Agitated, Callie rang a bell. 'It's alright Dulce will come. Go mingle with my other guests. They are all dying to talk of you and His Royal Highness. Talk to them, smile and be gracious, and any goodwill you may have lost is yours again.'

* * *

Julia took a shawl out onto the terrace. Daniel was there smoking a cigar, his shirt front white against the sky and the setting sun reflected in his eyes. He saw her and threw the cigar away.

She stood beside him. 'What a wonderful sky.'

'It sure is. Not as roaring as the skies over California but restful.'

'You miss your home?'

'I do.'

'And yet you travel.'

184

He shrugged. 'That's my job. I am a writer and a journalist.'

A telescope was mounted on the terrace. 'Are you star-gazing too?'

'Not with that. You wouldn't see much more than fog through that.'

'I have one that belonged to my husband. He loved to watch the skies and would probably have enjoyed the California roars.'

'He travelled?'

'Not as much as he would've liked yet I think where dreams and the skies and telescopes are concerned, Owen travelled a billion miles.'

'Are you recovered from this afternoon?'

'Poor Freddie! I put it down to the heat and artistic temperament.'

'I put it down to bad manners. It's not the first time you've borne the brunt of that particular artistic temperament. I would want it to be the last.'

Julia gazed out over the Rise. For a small place the cottage is the focus of much attention and not only now but in years gone by. What is it that makes it so? Is it the people that lived there or the land itself, magical perhaps, like a fairy ring. If I were to remove it stone-by-stone, she wondered, would I find a mushroom circle beneath? 'Gather here you thorny toads and elves with mischief in your fingers? Come dark spirits of the night and...!'

'A penny for your thoughts.' Daniel was smiling.

'I thought you Yankees dealt in cents?'

'We do and in pennies also. So what were you thinking?'

'I was thinking that a place can mean different things to different people.'

'As can a word.'

Julia smiled. 'You mean like "clever?" I must say I was startled. Until today I thought it an innocent word.'

'Freddie Carrington is in a jam. He doesn't know what to do with his life and looks to others for answers. It can be that way with those born into comfort.'

'You were born into comfort.'

'And there it ended. My pa worked hard and expected me to do the same.'

'You're not involved with the mining business?'

'I am not. Father and I disagreed on his treatment of my mother.'

'I'm sorry.'

'As a provider he could not be condemned. He was shrewd in business and lucky, though hearing me say so he'd probably pull a pistol and shoot me dead. Sam didn't believe in luck, though he and his fellow investors played a game of chance every day. If he thought the risk worthwhile he'd go for it no matter how obscure. If it didn't come good within an allotted time it was done. He lacked patience. It's why he never came to Europe. Why stare at ruins, he'd say. I live in Philadelphia not the Roman Coliseum.'

'So he never accompanied you abroad?'

'No ma'am. Until meeting with the Singer-Sargents in Paris, the Greville Massons were a caravan of four, Callie, Dulce, me and Watson.'

'Watson? Was he your man-servant?'

Daniel threw back his head and laughed. 'I've no doubt if he could he would've. He was diverse. Watson was my dog and my best friend.'

186

'Matty feels that way about Kaiser. He says the dog talks to him.'

'And of course he does talk. Watson talks to me and I hope always will. Just because he's no longer visible don't mean he ain't here.' Tears sprang into Daniel's eyes. The moment so filled with Watson, he couldn't speak.

Then, he swallowed. 'He was my boy. I loved him and he loved me.'

* * ** * *

Later, Daniel spoke of John Sargent. 'Our mothers share a love of Europe and of meeting new people. They shared each other's pain too.' He glanced at Julianna. 'I guess you've heard a little of what went on in this house.'

'Enough to know your mother was unhappy.'

'It wasn't always like that. As a girl she loved it here. She loved England, your cottage, and the woman who taught there.'

'Taught?'

'Justine Newman was Callie's governess. She and her sister Clarinda lodged in the gatehouse. Justine was a clever woman and by all accounts beautiful. Mom adored her. They were close but there was a problem.'

'Henry Lansdowne.'

'Yes, Henry. He and Callie were affianced. He died before they could wed, a hero going down with his ship leaving a hell of a mess here on land.'

'Henry Lansdowne loved Justine Newman?'

'Besotted, is the tale, and yet at the same time couldn't, or wouldn't, break his engagement with Callie.'

'Poor Callie.'

'Yes, poor Callie! Because when she did get back to Philadelphia she walked into more misery! My father was a philanderer of the worst kind. He left a trail of debris halfway across the State. Callie was drowning when she left England with only her fortune to keep her afloat. Sam Masson, ever with an eye to the future, was waiting for just such a treasure.'

'Your mother isn't well.'

'No and coming back here hasn't helped.'

'What was her hope in coming?'

'I suppose to lay Henry Lansdowne's ghost to rest. I was against it. She's too old to be grubbing up the past. I begged her find another house.'

'Why does she call it Greenfields?'

'This land was once owned by the Greenfield family. They were here long before the Lansdowne. Over time Greenfield softened to Greville. In the 1600s when pilgrims left for the New World there were Grevilles among them. Our branch of family settled in Philly and made a good life.'

'You don't like it here.'

'I do not.' He sighed. 'I have carried this house, and what happened here, on my shoulders the whole of my life. Living here is my idea of hell.'

'I'm sorry.'

'Don't be Julianna! Good came of it! You came! I wanted to tell you of Callie's obsession. I thought of writing but didn't know how to set it down in words that made sense. A seventy-eight-year-old Philadelphia socialite shinning over walls to pilfer her neighbour's daises? Where's the sense in that?'

'Is she seventy-eight? I thought she was younger.'

'Like most women Mom's constantly chipping at her age, but yeah, too old to be doing such things.'

'Why steal plants and then return? To whom does she give them?'

'The same person, I guess, Justine Newman.'

'The business with Susan Dudley didn't help.'

'It was never going to be helped. Mother's set on this house for fifty years. Sam died and suddenly she is free to pick up withered reins.'

'She wanted the cottage?'

'That above all! To own the cottage would be to own Justine and Henry. You beat her to it.' He turned. 'Earlier we talked of words meaning different things. Can I ask what you made of my words today, my clumsy declaration?'

'Was it a declaration?'

'It was and one I'd repeat again right now if you'd let me.'

'I beg you let me think on it awhile, Daniel. I am unsure of myself and my life. But do let us take Matty on that picnic.'

'We're still going to the Fens?' His face cleared. 'I'm glad. I did wonder if all this talk might've put thoughts of fun aside.'

'I'd like to go as will Matty...! Oh look!' She leaned forward. 'There's someone by the cottage wall, a prowler!'

A shadowy figure, tall and remote, stood by the gate.

'I see him but I don't reckon him a prowler. It's the fellow from the village, the one Matty calls Wolf.'

'Ah yes.' Julia's chest hurt. 'That would be Luke Roberts.'

'He seems anxious for your security.'

'That's probably because there's been trouble of late, someone tapping on the door at night and the greenhouse broken into.'

'I don't like the sound of that.'

'Neither do I. In fact I think it's time I went home.'

* * *

Red Riding Hood needn't have worried about encountering the Wolf. Hearing their approach Luke Roberts slipped into shadows. Daniel doesn't know the fellow but has seen his work on the cottage and thinks it first class. Hard worker and talented, pity Callie didn't employ him. He could fix the plumbing in the North Wing and the damp in the East. The house will never be right - you can scrape rot from walls but not from flesh.

Daniel feels a kinship with the Wolf, both outside of Julianna's heart and wanting in. It was John's painting *Girl Eating Strawberries* that did it for Daniel. He saw the first sketch. 'Who is she?' he asked John.

'Never you mind.'

'I do mind. I mind very much and you know me, Johnny, when I put my mind to a task it has to go my way.'

'And what do you want from this?'

'Her, the girl!'

'She's not a girl. She's a married woman. Go try your luck elsewhere.'

Daniel did go. On behalf of the Philadelphia *Bulletin* he went to China reporting on the rebellion. He left an open cheque with JSS and a plea that, married or not, he'll have her picture on his wall. Daniel and John have been friends for years, Callie and Mary Newbold Singer both ardent globe-trotters. They met at John's house in Montparnasse, John flying a kite; 'Hey, young fellow!' he'd called. 'Grab hold! See if you can catch the wind.'

Daniel will always be a young fellow to John and in many ways it's right. With his mother and father separated, Daniel's education was more the product of museums and churches in Florence and Rome rather than a schoolroom. But a man can't wander forever. If he wants to be taken seriously he needs collegiate backing and so Daniel went to Lehigh University where Uncle Lemuel is professor. From there he moved to University, and the *Inquirer*, which didn't last long, the editor thinking Daniel 'looking to die young.'

A spot with the *Bulletin* was followed by a stint with the *New York Herald*. Then Daniel hit the news with a best-selling bio of the American portraitist, John Singer Sargent, followed by another best-seller, on the Rights of Black American Citizens. The first book brought closer ties with John, the second, death threats from the Klu Klux Klan. For a while he was freelance, writing of wars and the making of wars. Then Pa died and Callie renewing a love-hate relationship with a house, which in turn, like sunlight on stepping-stones across a lake, led to him acquiring *Girl Eating Strawberries*.

Learning of Owen Passmore's death, Daniel had visited John saying he wanted to meet Julianna, wanted to paint her.

'What d'you mean paint?' John hated the idea. 'You can't paint.'

'I know but how else are we to meet?'

'You do what every decent guy does, you wait.'

'Yes, but what if in waiting another guy with a better address, and a responsible history, comes along?' Then he heard she was at the Carrington's and contrived an invite, ostensibly to paint her. John took some persuading. 'This is a low for a man like you. Can't you just come out with it?

'Come out with what; "How di-do, Mrs Dryden, sorry for your loss and more sorry that my mother is every night nipping over your wall to steal plants. I beg you, beautiful Julianna, don't call the cops! She can't help herself."

John surrendered to an introduction and the *Strawberry Girl* portrait. 'Take it! I'll get no peace until you do. As for Russell Square I'll introduce you as a friend *wanting* to paint Mrs Dryden. I don't like subterfuge but neither do I like the way Freddie sees Julianna as an answer to his problems.'

The year he died Sam Masson told Daniel it was time to settle. 'Marriage gives a man roots.' He said this on his way to meet a tart; that he survived as long as he did is down to mother's purse ready to settle a bill. Daniel once asked Dulce why his father needed so many women. She blew out her lips. 'Lots of gals make little guys feel big. Big guys are big and only need one gal to tell 'em so.'

They came down the Rise, Julianna light on his arm and her perfume in his nostrils. Her dog was at the door, every hair quivering.

'Easy fellow,' Daniel dropped onto his knees. 'I'm not the enemy.'

Julianna stroked the dog's ears. 'This is Kaiser.'

'And a good dog at that! He reminds me of Watson.'

'What a wonderful name. Is he a Conan Doyle character?'

'In those days the stories weren't written, yet when it came to detecting trouble my dog was on it. And brave? You wouldn't believe it.'

'My father said a dog takes after his master. You are a brave man. Watson would have been the same.' Daniel wanted to say wars don't make men brave but he liked to see her white hands against the dog's rough pelt. He had a mind one day to feel those hands against his lips and so took the compliment and went home to bed.

* * *

Julia sat at the piano wondering if she had been too open, and that she needed to be more discreet, as Freddie said, there's only so much darkness a soul can deflect before the glass cracks. Today he was a child throwing a tantrum. She would've gone after him but Daniel said no, 'that men like Freddie have another Freddie inside their head, and that no matter what anyone says that other Freddie only hears the shattering of dreams.'

A fog rolling off the Wash and the back parlour alight, the Needed and Necessary must shine through the mist like a faded jewel. Julia stood at the bedroom window, a fierce need to protect the cottage rising up. Hatred of the past must stay on the other side of the wall; it must not be allowed to cross over. Luke and his father secured the bricks and mortar. Julia must do the same for the memory of those once living there.

'Oh! Callie was out on the terrace bending over the telescope!'

Julia moved away from the window knowing why Justine Newman built the wall. It was to deny this, the brooding anger of a girl who, though decades have passed is again at the spy-glass, a ghost spying on ghosts.

Continuing

Matty stamped his foot. 'Not going!'

'What a shame!' said Julia, 'and here's me filling the basket with nice things to eat. I did think you might take your bucket and spade and dig for bait.'

A pause, his lip trembling, and then: 'Don't want to!'

Julia is losing patience. 'You're going, Matthew Dryden, and that's all there is to it. I am in the garden this morning. You have your music lessons and when Mr Masson calls we'll go together.'

'I won't!' He threw down on the floor. 'I really won't!'

Five o'clock this morning he climbed into her bed claiming a pain. When asked where, he pointed to his chest. Matty's not good at fibbing, he wriggles when attempting it. 'Is the pain here?' He claimed Mister Punch had bitten him. Julia said she thought Mr Punch was gone, that the Seed Lady's crocodile ate him up. At that Matty is silent, to fib about the Seed Lady unthinkable.

What brought this about? Last night Matty was excited about the picnic. This morning he was all sulk. 'What is it,' she asked, 'why do you behave so?' He wouldn't answer, only dragged away, his hand through Kaiser's collar.

Daniel is to collect them at three, Julia, meanwhile, lifts hyacinth bulbs. She loves hyacinth, amiable plants. Afterward she'll cut lavender. Most of yesterday was spent making lavender bags for tomorrow's Gala opening.

Ben Faulkner arrived, a cheery call across the green. What a difference regular work has made! No doubt he still drinks but that awful tired look is gone. Until he arrived Matty showed no real interest in playing piano but, as is often the case, a stranger ignites a fire. 'He has talent, Mrs Dryden,' says Ben. Today that talent is not in evidence, the mice in *Hickory Dickory Dock* trudging up and down the clock with leaden feet.

Matty sits under the piano wishing he could tell Mister Wolf of the Seed Lady. She came last night to sit by the bed. They talked of animals, her papa having Arabian thoroughbred horses. She spoke of County Clare when she was a little girl, and of trees called Sequoia that grew up into the sky. Matty asked if the trees were higher than Jack and the Beanstalk. The Lady said close enough, 'But there are no big bad giants at the top, only the sky and the stars and a thousand bright miracles.' Matty asked if Papa was in heaven. The Lady said he was continuing. Then she whispered a secret in his ear. It was a good secret, almost filling the hole that came in his chest when Papa died.

Matty woke thinking of the man, Daniel, on the Other Side of the Wall. The Seed Lady said not to worry, if it is Daniel's fate to be with Mumma, then he will be, but, that if Matty wanted to protest he is free to do so.

* * *

'I am most awfully sorry,' Julianna is all red cheeks and apologies.

At the second dunking of a tin soldier into a stream - and him having to retrieve it – Daniel began to wonder if being a bachelor was no bad thing.

'Don't give it another thought. I was the same when I was his age.'

'I find that hard to believe. You seem too calm and collected to be so.'

'Calm and collected? Is that good manners for boring?'

She laughed. 'I don't think so.'

'Perhaps you are saying I have gravitas.'

'Is gravitas important to you?'

'It's important to any newsman.'

'Why?'

'I suppose,' he lowered himself over the side of the skiff, 'because a newsman spends his life trying to access places he shouldn't go to learn secrets no one should tell.' All afternoon Daniel strove to make the best of it, but 'won't do this, won't do that,' the boy sulked throughout. Daniel itched to give him a beating. He hadn't thought Matty difficult but today he was a monster. By five in the evening, a glass of lemonade in a new straw-boater, he'd had enough and steered back to land. If the child had wanted to put a hex on the trip he couldn't have done better.

* * *

Mrs Mac was up early making pastry. 'If it's alright with you, madam, I thought a meat pie for lunch and lemon meringue to follow.'

Julia nodded. 'You might save a portion for Mr Faulkner. He's coming today to help put up tables.' Mrs Mac is taken with the tutor. He comes every Tuesday and every Tuesday she cooks extra (she also darns his socks and patches his sleeves). Seeing this helped Julia make a decision. 'There's a box of Doctor Passmore's things in the closet. You might go through it with Ben in mind. Oh, and yet again we are expecting Lady Carrington to call.'

This will be the third time of a suggested visit. They never did make it from the Nelson; instead Evie sent a note saying they'd been called away.

'Do you think they'll come today?' said Mrs Mac.

'I don't know but why not take this afternoon as a rest. It's a lovely day. You could take Matty for a picnic and have Ben accompany you.' Doubtless Evie would sail through any meeting, Mrs Mac's nerves, and Julia's, are less secure. Let's hope their picnic goes better than the trip to the Fens.

Parting that day Julia apologised. 'I don't know what got into him.'

'He doesn't want to share you,' Daniel had taken her hand and pressed it to his lips. 'I wouldn't want to share you either.'

In that moment, his lips warm and his smile beguiling, Julia knew how much she needed a man's arms about her. The need must have shown because Daniel bent closer. 'I'm a patient man. I can wait. But know this, a couple of days ago we spoke of words and what they can do. One word from you and it will take more than a troubled child to keep me away.'

* * *

Yet again the Carringtons didn't show. Everything ready, the rose-sprigged service down from the shelf and a sample of delicious pastries they plan to sell on Saturday. So ill-mannered and such a waste of time!

Maggie hovers. 'Nobody comes anymore, not the Missis from the Nelson or the German doctor. We don't see Mr Luke either him building his house.'

'Luke is building a house?'

'Yes and it ain't half big! I went to see it the other day. He was putting a new roof on. I asked if he needed a maid. He told me to clear off.'

Julia wished the same. 'It's time you were gone. Be back before nine or I'll lock the door. A repeat of the other night and you'll be out permanently.'

It's no good being sharp with Maggie. It's not her fault the Carringtons choose to stay away anymore than it's her fault Luke does the same. So he's bought a house? It will be beautiful wherever it is. Look at the cottage! His magical talent is everywhere even to a door knocker. A miniature version of a three-headed Cerberus that guards the Wall, the knocker repelled rather than invited. Now the brutes are tamed, a twisted leather leash about the many necks. What was it Evie said, 'charming and resourceful.' Julia knows Luke Roberts is charming but wonders exactly what was meant by resourceful.

* * *

Countdown to the Grand Opening! Local housewives promised cakes but not too many obliged - happily, that doesn't matter now Leah is here. A friend of Mrs Mac, Leah Ferguson is calm and courteous, everything one would want in a maid. The household is growing, the staff sitting room given up so that all might have a room of their own. Maggie sleeps in the high attic. She sulks but doesn't lose by it, Leah and Maud feeding sweeties to a spoilt child.

Wednesday started in dramatic fashion: seven am posts hammered into the ground and workmen, telegraph engineers, swarming all over the land.

'You'll be sharing a party-line with the Big House. Once linked, ma'm, I'll knock and show you the ropes.' Julia's not keen on the telegraph posts but appreciates the telephone, though who she has to call is another thing.

Mid afternoon the seamstress arrived, Maud, Leah, and Dorothy, a girl from the village, to try on their uniforms. Black being too harsh for Maud's sallow complexion Julia chose grey poplin dresses. Watching the maids parade, suddenly the tea-shop is real. As yet no one dare ask what if it fails.

* * *

Callie's carriage pulled into the yard. She frowned at the telegraph poles.

'I don't care for telephones. Ringing all hours, one might as well pay a chap to bang a gong just as you're dropping off to sleep.'

She walked into the parlour. 'You're expecting visitors?'

'I hoping Evelyn Carrington will call.'

'Oh, you won't see her today. She'll be at the Motor Show. Everybody's there. My Crosby is keen to go. Are you expecting many on Saturday?'

Julia crossed her fingers. 'I'm not expecting anything.'

'It's a pity I shan't be here to see it.'

'Oh but Callie why not?'

'It's one of those unfortunate clashes. I arranged to visit a friend in Berkshire and can't break a promise. You'll be fine. The world and his wife will come, downright nosiness will fetch 'em.' Callie picked up a tea-cup. 'This is rather lovely. Is it from the set your German doctor donated?'

'It is. I thought to use it on Saturday.'

'Beautiful! If it were mine I'm not sure I'd want strangers touching it. So, it was not so much a gift to you as for the business?'

'It was meant as a gift but also for the tea-shop.'

'I am currently transferring my sickly heart to your Stefan. He waits upon Her Majesty, who we hear is very low. All this time and the throne in sight, Bertie must be champing at the bit.' Callie picked up a cake stand. 'I have Meissen but nothing as good as this. Does his family know you have it?'

'I believe Frau Adelman knows.'

'And she's happy about it?'

'I don't know her feelings on the matter. They haven't been relayed to me however I am to visit her next week. I'll ask then.'

'You go to see her in the sanatorium?'

Julia chose not to answer.

Callie wandered about the parlour. 'Daniel's busy scribbling away at some book he's writing about the painter Georges Seurat. It won't sell. My son's another John Sargent, forever backing lame horses. But you can't tell him, always so sure of his opinions. There's the Greville pernickety side to the boy. Fastidious in manner and dress, he expects everyone to be the same.'

'I hadn't noticed that.'

'I don't imagine you had. It's a thing only a mother would see but it's there and the older he gets the worse it gets. I say to Dulce, keep your clay feet well inside your slippers. You don't want him seeing them. He's another who'll miss the opening. The news agency wants him.'

Callie swung the cake-stand back and forth.

Julia took it and set it down. 'We mustn't keep you.'

'I am in rather a hurry.' She picked up her gloves and left.

* * *

Daniel is angry. 'You're old Lansdowne, Mother, a monitor of all that is in and out. Being there you would've sanctioned the enterprise. Now you've left Julianna swinging in the wind. And don't say you're visiting a friend! This is you harping on that old business and letting a good neighbour down.'

'It hurts to be there,' was the best she could come up with.

'That's the past!' He wouldn't let her off. 'I'm hoping is the past and not you interfering with my wants...because if you are...if what you're really doing is getting between us, then we have a problem.'

'I've nothing against the girl,' Callie blustered, 'though you could do a whole lot better than a widow with dubious connections. I mean, what is a parson's daughter doing with Evelyn Carrington? I've been in the country less than a year and gossip about that woman is all I hear. And not just her, her brother, the Honourable Freddie! Downstairs are saying he's one of those fellows who don't know a duck from a drake. Talking at the Festival about how he's gonna be Matthew's pappy? I wouldn't let him near a child of mine.'

'The Carringtons have society friends. Frances likes them. They often dine at the Castle. John Sargent won't have a word said against them.'

201

'Frances Warwick does as he's told. Daisy calls the shots in that relationship. As for John he's an artist and closes his eyes to lots of peculiar goings on. But forget the Carringtons! What's about Stefan Adelman?'

'What about him? As far as I can tell Adelman is a decent fellow with a difficult domestic situation. Julianna is no more responsible for the madness in Freddie Carrington's head than the suffering in another.'

They wrangled most of the day. Now he's at the cottage and sees doubt in Julianna's eyes where there didn't use to be. 'Don't worry about Saturday,' he said. 'People will step up to the plate.'

'I hope they do. Thank you for organising a telephone.'

'I was glad to do it. If you've prowlers at night a telephone is essential. Oh hello, young fellow!' Matty appeared and then ran away. Daniel grimaced. 'I guess he's still unhappy with me.'

'I'm sorry,' said Julia. 'I'll have a word with him later.'

'Don't! He can't help the way he feels and pressure will only make it worse. Let him get used to the idea of me being around. Better yet...' Daniel took her hand to his lips. 'You get used to the idea.'

The cabbie was whipping up the horse when the boy came again, and panting, held out the toy soldier that was tossed in the river.

'Is this for me?'

Matty nodded.

'Thank you. I'll take him with me to South Africa and next time I'm here he can tell you of our travels.'

* * *

Julia was woken in the night by Kaiser barking. She pulled on a robe and ran downstairs. Maud and Leah were on the landing, hair in curling rags.

'Stay with Matty! I'll check the doors.' She opened the door and stood listening. A door creaked and Kaiser raced away. Lamp held high she ran along the terrace. 'Go away, whoever you are!' she shouted. 'I'll call the constable!' There was a scrambling noise and then Kaiser was back, leaning against her knee, hackles stiff but no longer snarling.

The following morning Joe Carmody fetched the constable. 'Yours is not the first house to be bothered,' said he. 'Lower Bakers had a similar thing. It's the telephone installation, thieves after the cable.'

'You think it opportunists and not a personal thing, because somebody was here last week, panes broken in the greenhouse and the back door tried.'

'Any other damage?'

'Not that I could tell. It was dark. I wasn't going to press too closely.'

'Quite right too.' The constable put away his note-book. 'I've had a look round and you seem secure enough. What d'you store in those sheds?'

'Only wash tubs and coal and wood.'

'Well then you're probably safe. It's a rare burglar that steals coal, though the price of things nowadays you never know.'

'Well?' Joe saw the constable out the yard. 'Did you see it?'

'I saw fag ends stubbed out on the floor if that's what you mean.'

'There ain't just fag ends, there was a cigar butt. I want to know if there's more than one bloke hangin' about. Did you say owt t'missis?'

'I couldn't see the point. It would only frighten her and we don't know how long the fag ends have been here. They might've been there years.'

'No they ain't!' Joe protested. 'I cleared up the last lot. This is some bloke, or blokes, spyin' on my lady.'

* * *

That night Julia went through Owen's things. Forty years he walked the earth but left little of personal value, his son his greatest contribution.

Last night Matty climbed on her knee. 'I want my own papa,' he sobbed. 'I want him continuing with us and not with angels in heaven.'

Julia sighed. The boots are too small yet there's a corduroy jacket and raincoat that might do for Ben. Beyond that it's books and gold cufflinks. The cufflinks belonged to Uncle William, the Flower-Finder. Strange that she should now live in a house once occupied by flower-gatherers. With Uncle William it was a hobby. A diary found in the Needed and Necessary attic speaks more of a crusade than a hobby, a log of travels abroad and plants he collected, the gold initials HLL suggestive of Henry Lambeth Lansdowne,

Owen kept a diary, the diary and a lock of Matty's hair among items returned from Cairo. Last night she dreamed her husband sat under the Sphinx teaching as he taught when alive, responding to the question, 'how did the Sphinx lose its nose,' how soldiers of Napoleon's army used it for target practice.

In the dream Owen turned. 'What is it, my love? Do you have a question?'

She woke thinking of Matty's word, 'continuing', and looking through the diary at the neatly penned entries, dates of sun-sets and the rising and falling of stars wished he continued on earth so that instead of reading of him she might learn from his lips what kind of man he was and why she misses him so.

CHAPTER SIXTEEN

The Kiss

When the clock struck twelve Julia didn't know whether to laugh or cry. There was something so horribly melodramatic about it all. It is midday rather than midnight but with the last chime of the clock - and not a single customer these three hours - surely her dress should be in tatters and the maids all mice.

Silver tea-pots glittering and napkins flared, a table in the window is laid for tea with cakes and chocolate bon-bon and little dishes of fresh strawberries, jewel red and succulent against white meringue glace – not to mention millefeuille choux buns oozing cream, and sparkling sugared ice marshmallow.

The table display is hourly changed for fresh. All will go to waste but not because of a lack of interest, scores of would-be patrons pass up and down the street or jostle for room outside the double-bay windows. All would sample the wares but are stopped by an invisible barrier. A couple with perambulator pause. Eyes round and mouths watering they lean toward the glass, but then afraid of crossing social boundaries they turn away.

Maud sighed. 'Oh madam!'

'I know.'

'What shall we do?'

'All we can do, continue to be hopeful, and alert and bright, and then if by three no one has come through the door I shall turn the sign to closed.'

Matty is in his bedroom. He's built a tent of blankets over a clothes-horse and hides inside with Kaiser. If the blockade continues Julia may well join him but for now she sits in the garden, a burned wrist gained by being overhasty with a treacle sponge bearing witness to folly. She ought to have known a minnow of wrong colour and tribe cannot expect to swim with the tide.

Five o'clock this morning she thought how enticing the parlour looked. Yesterday Maud and Leah hung bunting outside. In that moment Julia loved them as family. Now they stand with heads high but underneath are broken.

Yesterday evening the telephone rang, Stefan, her first official caller via the shared line. 'I learned you are with telephone and rang to wish you luck. I'd like to be with you today but thought it in your best interest to stay away.'

* * *

Five minutes to one the door bell jingled. Mrs Mac came through. 'We have a customer.' It was Joe Carmody tightly buttoned into a go-to-chapel suit, a wisp of grey hair slicked down and boots polished. Cap in hand, he hovered.

'I've come, ma'm.'

'Good day, Mr Carmody. We are pleased to see you. Please take a seat.'

'Where shall I sit?'

'How about a table in the nook? It's my favourite spot and has a view of the side garden and the white roses you trained across the lattice.'

'As you wish.' He sat with his cap on his lap.

'Let me take your cap.' Julia took an order pad. 'Now what may I get you?'

Joe screwed up his face. 'I don't rightly know. From what I've seen and smelt in the kitchen this last week I'd say pretty much anythin'.'

Seeing him flustered Julia smiled. 'Might we put together a selection for you to try?' Thinking of his slender means she added, 'and of course those you don't want you leave.'

'You mean not pay for them like?'

'Exactly so.'

'That sounds alreet. As always I'll be guided by you, ma'm.'

Julia was overcome. Bless the man! He came thinking no one else will. He'll hate every minute yet be faithful to the end. She put her hand on his shoulder. 'Ladies, be especially attentive with Mr Carmody. He is our dear friend.'

Joe was always going to come. Poor madam, folks treating her shabby! It's shameful, like pulling the wings off butterflies! He is here and will stay as long as his money and his nerve holds. Crunched up and uncertain, he sits mouthing an egg-custard. Gar! A mannequin in Bentalls Window with painted smile couldn't have been gawped at more. Look at 'em staring! They'd love to be in here but not one of 'em with courage to stand up. This custard tart is tasty but bound to give him indigestion as Bertha was quick to point out. 'Where you going, Joe, all dressed up like that and havin' takin' a bath?' she'd asked.

'I'm goin' to the cafe openin' in town.'

'Why are you going there? That's not for the likes of us.'

'Maybe not but I'm goin'.'

The doorbell chimed. A gentleman doffed his hat, a handsome chap in a white shirt and pinstriped suit. 'Hello, Joe. May I join you?'

It was Luke Roberts! Joe grinned. 'Nay, I didn't recognise you, lad, all spiffed up like that. Come in, sit down and welcome.'

Cheeks pink - and his more so - Dottie Manners who lives in the village took his order. The menu was mostly sweet stuff. What Luke really wanted was a slice of the steak and ale pie at the Nelson and a pint of Pipers best bitter, but for now will settle for strawberry tart and the gratitude in his darling's eyes.

'Good day, Mr Roberts.' She's here, her mouth a smudged peony.

'Mrs Dryden.' He got to his feet. It's likely as a customer he ought to stay put but no man is able to sit when Julianna Dryden speaks his name.

'I am so pleased to see you. Are you keeping well?'

'Thank you I am.'

'And your mother?'

'She's well.'

'Dorothy will take your order. If what you would most like to try is not on the menu please say. We shall endeavour to provide it.'

Knees shaking, he sat and stared at the hand-printed card but could only see her mouth and the burn on her wrist.

Joe leaned close. 'Is it on the menu, lad? The thing you'd most like to try?'

'No,' Luke sighed, 'and never likely to be.'

The strawberry tart arrived and was good but he was so anxious he could barely breathe. He was up before dawn getting jobs done so to be here on time. Then a trip to the barber and back to the Nelson for a bath and the new pinstriped suit - his mother's eyes red hot coals on his back.

'You're dressed up for it, aren't you?' she says.

'You want me to go in my boots and with my hair all easy?' he replies.

'Nobody else will be there!'

'There'll be somebody there,' says he grimly, 'and you one of them. I see it in your face, Nan Roberts, and in your best blue dress and feathered hat out on the bed. You can't bear the idea of her left standing alone.'

Nan had tossed her head. 'I may go and I may not. I haven't made up my mind. But if I do it's not about her, silly girl that she is! It's more about not lettin' Aggie Simpkin and her chapel friends rule the roost.'

* * *

The clock ticked and still only the two of them. Luke looked at his watch.

Joe stared. 'Why're you lookin' at your watch, you expectin' somebody?'

You bet your life he is expecting somebody, though not so much expecting as hoping a prayer brought to the ear of a fickle Society Lady will be heard.

Two o'clock she said she'd be here. It's quarter to. Evelyn Carrington doesn't have to come, only a promise binds them, she to bring her name and influence to the opening of the Tea-Shop and Luke to come to her house in London.

The deal, Devil's Pact as it may prove, was made the night she stayed at the Nelson, and though shamed to think it, Luke wonders if his part of the bargain wasn't more about eating a slice of Milady rather than strawberry tart.

'You'll come to my house in London and I shall paint you,' she said.

'I'll come to your house but I don't know about painting.'

'Are you making rules, Mr Wolf? I thought you needed my help.'

'I do! Or rather she does! She needs it bad.'

'Then place no barriers on friendship and I'll place none. Who knows we may both succeed in our desires.' A fairy goblin she'd paused in the moonlight. 'One thing more, I want you there when I bring friends.'

'Oh no, you don't need me! I'll only act like a fool.'

'You won't. You'll be what you are, rather splendid.'

Now he's here, Mr Splendid, crumbling cake and staring out as people stare in. The same crowd make the rules, August Simpkin's wife and her minions, talking of Christian charity but first to put the boot in. Every one of them peers into a goldfish bowl hoping to see a dainty little guppy gasp for air.

'Is your mam coming?' whispered Joe.

'She'd better. I told her straight - if she doesn't then me and her are done.'

'Women can be awkward about such things especially when beauty is involved. My missis was none too pleased but I can't help that. Madam's been kindness itself to me. I'll not stand by and see her crushed. Talkin' of standin' by did you hear some bloke's hangin' about the cottage again?'

Luke's stomach jolted. 'I didn't!'

'Aye, more fag ends on t'floor *and* a cigar butt. What do you make of it?'

'I don't know but I don't like it.'

'I got the constable to take a look, not that he was much use.'

'Maybe not but at least word will travel. That might keep 'em off.'

'Here hold on!' Joe craned his neck. 'Your mam's coming down t'road. It looks to me like you've won a battle, lad, if not the war.'

In best blue silk and a feathered hat, Nan bounced through the door. Luke got to his feet. 'Thank you, Ma.'

Nan sat. 'Don't be too hasty with your thank-yous, Luke Roberts. I'm here for a cup of tea and then I'm off. I've things to do.'

'You came.' Luke sat down, his heart a little easier. 'I'll not forget.'

'Make sure you don't!' Nan settled her skirts then waved at Dottie. 'I'm here young woman! If you're ready to wait on I am ready to be served.'

Colour high and eyes brilliant, Julianna arrived. 'Dearest, Nan!' She hugged Nan, and Nan hugged her back. 'Right then, Anna!' Nan blinked through blue parrot feathers. 'We're here and as friends shall sink or swim together.'

The tea-pot arrived. Nan is sipping and crooking her little finger and out-staring onlookers, her glance stern yet her ginger-up.

* * *

They sat a while, tea spoons rattling. Then Joe craned his neck. 'What's goin' on outside?' The window was clear, not a soul peering in. What's more, the road was free of traffic, not a cart in sight. 'Come look!' Joe stood up. 'There's a reet kerfuffle goin' on with Bobbies in the road directin' traffic.'

'Police directing traffic?'

'Aye, everywhere you look.'

A carriage rolled up with a uniformed chauffeur at the wheel. Two men got out. Toffs dressed in top hats and frock-coats they entered the tea-shop.

'What's to do?' whispered Joe.

'I've no idea,' said Luke whose brain was buzzing with a million ideas!

The two men, Court equerries they were to learn, talked with Julianna, who by degrees was pale then pink and then pale again. There was a buzz in the air and a murmur. The murmur became a roar. People were cheering! Another carriage pulled up and with it an open-topped landau, horses gleaming and pennants flying, and the cause of the kerfuffle sitting in the back smiling.

Nan is fumbling with her bag. 'It is him en't it?' she squeaks.

'Be still Ma,' Luke turned to Joe. 'And you, Joe! I reckon we're going to see and hear things today we're never likely to see or hear again.'

Lady Carrington has kept her promise. My word has she! One of the equerries was at the car, a brief conversation with the occupant and then he returned and approached their table. 'Mr Luke Roberts?'

Luke is on his feet. 'Aye, that's me.'

'Good day to you, sirs, and to you, Madam, Hugh Beresford Fitzwilliam, equerry to the Court of St James. Mrs Dryden is to receive a visitor and his friends.' The equerry read from a piece of paper: 'They are here to celebrate the opening of the Needed and Necessary Tea-Shop.'

Luke picked up his hat. 'And you'd prefer us to leave.'

'On the contrary, we would prefer you to stay.'

'That's if you want to,' Julianna interjected.

'We want what you want.'

'Then please stay.'

'And us staying?' Heart thumping in his chest and throat dry, amazed at his cheek, Luke kept talking. 'Does it meet with the visitor's approval?'

The equerry bowed. 'Mrs Dryden's wishes have been passed on to the visitor and thought right and proper. First come, first served, I believe, is the opinion. As such, I am therefore pleased to offer His Royal Highness the Prince of Wales' cordial greetings and beg you to continue to take your tea.'

'Well I'll be buggered,' said Joe.

'Yes,' said Luke. 'And me too.'

* * *

The rest of the afternoon went by in a blur; Luke's guts in a constant knot, not so much for himself but for Julianna. Gown rustling and hands steady, she seemed calm but having studied her face he knew when she was anxious. Matty meeting the Prince of Wales was her moment of joy, the little lad bowing, and Kaiser, the dog, extending a paw, a Union Jack kerchief about his neck. The Prince was heard to adjudge Matty 'a jolly little chap' and the tea-party a 'delightful interlude'. As for the rest, if their smiles - and the amount of running up and down by the maids to go by - they also found it delightful.

The person who did enjoy the day was Nan. Eyes bright as

raisins she sat observing all. Once she let out a squeak of laughter which was quickly smothered. Such delight in the sound, Luke knew memories were being stored away beneath that feathered hat, and that for the rest of her life an occasion would be found for Nannette Roberts to say, 'this reminds of the time I took tea with His Royal Highness, the Prince of Wales.'

* * *

Three-thirty the Royal Party was on the move. 'You wait til I tell the missis,' whispered Joe. 'She'll be talkin' about this from now until Doomsday.'

'And why not,' said Nan smoothing a fur-tippet. 'You can be sure I'll make plenty of it. Sippin' tea with Royalty is somethin' to talk about. Ooh, the church wives that now wish they were in my place! Hah! They'll be spittin' feathers!'

'Aye, up!' Joe nudged Luke. 'He's leavin'.'

There was movement to the door, hands shaken and kisses exchanged. Prince Albert reminded Luke of the German doctor, Adelman, the same build. Until viewed through the eyes of Majesty he might be as other men but he moves and is transformed into Light, Halley's Comet entrained by lesser comets.

Elegant and affable, he acknowledged Nan's curtsey.

'He likes our dear madam,' said Joe. 'Look at him smilin' fit to bust!'

'Yes and kissin' her hand,' said Nan.

Luke was silent. No need for comment. You'd have to be blind not to know what was going on. Lady Carrington may have charm, and the tea-party a delightful interlude, but a cup of tea and bun didn't bring this man to the door. He came to see the *Faun Surprised*.

Freddie Carrington told of the paintings. Sunday evening Milady dined out which left the Honourable Frederick alone, a wine glass in his hand and Black Dog curling at his feet. Black Dog, two words that aptly describe the way a soul howls when trapped in a pit, paws bloodied from trying to get out. Luke knows the dog, since Jacky's death a creature like that often mouths his ankles.

Sunday evening, and the Public Bar empty, Luke asked Freddie what happened to make him sad. 'My pa happened,' was the answer, 'Pa and the despair that comes with trying to set one's feelings down on canvas.'

Freddie reckoned only God and Leonardo Di Vinci can paint a decent picture, and that, he, Freddie, was so on fire for the world any brush he picked up turned to ash. 'Evie burns the same but as ice and able to set things down. You should see what she did with the woman you love, got her cold and clear.'

The first day of the Art Festival at Sandringham was by invitation only, the second for lesser mortals. The Central Marquee was where the *Fauns* were housed. Luke spent an age gazing at Eve Carrington's paintings. They were beautiful, the barley-sugar gold of Julia's hair and rose tint of her lips, yet more of a fairy story. The Julianna he knows is flesh and blood. She burns her wrist baking and loses patience with plant-stealers. She has a heart and feelings. The deity on those canvasses is as far removed from the world as the Unicorn on which she sits and glitters like the china in her kitchen. A man wouldn't dare to kiss those lips for fear she might crack.

What, Luke wondered, did the Prince of Wales see. His kiss was courtly yet deliberate, information exchanged and a gilt-edged Royal invitation offered.

Eve Carrington saw the invitation and smiled across the room, her glance arch as if to say, 'what did you expect. He is a man as well as a Prince.'

That kiss split the front parlour, the Roberts and old Joe on one side and Prince Albert and his friends on the other, and Luke an outsider.

* * *

The Royal car rolled back down the road. A box of macaroons dangling from his finger, Hugh Fitzwilliam bowed to Julia. 'My congratulations, Mrs Dryden.'

'Yes, well done, Ju-ju.' Evie adjusted her stole. 'You managed awfully well.'

'Everyone did well,' said Julianna acknowledging the maids.

'Indeed they did. I must say Mrs Mac has come on. I understand most of the day's delicious pastries were of her concocting.'

'Maud is an excellent cook.'

'You call her Maud? But then, why not! She is a friend and one needs friends.' Evie nodded to the window. 'The hordes are gathering.'

'So I see.'

'Let 'em wait! Once we're gone lock the door and keep it closed for a week, all bookings taken by telephone. Make the blighters sweat! They do not deserve you or your ladies.'

'Thank you, Evelyn, for being here. I am grateful.'

'It's the least I could do. But hold onto your gratitude! Your introduction to Society is only beginning. We are entertaining His Highness soon at the London house. I hope you will attend.'

'I'll try.'

'No trying, Julianna!' Evie's eyes were steel. 'You are asked for therefore required to be there.'

'I see.'

'It's as well you do see.' All smiles again, she took Julia's arm. 'I think you might let your people go now. They've waited long enough.'

'Thank you so much for coming.' Julianna took Nan's hand. 'But for you I don't know what I would've done.'

'You'd have managed. You didn't need us, Anna.'

'Oh I did and I do! You'll never know how much.'

Nan adjusted her hat. 'This time tomorrow when news gets around you won't need anybody. Isn't that right, Milady?'

'Mrs Dryden did make a success of the day but as I said, one needs friends and never more so than when scaling the heights. I wouldn't part with your friendship, however lofty the call. You too, Mr Carmody! How well you served your lady today. I would wish for gentlemen servers half as loyal.'

Joe was starry-eyed. 'Thank you ma'm.'

Evie turned to Luke. 'And what about you, sir, the fife and drum behind such chivalry? I confess to being envious of Julianna, and along with other ladies of our party today wonder how one might steal such devotion away.'

* * *

218

What kind of a wondrous beast is a fly on the wall if it sees all and hears all and yet remains unmoved! Luke was aware of Evie's hand on his arm, a hand that pulls the trigger on a twelve bore. He was aware of eyes staring and his mother's lips tightening. He knew that, though proud and pleased, Joe wished himself any place but here. He knew handsome Hugh Fitzwilliam, the man with medals on his chests, liked Julianna but preferred a man in his arms. Such a vivid, multi-layered moment - white linen tablecloths, sunlight striking a crystal dish, a wasp eating jam inside - he knew it all but could only comprehend Julianna and the moment hanging above them.

'Speak to me, Anna,' his prayer was mute. 'I don't care what you say. Talk of Matty, how his speech is improved under the care of a drunken piano player, and how he always adds Mister Wolf to his prayers. Tell of your studious husband, who cherished you as an artefact rather than a woman. Tell of your worries, how you fret about the wall, and the dead woman who abides in Greenfields, and the breaking of china. Ask me to help you! Ask me to put a lock on the damned laundry door because some arse is spying on you! Talk to me, heart-of-hearts! Don't let go of me in silence, or like a balloon lose on a string I'll float away never to be seen again.'

For a moment her gaze held his and then she turned away.

It wasn't much of a turning away but it was enough to swat the fly. From then on Eve Carrington's voice was all he heard.

'I believe you've recently developed an interest in art, Mr Roberts.'

'I am interested but know nothing about it.'

'Then, if you visit Russell Square one day next week it shall be mine and my brother's pleasure to assist you in that knowledge. So, will you come?'

'Aye, I'll come.'

'Excellent!' With a flick Evelyn opened up a parasol, her beautiful face half in shade and half in light. 'So that shall be our plan. A trip round the galleries and back home in time for tea. Do you think you can manage that, Luke?'

'I don't see why not. Like most men I'm open to learning.'

* * *

Seven o'clock the phone rang. Julia was watering the window boxes. It was Callie Masson. 'Pop up and have a nightcap.'

'I'm awfully tired.'

'Humour me. I'll send Crosby down to light you.'

Callie was in the small salon, her foot on a stool.

'You didn't get to Berkshire?'

'I was laid up. What about you? I understand you've had quite a day.'

'It was a surprising day.'

'Not least a visit from the Prince of Wales?'

'That too.'

'That too!' Callie's eyebrows shot skyward. 'You've had a bigger surprise than the heir to the throne in your front parlour?!'

'As I said, a day of surprises.' Julia offered a few details. She said nothing of Luke Robert's trip to London. She couldn't give the words space on her tongue. Weary, she concluding the day's events with Evie's advice of a week's break.

Callie nodded. 'It will make them hungry for more especially when the newspapers get busy.'

'Newspapers?'

'Of course! His Highness, the Prince of Wales, taking tea with a new lady? Come tomorrow morning you'll be the talk of London.'

* * *

All hope of sleep banished, Julia made her way down the Rise. All were abed, the maids worn out. Earlier she thanked them for their efforts.

'I was in the back washing up,' said Maggie. 'I din't see much of anythin'.'

'My knees were knocking,' said Leah.

'I hope you'll continue to be steady,' said Julia. 'Having been so honoured we may expect others and must behave in a dignified manner.'

Maggie rolled her eyes. 'Madam, must we always be dignified? Can't we ever be happy and laugh and sing?'

Rightly reproved, Julianna laughed. 'Of course you can! You surely deserve it. But let's make it a quiet sort of laughter and a mute sort of singing.'

Needless to say Maggie must be impertinent. She cast a sneaking sideways glance. 'Can we sing "*Come into the Garden Maud?*"'

'I'm not sure that's appropriate.'

Mrs Mac shrugged. 'Oh, let's sing it! Appropriate or not it'll be the only time anyone invites me into a garden.' With that she began singing and the maids with her. They danced about the parlour, Maud an ostrich lifting knobbly knees, Leah a mature

221

swan drifting to and fro, and Little Dottie Manners waltzing with Maggie. Later, outside watering peas, Julia wished she'd danced with them. Mother loved Tennyson's poem. 'It's about a man watching in a darkened garden hoping to see his love,' she would say. 'He shouldn't be there. He is Maud's secret and she is his.'

Watering can set aside, Julia sat on the swing, and gathering her skirts pushed lazily back and forth. It is years since she rode a swing. Time has moved on yet she's still on a swing, an image rocking back and forth inside her head - a kiss offered one human being to another.

It's not the Prince's kiss she recalls. The kiss she sees rose in a woman's eyes to float through the air and land on target. 'You will come to London won't you?' said Evie, her lips parted and eyes lambent.

Poets talk of Cupid's arrow piercing the heart. Today his arrow was sharp and coated with bitter aloes. Seeing that kiss, watching it happen - Luke Roberts about to be spirited away - an arrow had lanced Julia's breast. She'd wanted to call out, 'Don't go, Mister Wolf!' The words wouldn't come. Debt, money loans and Meissen china, how could she ask when entangled in so many webs?

Love is painful. Alone in the warm darkness Julia swung higher, her skirts flaring out and combs loose in her hair. She never felt that kind of pain for Owen. Their love was manageable. There is nothing manageable about jealousy. It hurts!

She went into the house, the swing swaying and the chain links creaking.

'Come into the garden, Maud, for the black bat, Night, has flown. Come into the garden, Maud, I am here at the gate alone; And the woodbine spices are wafted abroad, And the musk of the roses blown.'

Book Three

Thistles

CHAPTER SEVENTEEN

Dust

September 1900. Cairo.

Julia visits a private graveyard in the south side of Sarah Salem. She arrived in Egypt yesterday to a message from the Foreign Office asking to meet at the cemetery where she was told her husband's body had been removed.

'What do you mean *removed?*'

The Consulate mopped his brow. 'The remains were moved to another spot by Professor Radcliff, a colleague of the late Doctor's who works here in Cairo, and who I understand, is on the way to meet you.'

'They had my husband's body dug up and taken to another place?'

'I know that this sounds like a wanton act of desecration but..!'

'Sounds like?' Julia hissed. 'Don't you mean *is* an act of desecration!'

'This is Egypt, Mrs Dryden, a grave is despoiled and a body removed in the name of antiquity every day and no one so much as raises an eyebrow.'

'And was my husband's body removed in the name of antiquity? It can't have been for treasure. The only treasure to be had of Owen was the man himself.'

'I don't know why he was taken. I have heard rumours, this place a Whispering Walls, but as for veracity you must ask Professor Radcliff.'

'Don't worry I will. I would have thought the moving a body like that without the relative's permission to be outside of the law.'

The man sniffed. 'Where archaeology is concerned there is no law. This country is a trading post of the dead. The Embassy deplores the business but with British among the forefront of such scavenging can do nothing. Here comes the Professor! Hopefully she'll be able to set your mind at rest.'

A bullock cart rattled alongside. A woman jumped down. Dressed in Bedouin robe, the floating ends of a scarf wrapped about her head, she strode forward, her hand thrust out in greeting. 'Ah, Ju-ju! At last we meet.'

'Set my mind at rest?' Julia ground her teeth. 'I doubt it.'

* * *

A theatre of three, they sat in the cart, poor Dorothy suffering from heat at the back and Julia, and the woman, Radcliff, up front. A Texan, a blade of a body with an intelligent face and ardent eyes, Kitty Radcliff shook Julia's hand, remarked on the weather, and then proceeded to uproot any comfortable thoughts Julia might have on her marriage to Owen.

An expert in cuneiform writing, Kitty Radcliff said she was based at the Museum of Antiquities. 'Though what use they are to me and I to them I don't know. A woman carries no weight in this country. A lesser species, we must fight for every crumb. I don't care for Egyptian History, Persia my choice, yet bitten by the treasure-seeking bug - and lately bitten again by Flinders Petrie - I suppose I'm here, until like Owen, I am mowed down by a bullock cart.'

This was the tenor of Miss Radcliff's conversation, a mocking wit of her life and devil take the listener's feelings. It was a difficult meeting for Julia who, while repressing anger, knew a sense of guilt. Why didn't she know of Owen's life in Egypt? Who is this woman and why did he never tell of friends he had, close friends in this case with whom he could apparently jest of death.

'I had to move the dear boy, you understand.' Defiance in her eyes, Kitty Radcliff lit a cigarette. 'I couldn't leave him there. He hated Ex-Pat cemeteries and their beastly concrete markers. "Don't let me to stifle in one of those, Kitty," he'd say. "I'd sooner cook on a brazier than lie alongside stuffed pigs."'

'Stuffed pigs?' Julia stared in disbelief! The Owen Passmore she knew would never talk so scathingly of people whomsoever they are.

'I know.' Kitty Radcliff smiled. 'It's how he saw the pen-pushers here, the wives and retired Colonels and their dainty tea-cups and antimacassars. He had no time for bureaucracy. He said it smacked of India and other tyrannies.'

It appears Miss Radcliff knew Owen in Cambridge. 'I thought him brilliant, if a little disrespectful of female deities, in particular Lady Bast. He said he was a dog person. Cats lacked in affection.'

Julia listened with mounting indignation -nothing heard from this woman explained her highhanded behaviour. 'Why did you move his body?'

'Because he would've wanted to be moved! His place was with the people of Egypt not with those that profit by them! I knew this and so took him where he would want to be, the Great Pyramid of Khufu.'

'Why there?'

'He came as a boy. He and his father were hunting a species of lotus that grows on the lakes of El-Fayyoum. He said it was during that trip they visited the Valley of the Kings and how seeing it his heart had burned.'

Julia's heart burned. 'He told you that?'

'Owen believed the pyramid to be some kind of receiver and a point among the stars the transmitter. He once spent the night in the King's Chamber lying inside the empty sarcophagus hoping to learn of their intention.'

'And did he?'

Kitty Radcliff laughed. 'He learned how a million bugs can make a man itch, beyond that I couldn't say. His last wish was to be buried there.'

'His last wish? You were with him when he died?'

'I was. We were on El Sabtia Street when it happened, though street is an optimistic term for that dirt track. I saw it.' Kitty Radcliff pulled on the cigarette. 'I know I should've spoken to you before moving him but I hoped you wouldn't need to know.'

'What!'

'I thought you would never find out.'

'You mean if this hadn't come to light I'd be visiting an empty grave? My word, that's a dreadful thing to admit don't you think.'

'I dare say it is but you've no idea the fuss that goes on these days! Digs here in Egypt are not what it used to be, the government is cracking down. It was a matter of expedience! An archaeologist's life these days is one piffling form after another. Aware of the fuss if I sought permission I took a chance.'

'A chance with what?'

'Your feelings.'

* * *

Julia returned to the hotel struggling to come to terms with the day. Who is Owen Passmore? She had thought she knew him. Now she realises she had no right to know him. From the start he was a compromise - a home rather than a person - and when Matty came, secondary to his son. Any chance they had of learning of one another was lost with the tonsillectomy. Like the Wall in Bakers End, botched surgery came between them. That there might be another Owen behind the Wall beloved of another woman never occurred to her.

'And so what,' she whispered. 'Did you take your hopes to this Professor of Assyriology with the furious eyes? Did you die loving her and regretting me?'

How strange is the human condition? Before leaving England other questions of love occupied her mind, a frequent question, though never uppermost, how to fend off the Prince of Wales while retaining friendship. It's a question she's been asking these last three years. There have been spats over her non-compliance but no real issue; Bertie gets older, and while Mrs Keppel and other current favourites stay close his needs worry him, and Julia, less.

The night before leaving England she dined at Marlborough House where he suggested she might like to comfort the dog, Caesar, who was about to have his claws clipped. There in the Salon with the dog in her arms Bertie asked was he, like Caesar, always to beg for her love. In answer she kissed his cheek. 'You have my love, Sir, and always will.' Sighing and fondling the dog's ears he surrendered. 'I'll settle for that, Ju-ju, if only with hope of a change of heart.'

The issue that night was resolved with gentility. It's doubtful she can do the same with Miss Radcliff who, if not unhinged, is surely unkind. Who meets with a widow and speaks of prior intimacy with the husband? And who with any kindness talks of being privy to a dying wish?

Tomorrow they go to the pyramid. Miss Radcliff was dismissive. 'Women like you aren't meant to crawl through tunnels.' Julia lost her temper. 'Do not presume to know me. You don't know me as I certainly do not want to know you. Keep your opinions to yourself as I shall keep mine. You took it upon yourself to move him. To show me his grave is the least you can do.'

'I don't think you'll want to come,' says Miss Radcliff.'

Julia insisted. 'You will take me! If not, I shall make formal complaint to the British Embassy who will take it up with the American Consulate. I imagine you're here on a visa. I doubt you'll want your affairs scrutinized. As you're fond of saying, authorities and their petty rules can make life difficult.'

There was a moment then when hatred burned in Kitty Radcliff's eyes. Then she shrugged. 'You'll need trousers. Skirts are too much trouble. And as we are to climb in darkness best leave your wounded pride behind. I can lend you boots but you'll need to bring your own courage.'

* * *

They met at dawn. Julia had no need to borrow. With the help of the hotel concierge she was correctly attired. Dorothy stayed behind. Carts and wagons so thick it took an age to cross the city.

Last time Julia was in Egypt she and Matty took a boat down the Nile. It was dirty and foul-smelling, bodies floating in the river, yet there was a magical haze on the water and the snouts of Matty's crocodiles and graceful felucca boats. Owen was everywhere. Julia had stood at the rail with his breath on her cheek. 'Oh my dearest dears!' he'd whispered, 'don't you think this the most marvellous place?'

Memories of the man in dispute there'll be no voices today.

Time has moved on and Julia is stronger. Though never shaped for a king's mistress - father and the Rectory having too long a reach -the company of princes and their followers proved a powerful education and not always what she wanted to know. With the launch of N and N, the Nanny Tea Shop as it is now known, the past shimmered through the present as a series of colours interspersed by shadow, Evie the brightest colour and the darkest shadow.

The success of the Tea-Shop, and the life of the owner, might be likened to a runner in the Grand National, a cheer for every hurdle but the winning-post ever around the bend. A second shop, the Nanny Too, is to open in Cambridge. Evie had agreed to cut the ribbon but of late there's been a cooling on both sides, Julia wary and Evie evasive, especially in respect of Luke Roberts.

* * *

Julia has made the journey to the Great Pyramid. Last night a booklet was sent to the hotel, a scrawled note pinned to relevant pages: Flinders Petrie, the archaeologist, offers his thoughts on the King's Chamber.'

...a stairway cut into the rock and the only light carried by guides. It was not an easy climb, our way hampered by mounds of fallen debris and the air heavy with dust. For much of the way I had to crawl on my hands and knees, the ceiling scraping my scull. It was a daunting climb particularly for one troubled by confined spaces. I found it is worth the effort but only for the brave.

Like Mr Petrie, Julia is not good with confined spaces. A guide up front with a torch, Miss Radcliff, Julia, and a guide at the rear, they shuffle down a narrow staircase, perilous, yet judging the indifference of guides at the mouth of the tunnel tourists do attempt it, even foolish English ladies.

What happens if I fall and break my neck, thinks Julia, do they bury me beside my poor Owen or haul me back up as undeserving? Anger keeps her going. Professor Radcliff be damned! I'll not address her so. I mean, who is she? Owen never mentioned her and would write every day when on a dig.

Julia rarely dreams of Owen. She once dreamt he sat teaching beside the Sphinx. Last night he *was* the Sphinx and his voice rolling thunder. 'You have a question for me?' A gag across her mouth she couldn't answer. He asked again. 'Do you have a question?' Desperate to understand the Radcliff woman, and what she'd meant to him, Julia tugged at the gag but couldn't get it free. The dream Owen then leaned down, his eyes afire. 'You cannot ask! Such a question is unworthy of me and you!'

Now, she gazes at an empty stone coffin. 'He lay in that?'

Kitty Radcliff nodded. Julia is appalled. A scarf over the mouth to filter dust and the only light a lamp held over the sarcophagus, she struggles to breathe. It's all she can do not to make a wild dash back into the air, to breathe sweet sunlit air and not the foul excretions of bat and mice.

'And he was alone?'

'A guide led him down but wouldn't have stayed. Being a king's burial chamber, it would be against their beliefs.'

All night alone in this tomb and never a word to Julia! What else doesn't she know about the man? Numb, she peered through the gloom. Other than the collective corpses of flies and spiders, there's nothing to see. He died under an ox-cart, his arm flung out and his face turned toward the East. No one told her so - nevertheless, here in this sepulchre she knows it to be so. She knows too there was blood on his chest, bright red in the sun, but none on his face, and that his eyes were open and lips upturned as though smiling.

'Was it you he ran to meet, Miss Radcliff?'

'No, he ran to help a beggar! The chap had fallen and couldn't get up. Owen tried dragging him out of the way. The cart took them both. I saw it a terrible waste, but you know Owen, he saw all life sacred even that of a leper.'

Julia was bent over in pain! Until this moment she thought she'd mourned him but no. Any pain felt before was nothing to this. It hurt so much she couldn't weep, the tears locked up inside. It hurt! Oh it did hurt! What's more she knew back home in the cottage Matty was hurting too.

For the last two day's Kitty Radcliff's every comment on the man has been peppered with that rider, 'but you know Owen.' Last night Julia thought maybe she didn't know him. But hearing of this, Owen giving his life for another, she knew she did. 'Yes, I did know my husband. I knew him very well.'

Kitty Radcliff sighed. 'I'm sure you did. After all, what was there to know? Owen was an academic with history on his mind yet with his wife and son in his heart. You were the blood in his veins. Beyond that all else was incidental.'

The guide jiggled the lamp. 'It is late. We must go now, Missies.'

Julia nodded. 'Perhaps you'll show me the way then?'

Kitty Radcliff frowned. 'To what?'

'To his grave.'

'You're looking at it.'

Julia could only see the empty sarcophagus. 'Where is it?'

'Everywhere! For God's sake wake up, Ju-ju!' Kitty Radcliff flung out her arms. 'He is here in the walls and the stone. He's thick on the ground and in the air! Owen Passmore is dust! We took him out of that grave, me and Mohammed, and burnt him to cinders! Then we swept him up and carried him down in a five cent jug. How else could we manage?'

'Oh course!' Julia gasped. 'How else could you.'

'Look, Missy Passmore!' The guide swung the lamp back and forth and the walls and motes of dust hovering in the air sparkled. 'Doctor Sahib!'

'Yes!' Tears poured down Julia's cheeks. 'Doctor Sahib!'

Quartz glittered in the huge slabs of granite. Everywhere she turned there was light, splendid and beautiful, the effulgence of a thousand stars.

The guide moved the lamp higher. Light flashed on Kitty Radcliff's tear-stained face. 'Owen valued my opinion when others did not. I respected him and he respected me. I was there the day he said how it must feel buried among kings. I brought him so he might find out.'

'I understand,' said Julia.

'Do you?'

'Yes I do.'

'I couldn't leave him there. The tunnels are as Flinders Petrie said, filled with rubble and impossible to negotiate. But they won't always be like that. Fifty years from now the world will come marching down those steps. Day after day people from every country and every walk of life will see the mystery that is Khufu, and one of the mysteries - if not the greatest - will be the light that greets them in this chamber, the light of Doctor Owen Passmore.'

* * *

There was nothing left to say, or so Julia thought. First bitter anger was fading. There was even admiration for a woman that could do this, remove a body from a grave, reduce it to dust, and then spread the dust as a sower spreads seed. It takes courage to do that. That Kitty adored Owen is evident. Julia can forgive that. One can't help who one loves.

They made the journey back. The cart pulled up outside the hotel. Julia got out and wanting to part with civility offered her hand. Kitty Radcliff pulled away. 'I have something for you. Once given you might not want to shake my hand.' So saying she dropped a wedding ring into Julia's hand.

'Oh!' She gasped. 'It's Owen's ring. '

Kitty Radcliff nodded. 'It's amazing what you find when a body is cinders.'

'You wore this?' The ring was cold in her hand.

Kitty nodded. 'Yes. I wore it.'

'What were you doing, pretending to be Owen's widow?'

'Yes. I was not his wife, yet I loved him as only a wife would love a man.'

'So why do you give it to me now?'

'Owen would want me to.'

The day was hot but the ring cold. It felt strange to Julia, unfamiliar as though belonging to another. A choice lay before her, what she did next could harm or heal. She was angry, wanted to slap the woman hurting as she had been hurt.

Then, as though he were beside her, she heard Owen sigh. 'Poor soul.'

She dropped the ring in Kitty Radcliff's hand. 'Take it.'

A tear ran down Kitty Radcliff cheek. 'Why?'

'Because he would've wanted you to have it, and as you have so often pointed out, you knew Owen.'

CHAPTER EIGHTEEN

Servant

Luke is on his way back to the Villa. An evening at the Borghese is planned with Eve's friends, Robert Scholtz and his wife. No need to rush. They're not to meet until eight-thirty which gives plenty time to bathe and change.

Were it not for a chance encounter he would've been back sooner. Freddie in the Vatican City and Eve out in the hills painting, he'd spent the better part of the day in the Piazza Navona looking at the windows. It was the lintels that drew his eye. He was making notes in his diary when a breeze took a paper he'd been reading on the many Flying Buttresses in Westminster Abbey.

A chap nearby retrieved it, and interested in such things, struck up a conversation. Three hours they sat chatting. In Italy it's rare to talk of stone in any manner other than of statuary and Michelangelo. The chap in the square was an architect, thus their conversation was of the nuts and bolts of building rather than a sculptor's art. Luke came away from the encounter pleased. Not only was he able to converse on a topic he knew, he'd done so in Italian.

The high-spot of this trip has been the ease of conversation. Last year was his first on Italian soil. Experienced travellers, the Carringtons found the touring easy. Luke had hoped for a sense of belonging. What he got was an aching neck from staring at living history and the brain-numbing exclusion that comes with not 'understanding the lingo' as Freddie puts it.

Earlier this year he came alone and found in the Brenta Mountains a homeland and relatives he never knew he had. He will come again but first there must be this trip and the need to find freedom for him and for Eve.

Their association is a mistake - their regret immediate and mutual. Three years and they struggle to like one another. If asked why, he'd say they were offered a gift that neither wanted. They spend very little time together. He seldom visits Russell Square. Life with the Carringtons is all noise and movement, house-to-house and country-to-country they are never still, and with a grating sound of rocks rubbing they take their noise with them.

Even when painting Eve's talking, 'what does he think of this and what is his opinion on that.' He used to respond but learned to keep his mouth shut. Last night at dinner when asked his thoughts on Caravaggio's *Boy with Basket of Fruit,* he said the boy was unlike any child he knew but the fruit real enough, fungus and all. Evelyn was scornful, 'a snarl from a Wolf who only ever sees his lair empty.' She was taken to task by Robert Scholtz: 'Caravaggio was fond of pointing out perceived defects, as, it seems, are you, Lady Carrington.'

Luke is used to criticism, Nan Roberts an expert at the game, but with the constant nit-picking here in Rome he feels he is choking.

Such noise and never alone! There are scores of attendants, nameless and faceless, folding and pouring and carrying. Used to dealing for himself Luke finds it unnecessary. Under observation twenty-four hours a day, he drops a knife and a dozen elevated eyebrows stoop to pick it up. Same in the bedroom, he yawns and a manservant asks what nightshirt he favours and how does he like his bath. He can't blink without someone enquiring his need.

* * *

Grimacing, he kicked at a pebble. Miserable arse that he is making inventory of his woes! He wants to call quits but fettered by guilt, is a cripple waiting for a voice to say, 'pick up thy bed and walk.' Until he hears it he's stuck.

Eve Carrington is a broken person. Things said and done these last few years, the sharp tongue and violence, most men would be gone. Luke hangs on trying to tell himself 'you don't throw away treasure because it's damaged, you try using it gently.'

Trouble is you can't be gentle with Eve. She recognises a curse rather than a kiss. So changeable, she'll give the coat off her back one day then an inner voice from the past will see kindness as weakness and she'll snatch the coat back - and a layer of skin with it. Then there's Freddie who spends his life running from the past. At times he doesn't run fast enough and wakes in the night screaming. Harm has been done to them. It has made a counterfeit of Freddie, a poisonous, albeit fragile, blossom of Eve, and a coward of Luke.

Albert Roberts taught Luke never to lie. Now every day he lies, if not to Eve then to himself. Below stairs he's known as 'Milady's tame brute.' Tamed he may be but no brute hence he doesn't know how to extricate his body while keeping his soul intact.

Early morning and late at night, a child knuckling her eyes, she seeks forgiveness: '*Mister Wolf, please don't leave me. I don't know what I'll do if you leave me.*' Between times she rips him heart and soul. There are days when he is beyond freedom, when indifference dulls his senses, his thoughts so far from Russell Square his flesh may as well follow - it's then her body does the talking.

That first night - the invitation tea-for-two - he came to her a virgin. It didn't take her long to realise. Eyes flashing like a tigress, she cried out, 'you've not done this before! I am the first!' With that she'd leapt from the bed returning to empty a bottle of champagne over his naked body. Laughing she was, Jezebel, Queen of Desire. 'I name this ship Invincible. God bless this barque and all who sail in him.' She thought it exciting, and so did he, but then what man would not be excited by that first exquisite touch of mouth and hand. Her mouth a pump applied to his loins, passion - a dry underground river these thirty years - rushed to the surface. Whatever happens, however long he lives, memories of that first dazzling explosion will remain.

Luke is nothing to her. Other lovers call, but are merely a distraction, Eve on the outside looking in. 'Don't think you're the only one,' says Nan. 'She'll have others in her bed.' Freddie too hints of harm. 'Don't get too close, dear chap, she'll hurt you.' Too late for warnings, harm was done the day he walked out of the N and N Tea Shop with Eve on his arm.

Nan asks why he stays, can't he find a better way to live and a better woman to love. There's no clear answer unless it is of pity and he does pity Eve, because when she's happy she is ablaze with joy, a magnificent soul emptying beneficence upon the world - beyond that it is as he said, noise.

Lately the noise is inside his head which is why he stays away. If she misses him Eve doesn't say. Her questions are of Norfolk and Julianna. When he does come home he avoids the Nanny and the Nelson as too close to the woman he's never stopped loving. As for the Forge, he misses the solitude so much that often in sleep he follows his soul homeward aboard the cart, his good old horse, Betty, clip-clopping through the mist.

A ghost, he does as he used to, feeds the horse, beds her down, and then naked as a babe climbs to the loft to sleep with the stars for eiderdown.

* * *

'You're late!' Eve was on the terrace. 'What kept you?'

Luke took off his hat. 'I met someone.'

'Oh, who?' Hair piled high and dusted with white powder she came through the doors in a jerky side-step, the skirts of the crinoline gown swaying.

'Ah!' Tonight is the masked ball and he is to be her partner.

'Ah indeed!' she tugged at the gown. 'You're late. The carriage is due and you need to be dressed and ready.'

'Sorry, it slipped my mind.'

'And it shouldn't! I don't know why I bother with such things. You'd sooner be plastering walls in Wapping than pleasing me. Jamieson! Bring out the raspberry pink silk cutaway coat and the frilled jabot!'

Luke sighed. 'Raspberry silk?'

'It's an early French ball we're going to and you to be in character.'

'And what character am I?'

'Whoever you choose! It's that kind of an evening.'

'Then I'll go as myself.'

'Sorry, we haven't a wolf skin handy. Settle for a mask. It's your identity you're to conceal not your true nature.'

He went into the dressing room. She followed. He surveyed her in the glass. 'And you, Madame Pompadour? Is that a reflection of your true nature?'

'I see myself more a Madame de Montespan favourite of the Sun King.' She picked up a bottle from the wash-stand. 'Favourite or not, they were all whores and all died young. But then, courtesans aren't meant to grow old. They are as Roman Candles, a burst of glory and a dark pit.'

Luke unbuttoned his shirt. 'And from slant of this conversation I'm guessing you are in the same dark pit.'

'I was born in a dark pit. But make haste! Try to look divine if nothing else.'

His shirt was borne away, Jamieson appearing with hot water and towels, the raspberry pink cutaway over his arm. It was a large dressing room but shared with Jamieson and Eve's brooding anger it was stuffed to the gills.

Tipsy, a couple of upturned wine bottles already in a cooler, she leant against the mirrored wall, a porcelain doll in a powdered wig replicated over and again. 'Who was it you met?'

'Oh, some chap in the Square.'

'He must have been a fascinating chap to keep you so long.'

'He was.'

'And what was the fascination? I mean, apart from the fact that it kept you from doing your duty to me.'

'He was an architect.'

'Ah, ceiling elevation and joints, a case of like attracting like. Was it early Roman elevation you discussed or the more mundane?'

'We talked of Westminster Abbey.'

'Westminster Abbey!' She smiled. 'My word a high elevation indeed! And in this discussion were you able to hold your own?'

'I hope so.'

' *Lei ha parlato in Italiano?*'

'*Si, nella mia lingua madre.*'

'Well good for you, though hardly your mother tongue. Our Nanette too much up from t'North to chime with that.'

* * *

Luke walked into the bathroom and closed the door. He should never have told her of Lucca Aldaro. At the time, she heaping gifts upon him, he wanted to give her a gift and told how his real father was Italian. That he should have a history other than that of a plumber was not what she wanted. Now everywhere they go she scratches the secret hoping to wound. 'Do you think your real papa ever supped here?' she said of St Mark's Square in Venice where an ice-frappe costs a millworker's yearly wage; then on the train from Florence; 'Look at that hut nestling among the hills! It has your name of it, Senor Roberts. What say we buy it as a summer home? We can plant vines and sit and drink wine in the sun.'

In such moments he hates her. She knows and smiling waits his response. So far he's managed to swallow anger. To remain impassive is his choice and she, confounded by silence, loses her temper and boxes his ears. Last time she drew blood. Freddie goes crazy. 'What's wrong with you?' he shouts. 'Keep this up and one day you'll be found in the Thames with your throat cut, and it won't be Luke that does it. It'll be one you prize higher, some moronic Lord with a rustic title and a hefty fist.'

As always it is about Julianna. Eve can sneer at his beginnings; she can scoff at him not knowing a Caravaggio from a Ruebens, but she can't deride his heart. 'You're with her, aren't you?' He'll be walking along the street and she'll pull on his arm. 'It's Ju-ju you're thinking of, isn't it?' Nine times out of ten she's right, and if it's not Julianna he's remembering, then it's Matty.

Every day when writing to Nan he asks of the boy knowing that if he is well so is Julianna. That child occupies such mental space he might be here right now sitting on the wash-stand. It's this place! It's Italy. Here among the dusty magic imagination runs mad. Luke told Eve of his father but didn't tell of his visit to Italy last year and how he learned he has family in Madonna de Campiglio. These days his soul is a weather vane caught between the past and the future. He will return to England but doubts he will stay. He is for the mountains and silence, and God be willing, Matty and Julianna with him.

* * *

The evening went surprisingly well despite Eve's need to spoil it. A harvest moon low in the sky and lanterns hanging from trees, the party dined al fresco, food brought from the kitchens to tables on carpeted grass. Musicians played, couples danced on the Long Terrace, light flashing on jewelled masks. It is not so much a Masked Ball as a picnic, the Villa Borghese filled with magnificent works of art but rundown and stinking of mould.

Luke sat unmasked, his mind a thousand miles away.

Robert Scholtz smiled. 'Mr Roberts, sir, I believe I know what you are thinking. A fine building with fine things but not exactly home sweet home.'

'Can such a place be thought of as home?'

'Perhaps to a Papal Lord but not to me,' said Robert. 'This place needs constant managing and without the money and time to do it will fall into ruin. I'll make you a bet. This time next year the Italian government will have bought the family out. It's the only way the Villa can survive.'

Robert Scholtz owns an art gallery in New York. A businessman, his gaze is everywhere assessing and evaluating. His wife too knows to a cent the best rate of exchange. Scholtz is the man behind the Imperial Hotels that decorate the East Coast of America. For the last three years he's been in England looking to buy, and for the last two years has sought Luke's advice.

'You know, a man of your talent and integrity would do fine in Boston. You'd have so much work you'd be able to buy this mouldering heap and with change.' Robert tapped his cigar. 'These days I'm hard pressed to find men worthy of hire especially in the need for urgent action. Come home with me and Mamie! I could do much for you.'

'You already have. It was you put the Harrogate place my way.'

'I was happy to do so. I saw what you did in Derbyshire. Talk about a Phoenix from the ashes! You turned a ruin into a home and you saved my pal, Bernie, a lot of trouble from his ulcer. I hear you're into electricity?'

'I'm paying apprentices to learn the trade but that's where it ends. I don't need another string to my bow. I've too many as it is.'

'Sensible! A man should be master of one talent and not play with many. But remember what I said. I'd be happy to put business your way.'

It's sad. Every day Eve seeks to undermine Luke and to make him look foolish and yet she can't undo the good already done. He has confidence in his life choices. Three years of travelling and meeting with men like Robert Scholtz, knowledge rubs off and polish is acquired whether one wants it or not.

Luke is in debt to Eve. Whatever their personal regard for one another she opened up the world for him especially where business is concerned. A master-builder, he was doing alright, yet the name Carrington opened doors, and Luke working with beautiful houses for people with open minds and generous purses, that connection alone creates an obligation he cannot ignore.

Robert Scholtz leaned closer. 'Talking of Harrogate and hotels, I believe we have a mutual acquaintance in Mrs Julianna Dryden.'

Luke skin prickled. 'I am acquainted with the lady.'

'Did you know she is opening another of her coffee shops in Cambridge?'

'I heard it said.'

'Me and Mrs Scholtz have taken tea in the Norfolk place and liked it real fine. Didn't we Mamie?'

Mrs Scholtz nodded. 'We did.'

Luke shifted in his chair. 'I believe it is popular.'

'Popular? The phone was ringing off the hook! A pretty place with good china and linen, we saw things that day we liked. The name, for instance, the Nannies? Cute and clever, it makes a man feel cosy and warm. You'd buy anything just to sit and be comforted. Anyway, me and Mamie got to thinking and decided Mrs Dryden's Tea-Shops would suit us fine.'

'How do you mean?'

'We're thinking to have a tea-room in our hotel lobbies and would like her for sponsor. I meant to contact her last time we were in London but we were busy and she was tied up with the Royals.'

Mamie Scholtz leaned forward. 'We met a while back, sharing a box at the Garden. A pretty woman, such eyes and manner! No wonder the Prince of Wales is taken with her. We wanted to make more of the acquaintance back then but Freddie C was being silly at the time and it put her off.'

Robert Scholtz nodded. 'Still, that was then. Time has moved on and we mean to bring Mrs Dryden, and you, to the East Coast.'

'I think Mrs Dryden has a partner to consider.'

'You mean Doctor Adelman? We met him that night, a fateful meeting as it turned out. I shall give him, and the beautiful Julianna much thought.'

'Ooh!' Face flushed and wig askew, Eve dropped into a seat beside Luke. 'If I don't sit down I shall fall down.'

'My word, Evie,' Mamie Scholtz passed a fan. 'You're looking rather warm.'

'It is too warm for October and I'm too old for polkas. What were you discussing? Did my ears deceive me or were talking of Ju-ju Dryden?'

Luke considered slapping a hand over Robert's mouth but held off. Eve laying fuses all week, sooner or later a bomb is bound to go off.

'We were talking of installing coffee shops in the Scholtz Hotels.'

'You mean soda-fountains?'

'Heavens no! English Tea-Shops like those of your friend Mrs Dryden.'

'The Nannies? Capital idea! They'd go down awfully well in Boston.'

'That's what I was saying to Mr Roberts,' said Mamie.

Evie patted a hanky about her face. 'And did Mr Roberts agree?'

'He thinks it's a humdinger. Next time I'm in the old country I'm popping along to see that little lady, and while I'm about it I shall lean on our friend here to come to Boston to work his magic. What say you, Luke, shall I start leaning?'

Conversation passed back and forth across the table, the subject matter, English Tea-Shops on American soil. Eve was witty and joked of toasted crumpets and cucumber sandwiches. Everyone laughed. Then Freddie arrived with friends and the subject matter changed to who could balance a champagne glass on his nose and quote the Gettysburg Address without spilling a drop. Luke watched all and said nothing. Sooner or later the storm will break. It did break and a crystal water-jug with it.

* * *

Early morning he sits on the terrace writing to Nan. Eve hasn't slept and neither has he. Naked but for cotton-shift and coral necklace she's wandered the Villa these last three hours. At last she sleeps. If a maid enquires Luke sends her away. '*No grazie, signora! Diamo madam dormire*!'

At least asleep she is quiet. Eve and her problems! Migraine headaches and such he can tolerate. It's the mental stuff he finds hard. When she's low or had too much to drink madness takes over where she needs to humiliate or be humiliated. She throws things and punches and kicks. Usually he is on the end of her fist except he's not Luke to her then. He is a slave to be abused.

Such anger usually ends in her need for sex. 'Harder you useless creature!' she'll shriek. 'It's not working!' She wants to be raped and tossed aside. Every man has a darker self that given the lead will rise up with clenched fist; Luke is not prepared to meet that self, not for Eve Carrington or anyone else.

A lacklustre affair all flesh and no heart, they had sex. Then she spoke of Julianna. 'Your teeth are not so sharp tonight, Mister Wolf. Why don't you think of me as Little Red Riding Hood? I'm sure that will fire the engines.'

Angry, he told her to shut up, that he didn't want to hear such stuff. She laughed. 'Of course you do, you just need persuading.' That's when she bit him, her teeth grazing his flesh. 'I know you think of her.' She followed on her hands and knees across the bed. 'Inside or out, it's her all the time so you might as well have my sanction. Here!' She'd ripped the shift from her breasts. 'I make you a present. Call me your darling Ju-ju! Kiss my lips and sip my honey! Then we might both get the pleasure we yearn for.'

It was too much. 'I could never think of you as Julianna Dryden. In fact, when I'm with you I try not to think of her at all. Feeling as I do, utter disgust for me, and for you, why would I want her here?'

That's when she bit him, leaping on his back sinking her teeth into his flesh. 'Good God!' He came close to striking her. 'Is this what you call love?'

Eyes shadowed, she'd grinned. 'Why? Are you saying you love me?'

'I could never love you! But neither when I am with you can I love anyone else! You, or rather I, have made that impossible.'

Away she went, waltzing about the room, the coral necklace looped about her breasts and blood on her lips. He went to the bathroom to bathe his shoulder only for the door to be flung open and a water jug hurled at the mirror. 'Don't you dare shut the door on me!' She ran at him through broken glass, her feet cut and blood spraying. 'You're no companion or friend, Luke Roberts! You're here to be of service and don't you forget it!'

Now she sleeps. She'll wake and remembering what has passed beg Mister Wolf to stay. Luke Roberts, servant and hireling will stay, but she needn't bother begging the Wolf. The Wolf was never here.

CHAPTER NINETEEN

Warm but Unwilling

'What are you doing, Mother?'

Caught listening in on the shared line, Callie slammed down the phone. 'You are going to have to do something about this phone, Daniel,' she said, cheeks burning. 'I can't be doing with shared lines disturbing the whole house.'

Daniel picked up the *Times*. 'I'll get onto the engineer.'

'Yes do! I wouldn't mind if the calls were for me. They're not. They're for Anna and her precious tea-shop. "Can we have a table for four for Friday, and a party of eight for Saturday, and could Mrs Whosis hire the amusing piano man who played for Tommy on his birthday?" It's enough to drive a body crazy.'

Daniel sighed. 'Have you thought any more about seeing that doctor?'

'No and I'm not going to. He'll only tell me what I already know.'

'And what is that?'

'That I'm a pain in the posterior and that I have heart disease. For my heart I have the best cardiologist in Professor Adelman. As for the other thing, I know I'm a pain and don't need some two-bit horse-doctor reminding me.'

'Then why this weeping? Dulce says you're all the time moping.'

'Well she's no right! My tears are my business. It's the phone calls getting to me. And this darned weather! I'm so cold.'

'Then move to a climate that suits. Go live in France with Mary Singer Sargent. She's always asking after you. You don't have to be cold or miserable.'

Callie frowned. 'Are you trying to be rid of me, Daniel Masson? Is that what this is about, me moving out and you moving in with Julianna?'

'I want to be with her but not here.'

'I can't see her going to California. She's loves this country.'

'She can learn to love another.'

'I doubt it. It's not about a house or even a name. It's about heritage. And what of her family? I'm sure her sister wouldn't want her to go.'

'I thought she had two sisters, farmer's wives.'

Callie stared. 'Farmer's wives?'

It was Daniel's turn to stare. 'Who are we talking about? What woman and what sister?' Furious, he rattled the newspaper. 'This isn't about Julianna and her sisters. This is you obsessing on the Newman woman and *her* sister.'

'Not at all!' Callie spluttered. 'It's about Julianna Dryden and her rise to fame. You know she's setting up another place in Cambridge?'

'Yes, a spot close by the University. A smart business move, I thought.'

'It's not good for Matty. He needs a mother not a female Joseph Lyons.'

'He has a mother, and don't underestimate Matthew Dryden! He might be little but he's strong and with a mind of his own.'

'And him not wanting you for a pa is why you're still dancing attendance. Not that it matters. You've more obstacles to overcome than a fractious child.'

Callie is driving him nuts. He's trying to pack ready for Port Elizabeth and Boer prison camps. He needs time to prepare but all he hears is a whining band-saw. Dulce is worried. 'Your momma has unfinished business here.'

'And what am I supposed to do about that?'

'You can get rid of the shared line. She's driving herself crazy listening in on Mizz Dryden's calls and when she's not doing that she's writing letters.'

'To whom?'

'Ghosts! All day scribbling away, I say, you want me to post those? She says when I'm ready. The folks she writes to are dust in the ground. Then there's the telescope. I almost took an axe to it the other day.'

'What stopped you?'

'God stopped me. He said she's to figure it out. Your momma made an idol of Justine Newman. Then she learned not only did her Madonna have earthen feet she had hot blood and wasn't above sharing heat with your momma's affianced. *Elle était une Madonna mauvais! Une Verge noir!*'

Riddles and omens, Dulce talks like this all the time. To Daniel the situation is straightforward - Callie is getting senile. He takes her hand. 'I'm not trying to get rid of you. You're my mother and I love you.' Callie isn't listening. She's gazing down the Rise. 'I'm like Queen Victoria, I've overstayed my welcome. So cruel, why don't you take a gun and put us both out of our misery.'

'You think I'm cruel?'

'Not cruel. If you were you'd be less hogtied. You think you

253

have a relationship with Anna Dryden. You have lease-lend with half of London Society.'

* * *

Daniel thought on his mother's words. If he is hogtied it is by Julianna's willingness to give affection while retaining her heart, Stefan Adelman a case in point. Then there's the Prince of Wales. Of late her popularity with the Prince ever constant, gossip acquires a barbed edge. 'A tease, warm but unwilling,' was said of her last week at Sandringham, Daniel attending as her partner.

This thing with Bertie won't last. The Queen hangs by a thread and those close to the throne ready to repel boarders. It's likely in the push for space Julianna will be swept aside, then again Bertie may hold fast and she a Person of Note. The likely-hood of that was seen last week when Julianna, glorious in old gold and with pearls in her hair, entered the ballroom, the crowd parting to let them through and everywhere along the line locks applied to knees, a curtsey the natural inclination of those with an eye to the future.

The Prince was smiling, 'Mrs Dryden. So happy to see you.' To Daniel he extended a hand. 'And you, Greville Masson, always a pleasure.' So presented they took their place among the Marlborough Set. Then began the game of *Pass the Parcel* - the manoeuvring of a preferred beauty close to the prince. Soon, Julianna was side-by-side with Alice Keppel, the current *maitresse en titre*, and Daniel with Daisy, Cousin Francis's wife, the inspiration behind the song, '*Daisy, Daisy!*'

Daisy Greville Warwick is a thorn in the family paw. Callie

can't abide her. 'Francis married down. She'll bring us all to ruin.' Noisy, embroiled in many affairs and not afraid to tell, she's known in London as the Babbling Brooke.

At the ball she hung on his arm, Daniel dodging the Ostrich plumes in her hair and impertinent questions. 'Why aren't you and Julianna wed?' she said. 'Are you refused, or is she as with Bertie, warm but unwilling?'

Callie sighed. 'They say she won't dine alone with him. A cook at Sandringham says she doesn't toe the line, picky about invitations and refusing shooting parties. I'm with her on that. I hated being with your father when he was in the mood to shoot at deer and not me.'

Daniel doesn't ask questions of Julianna. The only right he has is to love. It was chilly Friday evening on the way back from Sandringham. He leant to pull the hood about her face. Then he kissed her. Hands flat against his chest, she at first resisted, but the kiss deepening she relaxed against the cushion, soft and compliant, her body an offering. Lashes lowered, she waited to see what he would do. Ardour retreating before pride, and with the thought, all or nothing, he did nothing.

* * *

Stefan is unwell. He's spent the better part of the year travelling to Osborne House, the journey, and a worsening situation with Karoline, taking the toll.

Julianna rang to see how he is. The phone was picked up. 'Hello?'

'Is this Doctor Adelman's residence?'

'I'm afraid he's busy. Can I take a message?'

'Thank you. Would you tell him Julianna Dryden will be making the trip to Bradbury next Tuesday as planned and would he meet me at the station?'

'Alright, ducks, I'll pass the message on.'

Julia replaced the phone wondering if she's awake. Three nights in a row she dreamt she phoned Stefan and a woman with a melodious voice answered: 'I'm afraid the Professor is busy. May I take a message?'

Now Stefan's cockney charlady breaks the dream.

The phone rang. 'Sorry, my dear,' Stefan panted. 'I was otherwise engaged.'

'Not to worry. I rang to say I'll be with you Tuesday.'

'Excellent. I shall see you, as my charlady would say, with boots blacked.'

'That was your charlady who took the call.'

'It was, my Peggy Carstairs.'

'And does your Peggy take good care of you?'

'She does. I am a fortunate fellow.'

* * *

Nan is here discussing bookings. It wasn't long before the topic turned to Matty. 'Your boy needs a strong hand.'

'You have a particular hand in mind?'

'Nay, not me! I'm as inquisitive as the next but not so foolish as to dip my oar in choppy waters. All this society gadding-about I'm sure you've plenty suitors. Is it true you're to dine at Sandringham again this evening?'

'I believe so. '

'Is Prince Albert a nice man? Does he treat you as he should?'

'I thought you said you didn't dip your oar in choppy waters?'

'Is the water choppy then, Anna?'

'It is certainly deeper and more dangerous than I ever imagined, yet I believe I am learning to paddle my own canoe with a certain amount of dexterity. Talking of deep waters, I saw Luke yesterday back from Italy.'

The smile fled from Nan's face. In drawing attention away from her secrets Julia had highlighted another's. 'Oh don't talk to me of Luke! That woman! If I'd have known what her coming to Bakers would lead to I'd have barred the door. It's not enough he follows her to London, she tries comin' here.'

'Why does Lady Carrington want to come do you suppose?'

'Probably to tighten her grasp on my deluded son, telling him how happy he'd be if he were to leave here permanently. It's my just deserts! I should've let him have the woman he wanted. I should've let him have you.'

That evening Julia pondered Nan's remark. Not so long ago a door was slammed in her face, now she's considered the lesser of two evils for Luke.

Nan says he's changed. Electric body, brooding eyes and mass of dark hair, from what Julia has seen the essential man looks the same. Last week she was at the theatre watching Mrs Patrick Campbell in the *Second Mrs Tanqueray*. Evie and Luke shared a box, Luke handsome in a midnight blue tail-coat, his waistcoat embroidered in a similar blue. There was much whispering behind fans, Luke likened to a new motoring car - '*plenty poke under the bonnet but in need of polish.*' Time will move on and gossip will wane, as, no doubt, in the case of Julia and the Prince of Wales.

Nan asks what kind of a man he is. Julia sees him as the insignia on his chest that, if gently pressed, allow a good man to appear with genuine acts of kindness. If the medals are mishandled, and good manners and protocol so meaningful to him not observed, then a bully appears - witness Marlborough House last year between Acts of The Mikado. 'Why deny me your company, Ju-ju?' he'd grasped her elbow. 'Am I not worthy of attention?'

'You are, Sir.'

'And what of love? Am I not worthy of that?'

'Every man is entitled to love.'

His answer was half humour and halt intent. 'I suspect you, dear Ju-ju, of withholding treasure in the way of a certain Lady would persist in forestalling an illustrious forbear of mine, an infamous forbear, I might add, known for the swift dispatching of errant wives.'

'If you're speaking of English History, Sir, then your description offers ample choice. But if the lady you refer to is the unfortunate Anne Boleyn, let me assure you, emulating her fate was never an ambition of mine.'

'I'm glad to hear it.' He'd leaned close, his breath smoky. 'As you say, every man is worthy of love. Kings too are worthy and must not be coerced into offering of a reward for that which should be freely given.'

Angry, she kept her distance and for weeks when invited cited illness or prior engagement. The prince regretted the incident, saying he had toothache at the time and his comments an attempt at humour. Julia stayed away until Hugh Fitzwilliam arrived at the cottage bearing the rubies she'll wear tonight.

'A pretty little coronet goes with that, Ju-ju,' Bertie suggested some weeks later. 'I would've sent it but thought the gesture excessive.'

Julia thought it all excessive and said so. 'I can't accept this,' she told Hugh. 'He insulted me and I'll not wear it.' Hugh laughed. 'You can't give 'em back. That would be tantamount to treason. My advice, Anna, is to see beyond the outer crust to the soft underbelly. That way you will both benefit.'

Last April an attempt was made on Bertie's life, he and Princess Alexandra shot at aboard a train to Brussels. The death of his brother Alfred scored another wound. Bertie was heartbroken. 'Affie will be remembered as a man who did something. I shall be remembered as the prince who did nothing.'

The day he said that, sun turning the velvet curtains ruby-red and he aging and bewildered, it was easy to kiss his sorrow away. That the kiss should lead to closer intimacy was not the intention. Bertie didn't press. To say they are friends would not be true, others having a greater claim. He writes letters to 'My Dearest Ju-ju,' nothing indiscreet, more the chronicles of a complex man. They don't always agree. Julia's refusal to attend the last Glorious Twelfth brought a public dressing down, '*if the patronage of the Prince of Wales is of so little consequence we suggest, Madam, you return to your tea-room.*'

* * *

Matty brought the name Nanny: the N an N clumsy on his tongue it became the Nanny, staff and patrons taking it up. The tea-shop doing so well Julia had August Simpkin draw up a deed of partnership and Mrs Mac, more family than employee, a third share. This morning Abigail Simpkin called to book next Christmas for the Good Wives annual luncheon *and* a date for their daughter's wedding. Julia offered a wedding cake as a gift to the bride. Abigail told her friends. By mid afternoon a trend had developed, the phone ringing for similar occasions. 'I hope you can make wedding cakes, Maud,' said Julia, 'I've committed you to more than a few.' Maud was in tears. 'As a partner I'm only too happy to see it. I just wish my mother could've seen it too.'

* * *

There is a musical soiree this evening at Long Melford Hall. Hugh Fitzwilliam is elegant and droll and not above poking fun at himself. An avowed homosexual, he offers to be her escort in hope of a glimpse of 'Delicious Daniel.' He gazed toward Greenfields. 'All the lights are out.'

'The Greville Massons are away.'

'And yet again I am on the outside looking in.'

Dorothy helped Julia with her cape. 'Hello, Dottie,' says Hugh. 'You're looking very bright-eyed and bushy tailed. Is it safe to leave you alone or have you some young chap hiding behind the wall ready with a bunch of mistletoe?'

Dorothy giggled. 'Ooh no sir.'

'What no one? Dearie me, what is the world coming to?'

Julia climbed into the carriage. Hugh bundled her train in behind and rapped on the roof. 'Drive on, my good man, but take your time. We're mixing with the riffraff this evening. No one there worthy of gaining more chilblains.'

The carriage pulled out the drive, a row of faces at the window, Matty smiling and blowing kisses to Hugh. 'That's a gorgeous little lad, Julianna.'

'I know. I do adore him.'

'And do you adore your Colonial neighbour?'

'I like Daniel.'

Hugh sighed. 'I've adored many a chap.'

'And never that one special person?'

'My dear, there have been hundreds of special people but never beyond a fumble. I can't let it beyond a fumble, not if I want to keep my job and my prize marrows. It's an odd world. A man can be all kinds of swine, he can lie and steal and beat his children, but he can't love another man.'

'Dear Hugh.'

'I'm alright, Anna. I manage my tied-cottage and my cats and my dowager's hump. I keep my garden. I go to Matins on Sunday and confess my non-existent sins. I take a warm brick to bed and tell myself I'm too old to care.'

'Daniel and I are friends.'

'Lord, how awful!'

'Why is it awful? Can't a woman be friends with a man?'

'Of course she can! I have masses of women friends and that - according to the Marquis of Queensbury – is because I am a sinful sodomite and harmless to women. Talking of sodomites, as we are at this moment, how come you, a vicar's daughter, are so *laissez-faire* about me and my delights?'

'That'll be father and ducks on the pond at Bentham.'

Hugh blinked. 'The ducks on the pond?'

'When I was girl we had lots of drakes as well as ducks and

all happy to share. Father said the Lord God liked variety.'

Hugh hooted. 'You're pulling my leg.'

'My sisters are farmers' wives. I was often there as a girl and saw that animals don't always follow rules as laid down by Adam and Eve.'

'Mrs Dryden, you are a puzzle and a chameleon. Just when I think I know who you are you slip into another colour.'

'You do know me, but getting back to Daniel, why can't we be friends?'

'Because you can't be and look as you do like Venus rising from the waves. Any man would see it as a waste, especially that man. We're talking of one who squares his shoulders and strides from the crotch, who exudes passion and warm beer, and who turns his bewitching eyes on the world and the world weeps. Oh!' Hugh shuddered. 'I could do much for a man like that.'

'It's as well Daniel can't hear.'

'He wouldn't care. He's a Yankee and a modern man. And who says I'm talking of Daniel? I might have another in mind. And don't say who or I'll think gossip right and you Tennyson's *Maud*, "*icily regular and splendidly null.*" '

'Any one gossip in particular?'

'Oh, you've several hatchet wielders, not least my Goddaughter, Eve Carrington. She's not above lobbing the odd dagger.'

'And her brother, does he also lob a dagger?'

'I should say not! The dear boy doesn't know how.'

'He did rather a wonderful portrait of me and then destroyed it.'

'Freddie destroys everything that means anything. With both of those unhappy children it's a case of those whom the Gods love they first maltreat! Evie is clever at a time when it's not good for women to be clever. Freddie is beautiful and so the ugly tear him apart. But let's not be miserable!' Hugh clapped his hands. 'This will make you smile. It is said you are a saintly icon to be sighed over while humping a Lady of the Bedchamber, and though saintly, not averse to giving Bertie a thrill but always at a distance *and* wearing gloves.'

'That is so silly!'

'I know but you have to laugh or you'd go crazy. And so back to our dark-eyed Adonis, you really don't know to whom I refer?'

'How can I know when according to you I am splendidly null?'

'Touché, my dear, but it won't do. You know as does everyone in Society that Evie's gypsy lover only has eyes for Ju-ju Dryden.'

'Oh don't call me that! I hate the name and the association.'

Hugh patted her arm. 'Now, now, my dear, don't get upset.'

'I can't help it. I am changed and it hurts.'

'It happens when one is near a fire. I've been where you are. Sooner or later you understand you have to make a choice, this feeble glow, the reflection of Princes, or a real love.'

* * *

Freddie sank down beside Julia. 'Evening, Ju-ju.'

'Hello, Freddie.'

'My God-Pa not with you?'

'No, he's away teasing another poor soulouse.. How are you?'

He rolled his shoulders. 'I'm managing.'

'Are you really managing, Freddie?'

'Oh don't you start!' he said wearily. 'I've enough dealin' with others. 'I am fine, just rushin' to finish my showin'.'

'Ah yes, the painting. I'm told it's good. I won't say clever.'

'Ah yes.' He grinned ruefully. 'I do regret spoiling the *White Lady*.'

'Are you happy with your new work?'

'I am but the National won't hang it. A man has to be dead a thousand years and his subject with dimpled thighs before they consider him. I don't put my brush to anything ugly and the subject in question can only be divine.'

'I heard you were in Italy.'

'We were.' He yawned. 'I sat in the sunlight drinking ver' good wine painting ver' bad pics, Evie did the same but with amorous overtones.' Amorous overtones! Julia closed her eyes but couldn't stop the visions his words conjured. 'Does sunshine bring out the lover?' He gnawed the handle of his cane. 'I'm an affectionate sort of fellow, don't you know. Evie's a clutching sort. In Rome she overstepped the boundaries. It's him bringing out the beast in people, though a one-sided beast as her things so often are. And behold! Even as we speak they appear, Romeo and his aging Juliet!'

Evie and Luke stood in the doorway. Freddie grinned. 'He don't look especially pleased to be here. Poor fellow, if he could cut and run he would but good country manners and bad sultry nights prevent him.'

The company seated, Adelina Patti began to sing an aria from Bizet's *Carmen*. Freddie sank into his chair. 'I know this aria,' he said, 'it's about people takin' what ain't there's to take. Evie's always takin' my things. She did it at Cambridge, took fellows out to lunch. She did it with Johnny. She tried to do it with Danny Masson. And she did it with Susan. I was fond of Susan. We had plans.' He looked up. 'Are you comin' to the séance? I tried for the first sittin' but could only get in the second.'

Julia thought of Egypt and starlight flickering over an empty tomb. 'You believe in that, do you?'

'I'm not sure I believe in anythin' but I'm willin' to give it a go. Wouldn't you like to hear from a loved one?'

Her smile was bitter. 'Not if it's Tennyson quoting his wretched *Maud.* I'd sooner that particular lady rest in peace forever.'

Freddie frowned. 'You're changed. You're nasty now, sharp as glass.'

'I don't mean to be. It's this world. Things simply don't seem to work out. Is there someone you'd like to hear from?'

He was silent and then nodded. 'Yes, then I might get some rest.'

Evie, her gown swirling, arrived with a rush. 'So, there you are, Ju-ju!' she cried. 'I've been looking for you everywhere.'

'She has been here,' said Hugh.

Evie bared her teeth. 'Yes, and as usual the centre of an adoring crush. May I steal her from you, Dear Godfather? She is wanted in the Blue Room.'

'Does Julianna want to be wanted?'

'I don't know but she must come.' Evie took Julia's arm - Julia rising as though on the end of a piece of elastic. 'A message has come through. She's to come to the table or Madame can't conjure the right spirits.'

Hugh scoffed. 'Such nonsense!'

'It may be, as you say, nonsense, yet she is required. And she will be among friends! There's Freddie, and Luke Roberts, who I'm sure she remembers. There's Mrs Langtry, the Jersey Lily!' Evie smiled. 'Julianna will like Mrs Langtry, a consummate actress, they have much in common.'

CHAPTER TWENTY

Séance

Madame Leonora gestured. 'And you, Senor Roberts, the chair in which you are seated is known as the North Gate or the Gate of Denial.'

Luke stretched his back. He's been sitting too long. 'And what am I denying?'

'You have bright energy, sir. It will repel negative energy.'

'Negative energy?' Lily Langtry frowned. 'Is such a thing likely to bother us?'

'Mrs Langtry, you are as safe as the need that brought you. We draw to ourselves a mirror image - like attracting like.'

Freddie grimaced. 'I'm not sure I like the sound of that. I'm an awful fellow, and if what you say is true can only draw to myself more awfulness.'

There was laughter about the table, Freddie laughed too but his eyes were empty. 'Truly,' he protested. 'I am a lame creature and beg my friend Luke to sharpen his claws. I'm at the National tomorrow before the hangin' committee. If I am to go to Hell I'd sooner it be *after* they agree to show my work.'

Madame Leonora smiled. 'I am sure Senor Roberts will stand fast. We must all stand fast. If among you there is one who would fail, it's best they leave now. Once the circle is made we must try not to break it. One does not invite friends to the dinner table only to eject them mid meal. Let us extend the same courtesy to those we call to our table.'

Luke sighed. Eve and her obsessions! Three hours they've been at this place and she a fevered creature talking. Now there's this: sitting with strangers to converse with ghosts. She invited him to accompany her, a rarity given that despite an avowed need of him they rarely attend public events together.

In Italy where nobody cares he can go anywhere, in England his role is of a servant passing Milady's fan. It's about acceptability and the line society draws between tolerance and outright scorn. Milady observes the line yet tonight pressed him to come. She said it would be fun. A conversation overheard between her and Stefan Adelman's housekeeper suggests otherwise.

Sunday it was, unshaven chin and eyes heavy from too much wine, Luke lay abed observing his reflection in the ceiling mirror. That's when he heard her on the telephone, the name Adelman leaping out. 'Thank you for the letter,' she was saying. 'I was concerned for Doctor Adelman and his wife. Poor woman, locked away in an asylum. How does she bear it?'

It seems she'd written to the housekeeper enquiring of Julianna. 'So Mrs Dryden stays overnight? Many hearing of this, and the doctor's wife incapacitated, would take it ill, but not you and I, Mrs Carstairs. We know that in times like this we need our friends...No! No one else shall know. The moment I put down the phone I'll destroy your letter.'

Seeing Luke at the door Eve dropped the phone. He asked what she was doing, she said offering help. He didn't believe her. 'If you're planning on harming Julianna Dryden and her friends you'll not see me again.'

Enraged, she'd snapped her teeth and tearing the letter strip-by- strip tossed the pieces into the air. Her robe followed, peach silk settling on the floor amid tattered threats, Luke's resistance scuffing the floor - lime-wood, a good base when stained and polished - malleable much like his will.

* * *

Madame Leonora opened the séance with a seating plan. 'Mrs Langtry sits south. The Honourable Freddie occupies the West Door in place of the setting sun. Lady Carrington the East and rebirth and Senor Roberts the North Gate, the rest of the group seated accordingly about these four gateways.'

A prayer was said, the letters of the alphabet spread clockwise about the table, and a glass tumbler upended in the middle.

A man laughed. 'A tooth mug and a child's ABC?'

'I had in mind bells and priestly vestments,' said Lily Langtry.

'Or one of those Ouija Boards,' said Freddie.

Madame said Ouija boards were prey to waif and strays, a glass was steadier, 'place a finger on top and go where it takes you.' They did as she bid. It wasn't long before the glass began to move in lazy circles.

Freddie was agitated. 'Surely it's us moving it?'

'It is you and yet not.' Madame sat with her hands in her lap. 'Think of it as vital energy, an engine in need of cranking or a telephone in need of a line.'

After a slow start the tumbler began rushing about the table, Evie calling out letters and a woman sitting aside copying them down. The first communication was for Mrs Langtry regarding a Cartier necklace previously thought stolen. The glass told her to telephone her maid, to *look in the stuffed bear's head, the head due to be shipped out the following day.'*

There followed a pause, the glass idling while a manservant made a call. The servant returned and whispered in Mrs Langtry's ear, the necklace was found. The glass said it was '*Kismet's fault,'* a pet monkey, had hidden the necklace in the bear's head. The tone of the evening set, there was much anticipation. A second message was for a nervous lady on Evie's left. She was not to worry about '*Dear George of the Sussex Regiment. He felt no pain when killed at Khartoum and is now reunited with Barbara and Little Basil.'*

Other messages followed, some accepted with joy others with tears. The glass came to a halt. Madame Leonora ordered the table to be cleared, the sitters then to lay their hands on the table little fingers connected to little finger.

That was half an hour ago, the candles burn lower, light recedes and Madame, chin on chest, appears to be sleeping.

Julia dares not move. Luke was on her immediate right, finger aligned with hers. Such a feeling; the need to pull away so strong her arms quivered.

The seating plan is meant, the printed cards on the chairs in Evie's hand, who now fixes Julia with basilisk gaze. Minutes tick by. People are nervous and sit joined together like shiny conkers on a string awaiting the first blow. Outside the soiree continues; a piano begins to play and Adelina to sing an aria from Madame Butterfly, Cho-Cho-San telling of the day Lieutenant Pinkerton will return to Japan, passionate words mingling with smoke from the candles.

'*One fine day we'll notice a thread of smoke arising on the sea in the far horizon, and then a ship appearing. The trim white vessel glides into the harbour…He is coming! I know. He will return*!'

All is shadows and Luke's face a pale blur. His finger creeps over hers and happiness fills her heart. Madame Leonora begins to speak in a voice recognised as from a dream and happiness dies.

'*I'm afraid the Professor is busy. May I take a message?*'

'Oh!' Julia's first instinct was to fly but Luke's finger bade her stay.

It came again. '*The Professor is busy. May I take a message?*'

Evie took charge. 'Bright Spirit? Do you have a message for us?'

There was a hushed pause, every heart beating madly. When the voice spoke again it was Luke that would bolt and Julia holding him steady.

'*Your mother saw in pounds and pence, it's how she was bred. Your Papa in sunshine and sin and that in his stead. Take of your mother's kin but only as you need. The rest seek of your homeland, my son, and be content indeed.*'

'Dear God!' Luke was shaken to the core. The verse had been changed, two words inserted, and a message given years ago subtly altered. He hadn't bargained for this and came this evening certain of fraud and assuming earlier messages prearranged. Now his world is turned upside down. He got this message as a lad. None knew of it then and none since. Only Justine Newman knew, and if this is to be believed she is the angelic messenger.

Julia gentled Luke's finger. She had no idea of the message yet knew it was for him. Then Madame spoke again. '*I'm afraid the Professor is busy. May I take a message?*' Again Evie took up the lead. 'We have no message to give you as yet. Do you have such for a member of our party?'

This time there was a longer silence and then the voice, the same musical voice, spoke. '.... *ich muss gehen! Dieses Leben ist mir...!*'

Freddie, hoarse and fearful, broke in. 'What is it German now? Are we to have Chinese and hear from Confucius?'

'Be quiet, Freddie!' snapped Evie. 'Bright Spirit continue.' The voice started up, repeating Karoline Adelman's plea for release. *'Dieses Leben ist mir und den Mieinen zu toten. Hilf mir, nehmen Sie diese Last von mir, und ich werde dich fur immer segnen... immer segnen.'*

The voice trailed away. All was silent. Then Evie spoke.

'Come on! This is meant for someone at this table!'

'I think it may be for me,' said Julia.

'And who is communicating?'

'I can't say.'

'Why can't you?'

'It's a private matter.'

'Someone must respond! ' said Lily Langtry. 'If my understanding of German is correct the communicator begs release from hell!'

Evie leaned forward. 'When did this soul pass over?'

Julianna shook her head. 'To my knowledge the person is still alive.'

'Still alive!' There was a buzz about the table. With no notion of what to do Julia could only sit. This is Karoline's pain and cannot be laid open to strangers.

The voice spoke again softly pleading. *'Julianna, wenden Sie sich bitte am Dienstag kommen! Kommen Sie, bringen Sie ihre Freundlich un Warme, und dann konnen wir uns endlisch verabschieden.'*

Evie was furious. 'Well?'

'I'm sorry. I have no real idea what is being said.'

'I know,' said Lily Langtry. 'You are asked to go on Tuesday, to say goodbye, and to bring kindness and warmth with you. This is clearly an important issue; perhaps one day you'll let me know the outcome.'

'If I can I surely will.'

'Is that it?' Eve glared. 'Can we move on now or is this a private séance, Julianna Dryden and the whole of the Spiritual Realm?'

'I'm sorry. I had no idea this would happen.'

'Why would you?' said Luke. 'Can any sane person know what goes on with these things?'

It was cold, the air and breath about the table white mist. Eyes glittering in the candlelight, Madame Leonora sat upright. 'Hush!' hissed Evie. 'Someone is coming.' A voice whispered like the soft susurration of waves on a shore. Slowly the sound clarified to be that of a child singing.

'*Where oh where has my little dog gone, Oh where oh where can he be, with his ears cut short and his tail cut long, Oh where, Oh where is he?*'

One-by-one candles flickered and went out, the room in darkness but for a single candlestick. A child sang and was accompanied by the swishing sound of Madame Leonora brushing her hand back and forth along the table.

'What is that noise?'

'It's Madame's arm!'

'That's only the movement! If you listen there's a sound beyond it.'

'I don't want to listen,' a woman protested.

'It sounds like a fan waving,' said Evie.

'That's not it,' said Luke, his finger tight about Julia's.

'What is it then?' she whispered.

'A dog's tail wagging.'

Julia knew the song. It was Susan's song. She said her lover used to sing it to her and he would..! 'Play the paper and comb,' whispered Freddie.

'Oh, Freddie, no!' The words burst from Julia's lips.

Freddie nodded. 'Jimmy Button, the Pater's groom, showed me how. He could get a good tune out of it, a real Scotch jig.'

'Be quiet, Freddie!' Evie was on her feet. 'We don't want to hear this! This is hardly the time or place to talk of childish fancies.'

'Yes it is,' he said wearily. 'What better time to talk of dogs without tails than in the darkness with Bella listening. I know this song. It's familiar to me as a lullaby. I hear it every night when I lay down to sleep.'

Julia closed her eyes. She knew now what Susan had known and kept secret even to the grave. 'Oh poor Susan!'

'I know and I'm awful sorry,' Freddie sighed. 'I wanted to tell you.'

A man coughed. 'I don't know what this is about and no wish to enquire. I think the whole thing in bad taste. We should break the circle.'

'No!' Freddie reared up. 'I beg you! I have been waiting for this! Madame Leonora!' he cried. 'Don't let them break the circle! I need to speak to Bella. I need to know if my little boy and his mother are at peace!'

Evie let her hands fall. 'The circle is made,' she said dully. 'It is not our hands that link us together, it is our minds. It doesn't matter now who stays or goes. As long as Leonora holds the trance the circle is confirmed.'

'I'm not staying!' A woman scrambled from the table. 'I find this talk of dead babies most distressing. Had I known it like this I'd never have sat.'

'Nor I,' said a man. 'I came to learn of my wife not wallow in muck.' He turned to Freddie. 'By all means wash your dirty linen in public but not in my time!'

One by one they left, Lily Langtry gathering her shawl. 'I too shall withdraw. This is an intimate affair. I wish you well to resolve it.'

That left only five at the table. 'What now?' said Luke.

Evie shrugged. 'Does it matter?'

'It seems to matter to your brother!'

'And to Madame Leonora,' said Evie. 'She'll not let go until all is resolved.'

'Then let's try and resolve it!' said Luke. 'I'd sooner walk out the door and never look back but if this is about Susan Dudley dare we leave it?'

'No,' said Julia, 'anymore than we dare leave Freddie.'

Freddie's heart is breaking. He wanted to run and keep running until he fell off the end of the world. Darkness, shadows on the wall and that same singing, he hears it every night, London or Rome it's there and always the same song.

'I don't hear the dog. Usually it's Bella singing. Oh, Ju-ju,' ashen, his hand crept to hers. 'You don't think that's my little boy singing? I mean not my son?'

'Of course not!' Julia hung onto him. 'It only sounded like a child.'

'No,' Freddie shook his head. 'It was a child. I heard it and so did you.' He squeezed Julia's hand. 'Was it an angel? D'you suppose that's possible?'

'Your little boy is in heaven with his mother,' she said, desperate to ease his pain. 'If we are to hear anything it would be an angel.'

'I wanted to keep them. I wanted to take care of her. She could've stayed with her mother and I maintained them. After all, it's not every day one has a son, but the more I thought the more difficult it became.'

Julia held onto his hand.

'You saw him, didn't you? You held him. Was he beautiful?'

'Oh yes, so beautiful.'

'I sent a Christening robe. It was my baptismal robe. I sent flowers, pink roses, ever so many.' He sighed. 'It was too late to do any other.'

'Freddie?' Julia squeezed his hand. 'You are tired. We should go home.'

'But I haven't said what I wanted to say. I haven't said sorry.'

'Then say it, dear boy, and be at peace!'

He began to weep, great tears sliding down his gaunt cheeks. 'I am sorry, Susan. I thought I could do it! You were sweet and kind and you liked me. It is easy to love when all the person wants is to love you back.'

For a moment there was silence and then from far away a voice echoing, '*love you back...love you back...love you back...*'

* * *

It was wet out and cold. No one spoke, and then in need of conversation Hugh turned to Julia. 'Will you be at the funeral on Tuesday?'

Julia shook her head. 'I can't. I am otherwise engaged.'

'It should be quite a spectacle. Sir Arthur wanted to be buried with his mother but Her Majesty thought St Pauls the only rightful place. Do you like his music, Mr Roberts? I seem to recall seeing you at the Savoy.'

'I don't know too much about it.'

'Do you have a favourite of his operas, Julianna?'

'I quite like the Pirates of Penzance.'

'*Pinafore* is my choice though I have a liking for *Patience*. I wonder if Schwenk will attend. They had a falling out, but then they were always at one another's throats. Clashes of temperament, pity really.'

Eyes blazing, Evie launched forth. 'I'll tell you what is a pity, you prattling on about Gilbert and Sullivan and poor Freddie in bits!'

'I say draw it mild, sister mine,' Freddie sighed. 'Don't be rattlin' at them. It's not their fault I can't fire a straight arrow.'

'I'm not saying it is. I'm simply asking for a little understanding. All this chatter of operas! Don't they realise you never meant to hurt Bella?'

'Forget it.' Freddie turned up his collar. 'It's done and dusted.'

'I think you should leave it, Evelyn.' Hugh's expression was bland. 'This is neither time nor place to scrape the bowl clean.'

'I'm not scraping the bowl! I am trying to speak for Freddie.'

'There's no need to speak for anyone. We're all grownups here. From what I've heard it's best no one says anything. We should all repair to our various caves to lick our wounds in silence.'

'I have no wounds to lick, Hugh, and resent the idea that I have. This vile mess is not of my making. All I did was try picking up the pieces.'

'Let go of it, Evie!'

'I will when people stop pointing their fingers. You'd think this time of the year, Christmas soon upon us, people would be kind. They're not. They're busy grinding meat cleavers ready to slice our good name to ribbons.'

'Nonsense!' Hugh snorted. 'Our name has been in tatters for centuries. How d'you think your grandmamma acquired the Fitz? It wasn't for serving Holy Orders, though on her knees was the likely position. We are what we are. If mud is thrown we've plenty to throw back.'

'It's so unfair.'

'Nothing is fair. Civilised people (and they are the only ones that count) are busy looking the other way. I suggest you do the same. This night needs to be sat upon and not drawn out for love of drama.'

'Are you saying I am dramatising this?'

'Well, it's not me flinging my cloak about! I don't know what occurred in that room other than what is already known. It seems your tamed parrot caused some of your company to take offense.'

'There were several very illuminating messages, not least a German lady, who for reasons of her own, Mrs Dryden chose not to identify.'

'Bully for Mrs Dryden! It sounds a silly business that if you're not careful will gather silliness until it is downright dangerous. In this, as with all misalliance, least said soonest mended. So please, Evelyn, go home!'

'Good advice.' Luke took Eve's arm. 'The carriage is here. Let me help you. The steps are wet and you might slip.'

She shook his hand away. 'Thank you, I am able to walk unaided. I'm not so in my dotage I need lean on you.'

'Take my coat you're shivering.'

'That's because in all the fuss I left my shawl behind. I like that shawl. It was a gift from my late husband. I wouldn't want to lose it.'

'I'll go and look for it.'

'Thank you, Roberts.'

Luke looked at her. 'Roberts?'

'Yes,' she said eyes cold. 'That is your name, isn't it?'

'That is my name.' Luke turned back to the house. 'I must remember it and not imagine any other.'

'God Evie!' said Freddie. 'You really are a mad bitch. Do you want to lose him along with everyone else?'

Evie slapped him. 'How dare you talk to me like that! Three years I've put up with you bemoaning your sins. Three years trying to stop you doing what you did tonight and a life-time trying to keep you from being hurt.'

He shrugged. 'Oh well, now the whole world knows.'

'The whole world doesn't care! I am ashamed of you Frederick Carrington. You're like your father. You don't care who you hurt.'

'And neither do you!' Freddie turned away. 'I'll go help Luke look for the shawl. Who knows, we might find your heart while we're at it.'

'It's true!' Evie shouted. 'You are like your father! He loved serving girls, especially if they were on the silly side and Bella was certainly that.'

'Her name wasn't Bella,' Julia could stand no more. 'It was Susan.'

'Julianna!' Hugh's fingers tightened about her wrist. 'Let's not add to this.'

'I hope I'll not do anything to add to this tragic tale but I beg Evie to remember Susan by her given name and not that of a servant.'

'Oh, this is all I needed!' Evie turned. 'Sanctimonious deceiver, if anyone is to blame it's you! You brought Bella to Norfolk. While she was with me she was well and every reason to stay so. Yes, she was with child. I didn't ask the father and she didn't tell. She was a maid! Why would I ask her anything! You brought the problem about smuggling her away in a questionable manner.'

'Questionable?'

'Yes questionable! I'm sure I'm not the first to wonder at that decision. There was no need for her to leave. Had she stayed I would've helped.'

Julia held back anger. 'When Doctor Adelman found Susan she was not in your employ. She was drudge and maid-of-all work in a slum with other half-starved children. No one forced her to Norfolk. She was happy to come, at least that was to my understanding. Clearly we remember events differently.'

'Yes, and you remember to your advantage. A girl and her baby die in your care? One can only hope your other protégés are better served.'

'Protégés?' Julia frowned. 'What are you talking about?

'Aren't you and Stefan Adelman responsible for a Girl's Home in Cambridge? Isn't it you caring for them and helping find employment? You capturing the attention of the good-hearted, even our own Princess of Wales. And why? What is your hope, a place in history alongside Florence Nightingale?'

There was silence, people turning to look and words digested.

'I am not going to enter into an argument with you,' said Julia. 'We are at odds over Susan Dudley and always will be, but I ask you not to malign Stefan Adelman when you know a kinder man does not exist. He lives only to serve those less fortunate than himself and deserves to be remembered so.'

'Is that why you sleep with him? Do you hope the goodness will rub off?'

'Freddie is right,' said Hugh. 'You say ugly things.'

'Ugly?' She shrugged. 'That depends on your point of view. The things I say become ugly only if untrue. I don't hear you rushing to defend yourself, Julianna. Do you deny that when you visit Bradbury you stay overnight? That you are alone, the two of you, no maid servant and no man?'

'I deny nothing. My life and my doings are my own. I answer to no one.'

'You see, World?' Evie spread her arms and turned in a circle. 'The truth is not ugly! Every word is honest and clear and simple.'

'Evelyn, that's enough!' Hugh barked. 'You are letting yourself down.'

'I'm not letting anyone down. I am sick of hearing of this woman, how good she is and beloved of Prince Albert. I said you and Mrs Langtry had much in common. You are both actresses. Bravo, Ju-ju! The beloved ingénue strides the boards declaiming innocence and every word a lie.'

A crowd multiplies, ears twitching.

'I'm sorry, Hugh,' said Julia. 'I can't stay.'

'Of course not! Let me settle Evelyn first. I can't leave her like this.'

'It's alright!' Luke pushed through the crowd. 'It's best you go. Julianna needs to be away. I'll stay with Lady Carrington.'

Evie rounded on him. 'Don't try managing me, Mister Wolf! I'm not to have a choke about my neck for fear I'd sink my teeth into the face you adore! You know what I say is true. Ju-ju Dryden is a liar and a cheat! She cheats the helpless! She visits a hospital for the insane to tend a sick woman. Then she beds the sick woman's husband. Ask her if that is not true. Ask!'

CHAPTER TWENTY-ONE

Big Question

Sick and sorry, Freddie kicked his hat out into the darkness. 'I have to talk to Julianna. I need her to understand I never meant it to end this way.'

'I'm sure she understands that.'

'I'm sure she don't! She's a parson's daughter and not the softie she was. It comes of mixin' with the Marlborough Set, brutes beneath the ermine.'

'Julianna Dryden is the opposite of hard and if you go at her hammer and tongs looking to offset blame it'll be me damning you to hell.'

'I'm not lookin' to offset blame. I'm sayin' she don't understand me and Evie.'

'Who does? You're crazy, the pair of you, and the only people to understand are crazy too!'

'Oh not you, Luke. I couldn't stand it.'

'Then stop whining! What's done is done! You must try to make a new life.'

'I'll never have a life with this hangin' over me. The best thing I can do is go where I won't have to listen to Evie tellin' me what a sorry arse I am.'

'I wouldn't worry about that.' Luke watched the carriage pull away, Evie with her face turned from the window. 'There's no one to tell you anything.'

Freddie swivelled. 'Is she going? God damn it, Evie, must

you always fly off the handle! I'd better find a place to stay.' He looked back to where guests stood at windows watching. 'I can't go back in there to be gaped at.'

'You can stay at my house.'

'You have a house?'

'No need to sound so surprised. Contrary to Carrington opinion under all of this dirt there hides a civilised brute.'

'Where is your house?'

'Not far from the Julianna. Come on!' Luke whistled up a cab.

'What about Evie?'

'Your sister's an enterprising woman. We were booked into the Swan. It's a popular Inn. No doubt she'll find a way of passing the time.'

Freddie's laugh was hollow. 'You are learning.'

'And not before time!'

'Don't take any of this to heart.' Freddie boarded the cab. 'She's seethin' now but come the mornin' this night and its absurdities will be washed clean. She'll contact friends, she'll laugh and lie and the damage mended.'

'Can such damage be mended?'

'Yes if you know the right people. A whisper to HRH and other whispers are mute. But that's not the damage you're referrin' to.'

Luke buttoned his jacket and his mouth. He's in no position to condemn another's weakness. He forfeited that right the day he went with Eve. But this about Susan Dudley is a shock. Freddie is an idle spendthrift but never a spoiler of kitchen maids. He's a "Mary-Ann", Albert would say. Luke knows he should be outraged for Susan but can only feel a desperate sadness for everyone, himself included. There was a moment during the séance when his mind was open to a loving word from brother Jacky, but with Freddie's disclosure and Evie's jealous rage, such hope dropped away.

* * *

The mud heavy, the horses had to struggle and the cab is slow.

'Do you have a comfortable house?'

'I like it well enough. I'd as soon live there as any other place.'

'You're a liberal sort of fellow, aren't you? Independent, free of mind and opinion able to come and go as you please, I do envy you. '

Luke closed his eyes in disbelief: if that's how Freddie sees things he really is a sorry arse. Truth is, he could not be more unsettled. Business thriving, money in the bank and plenty opportunities to make more, yet with every passing day England is more a prison than a home. 'I'm thinking of leaving England.'

'Where will you go?'

'Italy.'

'Of course! Everyone has a spiritual birthplace. Yours is Italy and sepia-tinted walls. Mine is Rhode Island and Jamieson with a pistol in his pocket.'

Oh Christ! Freddie sighed. Why must I exaggerate? It's Luke. He sees through a man stripping veneer away and exposing him to what he is. Every time they meet, even to shaking of hands, Freddie does foolish things, though where a pistol and Rhode Island is concerned he told the truth.

Freddie came to Rhode Island in July 1879, his seventh birthday. Evie's husband, Sidney Bevington-Smythe, brought him. Sid was accompanied by one Reuben Jamieson. They made the crossing aboard RMS Flagship Oceanic, Freddie sharing a cot with Sidney, and the mysterious Jamieson on the couch, a pistol in his belt and boots untied. 'Jamieson was a strong-arm.'

'What?'

'I said, Eve's husband hired Jamieson as a heavy-weight.'

'What was Evie's husband that he needed protecting?'

'It wasn't for him. It was for me.'

'And why did you need protecting?'

'I don't know.' That's not true! That's Freddie, the seven-year-old, saying that, who'd sooner lie than think on the past. Thirty-year-old Freddie knows why Sidney hired a gun. It was to stop George Carrington stealing back his son.

1879 – ten years would pass before Freddie would see England again. When questioned of that time Evie shrugs. 'Don't blow it out of proportion. Sidney was in England and went to Sir George at Charlecourt to take you for a spin in his new landau. He spun a little further than anticipated.'

Thousands of miles across an ocean is some spin. Freddie rarely asks questions. A question was asked of him the second week at Rhode Island. 'Now listen, son,' Sidney had sat him down. 'I'm gonna put a question to you. All you have to do is nod your head for yes and shake for no. You get me, son?'

Freddie got him and suspecting what was to come steeled his nerve.

'I wanna ask if your poppa did things you didn't like. Did he for instance ever touch you in ways that hurt? Did he try leading you into foul ways?'

It was summer when Sidney asked the Big Question, sunlight

through the veranda roof making patterns on the wall. One pattern looked like a circus elephant balancing on a drum - Freddie once saw an elephant do that from a circus pitched in the meadow. The elephant kept slipping and a man kept whipping. Freddie cried and so did Nanny.

Nanny Goldsmith was the one person he missed. She seemed to know he was going for a long spin and told him to be a good boy. 'Be a good boy.' Freddie hates those words. Had Susan's boy lived he wouldn't have heard those words from his daddy. False words they promise a gift but bring pain.

The day Sidney asked the Big Question the elephant was trying to stay upright. Not wanting it to fall Freddie had lied. 'No sir,' he said. 'Papa didn't lead me into foul ways.' Young Freddie decided that day to quit the Past. He was in America with an ocean between him and England - Evie said he was to stay with her, so it didn't matter what Papa had done.

There were times when he did remember things, like water spouts and painted fire screens. Even now he'll wake from a dream screaming. Evie will rush in. 'I'm sorry,' she'll say. 'I shouldn't have left you.'

Dear old Sid never asked the Question again but the week he died he came close. It was after an incident at college, an accusation. 'I've been all over the world,' Sid said, his face screwed up. 'I've seen miraculous things and terrible things and the older I get the more the line between miraculous and terrible blurs. You're a good boy but you're bruised and the bruises are beginning to show. Maybe if you said how they came about they'd go away.'

Sidney died soon after. The Question was never asked again. Until this day no one cared or dared to ask again.

* * *

'I don't know why I had to drag Susan into it,' said Freddie. 'I suppose I was tryin' to see if my understandin' of me was wrong.'

'And what is your understanding of you?'

'That I am a bugger. I have been beaten about the head for being a bugger. I've been kicked, whipped and spat upon, often at the same time. I have been accused of stealin' innocence and pervertin' young boys. I've been chastised for sayin' things I never said and beaten for doin' things I never did and all boilin' down to one thing. I can't love a woman.'

'And yet you tried.'

'I did and I'm sorry.'

'Susan was a simple girl. You must have known that.'

'I did and I'm not makin' excuses. I'm tryin' to tell you how it was. What we did felt unnatural to me. She wasn't over keen! It was only once. I didn't think it would lead to anythin'.' Freddie wrung his hands, that wretched song still in his head. 'She wanted the baby the way a kiddie wants a doll. Then she began to hate her condition. I must see Julianna! She'll stop this horror goin' round in my brain. She was there when they died. I need forgiveness.'

'That's crazy talk,' said Luke. 'You can't ask forgiveness of anyone but a priest. Go to church and seek absolution there.'

'Do you believe in God then, Luke?'

'No more than I believe in the forgiveness of sins. A man must have courage and live with his mistakes. If you're going to need forgiveness don't sin.'

* * *

They were at the house. 'I thought you lived in a Forge.'

'Before the big bang I did.'

'The big bang?'

'Yes, me realising there's more to life than taps and washers.'

'You are more than taps and washers. This house says so. It has space and is quiet. The light comin' off the Common I could paint here.'

'Then paint! Meantime get some sleep.' Luke flung a blanket over the bed. 'You've a bathroom alongside and usual amenities. There are clothes in the cupboard and shirts in the drawer. You might find them a bit on the roomy side, you the size of a sparrow, but they'll do for now.'

Freddie knuckled his eyes. 'Where shall you be?'

'On the couch.'

'I say, that won't do! I'll take the couch. You must have your bed.'

'I've stuff to sort, papers to look at and the like. Sleep and be easy.'

'I feel awkward takin' your bed.'

'No need. If I'm tired I'll sleep. I'm one of those that die when sleeping.'

'You have a clear conscience.'

'I doubt that.' When Freddie lingered Luke smiled. 'It's alright. No need to be spooked. I'm not going to steal up later and do you a disservice.'

Freddie blushed. 'Surely that should be my line.'

Luke stamped downstairs. 'I thought to save you time.'

* * *

Freddie dreamt he was in Charlecourt. He is four years old. Nanny Goldsmith takes him by the hand to lead him down the back stairs into the library. She sits him on a padded stool and places a screen in front of him, a big wooden screen with huntsmen blowing a horn and hounds running. Nanny is unhappy and mutters of sinners and the Wrath of God. She wheels the screen closer. Thinking they're playin 'peek-a-boo' Freddie laughs. She puts a finger to her lips. 'Be a good boy. Nanny will fetch you when it's all over.'

Freddie sits in a big brown room with a big brown desk. The door opens and Papa comes in leading a girl by the hand. They go behind the screen. Freddie sits inside the dream wishing he had Paul Revere, the knitted cat his sister sent from America. He wanted to bring the cat to the Library but Nanny said no.

Noises come from behind the screen, squishing sounds like the springs of the nursery sofa going up and down. Papa is whispering. The girl is weeping. Freddie sticks his fingers in his ears. The horror will not last. Nanny will fetch him back to the nursery. There will be an examination of his body. She'll remove his clothes examining every nook and crevice. She'll find nothing because there's nothing to see. Hands have pulled, and fingers have poked, and a child has wept, but there's not a mark on Freddie's body.

The noise behind the screen is loud and a boot stamps the floor. 'Open the door, little girl!' Papa is shouting. 'Open the door and let Papa in!'

Something awful is going to happen, a thing so ugly and sad Freddie will never forget! The fire screen will fall and the hunting scene, and pink-coated riders and horses, will smash to pieces and he'll know who Papa hurts.

There's a saying, 'what the eyes don't see the heart cannot grieve over.' Freddie grieves because even without seeing he knows what is happening. The girl is a servant who clears grates in the morning. She wears black stockings and the skin top of her stockings is very white and Pap hunches over her like a big black crow. Papa knows he is listening. He had Freddie brought there and will bring him again when there's another girl as young and as frightened. Papa likes that his little son can hear the squishing and weeping. Eventually the screen will fall and Freddie will see and he'll scream and scream...!

'Aghhhh!'

Luke heard the scream through his own dream. Unable to stay awake, he'd slept where he sat, face squashed among the papers, ink giving him an extra eyebrow. In his dream Luke is in Italy with his father. A storm is coming. They discuss the vines. The harvest is small this season and yet rich. Luke and his father board the cart. They take shovels to pitch a gulley above the vines to siphon silt away. Luke's wife walks alongside the wagon. He bends to kiss her. She tastes of wild strawberries and baby milk. She says take care. She needs him with her not scattered all over the mountain. A child is crying, the sound echoing about the mountains. Then the crying becomes a scream and his wife breaks away. He tries to hold her and to tell her it's not their son, she needn't worry, but she's gone, skirts fluttering, and the scream is getting louder.

It's Freddie screaming! Luke ran up the stairs. Freddie sits up in the bed, mouth open and eyes staring. 'Hey!' Luke shakes him. 'Wake up!'

Snap! He is awake.

'Good God, Freddie! What was all that about?'

Eyes and brain locked into another time Freddie can't speak.

'Come on old chap!' Luke snapped his fingers. 'Why the racket? Is somebody trying to kill you?'

Freddie nodded. 'I'm not sure he didn't succeed.'

* * *

It took a while to calm him down. 'So who was trying to kill you?'

'My father, George Reginald Stewart Baines-Carrington, QC, barrister at Inns of Court, a man fighting for justice and all that is right and good.'

'What about him?'

'We were all afraid of him, servants and family alike. Nowadays he's more insect than man and yet Iphigenia Carrington, my poor mother, is so afraid she bolts her door at night. But not to keep him away! No fear of that! Mater's old. George likes his flesh young and juicy, younger the better.'

'My God! Are you saying he...he hurt you?'

'Yes but not the way you think. He never laid a finger on me. Pater likes girls, young, timid girls, servants mostly with parents tied to the land so nobody dare complain. Evie says I take after him, son and heir to the Charlecourt rapist. And she's right, witness two innocent souls in a grave not far from here.'

'She's not right. You didn't rape Susan. It was an agreed thing.'

'It was no agreed thing! She a servant and me her mistresses' brother, how could she not agree? Evie is right. I am like my father except I have darker perversions. I'm queer as well as a brute.'

Head in his hands, Freddie began to weep. 'He liked to bring girls down the back stairs to the library, difficult to fight

in there with so many great men staring down. Ten or thereabouts, young and preferably pretty, he raped them and made
sure I knew. Young as I was he wanted me to watch. I was the
audience hidden away behind a screen. I wasn't meant to see. I
was meant to hear and imagine and be afraid, a dirty little boy
spyin' on a dirty old man.'

'No Freddie!' Luke took him in his arms. 'A child at the
mercy of a beast.'

'And for all I know still a beast! That stool and that screen!
When he dies I shall set fire to the lot. Shame Nanny won't be
able to join me.'

'Did she know what was going on?'

'She wrote to Sidney. He fetched me away thinkin' I was the
one molested. Poor Nanny! Be good she would say and I'll fetch
you when it's all over.'

'Monsters are everywhere.'

'I tried tellin' myself it was a dream but knew it to be more. I
pushed it away until Susan came, and then couldn't push anymore.
Tonight at the séance I thought I'd die, Freddie Carrington, the
queer who hangs about street corners lookin' to suck a man's cock.
My father made me so.'

'Did he make you so?'

'It was the screamin'! And they did scream, those little girls!
Why else would I be this way about women unable to have sex
with them at any price.'

'Maybe because you are a bugger.'

'What!'

'I said maybe you are a bugger. Your father is the worst of
men. To call him beast is to malign decent creatures. I am shocked

by your childhood but not surprised. Children suffer and pass their sufferings on. But why must it be that way with you. Why would you want to suck a man's cock because your father abused women? It makes no sense. If the thought of loving a woman is unnatural to you, might it not be you simply prefer men?'

'It's not a case of preferring. Loving a woman just doesn't come into it!'

'There you are then. I don't know why you feel that way. It's beyond my understanding. But I don't see you forced to it. More likely your father helped make up your mind. To love someone, to want to hold and kiss is natural. My mother says love begets love. She says nowt about hate begetting love. I don't know the world for what it is but I know you are not a brute. Best you regard your passion for men as natural and not the result of a crazy mind.'

'You said we were crazy, me and Evie.'

'And so you are! You're spoilt brats throwing your toys about but you don't rape children, Freddie, and your sister doesn't set fire to kittens. You love men and want to make love to them. Don't make it more of a curse than it is.'

Freddie wiped his nose on his sleeve. 'I want to make love to you, Luke Roberts, and have from the moment we met. Do you know that?'

'I do know but that's not who I am. Right now I am too weary to do anything but sleep so move over!' He lay down beside Freddie. 'Accept it for what it is and for Christ's sake let us both get some rest.'

* * *

Early next morning they called in at the Lord Nelson. 'We were booked in the Swan. It was closer to Long Melford for Lady Carrington and her party.'

'Lady Carrington and party!' Nan was scornful. 'You mean Eve Carrington and her seducing rogue of a brother and their bit of rough?'

'If by bit of rough you're referring to me, Mother, I slept at my own place last night. And if by seducing rogue you're meaning the Honourable Freddie I beg you remember he's but a couple of walls away!'

'Why when by all accounts I'd be telling the truth. There's talk about him and poor Susan Dudley, how he did the deed and then abandoned her.'

'There's always talk in Bakers End. They talk sooner than live. Dear suffering Christ! Is this how it's going to be all my life?' Luke stretched his hands up to the ceiling. 'How long must I endure this place?'

Nan slapped him and then slapped him again. 'Don't use language like that in my house! I don't know what you're used to in London but you'll not take the Lord's Name in vain in the Nelson. You may be my son and think you're entitled to come and go as you please but let me tell you this is my house, mine and Albert's, and while you are in it you'll treat it and us with respect.'

'I'm sorry.' Luke pulled his mother close. 'I've learned things about myself I didn't like and it's shaken me. I've lost my way, Nan, and I need to get back, not that that is any excuse for being a poor son.'

Nan kissed him. 'You're a good son. But you have lost your way.'

'... and soon as I'm done here I'm getting back. I need a loan of the Snug for a while. Freddie is to speak with Julianna where they won't be interrupted and where she's among friends. That is here, isn't it, Nan, among friends?'

'It is!' Nan sniffed away tears. 'You're among friends and if you're trying to help him the Carrington lad is welcome. Have you spoken with Anna?'

'I sent a note and a reply saying he need only say and she'll come. I'd like to stay, Ma, but I need to get back to London and pack.'

'Pack? What does that mean?'

'Move out.'

'Out of London?'

'Yes.'

'For good?'

'Yes.'

* * *

Freddie was sitting in the window-seat staring out into the road.

Luke came through. 'Did you order breakfast?'

'I've ordered. Whether I'll be able to eat is another thing.'

'Just take your time. You have my keys. Once you've seen Julianna you can go back to the house and maybe get some more sleep. I'm for the nine o'clock express. I'll pass on your messages to Jamieson.'

'Thanks. I need him to bring me a couple of things.'

'There's always the telephone? You could speak to the house direct.'

'Yes and Evie on the other end.'

'You'll have to face her sooner or later as will I. Shall you call on Julianna?'

'She's carried enough of the burden. I must heft my own baggage.'

'Good decision. I'd best be buzzing. I'm to be in Harrogate by Monday. I need to sort things with Evie and, hopefully, clear the air.'

Freddie got to his feet and fists curled deep in his pocket stared out of the window. 'And what about you and me? Do we need to clear the air?'

'About what?'

'I don't know. I thought there might be things to say.'

Luke thrust into his greatcoat. 'Need we say anything, Freddie? Some things are best left unsaid, that way we don't learn to regret them.'

'Do you regret last night?'

'I don't but neither would I want to repeat it.' Luke picked up his bag. 'We are what we are. I doubt either of us will change.'

With Luke gone the room is suddenly small and cramped. They talked so long into the night they hardly slept. Freddie doesn't believe his love of men was forced upon him. He worships the lean muscle and structure of the body. Women are softness and uncertain smells. A man's body has a scent of its own. A woman's scent is of need and highly charged likely to go off at any moment.

Freddie fell in love with Luke over a bottle of Madeira. Head thrown back and throat exposed, he was laughing and in that moment Freddie a vampire, mentally sinking his teeth into flesh and sucking until the body bled dry.

Man at a Window is the official title of his new work; *Fallen Angel Challenging God* is the subtitle. It shows Luke in a half light, head turned, the long planes of his back and buttocks relaxed, his right hand square on the windowsill and his left cupping his genitals.

'You know I painted you nude,' Freddie said last night lying alongside, his head on Luke's chest listening to the steady unaffected tolling of a heart.

'Eve mentioned it.'

'And it doesn't worry you?'

'It's done isn't it and up before the Hanging Committee?'

'It is.'

'Then it's too late to worry.'

'And this?' Freddie had lipped Luke's chest, breathing him in, the scent of olive trees in the rain and wet dog. 'Does this not worry you?'

Stomach hard, and sentiment equally so, Luke didn't move. 'Do you want me to worry?'

'No.'

'Then I shan't.'

CHAPTER TWENTY-TWO

Sinner

Luke is leaving. Evie sits in the window-seat watching. As with every day that follows a bite of the Black Dog, she's an empty shell sucked dry of feeling. Nothing she can do to fill the gap, no pills to swallow and no magical spell to lose the blues. Laudanum is a last resort which causes her to sleep when she shouldn't and wake when she'd sooner sleep. All that's left is to sit in the window and try not to mind sunlight making a concertina of her mouth.

Wrinkles in one's forties are inevitable. Perhaps she should smile more. Sidney maintained smiles exercise muscles. A jolly man inclined to wobble about the knees he would tug her hand. 'Forty-three muscles to frown and seventeen to smile? You could never resist a bargain.'

What a good man and what a beast she was to him. He gave her comfort and wealth - she gave tantrums and an aborted child. A Quaker, a descendent of the Boston Martyrs, Sidney Bevington-Smythe rolled into her life August '74 at St James' Palace and the Ambassador's Ball. He claimed the first waltz and by the end of the evening the hand in marriage of society beauty, Lady Evelyn Carrington, daughter of Sir George and Lady Iphigenia. 1882, victim of a brain seizure, he rolled out of her life into the Pacific Ocean, his remains sewn into a shroud at one with the seas he loved to sail. Foulmouthed but kind and so fabulously wealthy that when asked how his fortune was made, he said his money thrives as roses fed on horse shit - his particular brand of compost *'shat by the Iron Horses that hourly gallop the American Mid-Western plains.'*

Sidney was shrewd. Recognising despair in his young wife, he secured his railroad stock in a deal so tight that, though gone these twenty years, his roses continue to thrive: 'When it comes to property I'm with Charles Dickens, the Law is an Ass. I'll leave you wealthy, Evie, but not dangerous.'

Luke Roberts is not so much a fiscal mistake as a spiritual mismatch. Evie with flyaway temper and desire to die and him with stiff-necked pride, they don't meld. Look at him now packing things into a battered holdall! Last summer she bought a crocodile skin bag from Liberty's. He doesn't use it. Same with silver-backed hair brushes and the pearl handle letter-opener. For the good they do they might've stayed in Garrard's along with the monogrammed cufflinks.

The cufflinks were an Easter gift arriving on the breakfast tray with champagne and smoked salmon. He opened the box, 'EBC is your monogram?' When she nodded he bared his elegant arse. 'I think you'll find a brand is meant to go there. Upper left cheek, in and out quicker the way to do it.'

Evie had laughed and slapped his arse. He'd laughed with her but didn't wear the cufflinks. Occasion demanding, he chooses plain gold, a coming of age gift from his mother. When asked why he said, 'I'm comfortable with my own things. I don't mind them getting bashed about.'

Bashed about is what he does with her pride. His refusal to bend to her will rankles but not nearly as much as he, arrogant male, might imagine.

Evie stares out of the window. It is a beautiful day, cold yet bright and clear, a day for catching up on acquaintance and for purchasing shirts for Freddie in Jermyn Street, and then perhaps an after lunch stroll through the Gallery.

The Hanging Committee accepted *Man at the Window*. Evie is delighted for Freddie but also wary of the likes of Queensbury currently baying for homosexual blood on the corner of every Soho alley.

'I blame Oscar Wilde!' says Hugh Fitzwilliam. 'Him and his poetry! Had he lived life sooner than written about it the world would be a happier place.'

He viewed the painting when it was still on the easel. 'If society didn't know Freddie of the Greek persuasion they know now. And does anyone in this world care what pot we piss in? It's a game of chance whoever's in your bed.'

In company of other canvasses, particularly the French School of gluttonous derriere, Freddie's nude is refined. It's only when you query the stance at the window, the languorous lips and the hand on the genitals, covering and covetous, that you see the other male, the artist, equally nude, watching.

Freddie caused a fuss recently at Long Melford. Afraid for him, the Black Dog chewing her heel, and jealous of Julianna, Evie flew into one of her rages, the consequence of which, like the Walls of Jericho, now falls about her.

Nothing is heard of Julianna and nothing expected. Freddie went to the Sargent family, a usual bolt hole. Now Luke prepares to leave and Evie - the adjudged villain of the piece - wishes them all in hell! Thirty years she's agonised over Freddie. A magnet for rogues and hangers-on, he's always in trouble. During school years it was she who paid off the sharks that would otherwise have cut him to pieces.

* * *

Evie yawned. 'When will you be back?'

'I doubt I shall.'

'Oh, well, it is as it is. You gave me fair warning. You said if I were to hurt her you'd leave and we all know you a man of his word.'

'I'm not going because of Julianna.'

'Then why are you going?'

'I think it best for both of us.'

'*Je m'en fiche*!' She shrugged. 'It's all the same to me.' So damned sure of himself and his ideals, he blocks all attempts at reconciliation. It's been this way since Italy and him still bearing the scars - she shouldn't have bitten him but he drove her wild with his suburban pride.

Strange how men think they are being kind when at their most cruel. Some acts of cruelty are visible like teeth marks in flesh, others not so obvious but as hurtful, as with the averted profile and stony look. He is master of that, the bag he packs a metaphor of the man, high quality but tough as old boots.

Luke is not easy to love. In early days he was a lover sensitive and wild. That he soon cooled off was because he was asked for what he could not give. He loves Julianna as does Evie. It's more than three years since she and Evie lay on the bed, yet burns in memory as a defining moment. Desire for Julianna, to kiss and to hold, was there even on the steps at Cambridge.

There is that of her that makes a person want to touch as with caressing a gorgeous animal. It's what the gifts are about, Bertie's rubies and Evie's furs. In the slip of silk and satin the mind proposes undressing the beloved. Seeing diaphanous chiffon slide down a creamy thigh the mouth drips to follow.

Julianna walks into a room and that need is reflected in every eye, which is why, knowing it can't be returned, sweet turns to sour. The morning of the opera the need to express love was strong. Evie couldn't hold back and Julia, afraid of greedy love, fled. Had Evie toed the line there would have been no falling away. There would be friendship but friendship built on a lie.

Evie's not good with lies. It's why she gets on with the likes of Lolly Dupres. Lolly loves men and women with equal disinterest. When visiting London she shares many beds and goes away singing, body restored and heart intact. Evie forced the issue with Ju-ju as she forces the issue with Luke Roberts. It's as if her soul cries out, 'bring me love, Lord, but then for God's sake take it away.'

Where sex is concerned Evie is the opposite of Freddie, male flesh the antithesis of desire. Where she adores soft, were silken flesh conjoins with breast, he desires muscle and bone. She did think to soften Mister Wolf's tough exterior but look at him combing his hair with his fingers and shrugging into his jacket - a dark jacket, sober and industrious, chosen and paid with cash from his wallet. Evie stares out over rooftops and wishes him and his sober jacket away, affection begrudged is a damnable bore.

* * *

'Are you returning to Norfolk?'

'Not for a day or so. I'm in Harrogate tomorrow. The hotel is in need of major overhaul. Albert and his crew has been there a couple of weeks already.'

'You have done well in the latter years, your name known throughout the country and respected. In terms of men like Robert Scholtz don't you think your success is in some degree due to an association with me?'

'I do and I am grateful.'

'But not grateful enough to stay?'

'That wouldn't be gratitude! That would be me using you and I've done too much of that already.'

'One is never used until one thinks one is. I hope that Freddie and I shall still be a welcome acquaintance with you and your family?'

'Of course! I would hope you know that to be so!'

'*Mille grazie,* one takes what one can.' Anger licked Evie's skin. 'You are calm and composed and insultingly so. Sleeping in the same bed and drinking from the same cup, one would hope for a little less head and a lot more heart.'

'Forgive me. I don't mean to insult. Such talking leads to shouting.'

'An unwillingness to communicate has been your position throughout our association except in Rome when you said more than enough.'

'You communicated for us both with your teeth.'

'Well, you do bear a scar and scars are difficult to disprove. I must learn to be less vigorous when chewing. You didn't say much at Long Melford.'

'Would you have heard me if I had?'

'Probably not.'

'Words wound. I didn't want to add to your pain.'

'My pain!'

'Yes yours! You hurt a lot of people that evening. You were cruel. You said things purposely to wound and in so doing wounded yourself.'

'Did I wound you?'

'You did.'

'I didn't hear you yelp.'

'I've learned to yelp quietly.'

'You have suffered then as well as gained in business and wealth?'

'Eve, please! Let's not part bad friends.'

'Were we good friends before the Borghese?' Evie threw out her arm. 'Oh don't answer that! Go if you must! I shan't beg! As for the séance and what followed I said only what was true.'

'True to you but not to everyone.'

'Truth is truth. There can be no deviation.'

Head on one side, he regarded her. 'You can't believe that, not with what you know about poor Freddie.'

Evie turned to stare. 'If by poor you're referring to his sexual predilection I've always known. I never condemned him but neither did I urge him to seek his nature. Freddie's no Oscar Wilde. He doesn't have the veneer. It's why Bella happened. He thought to correct a sin. Poor Bella, I do regret her.' Evie sighed. 'I ought not to call her so. I'll do as Ju-ju says and give Susan her name.'

Luke shouldered his bag. 'I must go.'

'How long have you known about Freddie?'

'Since the day we met.'

'Did you not feel awkward sitting for him naked?'

'His feelings trouble him more than they trouble me.'

'I doubt your father would think that way.'

'I don't know what my father would think. I know what Albert would think but that's Albert. Did you think I'd be put out? Maybe take Freddie out on the street to punch his nose.'

'It crossed my mind.'

'Then you don't know me. If a man is decent with me I'll be decent with him no matter what others say. I'm in no position to judge Freddie's choices. As for the painting you know I never sat for him naked or otherwise.'

'I was only teasing. Have you seen how his imagination conjures you?'

'Not yet.'

'And when you do what will you see?'

'I imagine he does what you do, glorify.'

'Glorify?' Evie nodded. 'Yes, I suppose we do that. It's a mistake for which we both pay. You never did sit for me. Why is that?'

'You never wanted me to. It was Julianna you wanted.' He bent and kissed her cheek. 'It's why I'm here. I'm the closest you can get.'

* * *

He left and another hole appeared in the house. Wishing to be alone Evie cancelled the trip to a lecture by Annie Besant. Religion, Spiritism and the like is all very well but you can have too much of a thing. The séance on Friday was wonderful and terrible. Lord, what a shock to hear that song issuing from Leonora's mouth! It made the hair on one's head rise. Then there were messages for Julianna and Luke. Evie enquired of his message. He said it was from the past and of no particular interest but might have been from a lady he met when a boy. Sick at heart she baited him, what lady and was she vixen to his wolf until, white-faced, he'd turned. 'A female wolf is known as a bitch. You familiar with the state I thought you might've known.'

Life in Russell Square didn't suit him. The constant upheaval - spiteful servants, her temper and shouting - went against his Northern grain. It made life with Evie seem louche or as Sir George would say sinful.

Sinful was always Father's critique of her life. These days he seldom comments, Sidney's Iron Horse-shit putting an end to insults. Charlecourt, the family home on the Downs, is in need of repairs and Sir George and Lady Iphigenia the same. Sidney's money keeps them alive thus these days Evie is not so much sinful slut as beloved daughter. During their time together Sidney's dollars removed many a stain, alas, there are stains that cannot be redeemed. Freddie's sin was to be born different and trying to prove otherwise. Evie's was being born.

* * *

It is dark now, lamps glowing in windows across the way. Many of the stores are still open, hansom cabs busy with Christmas trade, the horses blanketed against the cold. Foolish to sit moping! She should paint but these days has a reluctant muse. She regards the *Fauns* as her best work. There have been offers, one excellent offer from Robert Scholtz. The Palace too made an offer, but as with all things Majestic, niggardly purse-wise. HRH will have them in the end or she'll do as Freddie and break them to pieces with a carpet beater.

The clock ticks. Evie sighs. She should've gone to the lecture rather than regretting a lover. Luke was not so much a lover as a mountain to climb. So reluctant, not once in all their time did he approach her with a kiss. He found pleasure in sex yet might've been in another room. It is the way of men. They do not need to adore. 'Love is sentimental hogwash,' Sidney said. 'If the woman is wet and willing she don't need to adore me. You don't adore me, do you, Milady C? If I can manage you, I can manage anyone.'

Sidney was a good lover. Stout and aging, he wasn't always able to rise to the occasion but took care of her needs. He liked women. In Rhode Island he attended all of Evie's soirees. A room filled with gossiping women and a loaded tea-trolley and he was happy. An unlit cigar in his hand, and Miss Fancy, the Pomeranian, under his arm, he'd circle the room bending and whispering and giggling. The ladies would giggle with him. Freddie maintained Sidney was one giggle away from batting for the other side.

Poor Freddie! It was the nurse, Mable Goldsmith, who alerted them to danger. She wrote to Sidney. '*I wish you'd come, sir, and take young Freddie to be with his sister. He's not a happy boy and not wonderfully loved by his papa.*'

'I knew it,' Sidney had raged. 'That place was wrong for you and for the boy. We must go and get him back.' She tried bringing him to America. Father would have none of it. 'He is the Honourable Frederick Erasmus Carrington. He is to inherit my name not that of a tradesman. Your brother, God bless him, stays under my roof where I can govern his future.' So Freddie remained behind with a cruel man on whose lips even a blessing becomes a curse.

* * *

Three in the morning and Evie thinks of Long Melford and how she shouted and society looking on. It was Luke that made her so angry, his hand on her elbow restraining a mad dog. Julianna should not have interfered! If she'd left things alone it is possible Bella and her baby might still be alive.

If Evie could turn back time it would be to the night of the opera and the moment Julianna asked why Bella couldn't go to Norfolk, what harm would it do? Evie wanted to tell of the harm already done long before Bella that caused another death. The second summer in America found Evie pregnant, happy, and more than a little surprised. Sidney was delighted. He made so many plans, if it was a girl she would be named Jenny after his sister who died.

The baby was born dead. Sidney stood at the bottom of the bed tears rolling down his cheeks. 'My little girl,' he sobbed, 'my Jenny.' Sidney had wrapped the tiny form in a blanket and carried it away. Baby Jenny was buried the following week Evie too ill to attend. Her parents wired their regrets.

Father never liked Sidney. Mother adored him. Once he took peaches fresh from the market glistening with sugar. 'Eat them now, Lady Effie, while your eyes are still popping. They'll taste so much sweeter.' Never leave for tomorrow what you can enjoy today was his creed. Finding joy in all things he planned for the morrow. Two babies are dead, Bella's baby and Evie's. They will never know life, never laugh and sing, but neither will they weep.

Freddie thinks Bella dying to be his fault. He said so. 'You were right to blame me. It's my sin. Please don't add to it by

309

saying I'm like father.'

Evie is sick of the word. It was father's favourite. 'You are a sinful slut, Evelyn!' He would say that unveiling his cock prior to plunging it into any of the orifices belonging to the slut. She once asked Luke, 'do you think this sinful?' They were in bed. 'You and me unwed and twined about one another?'

He was a long time answering, so long she'd heaved up on her elbow. 'You need to think about it?'

He'd shrugged. 'Maybe in the back of my mind I do think it a sin.'

'Why?'

'It's what my mother would think.'

Nanette Roberts has a strong hold on her son. She is one of the reasons he decamped today. Evie tried building bridges to Bakers End but her heart wasn't in it. Not that it matters! Daughter-in-law to a brewer was never her ambition. Luke was never an ambition. He was as he said - a surrogate, his love for Julianna, and the loyalty in his eyes Evie wanting for her own.

'Poor Freddie!?' Strange Luke should describe Freddie so and with affection or something akin to it. With the séance a family closet was unlocked and ugly skeletons stirred. One skeleton is hidden away right at the back of the closet. Sidney knew of it as does Evie. It will stay in the closet. She will never tell!

Evie knelt on the padded window seat watching a footman carrying his aged mistress through the snow. She doesn't know her neighbours. Nameless people they come and go as do post-men and milk carts. Mrs McLaughlin would chat with neighbours. Freddie liked Mrs Mac. Shame she had to leave and news of Bakers End no longer bought with thirty gold pieces.

Bella was a sweet girl. Freddie saw her as a playmate with whom he might share a dolly. Fly away Peter, fly away Paul, Evie had hope Bella would run home to mother, but *noblesse oblige,* the girl died never giving Freddie away. Freddie sees Ju-ju as the ideal. He said for her he could change his ways. Luke Roberts is in love with Julianna as is Stefan Adelman. Why? What can they get from a woman who loves from the mind rather than the heart? Mister Wolf seeks the passion of his kindred, claws ripping at silk, Julianna was wed to a Don Quixote scholar who tilted at Egyptian hieroglyphs and gave her a mute son so she might hide behind an aging German doctor.

* * *

Ho-hum! It's all such a coil. Crouched in the window seat, several trays come and gone, the bed turned down in her suite, Evie's heart aches. Luke slept as one dead. She could shout and scream. He would sleep on, his face pale and beautiful. History likens a handsome man to classic beauty. In Luke one sees a Greek profile but finds a temperament more suited to Attila the Hun.

'Oh!' Evie clutches her chest, sick and sorry. She hasn't eaten since yesterday. Is that why she feels so ill? It can't be because once again she is alone.

What is the day? Is it still Monday? Evie looks at the clock and sees it is four-thirty in the morning. The sky in the East is flushed with pink rays of the sun. It's Tuesday! That's why she feels faint. She's been in the window all day and most of the night. Not long until Christmas. Evie doesn't care for England at Christmas. She doesn't care for Christmas! What is there to celebrate? Next week

311

she joins Freddie in Paris and then back to Italy and the Villa Borghese. Why the Borghese she doesn't know, habit perhaps.

Weary, she climbs up on the window and standing on the padded seat stretches. Giddy, she slides down to the floor. It's a long drop to the Square. One wouldn't want to fall. Two floors and concrete pavement below, it would not be the way of Lady Evelyn Baines Carrington, internationally acclaimed artist - more the way of a whore and a sinner.

Hope

Just after midnight there was a scratching at the door. Kaiser stood gazing through the banister rails, his tail wagging. Julia went down. 'Who is it?'

'It's me, Dulce!' Julia brought her in - poor Dulce, her boots tied about with rags and a man's overcoat about her frame. 'I'm sorry to trouble you but Miss Callie's gone walkabout and in this snow I'm afeard for her.'

'How long has she been missing?'

'An hour maybe. Usually I know when she blinks, never mind walk, but this darned cold has left me deaf.'

'Have you alerted Mr Daniel?'

'Mr Daniel is out, ma'm.'

'Should I send for him?'

Dulce chewed her lip. 'Will you let me look first? She can't be far.'

'Mrs Mac? Make Dulce a hot drink and then ask Leah to sit with Matty in case he wakes. I'm going to take a look outside. Come, Kaiser!' Lifting his paws in the snow, the dog ran before. Bitterly cold, it's not the night for anyone to be out. Daniel is anxious for his mother. 'She takes no rest, Julianna! She's grows more ill every day. It's this darned house and its ghosts!'

Julia feels that way about the whole of Bakers and came away from the séance utterly wretched. So cruel, she'd wanted to leap across the table shouting, 'such secrets shared among strangers?

Have you no heart?' But a child singing and a dog's tail wagging, who should she accuse?

A figure loomed out of the darkness. 'That you, ma'm?'

'Oh Joe, thank goodness!'

He held up a lamp. 'What you doin' out here this time of night?'

'Mrs Masson's wandered away. Her maid thinks she might be here.'

'Aye, and not the first time! I'll go lookin'. You get back indoors.'

'I'll come with you, Joe. I wouldn't want to frighten her.'

'You think I might frit her? More likely she'll frit us.'

'If she's anywhere she'll be where the broken china was stored.'

'That'll be reet. She has a quarrel with the cottage and that perishin' wall. I see that wall a weed. There's purpose in weeds. They're meant to feed the earth and creatures that live on it. Some weeds strangle the life out of delicate plants. That wall and the reason it was built needs rippin' from the root.'

'Hush, Joe!' A cough was heard, Callie in the laundry room huddled against the wash tub. They led her back to the cottage. Julia poured Joe a cup of tea adding a tot of brandy. 'What were you doing out in the snow.'

He sniffed. 'I was keepin' an eye on things.'

'What sort of things?'

He wiped his nose on his sleeve. 'Nowt you need worry about.'

'Mrs Masson is ill. Please keep what you saw tonight to yourself. '

'No need to ask. I'd anythin' for thee.'

'I know, and am grateful.'

314

He got to his feet. 'Will you be wantin' me more?'

'You'd best go home. I can't have you ill.'

'I'll be off then.' At the door, beaky nose dripping, he wrapped a scarf about his head. 'What goes on here is your business, and I won't be talkin', but that lady needs to stop her madness before she does more harm.'

Callie sat clutching a sheaf of sodden envelopes. 'I was looking to post the mail. I thought with Christmas coming I need to post early.'

'Those envelopes are soaking,' said Julia. 'Let me take them.'

'No!' Callie snatched back. 'I haven't said all I want to say!'

Dulce rubbing her feet, soon the real Callie began to surface and to ask that Daniel not hear of her misadventure. 'He's so little patience these days, Anna, on account of you not treating him right, I'm afraid to speak.'

'Takes after his father,' muttered Dulce.

'I hope not,' said Callie, 'though he takes after him in bumptiousness. Once making up his mind there's no going back, which is why you must set his mind at rest or he'll marry another. I wish he'd stop picking on me. So what if I don't always know where I am? When one is old it's easy to lose one's place.'

Mrs Mac took the letters. 'Shall I post for you, madam?'

'They're not mine,' she said. 'All my friends are dead. I've no one to write except a son who wants me dead and a cold, empty house.'

'Stay here with Matty,' said Julia. 'You can have my bed.'

'I couldn't sleep here!' Callie shrank into Dulce's arms. 'It would kill me.'

* * *

An hour back and forth it went, the maids yawning, and Callie shifting between senses. 'Lovely china! Is it Meissen?'

'We think it might be.'

'Let me look!' A cake-stand was passed, Dulce's hands supporting wings. 'I had one like this. Great Aunt Greville gave it to me. I'd sit Prissy, my little foxhound, at the table, and we'd serve tea, wouldn't we, Dulce.'

'That was before my time, Miss Callie. I din't come to you until Philly.'

'That's right! You were one of Sam's leavings and very pretty you were. When I was here I had a maid called Jocelyn who ran off with a first footman. They say money is the root of all evil but I think it is love.'

They wrapped her in furs to pull her back up the Rise on Matty's sled.

'Should I stay and help?' said Mrs Mac.

'I'd surely be grateful for someone,' said Dulce.

'Do, Maud,' said Julia. 'I'd stay but am in Cambridge early. 'And the letters? Are they really for posting?'

Dulce shrugged. 'To what address, madam, heaven or the other place?'

* * *

Julia didn't return to bed. Bathed and changed she caught the express. It was cold in the carriage, ice on the windows. Julia was angry. Kept up half the night by Callie's wanderings *and* blamed for Daniel's bad temper. Damned cheek! From the first it was he suggesting he cared! Were he to propose she'd probably accept, similar tastes and interests it would prove a good match for both. But he makes no move. An odd affair - much like a waltz - they come together, swing one another about and then retire to separate chairs.

Weary, Julia slept and dreamed she shared the compartment with Justine Newman and Karoline Adelman. It was a dream and yet so real, Karoline's silver hair piled upon her head, and a scarlet feather on Justine's hat quivering.

Luke was right when he said Justine was beautiful. Clear and serene, her face draws the sun's rays. Clad in burgundy velvet, her skirt gathered over burgundy leather boots, she sits in the corner. Her hands are the pale narrow hands of an anchorite but her chipped nails those of a gardener. She reads from the same red leather diary Julia found in a trunk and appears to be making notes.

Karoline too is lovely, no wonder Stefan adored her. Dressed in a dainty tea-gown of pale material, she sits at a tapestry, head bent and lips curved in a smile. She embroiders with bright blue silk - Julia can see the image but like the words in Justine's diary can make no sense of it.

She woke questioning what she knows of Karoline. In the sanatorium she sees a haggard face and tormented eyes, yet here in the train carriage - albeit a dream - Karoline is young and vibrant. Justine too is vividly alive, no silhouette hanging on a wall, a living soul filled with hope.

* * ** * *

Julia looks forward to the trips to Cambridge. No meetings to attend, and no domestic crisis, she sees the visits for Julianna, the woman, not the mother or the owner of the Nanny Tea-Shops. She does stay the occasional night but always at a hotel never at Stefan's house. Today she drops off Christmas hankies at Karoline Adelman Home for Young Mothers. The home is not a charity home, as suggested by Evie; it is financed by Stefan, and latterly, with help from Julia. After luncheon she and Stefan will visit the Sanatorium. How long they stay depends on what they find. There are times when no sooner in than they are out again, doors clanging behind them, and Karoline raking the air with her nails. It is on such occasion Julia returns to Stefan's bed. They make a sad kind of love, he often so weary the only intimacy shared is that of compassion. Overweight, shy and unglamorous, he is no Winged Angel piercing the skies, yet Stefan is a good friend and Julia loves him.

Karoline calls Julia, 'my pale angel, *Meine blasse Engel*' and yet bitch is what she shouts when raging. Julia suspects more than one woman imprisoned in the emaciated form - the disease that destroyed the original Karoline leaving interchangeable women in her stead. Most days Gentle Karoline is present. On other occasions, as with the Prince of Wales, press the wrong button, and all hell is loose. Another soul hides among the Many, an ephemeral being ever seeking the best for Stefan. It is that Karoline who urges Julia to visit and who lingers among delicate china, and it is that Karoline who during love-making loosens her hair to mingle with the flesh.

* * *

Leaving the restaurant, Julia tucked her arm through Stefan's.

'You didn't eat the escalope. Was it not good?'

'I am not hungry. Shall we walk a little before the sanatorium? I know it is cold but it is a clean cold and I need to breathe.' They walked, Stefan's pace heavy. As always when seeing Julianna he looks forward to the day but now she is here, and Karoline obstructive, he wishes her away again. 'Doctor Davison has asked for Karoline to be removed from the Sanatorium. Nurses refuse to be left alone with her. The alternative is to increase sedation. I do not want that.'

'What will you do?'

'I shall take her home. With that in mind it was my painful duty last month to tender regrets to all of my patients, one of whom was Her Majesty.'

'She understood?'

'She did and though I cannot fulfill my duty to the Queen, I can at least try for my wife. We will go home to Dresden. We have a country house there, a pretty house we used to visit during the summer weeks.'

'Does she know she is going home?'

'I have not told her, which is why we will together beard the Lioness in her den. You have a softening effect. It will help.'

'My dear it is for the best.' Now, Stefan kneels before Karoline trying to explain. 'You will be better in your own home among your own things.'

He talked of the countryside and good fresh air and the necessity of her going to Dresden. For all the notice she took he might have been discussing the mitral valve or latest advances in anaesthesia - indeed a bright woman ever interested in his work it's likely his wife of old would've enjoyed such a chat.

'Professor Adelman!' A nurse knocked on the door. 'Doctor Davison sends his compliments. Could you spare a moment?'

'What right now?'

'If you would, sir? A patient is showing signs of cardiac distress.'

Stefan got to his feet. 'Stay here then, nurse, while I show Mrs. Dryden out.'

'That's alright, Stefan. I'll sit here with Karoline.'

It was warm in the tiny room and for once sweet-smelling, a miniature fir tree in the corner giving a clean odour. The tree is decorated with silver bells. 'That's a pretty tree, Karoline,' said Julia. 'We have similar ready for the Tea Room but as yet not decorated. Matty so excited, I thought to wait.'

Karoline continues to stare at the wall. The staff here say she does this, stares at the same patch hour-after-hour. Today Julia stares with her. She had hoped to be back early but that doesn't seem likely. This morning she gathered Callie's letters to return to Greenfields. As far as she can tell they aren't letters, merely reams of note-paper headed 'My dearest Justine'. Callie makes attempts to write down her thoughts but can't get beyond the heading. A pity, thought Julia, one letter complete and we'd learn much about the past, not least why she refers to the woman she professes to hate as 'dearest'.

There's something of Evie in Callie and something too of Julia, all searching for love in the wrong places. Julia stared at the little Christmas tree and thought of Owen and the Great Pyramid. Lost, we need an Oracle to tell us where to look. Perhaps we should send for Kitty Radcliff. Unhampered by good manners or laws she seemed to know what to do with her life.

Stefan away so long Julia thought to feed Karoline.

The nurse grimaced. 'Are you sure? The lady can be very tricky.'

'She seems calm.'

'Begging your pardon, ma'm, but seeming isn't exactly being.'

'I'm sure you are right but it is only food.'

'Yes and you could get bitten as have two or three here.'

'I think I shall risk it.'

'As you wish but don't say I didn't warn you.'

Julia knelt down offering a morsel of pie. 'Might you try this, Karoline?'

For a while there was no reaction. Then Karoline turned and leaning forward -and momentarily creating the whimsical image of a graceful Giraffe bending from a great height - opened her mouth to receive the pie.

'Quick, ma'm!' The nurse leaned forward. 'Put the dish under her chin and lean back. You don't want her spitting on your gown.'

Karoline chewed and then swallowed.

'Did you see that?' Julia turned to the nurse. 'She swallowed it!' Such joy to see the pie stay down she might've been an anxious mother and Karoline a stubborn child! 'Again?' Another piece that was chewed and swallowed. So intense was the moment Julia found she was chewing along with Karoline.

So it progressed until the whole of the pie was gone.

'Should I offer a drink?'

The nurse shrugged. 'Why not? You got further than any of us.'

'Karoline?' Julia asked. 'Would you care for a sip of champagne?'

No words, only haunted eyes staring, and then Karoline nodded.

'Oh Stefan!' Julia whispered, 'why aren't you here to see this?'

A measure of champagne was held it to the lips, sipped and swallowed.

'Is it because you're going home?' said Julia dabbing Karoline's chin with a napkin. 'Are you happy to go? Is that why you eat and drink today?'

Still no words only a sense of observation and sad humour back of the eyes.

Hands washed and things tidied away, there was nothing to do but wait.

Karoline is again staring at the wall, silver bells on the tree against her robe like fireflies on lint. Why sit hour-after-hour like that? What is it she sees?

Stefan once said it was being parted from the wall that unsettled her.

Last night a poem was among Callie's unwritten letters. Now, recalling the dream and the beautiful young Karoline at her tapestry, Julia took it from her bag and began to read: *Hope is a thing with feathers that perches in the soul...*

* * *

At the station they clung together. 'We shall soon be together again,' said Julia. 'It's only Germany, not the far side of the moon.'

'No it is not the moon. We shall meet again and chat as though never apart.'

'Yes, as though never apart.'

'And there is always the telephone!'

'Yes! The telephone!'

'And the business to run, the Nanny Tea-Shops, sugared buns for heartache, and all that is needed and necessary? I mean to say we are still partners.'

'We are partners, Dear Stefan, and always will be.'

One last hug and then Stefan wept. 'Kiss me then, dearest Julia, and hold me in your heart so it is *au revoir* rather than *Auf Wiedersehen.*'

On the train back Julia slept. Then, as though only marking time before renewing her acquaintance, they arrived, Justine in the corner reading the diary and Karoline still at her tapestry. Julia dreamed and wondered: Why am I seeing this? What is it you sew so tenderly, Karoline? And you, Justine, why do you haunt the cottage? What is it that holds you?

Joe is right when he speaks of weeds strangling delicate plants. Once Julia might've thought Justine Newman a weed, and Callie the fragile plant, but last night having felt the iron will she wonders if Callie was the stronger plant and Justine, though older and wiser, the strangled one.

Silent and beautiful, maintaining a secret, the ladies read and sewed. Aware of being carried away from Stefan panic rose in Julia. God bless you, Dear Friend! Believing it would hurt him rather than please she didn't mention the food. There was nothing to tell because minutes after eating there was a cry from the nurse, 'look out!' and Karoline with her fingers down her throat.

So much for female partisanship! Karoline had no intention of pleasing anyone, the look in her eyes when finally ceased retching said so. 'There,' said the sad eyes. 'I'm in charge of this agony not you, so don't give yourself airs.'

Brakes screeching, the train pulled into the station. Lamps

on the station platform swing back and forth in the wind. Light flickers over the phantoms as starlight on marble. All is still but for Karoline, and her needle, and the bright blue thread, and the blue cherub she sewed.

Then Julia knew the secret of the wall, the young and lovely Frau Adelman is awaiting her child - this is what Karoline sees in her patch of wall, this is her memory and her dream, a woman, belly swollen under her robe, embroidering a blue cherub in anticipation of a son.

'Oh Lord.' Knowing what was to come, sorrow and madness, tears filled Julia's eyes. No wonder Karoline holds onto the dream! Who would not?

Lamp-light shimmered on the tapestry and Julia's tears were stilled. Why be sad, whispered the Lord God. This patch of wall is My Gift to Karoline. It tells of a time when there was no sadness, there was only love and hope.

Blip!

Karoline is gone, fading away, a flashing needle and blue thread the last glimpse of yesterday. Yet all was not done, God ever Merciful, the Giver and the Gift continued to enchant. Justine Newman put down the diary and turning to Julia began to chant in soft Irish lilt the Emily Dickinson poem.

'*Hope is a thing with feathers that perches in the soul*
and sings the tune without the words and never stops at all.
And sweetest in the gale is heard and sore must be the storm
that can abash the little bird that kept so many warm.
I've heard it in the chilliest land and on the strangest sea,
yet never in extremity it asked a crumb of me.'

Messages

Port Elizabeth, South Africa.

The fellow died in his arms! One minute they're talking, the next the guy from the *Pretoria News* is dead, eyes wide and fists locked into Daniel's shirt. They were in a wagon on the way back to Camp. 'I'm off home tomorrow,' the chap was saying. 'It's my boy's first Christmas. I got him this!' Then a guerrilla sniper took a shot and the rabbit's foot charm for the boy wet with blood.

In Port Elizabeth Daniel couldn't get past the look on the guy's face. Some say when close to death your life rushes before you. There was nothing in that fellow's eyes but a future snuffed out. Seeing it a Message from Above, Daniel decided the next time Julianna presents a smile but not her heart, it's over. Life's too short to wait on one woman no matter how desirable.

The shirt he burnt it along with the letter from his publisher who said the market wasn't ready for an obscure artist like Seurat but there was a money-maker closer to home, *'anything about your cousin, Lady Brooke, would sell.'*

It seems *Le Grand Jatte* is Le Grand Waste of Time as is his passion for Julianna. It's time to marry and have sons of his own. Matty Dryden is a good kid. In Norfolk he dredges mud for worms, in the evening, face washed and hair smarmed down, he's dredging magic from the piano keys. Last week Daniel suggested music as a career. The boy debated and then in that crushed larynx voice, said, 'Papa says I must listen with my head and play from my heart.' Matty used to show animosity toward Daniel; now he sees him as yesterday's contender for his mother's hand and is amenable.

Why not break away? It's not as if his mind is closed to other opportunities. Mona Dobson, a woman here investigating the camps is worth a second look. She is that rare thing, a do-gooder who does good, though the way she's going she's likely to be on the next boat home. 'Better calm down,' he says. 'If you're here to access information you should at least pretend to be impartial.'

'Impartial?' Her eyes had flashed, nice eyes but red-tinged with fatigue. 'Don't speak to me of impartial. These places are of Satan.' She pointed to a tent. 'Do you know how many families are closeted in one of those filthy bivouacs, and how many babies, even as you prattle of impartiality, are dying of malnutrition? The British Government should be ashamed.'

She'd grabbed his hand. 'You want news worthy of the good people of Philadelphia?' She took him to a tent where children lay dying of typhoid. 'They don't have water never mind medicine. Something must be done, Mr Masson, and something true, not a parcel of lies.' She then asked why he was in the Transvaal as a news correspondent if not to tell the truth.

Mother said much the same. He argued it was his job and that he didn't have a choice. 'You've plenty choice,' says she. 'You were born with money in your diaper.' She waved the *Times* under his nose. 'They've finally tracked down the names of the English dead at Ladysmith. One hundred and fifty dead and close to three hundred wounded? Why put yourself in that kind of danger?'

He said not to quote statistics. 'A lot of men died fighting the Boers and not just the English. Until you know what you're saying, Mother, say nothing.'

'Why insist on calling me Mother,' she'd replied. 'You make me feel old.'

'You are old. I'd hardly call eighty next birthday young.'

'I'm not young but not in my coffin either. Go find a nice California gal, get married and make babies, then at least I can die happy if not live so.'

That's Mother, when sane she berates Julianna, and those associated with her; when hanging on the edge she tries contacting the dead. Last week she confessed to writing to a Spiritist. 'I thought we might have her over.'

When he said bringing a quack to the house was unbecoming to a woman of her age she hit the ceiling. 'I swear you'll age me into the grave!'

'At least you'll get your information first hand.'

'Oh do be serious! I want to hear what she's got to say. It might be interesting. It might even be fun! We don't have fun these days.'

'Turning tables is not my idea of fun.' Over the years the Lansdowne Estate has been the backdrop to all conversation but little said of the man centre of the coil. 'What about Henry Lansdowne. Did you love him?'

'I liked him well enough.'

'Enough to mourn him these sixty years?'

'It would have been a good match.'

'And what of Justine, have you mourned her as many years?'

'Yes,' she said, 'every hour of every day.'

There'll be no séance at Greenfields, not if he has anything to do with it, there's enough undead walking the battlements without inviting more. Why would you lay out your personal life before strangers in such a manner?

Daniel knows of the Suffolk Séance and can't think why Julianna got involved. John Sargent says the Carringtons are okay. Daniel sees Freddie Carrington for what he is, a fag who uses women as a smokescreen. Julianna needs to get away from such. Sooner or later there'll be one rumour too many and even the Prince of Wales not able to haul her up again. Daniel is no snob but knows who he is and wants to be able to bring his wife to dine with cousins, the Greville Warwicks, and not be embarrassed. Reluctant to surrender his heart's desire he closes his eyes to Messages from Above and dashes off a cable: *Julianna, I hope to be home in time for Christmas where I shall put to you a question I have long wanted to ask. Please give thought to your answer. The right words and the coming New Year will be the best year of my life, your Daniel.*

* * *

Julia took off her hat. 'Dorothy, is Master Matthew at piano practice?'

'He was, madam, but he's in the yard now building a snowman. Sir Hugh called to remind you of the charity dinner.' Dorothy giggled. 'He says he's practising kisses and you're not to forget the mistletoe.'

Everyone likes Hugh. He is charming and amusing and Julia is glad of him but not so glad she'd marry him - no matter his argument of yesterday.

They were at Holkham at the Point-to-Point. It was cold and a wind blowing, no one was happy. Hugh stamped his feet and cursed. 'Forgive me, Julianna, but this is a damnable bore. Why do we come to these things?'

'I know why I came,' she'd stuttered. 'I couldn't bear another scolding. Last week I missed a luncheon and thought HRH would have a heart attack.'

'Ridiculous! A man of his standing ought to be above such tantrums. Does he really need the same clutch of broody hens bolstering his feathers?'

'He's anxious for his mother.'

'As are we all, but ought that to prevent him from being kind to those that are kind to him? I was up half the night with a bad case of gout. Did I cry off? I'm here willing to do his bidding and still he treats me like a chambermaid.'

'Poor Hugh! Does your toe still ache?'

'Yes it does, or would if I could feel anything. I mean why are we here? Can you see the runners through the sleet? And don't bother offering field glasses! My lashes are frozen solid.' Later inside in the Hall and Hot Toddy passed around he was in a better mood. 'You must think me a wretch.'

'Are you feeling better?'

'I don't know. Three tots of this and I'm past caring.' He'd taken her arm and dragged her aside. 'What's this I hear about you leaving Norfolk?'

'Good grief! I only thought of moving, that's all!'

'A thought is all it takes. "I think therefore gossip makes it so!" It is a principle worthy of Descartes. Why didn't you say you're thinking of moving?'

'It occurred to me I might do better elsewhere.'

'You mean Matty might do better.'

'It's the same thing.'

'Why would he? What's wrong with Norfolk?'

'There's nothing wrong with Norfolk. It's Matty and certain friendships that shouldn't have been formed.'

'Since when did friendship become a hindrance?'

'You know Matty. If he likes a person he weaves his life about them, taking them where they are not meant to go and making demands of them.'

'You're referring to Mister Wolf, of course.'

'You see that's it exactly! It was Matty who made the man into a fairy story. Now Luke Roberts is known to everyone as the Wolf.'

'Well,' Hugh had smiled. 'There is that wild and hungry mystique about the man and you surely can't think he'd hurt Matty. For a wolf he is an honourable creature. I was with him recently and know it to be so.'

'You were?'

'I asked him to take a look at my roof. He did more than look he stripped off his jacket and climbed up there. He said the chimney stack had shifted and not to worry he'd fix it and fix he did. He sent a couple of his musclemen. Now I can go to bed at night and not have to watch water dripping down the wall.'

'He is good at things like that. You could not ask for a better man.'

'Then what's the problem? Why can't Matty have him for friend?'

'Matty doesn't want a friend. He wants a father.'

'Ah! Matty's looks for a papa and you don't think the Wolf right for the job.' It was then, Julia remaining silent that he thought to propose. 'Do you have another candidate in mind,

Delicious Daniel perhaps?'

'Now, Hugh, don't make a thing of it. Matty misses his papa.'

'And seeks a replacement?'

'Yes.'

'Then why not me?'

'I beg your pardon?'

'Why not me for papa?' Julia stared and he shrugged. 'I know I'm a bit long in the tooth to be anybody's pa but if it gives Matty a man to rely on, and gets you out of a bind, why not. We like one another, me and Matty, and we like one another too, don't we, Anna? We could grow old gracefully without the stress of the marital bed, and since I have neither property nor money you'd never be worried by horrid things like inheritance tax and Wills.'

'You are very kind.'

'Not kind, Julianna, desperate! I live in a cottage loaned Grace and Favour. When Her Majesty dies I'll be out. Bertie won't keep me. He doesn't care for us fairies. Married to you would be the answer to a prayer. I'd have a home with someone I like and not worried about being tossed out on my ear.'

'Oh Hugh! I didn't know.'

'I don't know why you didn't. My situation is common among many such households. The outside world thinks we do well to serve the Household. Some do well, those that crawl on their belly or have the good fortune to sniff out the odd Gunpowder Plot. I don't crawl on any part of me and though I served in the Hussars for years never came across Guy Faulkes.'

'I am sorry.'

'Oh do say you'll think about it? Life with me would have advantages. Imagine the young bucks who'd try their luck thinking you an old man's darling? I wouldn't complain. In fact I'd help sort the wheat from chaff. You'd be safe. No one would dare beset your name with me in tow. Fitzwilliam are as poor as church mice but have a lineage harking back to the eleventh century. And you must admit Lady Julianna Beresford Fitzwilliam has quite a ring.'

Then he'd smiled, God Love him, with his dyed eyelashes and single blonde curl stuck to a bald pate. 'But don't worry, my dear. If you truly can't bear the idea I have a couple of aging Ladies of the Bed-Chamber in tow with hefty bank balances and meagre hopes. One of them will do at a pinch.'

* * *

Ben Faulkner wants Matty to go to music school. 'He can remain as he is, a talented child, or he can assert discipline and become an artist.' Ben is not the only one to take an interest in Matty and his music; the Royal College of Music is suggested by the Prince of Wales. 'He should be heard, Ju-ju, and not by some determined lady pounding an out-of-tune piano in the school gym.'

Beset as Bertie is by problems, Julia thought nothing of it, yet, that same week she received a call to take Matty to the Royal College. The tutor listened and then taking Matty's hands asked why a piano and not another instrument. Matty said he heard Mr Doodle playing.

'Mr Doodle?'

Julia grimaced. 'He means Mr Faulkner, his piano tutor.'

Matty nodded. 'I saw the keys spring up and down and I remembered.'

'What did you remember?'

'I remembered making them spring higher.'

The tutor smiled. 'Your son has chosen well. He knows a pianist doesn't need vocal chords, his hands will speak for him.'

Matty took all in his stride and when questioned later if he would like to go to such a place to study asked if he could take Kaiser with him. The dog is everything to him. Knowing the brevity of life Julia tries preparing Matty for the inevitable. 'Such a dear dog! We shall miss him when he's gone.'

'What do you mean gone?' Matty flashed a look.

Having got into it Julia didn't know how to get out without making things worse. 'One day Kaiser will grow old and die.'

'Can I have a toast soldiers with my egg for breakfast?' Such a switch, Julia thought to bring the subject round again. 'We could get a puppy, and then when Kaiser does go you won't miss him so much.'

'I shall miss him but he'll be with Papa and so I'll see them both, and I shall still have Mister Wolf.'

Matty looks to the dog and sees Luke. Truth to tell, Julia does the same. It's another reason to leave. It's months since Luke set foot in the cottage but like Kaiser he is always here and the bond between him and Matty strong. That her son loves and is loved in return can only be good yet such ties deny other possibilities. Daniel would make an excellent father, and California, she has heard, a place where one could be happy and with no swishing of tails and worries of the dead. With that in mind Julia thought to pour oil on existing troubled waters and sent Maggie with a note inviting Callie Masson to tea.

* * *

Callie wouldn't come to the cottage, her cold prevented her. Julia will go but doesn't plan on staying. Joe Carmody is ill. She went earlier to enquire but learned he was too ill to see her. From one sick person she came to another, Callie's skin hanging on her bones. 'Does she sleep at night now?'

'She still wanders,' said Dulce. 'I've brewed a sleeping draught for tonight. If she don't sleep, and me for that matter, anything can happen.'

'Do you not get help?'

'I don't ask. I have been with Mizz Callie a long time. It's too private a thing to share, though I do wish Mister Daniel were here.'

'It's Christmas. He won't leave his mother at such a time.'

'The old Daniel never would but I'm not sure of the new.'

Dulce thinks Daniel changed, Callie suggests the same. 'The war has changed him but then war changes everything. Henry was the same.'

'I believe you said you were childhood sweethearts.'

Callie snorted. 'Not sweethearts! He thought too much of himself.'

Looking for calm ground Julia steered conversation toward forthcoming celebrations and the Nativity Play. 'Matty is to be a shepherd.'

'I should like to see that,' said Callie wistfully, 'but I can't manage that cold church. Do you suppose the children would bring the play here?'

'I don't see why not. Would you like me to enquire?'

'I sure would!' Callie's face was bright. 'It would do this old house good to hear children's voices instead of adult squawk.'

'I'll speak to the Rector and see what he says.'

'Tell him St Bedes was singing carols here long before he was born. Tell him I'm a wealthy woman and that it won't hurt him to keep that tradition.' Soon she was back with Henry Lansdowne's passion for Justine. 'She said his behaviour was unworthy, that he took advantage of her position.'

'So it was he who caused the split.'

Callie nodded. 'I went to Aunt Maynard accusing Justine of leading him astray. I didn't stop there. I accused her of making improper advances to me.'

'Oh Callie!'

'I know.' She buried her head in her hands. 'It was the damned spy-glass! I was wrong about Justine and in the end I was wrong about Henry.'

'What happened?'

'They tried beating her and her sister out of town but couldn't. He'd left Justine the gate-house and she wouldn't go. Clarinda suffered a bone disease that made her awkward. It's likely Justine did stay for Clarinda but then she may have just dug in her heels. She knew she'd done no wrong and wouldn't be pushed. They did push! The Aunts, the Maynards and Grevilles, made her life a misery, cut her from society ruining her name and her gardens.'

'And that's why she built the wall!'

'It was Easter time. She was in Japan hunting plants. The Aunts hired men to cut down trees and smash her greenhouse and everything in it. They didn't set fire to the house but they killed birds on her pond and pigeons in her loft.'

Julia could only shake her head.

'Horrible,' whispered Callie. 'She came home and built the

wall. I never spoke to her again until the day I left for America when, fool that I am, I went to see her. That's when she said he was the pursuer.'

'And what about Henry when he saw the destruction?'

'He never got to see it, at least not from this side of the grave. I was thankful and sorry for that, sorry he never got to witness the destruction he caused, and glad he was dead. I felt it was God's Hand that thrust him under the waves. He ruined my life. But for him I never would've gone to Philadelphia where for the next fifty-odd years I was tied to another selfish man.'

'Good things came from those years. You have Daniel.'

'Yes, Daniel, my pride and joy, but also his father's son and thus his future happiness in doubt.'

'How is that?'

'Samuel Masson was a gambler. Daniel doesn't study money markets but gambles the same and the stakes higher. He loves danger. He says not. To hear him talk covering those Chinese rebellions and the Boer War is a grind. But don't be fooled, he loves being in the thick of it.'

'And yet he seems a quiet man and steady. Matty really likes him.'

'Yes but not enough, Julianna! Neither of you like him enough! If you did he wouldn't be in South Africa messing with guns! I'm not blaming you. As I said he takes after his father. Dulce saw it straight away. It took me a while. His father made plenty money but lost as much paying off enraged fathers. When he marries - if he marries - Daniel won't be unfaithful. You won't catch him risking reputation for some little dolly, too much of a Greville high-hat. But free and rich of blood, he'll risk the world to be different. Before he came to Norfolk he was champing at the bit, an explorer in the mould of Cortes.'

'I heard him described in that manner.'

'And it was right! Shake a red rag under his nose and he'll charge. He needs to settle while he can. Left to his own devices he'll end up a monk or a martyr. Why do you think I was so keen to get you together?'

'I didn't think you were.'

Callie sighed. 'I was, Anna, at first very keen. But a lot of water has rolled under the bridge of late and most of it poled by your friend, Eve. I told you, Daniel can be pernickety. He is proud and resents what he considers a lack of proper pride. I am sorry to say it, Dear Anna, but where my son and his prejudices are concerned Eve Carrington has done you no good.'

* * *

Daniel is in a pew in the Trinity Church, Port Elizabeth, eating a cheese sandwich and chugging on apple cider. The Pretoria newsman told him of this place. He said they had a willing clergy and a generous congregation: 'If you're lucky you get a blessing from the Lord, a sandwich and a jug of cider.'

Daniel was lucky. He got cider, a sandwich, and Miss Dobson.

Mona Dobson is all fired up. It seems she's acquired transport to deliver aid to the camps. 'I jogged the family elbow and got help from Sir Robert Peel and got railway trucks and several tons of supplies which I mean to distribute.'

'You have a useful elbow.'

Freckles wrinkling, Mona smiled. 'My family is a busy family. My grandfather is Permanent Under-Secretary at the Home Office, my father an Archdeacon, and my aunt is married to the British High Commissioner.'

'Busy indeed!'

'There are forty prison camps here, Mr Masson. We need to be busy. I'm told Bloemfontein is as far as we can go. It's not much but it is a start.'

'Isn't that rather dangerous?'

'Not so very much. We travel under a flag of truce and should be safe.'

Daniel made no comment, his thoughts being the guy from Pretoria News probably thought the same thing. 'How many are you?'

'We are eight, me, my friend Mary Osborne and six other Baptist people.'

'Do you have armed escorts?'

'We don't need them. The supplies are meant for refugees, for farmers' wives and children, not rebels. No one will fire on us. The word has gone out.'

'Let's hope for your sake the word has been heard. A fellow was shot only a couple of days ago, a newsman not a mercenary. If the word went out about him the guerrillas sure weren't listening.'

Mona regarded him. 'Mr Masson the word I am referring to is prayer. I promise you that will be heard no matter where we are.'

Daniel's stomach contracted. What a woman! Tight riding britches, freckles and an evangelical soul is an alluring combination. 'What are your thoughts regarding hangers on? I mean, how do you feel about me coming with you?'

'In what capacity?'

'A helper?'

'Do you want to help?'

'Why not? I'm bound to see things that need seeing.'

'Would you give out supplies and help with cooking and washing?'

'Washing? What cooking pots and so on?'

'No, bodies, arms and legs and other parts of the anatomy! People that are sick - people with Typhoid and other infections - need washing. They can't do it themselves. Are you prepared to roll up your sleeves?'

'Washing sickly bodies is hardly my remit.'

'What is your remit?'

Daniel shrugged. 'Until today it was to get news from where news is most likely to be got and to get it posted so the world can read it.'

'Then it's time you did something more worthwhile.' She walked away. 'We leave at dawn. We could use a strong pair of hands, Godly hands, that don't mind dealing in dirt. Slack hands are no use to us. It's like life, Mr Masson. You can't come along for the ride. You have to be part of it to live it.'

* * *

It was warm in the church, flies buzzing. Daniel was sick of dirt and heat. He'd seen enough to last a lifetime. He should do what he came to do, put Julianna's letter in the post and book the first available birth back to England.

Right now it's cold in England, snow on the ground, icicles hanging from the trees and Julianna's cool beauty. The envelope rustled in his pocket reminding him that once posted there will be no turning back. A ship leaves at dawn that will take the letter. When he returns to Norfolk it's likely the letter, and an answer, will be waiting. On the other hand if he hesitates he won't get home in time and Callie, and Julianna, will be alone for Christmas.

Daniel thought of Mother's endless struggles. He thought of Greenfields, that miserable house with leaky roof and rotten plumbing. And then, there's the holiday programme, that like death and taxes, inevitably lies ahead: the pre-Christmas Lunch at Sandringham with HRH, and then a visit to the Warwicks with over-rich food and poor wine, and the cigars, the heaving tables and port to be passed, plus the heehawing and the interminable waltzes, and the bowing and shaking of hands - the whole weary business.

God, how dull it all sounds! Then he thought of the Pretoria news-man, whose name he thinks may have been Jack, the way the bullet parted the air, the snap of light and Jack's body sagging, and those sad fists clutching his shirt.

It could have been Daniel, six inches either-way and it would be him trussed up the hold of a steam ship along with sides of lamb.

He thought of Jack's little boy who never got to decorate the Christmas Tree. In Norfolk there's Matty. There'll be a fir tree in the cottage which he and Matty might decorate, but then Matty already has a pa, who, though not living, may as well be. Must Daniel be a substitute father as well as a lover?'

If he stays here it'll be hardtack and sleeping in bivouacs. There'll be guerrillas who want to kill him and refugees with typhoid looking to do the same. It will be hardly the jolliest or most comfortable of holidays.

Look! Mona Dobson drives a pony cart by the church. She handles it well. She has strong hands, Godly hands, as she said, hands that (if so inclined) would make a man stretch with pleasure. She's not beautiful but has nice eyes and riding gunshot on a train through the Transvaal sounds like fun - and as Callie pointed out recently, they don't have much fun nowadays.

He tossed a coin, heads to stay and tails to go. When it hit the ground he didn't bother looking. He left it where it was, and the note to Julianna dropped under the seat.

Nativity Plays

Saturday Julia called on the Carmody cottage for news of Joe. The door opened and Bertha, his wife, peered out. 'Oh, it's you, Mrs Dryden,' she said, her tone colder than the snow. 'You're about early.'

'I hope it's not inconvenient to call. I wanted news of Joe.'

'He's no better. I put a poultice on his chest but he's up there wheezing. It's his own fault. The silly beggar was up half the night fiddling with the tree.'

'What do the doctors say?'

'We haven't called any. Joe said not to fuss.'

'Is that wise?'

'Wise or not he's made up his mind.'

'Oh right. We've brought a few things, haven't we, Maggie? We thought it might help at such a busy time.'

Maggie Jeffers thrust the basket forward. 'There's a goose I helped pluck and a puddin' boilin' all night and mince pies as we sell in the Nanny.'

Bertha Carmody peered into the basket but made no effort to take it.

'Bertha!' Joe, his voice cracked from coughing, called down the stairs. 'Where's your manners, woman? What you doin' keepin' madam on the door step?'

The door was cracked wider but with no real enthusiasm.

'No need!' Julia was embarrassed. 'You're busy.'

Mrs Carmody folded her arms. 'I do have a lot to manage at the moment. Joe's always complaining of one ailment or other but never really ill until now.'

'Then perhaps he ought to see a doctor if only for an opinion.'

'If you mean your German doctor I doubt we could afford him.'

'Bertha! What's goin' on?' Joe shouted again. 'Quit gabbin' and bring madam in. And tell that Maggie Jeffers to mind her manners talkin' of her betters in that way! She wouldn't dare if I were up and about!'

Mrs Carmody gestured. 'Might I invite you in for a cup of tea?'

'Thank you no.' Julia stepped back. 'Matty's in the Nativity play this afternoon at Greenfields and I'm in rather a rush.'

'So I heard. I would have liked to have seen it but not with Joe poorly.'

'The whole of Bakers is invited,' said Maggie. 'My sister Flora's girl is an angel and Matty is a Wise Man. He's to wear a turban and ride a camel.'

Julia sighed. 'Matty is to be a shepherd and carry a lamb.'

'Does he have much to say?' said Bertha, 'him and his poorly voice?'

'He has eight words, "I bring you a lamb, Dear Baby Jesus." '

'That's nice. Joe will be disappointed to miss it.'

'Perhaps Matty could drop by tomorrow and tell him how it went.'

'No thank you. Our Clifford is coming. I'll be too busy.' Maggie was poking about in the basket. 'There's bramble jelly. Joe likes bramble jelly.'

Mrs Carmody snatched the basket. 'It's *Mr* Carmody to you, Margaret Jeffers! You need to mind your manners! You've far too much to say for yourself which might be alright for some around here but doesn't wash with me!'

Julia thought it time to move on. 'You'll find a gift in there for Mr Carmody in appreciation of his work and something too from Matty. Do please give him our love and tell him to get well. We can't manage without him.'

'You might have to manage.' Mrs Carmody's face was harsh in the morning light. 'Joe's not as young as he was and must be stopped going out in all weather. I've tried telling him but he won't listen. Maybe if you do he will.'

Bang - the door slammed!

Maggie sucked her teeth. 'Not very friendly is she, madam.'

'I imagine she has a lot on her mind.'

'Is Joe going to die?'

'Mr Carmody has bronchitis. I hope there's no need for anyone to die.'

'Mrs Carmody blames you for him bein' ill. She says he's always lookin' to your interests. She thinks it'll be your fault if he dies.'

'Good God, Maggie, how can you say such a thing?'

'It's what she's thinkin', madam, as plain as day. And if he does die it'll be what the whole village is thinkin'.

* * *

Maggie wouldn't go in the churchyard. 'I don't like walkin' on graves.'

'Then go!' Julia held out a package. 'And take this with you. It's the blue ribbons you wanted.' Maggie snatched and ran. She is with her mother over Christmas. The tea shop closed and Mrs Mac and Leah in Dorset, that leaves Dorothy, and hopefully peace on earth and good will to all men.

'Hallelujah!'

Susan's grave is by the wall, not exactly beyond the boundary but close enough to appease St Bedes' Good Wives. The grave has had a visitor, boot marks in the snow and circlet of roses crowning a marble cherub's head.

Stefan bought the monument. 'A cherub guards my son in the Adelman vault. God willing, we shall all be together one day as will this little family.'

Wings drooping and baby rabbit under his arm the cherub kneels in tender care, his crown of roses a beacon through the snow. There's a card in Evie's handwriting, *Sleep in peace Susan.* Freddie's involvement is known throughout Norfolk. 'I'm not surprised,' Mrs Mac was heard to say, 'gentry do what they like and get away with it.' Recalling Freddie at the séance, staring eyes and trembling mouth, Julia doubted he got away with anything.

* * *

The Nativity Play is a trial for Matty. Every Sunday Matty goes to church happy but returns pale and worried. 'If you don't like being a shepherd,' said Julia, 'what about a cow? They only have to moo.' He shakes his head. It seems Matty had promised the Knitted Lamb. 'I said he would meet Baby Jesus.'

The lamb belonged to Owen. Matty won't be parted from

it. It sits on his bed during the day. Kaiser is allowed to carry it hence the Lamb is a grubby grey. It's the words. Matty practices all the time, 'I bring you a Lamb Dear Baby Jesus.' He's only to misplace a word to start all over again.

Julia spoke to Miss Perkins, the teacher who had '*a lot on her mind at the moment and would be glad if Matthew's mother would sort it out.*' Short of a miracle Julia knows it will end it tears but promised to be in the audience. 'When it's over we'll have a party,' she said. 'We'll spread cushions on the floor and toast bread.' Bread blackened by fire and thick with butter being the height of decadence to Matty he said he'd do his part.

The wreath laid, she hurried on to the post-office. So many packages! She's sent packages to Germany, but hasn't had a reply and thinks Stefan is finding things hard. Packages for Charlotte and May went last week along with those to Greenfields - laven-der-water for Callie and a book on Christina Rossetti for Daniel. He is another slow to reply. Yesterday Callie asked if Julia had heard from South Africa, her parting shot (Julia again the villain) was that 'if he'd expected a warmer welcome from England he would've returned.' The Nelson packages are last to post - it is rumoured Luke Roberts is home.

* * *

Nan is happy. Luke is home. He is here now gnawing a chicken drumstick.

'Hey!' She slapped his hand. 'They're for the public bar and folks that pay our wages not cheeky sons. Look at all that snow!' She peered through the window. 'If the forecast is right there's

346

more to come!'

Luke took another drumstick. 'And you snowbound and the public bar empty so I may as well have another of these. Which reminds me...' he turned to Albert. 'Did your lads look to lagging the pipes in the Harrogate place? Only the last thing we want is burst pipes on a newly carpeted floor.'

Albert nodded. 'We did. And for heaven's sake, lad, settle down. It's Christmas and we're supposed to be on holiday.'

'Talking of lagging pipes,' said Nan, 'are you warm in that house of yours? I popped in the other day to tidy and thought you live like a hermit.'

'Some hermit!' Albert yawned. 'He owns half of Manchester. A chippie the other day called him Mister Rockefeller.'

Luke laughed. 'And does he know who Rockefeller is?'

'I doubt it, but be careful! You know folks like to bring a man down.'

'I'd like to see 'em try!' said Nan. 'I'm glad he makes his money work for him. He works hard enough. I just feel his position should be reflected in his house.'

'And what position is that?' said Luke.

'Aubusson rugs on the floor and linen sheets on his bed!' said Nan. 'He wants fashion and colour and mirrors that light up the room.'

'I have linen sheets on the bed and a sheepskin before the fire. That'll do for now.' Luke straightened. 'I'm going to look at Betty and I'm taking a currycomb with me. Her coat is rough and her tail full of burrs.'

'Betty is the pot boy's job.'

'Let him leave her alone. If he can't be trusted to do it right

I'll find someone who can.' Luke saw to the horse and then went home to change. Children of St Bedes are putting on a play at the Big House, Augustus Simpkin, newly elected Mayor, and others, invited to share a cup of punch. Nan says her invitation is due to having taken tea with the Prince of Wales. Luke thinks it is because Greenfields's roof is leaking.

Earlier this year Daniel Masson asked A Roberts & Sons to put in a tender for a complete overhaul. Luke said he couldn't do anything until the end of 1901, which led to the old lady on the phone begging for help and Luke agreeing to the roof. There was a time when he'd think twice about doing a job that size, never mind refusing. Those days are gone. Luke is not as he was, a bruised fingernail skirting the edge of life; 'Master' they call him now and not only the gangs of workers he employs, the bank manager.

Money was never the objective, it was more a by-product. It's the same with property. Last week in Manchester he bought worker's cottages. He hadn't gone with the thought of buying but they were derelict and the council looking to sell. Windows boarded up, and dandelion clocks blowing, he looked at the street and thought of his father and the kiddie that fell into the lock. Then he thought of Susan Dudley and knew he must help otherwise what's the point of living. He's no philanthropist. Too many years hard graft made that way of thinking impossible, but when renovated he will let the cottages at a reasonable rent, and if children thereabouts need a school one day he will build one - and his son, when he comes along, will go to University, to Cambridge, perhaps, where Julianna's husband taught.

He dreamt of Owen Passmore last night; a familiar dream it

was of Italian mountains and digging gullies. He and his father sat aboard a wagon, Luke's wife walking alongside. He can see her now clear as day, blouse dipping over her shoulders and the rich cleavage of her breasts inviting a kiss.

A child cries. Anxious, she turns back. 'Don't fret!' He says. 'That's not our son.' Last night a third man sat aboard the wagon. Tall and scholarly looking he stared at Luke. 'No,' he said. 'He's mine.'

This is about Matty. Luke's always worrying about that lad especially after that foolish séance. For some reason he sees that child singing and dog's tail wagging as a warning of danger. According to Nan it's a two-way love. She'll phone when Luke's away, 'the kiddie was here asking when you were coming home.' It's why Luke wanted to be home for this Christmas. There's something in the air, a rustling sound, snowflakes in the wind and hidden voices in the crackle of ice. He's never been one for praying, but these days pray is all he does, a silent thing, like a nursery rhyme back of his mind, 'Dear Lord, keep Matty and Freddie safe, and bless my brother Jacky.'

* * *

A crisis with the fire range in the kitchen caused Julia to be late to the play. Matty had gone ahead with the children 'to rehearse our entry,' said Mrs Perkins. 'The donkey must not get ahead of the sheep when entering the stable. They must enter together and not pushing and shoving.'

Julia was all but ready when the wretched range began belching smoke and had to be raked back. Normally, she'd call Joe but

349

can't now. With everyone else away, and Dorothy on her day off, there is only Julia. She shut Kaiser and the cats in the laundry room, and then, an apron over her dress, raked out the embers and in transferring coke to a bucket dropped a live coal on her skirt.

Nothing for it but to bath and change. Conscious of Matty waiting, she quickly wove her damp hair into a braid, and grabbing a cape went out into the snow.

The House is a blaze of light and the Hall arranged as a theatre, chairs drawn about a raised wooden dais. Overtopped by a pink hat and clutching a pink feather boa, Callie, occupies a huge throne-like chair on the front row.

Julia smiled. 'Callie and her hats!'

Dulce nods. 'The smaller she gets the bigger the hat.'

'She looks happy.'

'It's as well she is, considering Mr Daniel won't be back for Christmas. He sent a cable, he was sorry he was with a missionary giving out food.'

'That sounds important.'

'So is giving his mama a joyous last Christmas.'

'Last Christmas?' Julia drew back. 'What do you mean?'

Dulce shrugged. 'It's always somebody's last Christmas.'

* * *

'It's a pity Daniel isn't here. When he learns of it I'm sure he'll be sorry he missed it.' Spying an empty seat, Julia moved on.

Dulce watched her go, the beauty in the flame coloured gown. 'Yes, fool of a man,' she whispered, 'and Christmas won't be all he'll regret.'

Julia shuffled along the row. 'May I sit with you, Nan?'

'Of course! Nan smiled. 'You cut it a bit fine. I wasn't sure you were comin'.'

'I had trouble with the stove.'

'Say no more! They can be so very temperamental.'

'Mine certainly is.' Julia gazed about. 'Is Luke not coming?'

Nan laughed out loud. 'Now what prompted that question? Might it have been the word temperamental? My poor lad! Man of property with half the country beggin' his time and yet he still carries the mark of Cain.'

'That's not what I meant!' said Julia. 'I suppose I was thinking of the stove.'

'You mean overheated and in need of rakin' out?'

Julia glanced sideways and meeting Nan's twinkling gaze laughed. 'Yes poor Luke! Is he coming to see the play?'

'He's here already with the kiddies. It was him made the wooden stage and a crib for Baby Jesus. Mrs Masson wanted it like a real theatre.'

'He is very much sought after.'

'Indeed he is, especially with Mrs Masson's son away.' Nan smoothed her gloves. 'You know he's not coming home for the holiday?'

'I did hear.'

'It's a bad sign.'

'A bad sign?'

'Aye, for you.'

Julia understood Nan's meaning. Daniel Masson is a Greville Warwick. He is au fait with the customs and mores of courtship. That he chooses to stay away at Christmas (and not bother to

351

inform her) suggests a casual handling of their association. Nan and Dulce seek an answer to Julia's thoughts on this but they will have to wait. If she's unsure of her feelings she can hardly enlighten them.

There was a shuffling back of the Hall and a sudden drop in noise. The church organist sat at the piano and began to play. Then there was Luke.

Nan nudged her. 'Here he comes.' For an absurd moment Julia entertained the notion of him dressed as an angel but he came as himself carrying a wooden crib. He set it centre of the dais, glanced out at the gathering and returned the way he came. 'I took his seat?' Julia whispered.

'Don't matter,' Nan whispered back. 'He'd sooner it you than anyone else.'

* * *

Luke returned to the anteroom to find Matty with tear-stained face and the Knitted Lamb crushed in his arms. 'Is Mumma here?'

'Yes and Nanny Roberts so no need to worry.'

'Is Matthew alright?' The teacher was fussing. 'We must go on.'

'Then go on.' Luke sat beside Matty. 'It's only a touch of stage fright. I'll stay with him until he's ready.'

Out in the Hall the piano is playing and the audience singing '*Once in Royal David's City*.' The teacher rallies the children. 'Come along now! Mary and Joseph lead the procession, the sheep, cows and the donkey to follow.'

Luke sat with his arm about Matty. He's not sure how he got

himself into this other than when he came to set up the crib he found Matty in tears. It's the words, bless him! He's afraid he'll mess it up. 'You'll be alright. All you have to do is kneel at the crib and say, 'I bring you a lamb, Dear Baby Jesus.'

Face ashen Matty croaked. 'I bring a lamb, Baby Jesus.'

'Aye, that'll do.'

Luke could feel the child getting more wound up. 'When you've done here we'll go fetch my old horse so you can look after her?'

'Betty?'

'Yes. She's not being cared for as she should.'

Matty gave a great shuddering sigh. 'I love Betty.'

Again they waited. There was a lot of mumbling from the kiddies and then the teacher was heard declaiming, '... *and there were shepherds abiding in the fields keeping watch over their flock by night.*'

'That's you, Matty,' said Luke drawing him to the door.

Matty dug in his heels. 'No.'

'Yes! It's your cue.'

'No! I can't do it.'

'You can. You'll be really good.'

Matty tugged his hand. 'You come with me!'

'I can't, my love. It's for you to do it.

A tear rolled down Matty's face. 'Come, Mister Wolf, please.'

'Alright then.' Hand-in-hand they entered the Hall. They both knelt at the crib; Matty held out the Knitted Lamb. 'I bring you a lamb, Dear Baby Jesus.'

* * *

The Play over the gathering quickly dispersed. It was Matty's idea to bring Luke back to the cottage. 'You'll come won't you!' he said hanging on his arm.

'Nay, you don't need me. You've done your bit. You laid the lamb in the crib and spoke your words clear as any London stage actor.'

'I was good, wasn't I, Mumma?' Matty turned to Julia.

'You were excellent, as was the Lamb. When you said amen at the end of the play I am perfectly certain I heard him bleat.'

'Silly Mumma!' Matty laughed. 'Lamb is made of wool. He can't bleat! Mister Wolf says I can have Betty. Can I Mumma?'

Luke grimaced. 'It's my old horse. I'm having a problem getting folk to look after her. Matty was upset. I thought to sort two birds with one stone.'

'Betty is welcome. She can keep the pony company.'

Matty tugged Julia's skirt. 'Can Mister Wolf come for tea? You said we'd have a picnic. You said we'd lay cushions on the floor and toast bread.'

'I did say so. And if Mr Luke is willing to come we'd be so very happy.'

'So will you?' Matty leapt at Luke. 'Will you come?'

'I'd like to but I'm to see Nanny Roberts home.'

'Don't worry about me,' said Nan adjusting her furs. 'The Mayor and our Lady Mayoress have offered me a ride home in their new carriage.'

'Aggie Simpkin?' Luke grinned. 'Are you sure?'

'Sure I'm sure. I am your mother and keen to visit with you but you would use the trap and in this weather I'll not look a gift-horse in the mouth.'

'Then can you come?' said Matty.

Luke swung him up in his arms. 'Try keeping me away.'

They walked out into sunshine. Julia was happy. Seeing them together, Matty's hand engulfed in his, made her dizzy with joy. Then Matty pointed. 'Why is all that black stuff coming out our chimney?'

Thick smoke oozed from the cottage chimney. 'It's the fire range!'

Luke set Matty down and stripping his jacket as he ran left them to follow. He has a key. He meant to return it but was never able. Slipping and sliding, he came down the Rise as Dottie Manners stepped down from a cart.

'Dottie don't go in! Wait for your mistress. And you!' he yelled to the lad on the cart, 'stay put! We may well need you.'

He went in through the back shutting the door so not to create a draught. Luckily, the door to the back stairs was closed as was that to the Tea-Shop. The back rooms had borne the brunt of smoke, a fine layer of soot everywhere.

Coughing, eyes watering, he damped the fire throwing doors and window wide. Nan was already out front with Mrs Masson's man, Crosby.

'Is there much damage?'

'It's mostly smoke but there's a fair bit of soot.'

'What can we do to help?' said Nan.

'You can take Matty,' said Julia.

'Yes, and you Anna! Stay with us over Christmas.'

'Go!' Luke nodded. 'You'll be better at the Nelson than with this lot.'

'I'll stay,' she said, unfastening her cape.

'It's filthy in here.' He touched the window sill. 'Not a clean surface anywhere. The back rooms will have to be emptied and the walls and ceilings washed.'

'I realise that.'

'It's not a major job. I'll send the lad back with his cart to collect various bits and pieces and start right away but it'll take a couple of days.'

'And that's why I am staying.' Julia tied an apron about her waist. 'It's a while since you were here. I know what works and what doesn't. Don't think I'm being difficult! I understand what you say, and God knows I'm glad you're here, but this is my home.'

'As you will.'

It was settled then. Matty went with Nan, and Kaiser and the cats, now released from the laundry room, with them.

'It's as well the dog wasn't in the kitchen,' said Luke. Julianna was pale and subdued. He didn't like to see it but there wasn't time to worry. He and Crosby got going lugging furniture out in the yard. Albert arrived with men and began washing down walls and ceilings while Julianna and Dottie rolled up rugs.

'Lay them face down on clean snow,' said Luke. 'It'll absorb the soot. Same with the curtains! Think of the snow as lint. They'll come up better than new.'

* * *

It was around three-thirty when they started and light already fading. Soon it was pitch black. Then Dulce from the Big House loomed out of the darkness dragging a baby's pram filled with oil lamps. Luke couldn't help smiling. 'Coming down the Rise all lit up like that I thought you were an early Father Christmas. All you were missing were the reindeer.'

He tried making Julianna smile because it wasn't that bad. No one got hurt! It's muck, that's all, and you can always do away with muck. Sleeves rolled up and a pinny about her waist, she looked a sight but he'd never seen her lovelier. She was alongside and he didn't care if the sky fell.

By eight o'clock the ceilings and walls were free of soot. Albert went home promising to return the following day. Julianna wandered about fussing over china and the piano. God knows what was going on in her head; likely she was imagining what might have happened had the place caught fire.

Dottie's young feller arrived back with white-wash and the like. Luke unloaded the lot, covered it with tarpaulin and thought enough was enough. 'We can't do anymore,' he said. 'We need to rest.'

Julia drew Dorothy aside. 'If you were to go back with the cart now would you have a place to stay?'

Dorothy nodded. 'I could stay with Reg's mum and dad.'

'Then go. You've been a great help today. Take this,' she pressed a pound note into her hand, 'and take the next two days as leave.'

Luke didn't want to eavesdrop but the house so quiet it couldn't be helped.

Anxious, he watched the cart roll away into the night and thought it time he said something. 'So what have you decided? You can't be planning to stay here alone. We've cleaned up but it's a cheerless place.'

'Yes but as I said it's my home and I can't abandon it.'

'Come to the Nelson! I'll sort this. A lick of paint and it'll be as good as new.'

She gazed about. 'That's what Nan said when we first came here, a lick of paint and it will be good as new.'

'And it will, you see.'

Then she was weeping, tears making runnels in the soot.

'Oh don't!' He drew her close. 'No one came to harm. All are safe.'

'It's Kaiser,' she said. 'He could've been burnt to death.'

'But he wasn't. He was with the cats in the laundry room.'

'Yes, and I forgot they were there,' she sobbed her tears wetting his shirt. 'I was in such a rush. I never gave them a thought.'

'Yes you did.' Luke held her tight silky curls tickling his nose. 'The cottage told you they were best moved and you moved them.'

'You think so?'

'I do. So don't cry, lovely girl. It hurts me to see it.'

Eyes like great watery pools she looked at him, and then she said it, just came straight out with it and blew him, heart and soul, to smithereens.

'I love you, Luke.'

Many a Slip

It is the day before Christmas. Luke plans to be at St Bedes for the seven am service. He woke, bathed, and was ready by six. An important day, he took a while deciding what to wear, finally choosing the dark broadcloth overcoat and soft black hat. He bought the hat in Milan, the shopkeeper bouncing all over the place, *Il Principe tra gli uomini!* A prince among men is going a bit far but it is a good hat. When he looks in the mirror a man with a smooth jaw looks back, a dashing man, you might say. Today this dashing fellow, this 'Prince among Men' who owns half a street in Manchester, goes to church to hear the vicar calling the Banns -four weeks from today Luke is to wed the most beautiful woman in the world, Mrs Julianna Passmore nee Dryden.

Nervous, he struggles with his tie. He smiles and his reflection smiles with him. Will she tie this for me, he thought. Will I look in the mirror one day to see my wife's arms clasped about my neck? 'Let me, darling,' she'll say, exasperation in her voice. 'You're hopeless at this.'

Crazy! He laughed outright. Just the thought of being married long enough for Julianna Roberts to feel exasperation is a source of joy. That night on the steps he said, 'I want to kiss every bit of you - from top of your head to the sole of your foot.' She'd sighed. 'I know and I want it to.' At that he'd dropped on his knees. 'So will you marry me?' She'd reached down. 'Yes and gladly.'

Pressed against her body he breathed her in, a million gossamer blessings of snow falling on his face. 'This is real?' he'd said. 'It's not me making it up?'

Arms wrapped about him, she nodded. 'It is real.'

'Then kiss me.'

Luke closed his eyes. He can't dwell on that kiss. Three years he's waited. He can wait a little longer. They're not wed yet and as they say there's many a slip between the cup and the lip. Where Julianna's concerned memory is precise. One word sticks out of time like a jagged nail: the word 'can't'. It's what she said when he met her off the Cambridge train - she 'couldn't' love him. Now she says she does. He accepts that but keeps his feet firmly on the ground. He'll go and look at Greenfields' roof and mouldered walls; there's nothing brings a man back down to earth quicker than the stink of blocked drains.

* * *

The Meissen is none the worse for the fire but unable to sit she'd washed every piece. Now other than the smell of fresh white-wash you'd think nothing had happened when in fact the whole world is changed. Today they call the Banns, their commitment becoming public property. It is already known, the news bringing Hugh Fitzwilliam yesterday. 'You can't do it, Julianna!' He'd rapped the table. 'Good fellow though he is, you cannot marry him.'

She'd smiled. 'How news travels!'

'Your news isn't news! I heard it yesterday from the green-grocer who heard it from his wife, who'd heard it from the under-housemaid to my intended wife, Lady Charlotte Walbrooke. You cannot marry him.'

'It sounds to me like I've little choice.'

'You have a choice. Deny the rumour! He's too far down the scale.'

'What scale?'

'The scale that allows me to meet with you and you to dine with a King.'

'I'm not aware of any such scale.'

'Nonsense! You're perfectly aware! You were born aware. Your father knew a fellow from a chap as your mother knew who to call friend and who to call maid. You must forbid the Banns.'

Julia had laughed. 'Forbid my own wedding?'

'Yes. You must call halt or suffer the consequences.'

'And what consequences are those?'

'Every door beyond your own will be closed to you, although HRH being so liberal with you, it's likely His door will be the last to close.'

Furious, Julia protested. 'What's wrong with Luke? Wasn't it you who only recently said he was a charming man?'

'That doesn't mean I'd have him at my dinner table! He's Trade and lowly trade at that. Yes, he's climbing a ladder and the way he's going soon be at the top, but it's his ladder not ours. His work is to do with sewers and the conveying of human shit, dear Julianna, in a time when most ladies have the vapours when referring to a piano leg! He is not for you. You weren't born with name to lift him higher, and he not yet moneyed enough for it not to matter!'

'This is nonsense! You are surely talking nonsense, Hugh.'

'I am not. I'm trying to make you understand how this will affect your life. It won't do your business any good.'

'What the Nannies? What has my marriage to do with a tea-room?'

'Nothing at first. You'll do good business, people coming to look at you.'

'They do that now.'

'Yes, an admiring look! They want to know how you wear your hair and what you eat for breakfast. They see a woman beloved of Royalty. Marry Luke Roberts and you won't be admired. You won't even be Mrs Roberts. You'll be the woman who wed Milady Carrington's cast off.'

'Ah! And that's a reason isn't it?'

'It has to do with it! With Eve he was invisible. Lap-dog or artist's whim, she could take up or discard without harm to either. Beautiful Ju-ju Dryden takes him up and the world sees him as a fortune hunter and a rogue.'

'Luke is no fortune hunter with me. I have no fortune to hunt.'

'You have the Prince of Wales' favour! Marry Luke and he'll be seen seeking the same and you aiding him.'

'I never sought anyone's favour. I would hope any such favour was given in friendship. It was certainly returned so. My position in Court, if I have one, is slight. If as you suggest I should drop into the shadows no one would miss me. I would share the shadows with my husband and I wouldn't be lonely. As for Luke seeking favour if you knew him you'd know he scorned such things.'

'I do know Luke! I am not here out of chagrin! I'm here to make you see any hope of maintaining a position in London ceases with this marriage.'

'Who sent you?'

'No one sent me. I did have a call from Eve and mentioned the situation.'

'And what did she say?'

'Nothing, but then she's another who cares less for consequence! It's only people like me and Charlotte who try keeping order. All this swapping sides it's no good. A hundred years from now there'll be chimney sweeps marrying countesses, and Lords out of tin-men, or even a bugger on the throne, though that won't be new. The sad fact is the country's going to the dogs.'

When Hugh left it was with a sad smile. 'It's not likely we'll meet. I too plan to marry and can't afford to maintain suspect connections. I am a poor man and getting poorer. I must consider my rustic joints. Give Matty a kiss from me.'

* * *

The church was full. Luke helped Julianna down from the cart. It's likely he should have come by carriage but pride made a stand. He came as he is, Luke Roberts, builder and plumber. 'Are you alright?' he said.

Julia brushed snow from her cape. 'Yes.'

Nothing more to be said he offered her his arm and in they went.

The early service is for farmers and workers of the field and kept brief. Usually, there's a bit of preaching followed by communion for those that want to take it. Today it seems longer and the vicar red of face. They sang the hymn *Fight the Good Fight*, which Luke thought appropriate, and then everyone sat.

The vicar got to his feet and called for silence. He needn't have bothered, woodworm gnawing the pews made more noise than the congregation. Four couples were named, three in St Bedes and one at St Marks. The vicar read the Banns in such a monotone you'd think there was a tragedy at sea rather than forthcoming wedding. When he got to the '*anyone knowing impediment should speak up*' someone coughed and Julianna trembled.

Undercover of a bible Luke took her hand. Their names were called, Luke Claude Roberts and Julianna Passmore. Hearing them coupled together the blood drained from his face; it was Julianna then that held him.

* * *

Albert popped a bottle of champagne. 'Will you take a glass of something, Mrs Dry... er...Anna?' Albert is uncomfortable, things said and done making a divide that will never be bridged. As yet no one has thought to ask where the happy couple plan to live - Julia thinks it cannot be Bakers End.

Luke called yesterday evening. 'I'll collect you tomorrow for church.'

'I shall be ready.'

'Then maybe I'll drop by later with presents for Matty.'

A kiss of her hand, a tip of his hat, and he left. So formal and polite, if Julia didn't understand she'd be worried by the distance yet she does understand and is moved by his sensitivity. It is because of Stefan Adelman and Daniel Masson and maybe even the Prince of Wales that he sets himself apart. He gives Julia, and himself, a new page on which to write. 'You are to be my wife, my one and only, and I am to be yours. Use this time to be certain of what you do and if not certain then set yourself free.' Not a word of this passes his lips yet the message is clear, not least from his body and his kiss.

One kiss but such a kiss! In that first touch of lip to lip she knew why she'd kept a distance and why he did the same. The kiss burned. It burns still, and he knows it and arms folded he stares across his mother's table.

And this is the man Hugh Fitzwilliam would not have at his dining table, a man in trade too far down the scale to be lifted higher!

She collected her gloves. 'Do you think perhaps we ought to go now, my dear? I have things to do and I'm sure Nan is the same.'

Sunlight breaking into blue, he smiled. 'I'll collect Matty from the yard.'

* * *

That 'my dear' was a gift to Luke - it kept him warm, which is good since as the day progressed more than one disapproved of the union.

He went to Greenfields via the jewellers.

'Did you manage it?' he said. 'And in a box and all?'

'The best, Mr Roberts, velvet lined.' The box in his pocket, he called on Mrs Masson. Twenty minutes he was kept waiting and when she did arrive she was cool. 'Oh it's you, Roberts,' she said. 'I don't know that I can see you now.'

'Right!' He nodded. 'I'll be on my way then.'

'Yes do,' she said, 'the weather is closing in, though perhaps I should say if you called in respect of the roof I mean to offer it elsewhere.'

'As you wish.' He made for the door.

She followed. 'Don't you want to know why?'

'Not especially. It's your roof. You must do as you think best.'

A little woman, old but fast, she slid in front of him. 'I'll tell you anyway,' she said. 'We Yankees prefer doing business with people we trust. We don't commit our business to anyone if we're in any degree uncertain.'

'Uncertain?' Luke weighed his hat. 'Are you suggesting the firm of Albert Roberts and Son is in some way untrustworthy?'

'I'm not saying that.'

'You think us unable to handle the repairs to your roof, and the people my father and I have served the last twenty years - the churches and the private houses, the major and the minor - have cause to regret our services?'

'I would hardly think so.'

'Me neither, ma'm, or my diary wouldn't be booked solid these next two years, nor would we have people calling all hours begging help!'

'I imagine you are worthy of hire.'

'I know we are.' She was pink about her cheeks and flustered. Luke knew he should stop but he was good and mad, puffed up little peahen!

'I didn't mean to suggest you were anything other than worthy.'

'Then what did you mean to suggest?'

'I was referring to a situation entirely unconnected.'

'Then you'll excuse me!' He put on his hat. 'I've things to do.'

'No wait!' She pulled on his sleeve. 'I do want you to look at the roof and I do want your help. It's just that I am so darn cross with you throwing your life away on a woman like that when you could do so much better.'

Luke should have walked away, should've turned on his heel not stayed to defend a person who didn't need defending. 'A woman like that?'

'You know she's not the thing.' Julianna Dryden not the thing? He could only stare. When she began to ramble he began to wonder if she wasn't a little mad. 'These women are like spiders. They come with clever minds and winning ways and take up residence close by to lure us into their webs.'

'I beg your pardon?'

'Emancipation! It's all you hear nowadays, modern misses needing to be on top of everything. Do you know they're asking for the right to vote? I never had the right to vote. I did as I was told. It's why I left England. Education does it. They get a few facts in their heads and think they know the world.'

Luke pulled away. 'I'm sorry but I must go. If you want me to look at the roof let me know, better yet, I'll talk to your son when he's here.'

'Oh it's no good talking to him! He's besotted with her. It's why he is away and I alone. He's hoping distance will make her fonder. It won't and you the living proof. He's lost her and I shall get the blame.'

Luke tried to break free but her fingers were gnarled matchsticks. It made him afraid to touch her. 'Mrs Masson. I think you need to sit down.'

'Not sit lie! Lie down in my grave! Oh!' she groaned. 'I don't know why I should be alive when she is dead. But you are young and must steer clear! You don't want to be caught in her snare as I was caught. Did you know she can speak Latin? I stood where you are once. She and Henry were talking Ovid. They were quoting some tract. I had no idea what they were...'

Mid-sentence she stopped, a light gone out.

'Mrs Masson?'

'What?' She gazed at him and then the light came back on. 'Mr Roberts!' she said. 'I'm glad you dropped by. I wanted to thank you for the crib.'

'The crib?'

'I thought the play went well. And the children were so cute, especially Matty. I liked the way you came together, father and son, so to speak. He loves you - that much is obvious. He didn't care for Daniel and so even if I had encouraged them it wouldn't have worked.' She looked about her. 'Doesn't the tree look nice? Good of you to call at Christmas. It is Christmas isn't it?'

'It is.'

'Kiddies make Christmas and if you don't have kiddies you don't have Christmas. It's no holiday for me, not with my son away.' Click the light changed. 'And that's her fault! If she were to do right he'd be here, but she plays fast and loose with the Prince of Wales. You need to bear that in mind, Luke Roberts. Call all the banns you like but you're not married yet.'

'Mizz Callie!' The maid, a black-winged bat, swopped down the stairs. 'It's time you were taking a nap!' A forlorn child now the old lady stood still. The maid covered her with a shawl and called on the manservant for help.

'You must excuse my mistress! She's not too well.'

'Is there anything I can do?'

'Depends on what you heard.'

'I heard a lot but none of it made sense.'

'My poor lady's wits are befuddled. It's best you forget what she said, Mr Luke, and carry on as before.'

Luke buttoned up his coat. 'I'll wait and speak with Mr Masson.'

The maid eyed him, a plea for kindness. 'About what?'

He shrugged. 'The roof! What else?'

* * *

'Mister Wolf!' Matty threw himself at him.

'Whoah now!' Luke swung him up. 'It's only a while since we parted. Anyone would think we hadn't seen one another in years.'

'Yes and while we're here together, Matty,' said Julia, 'I want this to be the last time you refer to Mr Roberts as Mister Wolf.'

'Why, what's going to happen?'

'Yes.' Luke smiled over Matty's head. 'What is going to happen?'

'Mister Wolf...I mean Mr Roberts and I are to wed.'

'What does that mean?'

'It means we will be together all three of us.'

'Here at the Nanny?'

'Well,' Julia hesitated. 'I suppose here from the start?' She looked to Luke for help but he wasn't helping. He was hugging Matty and loving her with his eyes.

'Do you mean here at nights?' said Matty, who was playing with Luke's tie, tying and retying. 'With me, and you, and Kaiser?'

Julia blushed. 'Yes, you, me and Kaiser.'

'Does Maggie Jeffers know you're coming?'

Luke laughed. 'I reckon so. She knows everything else.'

'And isn't overly quiet about it.' Julia lifted him away. 'Time for your bath!'

'Can Mr Roberts do it?'

'Not yet, dear heart, perhaps afterward we are married, if he wants to.'

'Of course!' Luke grinned. 'Why else would we be getting wed?'

'Can he take me tonight?'

'Then this one time, as it is Christmas Eve. We will both take you. But you must be good and not try to hang it out.'

* * *

Matty safely in bed Luke looked at the clock. 'I should be going.'

'I suppose.'

He took her hand. 'You know I'd sooner die than leave you.'

'Oh don't die, dearest. I need you alive.'

'It kills me to walk away from you and Matty, but knowing I can come back makes me better.' He took the box from his pocket. 'I have this for you.'

She opened the box. 'It's your ring.'

'It's yours now.' He slid it on her finger. 'I had it made smaller. Not too loose, is it? I got it in Italy. The stone is of the mountains.'

She turned the ring on her finger. 'You were there with Eve Carrington?'

'Not when I bought that.'

'You and Eve? Is the connection broken?'

'It is. What about you and Stefan Adelman?'

She was a while answering. 'Stefan is my friend. If he were to ask my help I would go to him. I'd want to be loyal whatever my situation.'

Luke was silent.

She took his hand. 'If Eve came seeking help would you deny her? Surely time spent together makes such a refusal impossible?'

'I wouldn't see her struggling but I'd go as a friend and a friend only.'

'Then let us cherish our friends while we have them.'

He drew her close, cosying her head on his shoulder. 'And let me then cherish you for as long as I have you.'

'You mean for better or for worse?'

'Aye.' He nodded. 'And for richer and for poorer.'

'In sickness and in health?'

'Until death us do part.'

* * *

A cable arrived this morning from Stefan offering the season's greetings. Sensing his loneliness, Julia thought to cable back but settled instead to write. She wrote a cheerful letter telling of Christmas preparations and Matty's Nativity Play. She described Greenfields and the tree, she told of Callie's pink hat and the donkey's crooked tail, and the little angels with tissue-paper wings. She said how much she missed him and she sent love to Karoline, of Luke she said nothing thinking that news best left to the New Year. Then Matty wanted to add his love and a pencil drawing of Kaiser and the Knitted Lamb. The letter sealed, Julia put on her cape and walked to the village.

The post office was crowded with last minute mail. She posted the letter and was turning away when a voice whispered in her ear, '*tell him of Luke.*'

'What?' She turned to see who'd spoken but everyone else was busy with their own affairs. Thinking it imagined she walked on. '*Tell him of Luke.*'

Shocked, she ground to a halt and stood listening but could only hear the world turning about her, horses neighing, a child in a garden building a snowman and postmen collecting mail.

When it came again, '*tell him now,*' she sent a cable. It was brief, what else could it be: 'Luke Roberts and I are to wed. Be happy for me.' It was a long walk back to the cottage and a long time before she forgot the message. You see, she knew the voice. She'd heard it in dreams and again at the séance, a woman's voice, musical, who three times said, '*I'm afraid the Professor is busy. May I take a message?*'

Last Christmas

Sunlight on snow-covered willows making a second Hanging Gardens of Babylon, it is Christmas Day. Karoline gazes out on the scene, hand on the sill and her breath misting the window. 'My darling?' Stefan covers her hand with his. 'When the air is warmer we'll take the sleigh around the Lake.'

Lips stretched over teeth she smiled, an odd smile but a smile nevertheless.

'Frau Adelman is happy today,' said the nurse.

'I hope so.' Stefan sighed. 'Did she sleep at all during the night?'

'The new drug helps. She lay quiet but her eyes are red and inflamed. Might I suggest a bandage?'

'No bandage.'

'Then perhaps at night? It would shut out the light and give her rest.'

'No! It has been tried before. Frau Adelman tore it away,' said Stefan. 'She shall not be bandaged or restrained. My wife isn't a naturally violent person. She is ill and needs to be watched not tied down as by that other woman. A hint of such and the perpetrator will be instantly removed.'

'I understand.'

'Make sure you do. You are paid to assist Frau Adelman not to be her jailor.'

Stefan left them to it. God knows what he'd hoped in bringing her home. If he thought life easier he could not be more mistaken. She can't be left. She hates the nurses and those whose job it is to keep her clean. She hates that she soils herself and will spit and scratch. Today she smiles and that because all former objections regarding the use of opium are withdrawn.

Such a relief! No shouting or throwing things, a push of the syringe and it is done, Stefan often tempted to inject himself if only to sleep free of guilt.

He used to think he was a good man, no trail-blazer yet a hard-working God-fearing soul. Such self-endorsement comes of years of listening to grateful patients. Earlier this year he received a letter signed by Her Majesty, Queen Victoria, saying how much she had appreciated his loyal service.

This from a Queen! Now he sees Stefan Adelman as he really is, a weak man who'd sooner give morphine to his wife than suffer discomfort.

The trouble began the moment they left Bradbury. Parted from her wall, she screamed and continued screaming until they reached Dresden, by which time she was hoarse, and Stefan close to throttling her. Even with a partition between them the chauffeur quailed at the thought of another such journey. 'I'm sorry, sir,' he'd said, 'you'll have to hire another driver.'

She'd be better dead and so would Stefan!

He stares into the morrow and the horrors it will bring. *His* Karoline was meticulous of person, her clothes dainty and manners precise. The woman who spat at him on the ferry, calling him whoremonger, is a devil-woman who cries to the world, saying Herr Doktor is a liar and a cheat.

It was here in this house she miscarried. So many years ago

nonetheless he remembers it as yesterday. Karoline was out walking and tripped over a root and fell; eight months pregnant she called for help but none came.

Stefan was not at home, his message that morning, 'I have business in town.' His business was at an apartment in Wilsdruffer Strasse with Maria Boucher, a theatre nurse. No one asked why he couldn't be found that day, Karoline didn't ask, her husband is a doctor and needed elsewhere. No one asked but someone knew - the truth an iron fist between him and the world.

Karoline blamed herself. 'You said not to go. I thought to catch the narcissus in bloom. I am sorry.' She apologised and he with the stink of Maria on his fingers! For months she continued to apologise but then someone talked. Now every minute of the day he asks why Maria Boucher when all he wanted was at home. The answer is simple - availability and Maria's breasts.

Maria had breasts the size and shape of melons. Working with her every day, the melons jiggling as she walked, was an intrigue. One lazy wet afternoon in autumn he asked over a glass of tea if he might touch. She said she didn't mind, availability - and no particular price to pay - what man could resist.

There was a price, a miscarried son and post-partum depression. Karoline refused to try for another child. Her eyes would start out of her head if he approached her. 'You can't ask it of me!' He didn't argue. Without the burden of guilt he might have tried harder but being guilty he retreated.

One brief summer things improved. It was when her mother brought redcurrant bushes. Karoline found peace that season in the garden. One day, the bushes heavy with fruit, she allowed him into her bed. They made love, her lips sweet with juice of the fruit, the following morning the redcurrant bushes were found stripped of fruit - not a berry left, the birds eaten every one.

For some dark reason she associated the overnight reaping with the loss of Anselm and from that moment she too was dead. One day they fought, he told her to stop being crazy or he'd have her committed. Next he knew she's in his dressing room stabbing her wrists with his razor. She was confined to Sonnenstein Asylum. 'Your wife may never recover,' said the doctor. 'As with many such fragile blossoms they perish if left too long in the cold.'

* * *

The sleigh ride will be their first time out together in years and their last. He has decided it must end, that today shall be their last. It cannot wait. His heart is failing - he must not allow his nerve to do the same.

He has suffered two major infarctions and now his heart is compromised. The last time he was at Osborne House he asked James Reid for his opinion. Sir James smiled sadly. 'Haven't you worked it out, my dear fellow?'

Stefan has worked it out. The last attack was here in Dresden. He fell to the floor and lay unable to rise. A strange thing happened then, he could hear Karoline, and as absurd as it sounds could see her! She was in the long sitting room, wheel-chair parked against the window. A bag of nuts thronged with birds hung from the Cypress tree. She was trying to touch it but unable to lift her arms since she was tied to the chair, cords cutting into her skin.

Outraged, he'd shouted out but no sound left his lips. When he did recover and make his way downstairs the restraints were gone. He fired that nurse and hired another but the scene haunted him. What happens if he dies? Who comes between her then and torture?

Today they will take a sleigh ride. He will take champagne in a flask and strudel and napkins. He will take his cello! He will also take a syringe.

He's drawn his Will, three envelopes to be posted, one for his lawyer, one for Peggy Carstairs of Stepney another for Master Matthew Dryden in Norfolk.

This morning he received a cable telling of Julianna's forthcoming marriage and asking him to be happy in her choice. Silly girl! An old man sick unto death is in no position to challenge. Luke Roberts is a good man. A workhorse proud and stiff of neck, he will be there when others fall away. That she weds for love is certain, being Julianna it can't be any other way, yet if she sees this marriage as security then Stefan's Will offers another choice.

* * *

Stefan sits every night by Karoline's bed. In Bradbury she'd stare at the same patch of wall. Here in Dresden before sedatives were applied she lay night-after-night staring at nothing. Dreadful to behold! He told Julianna about it who wrote back of tapestries Karoline used to sew, he was to 'look for the blue cherub and give his wife back her wall.' A tapestry with an embroidered cherub was found hidden in an ottoman. With no particular hope he left it on Karoline's pillow as a pretty memory to look on. When he returned it was to find her asleep and the cloth held to her breast. Now the tapestry is her wall, it offers peace if only for a short time.

Last night he went to Mass. Seeking hope at the feet of the Saviour, he knelt at the altar rail, the organ playing the fifth movement of Brahms' Requiem, an Angel consoling those in grief. '*You who suffer in sorrow shall meet again and your hearts rejoice.*' There and then a pain flashed through his chest. He staggered and a soldier helped him to a seat. 'Better rest old man,' he said. 'Leave the drinking and celebrating until tomorrow.'

From the church he took the carriage the long route home. The way was thronged with many carriages. Church bells were ringing and people spilling out of houses, the doors behind them flung open and lights blazing. Many were singing. He rolled down the window to listen. Christmas, holly berries and singing, are for the young. They can have it and welcome.

* * *

Two o'clock and the sleigh slides into the yard; Gustave, a good and sober horse in the shafts and a carillon of golden bells attached to the reins.

The gardener would've carried Karoline aboard but Stefan wanted to do it.

'I can manage. She is no weight.' She is no weight yet he thought her the weight of the world and he exhausted. The maid tucked a rug about her knees.

'Madam is beautiful today.' Indeed she is so beautiful he wonders if he is doing right. Wrapped in silver fox, mittens on her hands and a fur cap on her head, she sits in the sleigh as Snedronningen, the Snow Queen.

Last night he told of his plans. 'So many times you have wished to die. The time has come to grant your wish.' So quiet in her room, just the tick of the ormolu clock on the console table, Mutti's clock, Stefan had it as a boy. It has an odd tick. 'I hear a mouse cough when I hear this,' he once said to Karoline. 'Yes,' she replied, 'and hurrying home with bread and cheese for his tea.'

It's how they used to be, imagination overflowing. It is how Anselm would have been had he lived.

'You'll be with Anselm again,' he told her. 'He will be there waiting.'

Stefan has seen many people die. There have been those who screaming in pain he helped crossover. If such pain can be eased surely the Lord God would not want His children to suffer. Karoline is as precious to the Lord as a sparrow. She will be welcomed into heaven and find Anselm waiting. If a soul must be cast into the Flames then it must be Stefan. To take another's life is a mortal sin. When the police come, as they will - Stefan ready to admit the deed - then if death hasn't claimed him a prison cell will.

* * *

He parked overlooking the lake. He can't handle the horse as he used to, the reins pull on his arms and make his chest ache worse. 'We shall rest here, Karoline. It is a good spot. You can see the house from here.'

Now that they are here he doesn't know why he brought strudel. Karoline is fed via a nasogastric tube! He took her hand, cold and thin, a child's hand.

'Thank you,' he said, 'for being with me all these years. I know

I haven't been the best husband but I do love you and hope a part of you loves me.'

Her hand hangs limp, no tightening of grip to show acknowledgment. If she does understand why they are here she doesn't show it. With nothing else to do he prepared the syringe, drawing up a lethal dose. Then, thinking he'd better unhook the horse, he climbed down. Gustave, sensing wrongness treads the ground, and then skitters away toward a knot of trees. 'Cheerio old boy!' Stefan panted. 'Pip-pip as the English would say. I'll see you in Paradise.'

Now for the cello! He dragged the cello out, setting it and the stool in the ground. Gloves removed, he blew on his hands trying to get them warm and then, back braced swiped at the strings playing the introductory chords.

Karoline observes all with what looks like amusement on her face. Who could blame her from thinking him ridiculous? He is ridiculous! His hands are so cold he can barely grasp the bow, and the sealskin coat is a hedge between him and the cello! It is all so ridiculous he weeps as he plays, tears turning to ice.

'Ah!' The pain grabbed him and tossed him sideways. He vomited the luncheon turbot into the snow. In his mind he saw their parting as a tragedy, a one act opera similar to Madama Butterfly, and he the suffering hero, instead it is farce, and he a foolish old man face down in his own vomit.

The pain hit again and he screamed the sound cutting through Shubert's *Die Forelle*, her favourite piece. Oh, he thought, I am dying and haven't done what I came to do. She is alone in the snow. I have again abandoned her.

* * *

Karoline watched him die. She wanted to offer comfort but has little strength and what she has she harnesses for the syringe.

It's there. She can see it poking out of a leather bag. Karoline loves that syringe and the magic it holds. If she can get to it she'll put an end to this horror. She knows how to do it. She has watched nurses do it, the gentle hands and the coarse, the good natured and the casual. If she can get to that needle there'll be no more nurses and no more unhappy men who sit by her bed feeding her apple strudel and lies.

Karoline doesn't like apple strudel. And she doesn't like lies! That man there on the ground, poor fellow, face buried in the snow, tells lies. He says she will get better one day. She will never get better. She doesn't want to. What she wants is to die and the liquid in that syringe will help her do that.

Carefully, she inches across the seat, a Lighthouse or Siren luring her onto jagged rocks she neither knows nor cares, the syringe is all she sees.

Now she has it in her hands but finds it's harder to use than she thought.

Jab! Jab! It's hard making contact needle to vein, all she does is rip her skin.

'Oh no!' She almost dropped it!

Feverishly, she scrapes her clothes sorting through layers of fur and silk, trying to pull her skirt up and her drawers down, but the maid, Misha, who likes things to be correct, has pinned Karoline's drawers to the bodice.

Nothing for it but to stab through the cloth, and quickly

before a passerby sees the abandoned sleigh and raises the alarm.

'Help me,' she whispers. 'Dear God, please help me! She pulled back her arm, and taking a deep breath brought her fist stabbing down into her thigh.

She bore down with such force the needle pierced cloth and muscle. Nerves reacted. She was thrown backward over the sleigh onto the ground. She hung on, both hands clamped about the syringe, and then she pressed the plunger.

It's done! It is in! Every last blessed drop!

Exhausted, she lay still. Peace will come, she knows it will. Already she feels the slow burn beneath her skin. Freedom will come and with it the Blue Angel.

Now she is sure of what is to happen, and no longer afraid, the man on the ground barely a hand's clasp away is of concern. Oh poor Stefan! Life has been hard on him. A wife confined to an asylum? It's not easy living with that, especially for a professional man. Madness carries a stigma. People ask questions, why is she there, poor woman, was it something he did?

He had few friends. There were those along the way who offered comfort. There was a fat house-frau he saw who wore cheap face powder and lived in a hovel and didn't always wash. They fucked occasionally.

Yes fuck! Leaning against a wall half clothed, you can't call what they did love, more the scratching of an itch, mutual consolation, sex and rice pudding enjoyed by the fire, and then he to be cast out in the cold again.

Stefan and his women! He was with a woman the day Karoline lost the greatest treasure of her life. Anger burns, it keeps the motors running even when dying. No other fuel - not love or forgiveness, just bitter, bitter anger. She's weary of it. She wants to be free. This needle has made it so.

The magic is working, anger abates. Gustave, poor beast, is afraid, and stands on the edge of the trees trembling. Animals are sensitive to death. Karoline seems to think she once had a horse of her own, a hunter - a *Schwarzwalder Katblut* called White Fire. She had many things, a house in a city where church bells rang and where pigeons fouled the windows. She had silks in the closet and lofty rooms and fine furniture, eighteenth-century Italian looking-glasses with gold lacquer edges, and Mutti's china glittering in cabinets, gardens filled with apple trees - the fruit so heavy it broke the branches - books, paintings and music. Now she has madness and shit under her fingernails.

The cello lies in the snow like the prow of a sunken ship. To remember *Die Forelle* was a nice thought and typical of the man. A great romantic, he was never comfortable in this modern world, preferring to walk with Siegfried through the hallowed Halls of Valhalla, a Hippocratic Oath for a shield.

The horse draws closer curious to know why his master and mistress lie in the snow. 'Come, Gustave,' she whispers. 'Let me rub your nose one more time.' Gustave is the gardener's horse. A good horse, he comes every morning to the kitchen window. The maid gives him a carrot. She shouldn't, the cook doesn't like it, but Misha is young and cares less about rules.

The drug is working well, the part of her brain that determines real from unreal is detaching, and she, unhappy Karoline, lighter with every breath.

In a while the Blue Angel will come. Such a beautiful angel, Karoline would like to ask his name but never dares - it would be as asking God of His name.

The Angel comes when she is overwhelmed with sorrow and snakes hiss at her heel. 'Come with me and I will keep you safe,' he says. In early years she was reluctant. Now when he comes she leaps to take his hand.

He is different every time. First he came as a child, then as a youth, handsome and bold. Now he is a man with mighty wings the colour of sapphires.

He shows her the world - the wonderful and the terrible - when all she longs for is the next world. Sometimes she asks of Stefan. 'What is he doing?' The Angel will look at her. 'Are you sure you want to know?' To spite her soul she says yes and learns of the smelly house-frau and sex and rice pudding.

'Hello Gustave!' The horse is here. He breathes on her cheek, anxious. She strokes his nose and he jumps away to lip up strudel.

Snow falls and the light dims. The magic is almost complete. A sweet lassitude seeps through her veins not unlike the after-glow of making love. The Angel is coming, she knows it. She feels movement within and without, and a sound like thunder, a mighty staircase sweeping down from the skies.

Then she remembers it is Christmas and sings, or tries to. *'Away in a manger, a crib for a bed, the Little Lord Jesus lays down His Sweet head.'*

No! She mustn't think of children, her mind will not let her. Think of children and a door spiked with baby's skulls stands between her and a scream. What baby? Cannot think of his name! Does not want to know his name!

'Do Not Tell Me His Name!'

All she wants is the Blue Angel. In the latter years Stefan

found an angel of his own, beautiful and kind. She visits Karoline. Breath scented with roses she kisses her cheek - a real kiss not a flinching away. They dream together, Karoline and this beauty. In such dreams a door creaks open offering glimpses of another life where Mutti's china sparkles on unknown shelves. Through this woman's eyes she sees a country cottage and white roses growing at the hand of a gardener who whistles through his teeth. Blessing after blessing, she sees a boy with dark hair and laughing eyes who races up and down stairs, and who teases the maids, and who sleeps with a dog on his bed, a vigilant dog who knows of secret watchers and wags his tail, guardedly.

Karoline sees this and sometimes when lonely, and when the co-dreamer is willing, she shares Stefan's love. Gift or curse, she neither knows nor cares. Such peace as can be found she takes and tries not to mind she can't eat from her own plate or drink from her own cup. Best of all when seeing through other eyes is recognizing Stefan again as a good man.

The snow continues to fall. She stares into white and wonders if they will all disappear, the sleigh, the horse, and poor dear Stefan who tried even to the last. Last night he carried her to a chair and kneeling brought gifts from under the tree. There was a book of poems. Stefan took the book and read:

'Hope is a thing with feathers that perches in the soul
and sings the tune without the words and never stops at all.
And sweetest in the gale is heard and...!'

Someone is coming! A doorway opens in the snow. Gustave snickers softly in welcome. The Angel comes to her. 'What are you doing down there?'

'I fell.'

He smiled. 'As do we all.'

Kneeling, he covered Stefan with a rug. Then he kissed him. That kiss broke Karoline's heart. She felt it snap. Her life is done. Nothing hurts now not her head or her heart. She hugs worn tapestry to her breast and is ready to go.

'Will you come back and bring my Stefan to me in heaven?'

'Your Stefan is already there.'

'Truly?'

'Truly.'

'So?' The Angel leaned down. He is so beautiful, his hair the colour of ripened corn and his eyes known. 'Will you come with me and let me keep you safe?'

'I will,' she said, 'if you tell me who you are.'

'Don't you know who I am?' he said.

'No,' she whispered, fearful of the Gift bursting upon her.

Anselm reached down and took her in his arms. 'I am your son, dear mother, and the answer to my father's prayer.'

CHAPTER TWENTY-EIGHT

Cup and Lip

Dorothy knocked on the parlour door. 'It's Reggie, madam!' She twisted her hands. 'He keeps going on about getting wed.'

'And how do your parents feel about that?'

'They like him well enough. He has a good job at the bakery and is promoted to foreman and wants his own shop.'

'He sounds a respectable young man.'

'He is though I don't know why he keeps on! It'll not happen for ages. We can't afford to buy the tandem he wants never mind marry.'

'Then why so anxious?'

'I was worried what you'd think. My last lady wouldn't let me think of Reg never mind walk out with him. She said I wasn't to have callers.'

Julia laughed. 'That was then. This is the twentieth century. As long as you do your job I have no problems with you looking ahead. After all I'm doing much the same, aren't I?'

Dorothy grinned. 'You are, madam.'

'So let's think ahead. With the tea-shop closed until Tuesday I thought to buy new linen. Would you like to come with me?'

'Oh, yes, madam!'

What fun to laugh with a female who won't take offence, and who won't offer advice, and who is young enough to remember how it is to be in love. Love for Luke grows every day. There is that about the man that pulls. It might be his walk, or his square shoulders, or his smile - whatever it is it draws like a magnet. The maids react to the power, and Delilah, the cat, is forever crawling over his legs and feet. Who could blame Julia wants to do the same.

And all this in four days! Why so blind and stubborn before? But no matter she sees him now and the needs of yesterday under change. Moving was mentioned earlier when Luke came with the old horse in the shafts.

Matty, ecstatic, ran out the door. 'Oh, you've come, Betty!'

'This old lady will be coming to live with you soon,' said Luke, 'You might want to put out a paw and say "good day, Mrs Betty, and how are you?" '

Matty held out his hand. 'Good day Mrs Betty and how are you?'

'That's it. Then maybe she'll come closer.' Over the horse's flank Luke smiled at Julianna. 'Good day to you, Mrs Dryden, and how are you?'

'Good day, Mr Roberts. Thank you, I am well.'

'That's good. I wondered if I might call this evening. I've a mind to talk about where we plan to live. Have you seen my house on the Common?'

'From the outside yes.'

'Then why not take a look from the inside? It might help to give you an idea of things. Of course, we don't have to stay here in Bakers.'

'No, we don't.'

'We can go anywhere the three of us. Right then!' He lifted Matty onto the horse. 'Me and Matty are off to work on his room.'

'Matty has a room?'

'Didn't he tell you? We've been arranging things in case you fancied coming. There's Matty's room, rooms for maids, if you want them, a room for you and me, and a spare room, and, though nothing hasty,' he reached over the horse resting his forehead against Julia's, 'a little room tucked away out back for Matty's brother or sister for whenever they're beautiful mother is ready.'

* * *

'That woman!' Mrs Mac came in from the front parlour. 'I wish she'd make up her mind. Her and her headed note-paper! I've better things to do.'

'I take it you're referring to our new Mayoress.'

'I am. Aggie wrote last week confirming her bookings. Now, she's cancelled her daughter's wedding breakfast *and* the Christmas Luncheon.'

'But her daughter's wedding is not until the spring of '02.'

'She unsure of dates and cancels now to avoid problems later. The only problem she has is with her silly mayoral chain and how to hang it!'

'Did we take a booking fee?'

"We did.'

'Return it and no scrimping.' Julia picked up her gloves. 'I'm taking Dorothy into Kings Lynn to look at linen. Is there anything you need?'

'No, unless it's more patience for dealing with foolish people, but then I'm not sure Bentalls will sell that by the yard.'

'And if they did it would be sold out by now. Have there been other cancellations? I was to attend a luncheon at the Dower

House but had a letter saying due to unforeseen circumstances the luncheon is cancelled. Judging similar cancellations there's a lot of unforeseen circumstances about.'

'Oh, madam, I am sorry.'

Julia sighed. 'So am I. Not because they're withdrawn! People must do what they do. I don't want the school to suffer because of changes in my life.'

Mrs Mac coughed. 'Has His Royal Highness cancelled any meetings?'

'We didn't have any meetings to cancel. Her Majesty so ill there were other more immediate concerns. I did write when I knew what was happening, I thought it only polite. The Prince of Wales is an honourable man. I shall hear. Have there been cancellations in Cambridge?'

'Everything there is fine.'

'So it's just here at the moment?'

'Yes and it will rally and we'll be serving people who want to be served and not silly fools trying to make a silly point. I mean Mr Luke Roberts!' Mrs Mac tossed her head. 'A finer gentleman you couldn't wish to meet.'

Julia smiled. From a dithering mouse to a lion that roars Maud really has come on, and an attractive lion at that with hair suspiciously darker of hue and lips tinted a gentle red. 'Is Ben Faulkner coming by today?'

Mrs Mac coughed. 'He said he'd pop in.'

'Do give him my regards. And thank you, Maud. You are a good friend.'

'I am a grateful friend and always will be. Is Matty home for lunch?'

'I doubt it. He's at the house on the Common decorating his room. By-the-by I found him upset this morning. He said he'd had a dream.'

* * *

Matty is painting the wall but very slowly. There is a spider. He is afraid of splashing it and tries shooing it away.

Luke looked across. 'What's going on?'

'Spider.'

'Knock him down.'

'No, he might smash!'

Luke dropped the spider out of the window. Matty continued pushing the brush up and down. 'You're quiet,' said Luke. 'Don't you like painting?'

'Why did Susan die?'

'Why are you asking? Has Maggie Jeffers been spinning her rubbish again?'

'Maggie says she'll lose her job when we move away.'

'That is a distinct possibility.'

'If we move we'd leave Susan and her baby in the churchyard.'

'Susan and her baby are not alone. They are in heaven.'

Matty wasn't weeping but was close. 'The Big Bear is with Susan.'

Luke set down his brush. 'What you talking about?'

'Mumma's friend the German Bear is with Susan and her baby now.'

'Do you mean Doctor Adelman?'

'Yes. He and Mrs Bear came to see me last night. He said

they were with Susan and I wasn't to worry because the blue angel would watch over me.'

Luke took Matty home. Julianna wasn't back from shopping.

'Go have your tea and tell your mother I'll be along at seven to pick her up.'

'Will you show her my bedroom and my painting?'

'I will. Did you tell your mother about your dream?'

Matty shook his head. 'No.'

'Why not?'

'The Bear said I was to tell you.'

'To tell me?'

'Yes. He said tell the Wolf I didn't do it.'

* * *

Julia and Dorothy were weary and ready to go home when they saw the toy-shop and a train driven by steam. 'What do you think, Dorothy?'

'Oh yes, madam, though I'm not sure Mrs Mac will like the mess.'

'She'll love it. She's more of a child than Matty.' Julia bought the engine and several boxes of crackers and was preparing to leave when she saw Hugh Fitzwilliam and Charlotte Walbrooke. 'Good afternoon Hugh.'

Hugh bowed. 'Good afternoon.'

'Good afternoon, Lady Charlotte, a beautiful day if a little cold.'

Lady Charlotte nodded.

Julia gestured to the cabinet of toy soldiers. 'Are you considering taking up arms again Hugh?'

'It's not likely.'

'Aren't they wonderful?' She bent over the cabinet. 'The colours!'

'Yes indeed, quite realistic.'

'But not for you, not even as a boyhood dream?'

'I'm too old to dream. Excuse us, won't you? We have business elsewhere.' Hugh bowed. 'Good day to you.' He took Charlotte's arm and walked away.

'Good day.' Julia gazed after him.

Dorothy touched her arm. 'Are you alright, madam?'

'Yes. I'm alright. I'm a little disappointed.'

'With what, madam?'

'With myself for expecting more.'

They had crossed the road and were buying tobacco for Joe when Julia heard the newsboy calling: '*Murder in Dresden! Double Death in Dresden!*'

Julia turned. 'What is that, Dorothy?'

'What is what, madam?'

'What is that boy calling?'

The shout came again: '*Her Majesty's Doctor's slays wife and takes own life!*'

'What?' Julia stared at the words chalked on a board: '*German Heart Surgeon Commits Suicide after Killing Wife.*' She snatched up a newspaper. There was his name, Stefan Adelman and headlines declaring him a murderer.

* * *

Luke had taken a bath and was trying to get paint from under his fingernails when there was a knocking on the door. It was Bertha Carmody.

'Mr Roberts, is your lady here?'

'My lady?'

'Mrs Dryden? Is she here? I tried her place but they said she wasn't back from shopping so I thought to come here.'

'What's to do, Mrs Carmody?'

'It's Joe.' She wrung her hands. 'He's terrible poorly. I can't get him to eat or drink or do anything. It's like he's turned himself off.'

'Why did you want Mrs Dryden?'

'I thought if she'd come and hold his hand maybe he'd get better.'

'I see. Well I'm sure if she were here she would come. She's fond of Joe.'

'Aye and he's of her. I'm that worried. I think he's leaving us. Tell her to come, though I don't know why she would. I wasn't very nice last time she called.'

'She'll come.' Luke stepped into his boots. 'She'll have gone by tram. I'll take the cart and wait at the stop. You go back to Joe.'

'Please tell her to be quick.' Mrs Carmody hurried away. 'And tell her I'm sorry about the bramble jelly.'

Luke waited at the bus-station. The tram pulled in. One look at Julia's face and he knew Joe Carmody wasn't the only problem. 'What's the matter?'

'I'll tell you later. Why are you here?'

'What d'you mean why? Can't I meet my best girl at the tram without her needing to know why?'

'Of course you can but what has happened?'

'It's Joe. His wife came looking for you.'

'I see.' She put the parcels in the cart. 'We'll drop Dorothy off first.'

'I'm alright, madam,' said Dorothy.

'You're tired. You need to rest.'

'But what about the poor man in the newspaper?'

'Don't worry about that.' Julia climbed aboard the cart. 'Let the dead bury the dead. We have the living to worry about.'

They left Dorothy at the cottage. Luke didn't ask what Julianna meant by dead burying the dead. She'll tell him when she can.

'Shall I come in with you to Joe's?' he said.

'Please. I don't know what we'll find.'

* * *

What they found was poor Joe in a right state. Unshaven cheeks and rheumy eyes, it would take more than a loving hand to fetch him back.

'Hello Joe.' Julianna sat by the bed.

'Aye, madam!' He struggled to rise up. 'What you doing here?'

'I called to tell you about the Nativity play.'

'The what?'

'The play Matty was in.' She shed her bonnet. 'What a nice fire you have, so deliciously warm.' She took his hand. 'Would you mind if I sit awhile? I've been thrashing about Kings Lynn all afternoon.'

Joe's hand was so tiny. Surely his hands were bigger? When he's digging or pulling weeds they seem massive and when planting seedlings fairy fingers. Such a gardener, whatever he does he puts his heart and soul in it.

'I say, Joe, do you remember when I was greedy with the lavender and all the bushes in the kitchen-garden died back?'

'I do, and I remember you pruning the *Cecile Brunner* when you shouldn't. You had branches crossing over. You made a reet mess of it.'

'Yes and pretended I hadn't done it.'

'So you did, you bad lass.' They talked or rather Julia talked and Joe listened.

What a true friend. He was always there, a bowl of flowers, a scuttle of coal and a smile. Look what he did at night keeping watch! And am I really responsible for this? Did I get him wet and cold and ill? 'Oh dear Joe!'

'Bertha?' Joe flapped his hand. 'Give me that paper I've been writin' about plants! Now if you don't mind I'd like a few minutes alone with madam.'

'It's alright,' said Bertha seeing Julia nonplussed. 'He wants to tell you how to live. Like most men he thinks the world will grind to a halt if he ain't here. I'm going to make a cup of tea. Can I get you a cup, Mrs Dryden?'

'Thank you no.'

'What about you, Mr Roberts?'

'Aye, go, lad! This room's too small for a big bloke like you. You're using all the air. Just...!' He bowed over coughing, his whole body wrenching.'... just make sure you say goodbye afore you go.' Joe waited until they were gone then gripped her hand. 'You've got to get out of that house! I know it looks cosy and well-meaning, but there's bad feeling in the walls and you'll not shift it.'

'Now don't get excited,' said Julia. 'I'm here to tell you how much we miss you at the Nanny, not to make you ill!'

'I know and I am glad to see you for I couldn't rest easy without you knowin' it's a queer place and sooner you're out of it the better.'

'What do you mean?'

'I mean your cottage and the House across the way are crammed full of other people's feelings. It's in the air buzzin' like a swarm of wasps. It drains you dry. Take the Yankee lady. She was alright when she first came, an old woman yet fit. Now look! She's a bag of bones and crazy bones at that!'

'Be calm.' She put her hand on his chest. Joe knew she could feel his lungs rattling and saw him not long for this world. 'Forget what Bertha said! My bad chest is nowt to do wi' cold. It comes of bein' down the pit as a lad.'

'Oh, dear Joe. I am so sorry.'

'So I am. I wanted to be here a bit longer if only to see them Persian roses I put back of the sun-room take flight. Persians can be difficult. They are like people, they grow where they'll grow and no place else.'

'They are beautiful. I especially love the pink rambler.'

'Aye, it's called Maiden's Blush' he cackled. 'I bought it wi' you in mind. It's an Alba rose, dewy petals, tender heart and a wondrous scent. It's you.'

Bless her, she blushed a pretty pink and Joe had a mind to beg a kiss before he died. Lord, he does feel poorly and light-headed the way you feel when you step out in the morning and breathe the air and a blackbird is singing and plants rustling under the sod and worms are doing their bit.

'I like worms,' he said softly.' They're hardworking little beggars and we can't do wi'out them. You make sure your new gardener knows what he's doin'. I've written it down, what to do and when to do it... not that these youngsters take notice. Chaps nowadays are full of fancy ideas and new fangled poisons to kill the land. Keep your land clean and it will look after you.'

He turned to the window. 'I don't mind bein' put to soil. I know the earth and it knows me. We've worked together hand-in-hand these fifty years, and though I'm goin' the Lord will find me somethin' to do if only swattin' greenfly. Talkin' of greenfly, what's upset you?'

'I've had some disturbing news about a friend.'

'What happened to your friend?'

'If the newspapers are to be believed he is dead and his wife with him.'

'The newspapers!' Joe blew out his cheeks. 'You don't want to believe what they say. Most of what they say is lies. How did he die?'

'They say he committed suicide.'

'And you don't believe that?'

'I do not.' A tear slipped down her cheek. 'He wasn't that kind of man. He was a good man. He was my friend.' She laid her head on her arm.

Joe stroked her hair 'Nay lass, don't weep or I'll be weepin' with you.'

'But to lose such friends! And now you, Joe! I can't be without you.'

'And you won't! Don't think because I'm out of sight I am out of mind. I looked after your interests on earth and I shall carry on lookin'. Bertha will get her share. She's been a good old girl and

I won't let her down. But love can be stretched to go wherever it wants. Life is full of sorrow but it's full of joys too. You have to know which way to look. I have a memory of you.'

'Do you?'

'I do. Nobody sees a gardener. He blends with the land. He can dig and prune trees and clean a duck pond and nobody will see him. You always saw me. You always smiled and made sure I was welcome. Even when that silly stuff was goin' on and plants stolen you didn't blame me.'

'Why would I blame you? I knew it wasn't you at fault.'

'Not everyone would see it like that. They'd think I should've been on top of it.'

Joe is tired. Heart banging ten-to-the-dozen he shouldn't be talking but wants her to know. 'An unseen person gets to see things. I've seen you happy and I've seen you sad and I've been helpless 'cos it was your life and none of my business. But the garden is my business and I like that you cherished it.'

'You made it easy to cherish.'

'I saw you with the buttercups.'

'Buttercups?'

'It was last year. You were on your knees with a pair of shears cuttin' by the terrace. I watched you. You got nearer and nearer the buttercups but couldn't bring yourself to chop them. When you'd finished that grass was smooth as silk but right in the middle, spoilin' the line, was a bunch of buttercups.'

'I don't remember that.'

'I don't suppose you do, but it's my memory of you, how you couldn't kill a beautiful thing. It'll stay with me and it will bring me back.'

* * *

At Fairy Common Luke settled her in the chair. He could see she didn't want to speak and neither did he. Poor old Joe. 'You'll take care of my dear madam won't you lad? She said she'd a pension for me and I wasn't to worry 'cos Bertha would get it.' Then Joe had frowned. 'I meant to tell her of fag-ends in the shed but it went clean out my mind.'

Luke tried reassuring. 'Don't worry about it. I'll see to it.'

But he wouldn't settle. 'You see, me not bein' there of late that chap will think he's been forgotten and has a free hand.'

'He won't! I'll be on it.'

'You must. Some folks like to hurt lovely things. I've seen it with flowers in the park, folks stomping on 'em. Make sure nobody stomps on her.'

Luke put coal on the fire. 'What happened today, Anna, other than Joe?'

'Stefan Adelman. The papers say he killed his wife and took his life.'

'How did he kill her?'

'Morphine. They were found by the lake on Christmas Day, Karoline with the syringe still in her body.'

'And Doctor Adelman?'

'They're waiting on an autopsy.'

'I am sorry.' Luke knelt in front of her. He'll not tell her of Matty's dream, now is not the time. 'Do you think he might have done this?'

'If the situation called for it I am sure he could do it, and if reported there was a syringe then that would indicate an intention.'

'An intention yes but not the deed! There might have been a plan but as with any plan things can go wrong.'

'That's true.' She leaned forward her head in her hands. 'Look at me. The day the stove caught fire I had a plan that didn't work.'

'What was your plan?'

She sighed. 'I wasn't sure I had one. It's only looking back I see that I did. I sent Dorothy home when she needn't have gone.'

'So why did you send her home?'

'I wanted to be alone with you.' Eyes heavy with tears, she looked up. 'I understood what you are doing. You are being you, proud Mister Wolf. You are aware of things said, of Stefan and the Prince of Wales, who I assure you behaved as a gentleman and only ever so. You wanted holy vows to make it right, and of course they will make it right. But I can't help thinking love between us could never be wrong. I wanted you to love me that day as I want you to love me now. So please, dearest Luke, don't say no.'

'Ah, my sweet and lovely darling.'

Luke drew her onto the rug before the fire and kneeling unlaced her gown. Fingers trembling, she helped him. 'No' He pushed her hand aside. 'I've looked to this moment since I first set eyes on you, Anna Dryden, so let it be mine.'

One by one he removed her clothes, hooks sticking and silk catching on roughened hands. He took it all not stopping until she was naked. He wanted her like that, a creature new born, not defenceless so much as capitulating, accepting her need as he accepted his and nothing between them but the truth. Then shirt over his head and pants trodden down he lay beside her.

She didn't move. Mouth sad, she lay gazing into the firelight.

That's alright, he thought, I'll kiss sadness away. He drew her close. 'I love you as I have never loved anything. What I did before this moment, how I lived and thought was of another man. With you in my arms I have everything I need. As for being proud, when it comes to loving you I am what I am, and what I am, holy vows or not, is husband to you. This is me, your husband,' he kissed her. 'This is me.' He closed her hand about his penis. 'This too is me,' he whispered, his hand between her leg. 'Now hold me, dear wife, and never let me go.'

* * *

Betty hiked out of her warm snooze Luke took Julianna home. She said she needed to be there when Matty woke, that he was out of sorts due to a dream. Body loose and soul singing, the living flesh of his flesh beside him, Luke was still within his own dream. 'He told me of it.'

'Of course.' She laid her head on his shoulder. 'He tells you everything.'

'He dreamt of Stefan Adelman. He called him the German bear. He said they were together at the end of his bed, Mr and Mrs Bear.'

Her grip on his arm tightened. 'Karoline and Stefan were in his dream?'

'The Bear told Matty they were with Susan Dudley and her baby.'

'Oh!'

'Don't cry, love. I think they came to comfort and not make you sorry.'

'But it's so sad. This world is so sad. Is it ever going to be happy again?'

'Weren't you just a tiny bit happy earlier?'

'I was! Yes I was! I was so very happy. It's just that everything changes.'

'Come, sweetheart, kiss me and make me happy!' Tears wet on her cheek she clung to him. He whispered. 'There was more to the message. Our little lad didn't know what but I do and I think you will. There may have been a suicide but I doubt there was murder.'

'What was the message?'

'The Bear said he didn't do it.'

* * *

Luke opened the door at Fairy Common and she was in the room, her scent in the air! Once again he was inside her and her legs were about him, a tangle of images, white skin and pink nipples, lips and a mouth that opened to his probing tongue, silken flesh open and wildly hungry.

'Aggh!' He drubbed his head with his fists! Enough of that, a man must sleep as well as dream. Stripped of clothes he fell into bed. Eyes closed he lay thinking and then got back out again and bare-arsed knelt down by the bed.

Prayer is rusty on his lips but this wonderful night, this night-of-nights, he managed to get the wheels going long enough to say what he wanted.

'Dear Lord, thank you for bringing me to this moment. I am grateful for Julianna and Matty. I will try and make them happy.'

He was about to get back into bed when with a half smile on his lips, and a hope that God wouldn't be offended, he added a postscript, thanking the Gods of War for luring Masson away. Had he been at the Nativity Play it would've been him putting out a fire and Julianna wouldn't now be wearing Luke's ring. Life isn't only about love. It's about opportunity and chance and being there at the right time. Luke was there. Daniel Masson was not.

CHAPTER TWENTY-NINE

The Slip

'It's been fun but I'm sure you'll agree our little fling is flung.' Mona Dobson said that in a hotel in Port Elizabeth, he at one end of a marble bath and she the other, her hair piled on top of her head and breasts bared - lovely breasts, delicate. Long legs and smooth hips, Mona is all woman, but not the woman for him, as he - she took pains to point out - was not the man for her.

Fling! The remark burned and later when dressing, a spiteful kid, he bit back. 'For a Christian lady you are generous with your affections.'

Head down, she laced her boots. 'What has my faith to do with it?'

'Nothing, I guess. I'm making comparisons, the buttoned-up women who shake tambourines in London slums and you.'

'And buttoned-up and shaking a tambourine marks a woman as chaste?'

'Forgive me.' He was repentant. 'That was a stupid thing to say.'

'Yes, and ungenerous given the circumstances! I don't shake a tambourine and hope I'm not buttoned up against anything of value but I do love the Lord. As for generosity I thought it a mutual giving.'

'It was. Again, forgive me, I am not myself.'

'Who are you then?'

'A fool bent on ruining his life.'

She'd dragged a brush through her hair. Beautiful hair, a thick mane, he'd watched fascinated. Two minutes and she'd forgiven and hopefully forgotten his comment. 'Well, fool, I must go. I'm called to England.'

'Who calls you apart from your Baptist people?'

'I am here at the invitation of the British High Commission and I am called, as are you, by the Lord God Almighty and His Holy Word.'

Daniel closed his ears and what was left of his heart to Mona. Bible tracts and the reading of psalms make him uneasy - not that she preached to anyone, she was too busy scrubbing their filthy bodies to care about their perjured souls. She gave love without thought of return. The better part of Daniel wishes he could love her. Truth is he's always known who he wanted and how foolish is that, to be certain of the heart's desire and still turn aside for a fling.

He wrote to Mother, a miserable mix of apologies and excuses, sorry he missed Christmas. Point of fact he spent Christmas Day combing bugs out a kiddie's hair and in the evening out of his own. Mona with all that hair and he gets the bugs! She laughed: 'The Lord's Word is Mighty. We don't need armed escorts and I don't get nits.' The Word did go out. Seven days and the hills massed with rebels and not a cross word exchanged! What was it he saw in the trip? It can't be the thrill of danger. The only danger was in keeping up with Mona, who rode like a wrangler and bathed babies with the tenderness of a mother. She wore him out. As for twilight activity her orgasms were plentiful and silent, appreciation translated via the rapid semaphore of her eyelids. Once achieved she'd wait for him to catch up! Mona's hands put the merry into Christmas. It was the only way she'd have it, saving her virginity for a would-be husband. In the afterglow of sex he joked: 'Maybe he's here.' Her denial was emphatic. 'You are not good husband material.'

He challenged her opinion. 'And yet you're with me?'

'I was lonely. I needed human contact.'

'And marriage vows?'

'What about them?' She'd frowned. 'My skin doesn't need a signature on a form to thrill at a man's touch anymore than manhood needs a ring on my finger to make it hard. We are creatures of need.'

'So what happens when the beloved does come?'

'Then I am his. His past is of no use to me as mine is no use to him. You worry a lot about rules, Daniel, and yet you continually break them.'

'What do you mean?'

'I mean you love a woman. I see her in your eyes if not in your heart, which begs the question, what are *you* doing here with me?'

That night in camp he had no answer, his breakaway reeking of the past and his father. The refugee camp was a combination of the guy from *Pretoria News*, boredom, and Mona Dobson. His letter to Callie will smooth his path to Norfolk; his letter to Julianna was tentative, and, if the cable from John Sargent is right, a waste of ink. December 23 rd, it came to the office in Durban. Short and to the point every word a punch in the gut: *Damned Yankees. Stop. You left the garden gate open and a wolf carried the strawberries away.*

* * *

He arrived in England to flags at half mast and shops closed. Everywhere he turned there were draped portraits of the late Queen alongside those of the new King. A black bombazine night had fallen, horses draped in funeral cowls and men and women in mourning. The lethargy affected transport, trains delayed, which meant he didn't get into Kings Lynn until gone ten.

Crosby was waiting at the station. Peter Crosby has been with the family forever. A quiet man, a cleft palate leaving him monosyllabic, he's always been there. Dulce is another, a polished Niobe she came as a girl and stayed. A more loyal servant you will not find nor one more dour. She rarely smiles. Callie says 'given her beginnings why the hell would she.'

Daniel climbed into the carriage. 'Good evening, Crosby.'

'Evening, Mister Daniel.'

'Mighty cold.'

'It is.'

'The Queen is dead then.'

'God rest her soul.'

The carriage rattled on. Daniel is looking into Ford motor-cars thinking of investing. According to Callie it's the way forward. Money and how to invest was the one thing on which she and Sam agreed. How to spend it was another issue. Sam bought baubles for his dollies. Callista Greville Masson buys the rare and unobtainable. Necklaces, bracelets and rings, if she wants it she'll get it via her broker, the latest acquisition a six string black pearl choker said to have belonged to the Tsarina.

Last October Daniel stayed with Cousin Francis. One night Daisy came to his bedroom, jewel case in hand; 'did he think Great Aunt Callista would be interested in this ruby ring.' He knew damn well Great Aunt Callista would be interested but the ring is a family heirloom, and the Warwicks union already shaky. Now he wonders if he'd done less thinking and more giving of ruby rings to Julianna he wouldn't be on the outside looking in.

The carriage turned into the Rise. As usual the House is a wedge of shadows, only the Hall and first-floor front showing light - a marked contrast to the cottage down the Rise where lights blazed.

'Is the Tea-Room open for business?'

'I don't think so, sir.'

'So what's going on?'

'Mizz Dryden is throwing a party for her maids. Mizz Callie said she'd pop along later but you coming, I doubt she'll bother.'

Daniel gazed down the Rise. Music and laughter drifted on the evening air. It made him miserable. Julianna should be missing him, the cottage in darkness and a solitary candle in the window bringing the wanderer home.

* * *

'Anna's getting married.' He'd barely a foot in the door when Callie came running looking like the Crone in the Gingerbread House, black silk dress, hair frowzy, and a front tooth missing. 'What happened to your tooth?'

'I fell. They've called the banns.'

'What do you mean fell?'

'As I said, I fell. They've called the banns in St Bedes Church.'

Daniel took his bag. 'Is there hot water in my bathroom, Crosby?'

'Yes, sir. It's been fixed.'

'Well, that's something.' He took to the stairs.

Callie followed. 'Did you hear what I said, they've called the banns?'

'I'm not sure what you're talking about.'

'I'm talking about Julianna and the builder! She's marrying him! They've put up banns and are to wed.'

'Good for them.'

'Good for them?' Callie scuttled alongside and with Dulce trying to haul her back. 'You can't mean that.'

'I do mean it because Julianna married means I'm free of this pathetic charade!' Door slammed, he set down his bag. He spun taps in the bathroom. Hot water gushed out, clean water, none of your rust-red poison. For a moment he dithered. He wanted to leave and never come back but with the Gingerbread Woman falling to pieces before his eyes couldn't.

Leaving the bath he went down to the small sitting room and a large whisky. Under normal circumstances Callie's talk would be of the death of Queen Victoria, but such is the grip of the past Julianna holds all. 'They call him the tamed brute,' said Callie, 'and threaten to cast her from society.'

'The British are such snobs!' Daniel sipped his whisky. 'It's Carrington that's the brute, him and his crazy sister!'

'They don't want the Old Order changing. I should've wed Henry. Had I done so it might be you with a title and not Frances. '

'Then bless you, Mother, for not marrying Henry. I am an American. Why would I want to live in this backward place? The Pilgrims knew what they were doing when they shook this archaic dust off their boots.'

'But what about you? What do you plan to do now you're a free man?'

'I was always a free man.' Daniel went out on the terrace. 'Crosby says they're having a party for the maids.'

'There's always a party going on. The noise those women make! Music playing and carriages coming and going, Henry should close the avenue.'

There it is again, Callie hovering between worlds. 'I called your doctor. He'll be down tomorrow to see you.'

Callie snorted. 'Did you dig him out the ground? "Arise, Doctor Adelman! Take up thy coffin and walk!"'

'I didn't mean Adelman. I meant the chap in the village.'

'Oh him,' she screwed up her face. 'I'm not seeing him.'

'Then who are you seeing?'

'I don't want to see anyone. I want to sit here on the terrace waiting for the spring and watching history repeat itself.'

'History is not repeating anything. Julianna Dryden and Justine Newman are two entirely different people.'

'They have the same initial.'

'So do I and a donkey but it doesn't mean anything.'

'On its own it doesn't but things add up.' She wiped snow from the telescope. 'To get this to work properly you must have the images one over the other, a triple world. Who's to say your world doesn't overlay mine?'

'Don't draw me into your craziness, Mother. We're not adrift in any serendipitous Universe. I control my own destiny.'

'Then control it, Daniel Masson! You're not invincible! You can be hurt same as any other man. I'm haunted by thoughts of

Stefan Alderman and worry his isn't the only death coming. It's why I invited Madame Leonora.'

'I thought I told you not to get into that!'

'I don't care what you told me. This is my house and I'll do what I want. I never expected your support. You're just like your father selfish to the end. Leaving me alone at Christmas? What kind of son does that?'

Daniel snatched up his jacket and vaulting the rail dropped into the snow. 'I'm the kind of son who wants to get the hell out of here and start living again!' Hands in his pockets he trudged toward the village but then, a fish on the end of a line, did a U-turn heading back to the cottage.

* * *

They pulled the tables together, Luke at one end and Julia at the other, and hung lanterns from the rafters and redecorated the tree.

'Shouldn't do that,' said Maggie. 'It's bad luck.'

'You don't want a gift from the tree then?' said Julia.

'I do. I'm just saying it's bad luck.'

A saddle of lamb followed by Mrs Mac's apple dumplings and fresh cream, it was a good meal. Now they are settled about the table with mugs of beer. Ben Faulkner is at the piano, and Reggie, the baker, about to sing. 'Don't let him, madam!' squeaked Dorothy. 'He thinks he sings like a bird but he don't!'

Reggie began to sing, or rather to bawl: '*Tom Pearce, Tom Pearce, lend me your grey mare! All along, down along, out along lea.*'

'Not that one!' Dorothy groaned. 'We'll be here forever.'

Julia called halt. 'I think we might be a little less raucous.'

When he began to sing again she went into the kitchen. It is the maid's party and as such she does the dishes. The party is Mrs Mac's idea and gathers quite a crowd: there's Ben Faulkner, the pot-boy from Greenfields, Mr Croft, the greengrocer, Nan and Albert and bar-staff from the Nelson. It was meant for next Saturday but brought forward on account of the wedding.

Luke came into the kitchen. 'You want help with that?'

'I'm alright. There's not too much.'

''E'en so.' He took off his jacket and rolled up his sleeves. 'I'll help.'

'I know what this is about.' Julia filled the bowl. 'This is not you helping with dishes. This is you trying to get away from the singing.'

'Darn right! The fellow's got a voice like a cow with bellyache.'

They worked together. They didn't speak. Aware of one another, of soap bubbles glistening on her fingers and of the white of his shirt against a sun-beaten arm, words are unnecessary.

'You know Nan offered the pub for the wedding breakfast?'

'I'd rather a small dinner party here.'

'Are you sure? It suits me but doesn't seem much.'

'It's fine.'

Silence and then: 'You are very quiet.'

'As are you.'

'I am a man of few words.'

'So you are, although...' she bent her head, 'not always.'

The tea-towel small in his hand, and a tide of red creeping over his cheek, he polished a plate. 'Aye well, there is a time for saying things.'

Bit-by-bit the shelves are restocked with china. He took the last dish. 'I don't seem to remember you saying much on such occasions.'

The tide of red was then hers. 'I needed my breath to survive!'

He glanced back at the door and then leaned across pressing his lips to curve of her throat. 'You have made me the happiest man.'

'And me the happiest woman.'

'Madam, come quick!' The moment was snatched away, Maggie at the door. 'Ben is playin' piano and we're to push back the table and dance.'

Mrs Mac proved to be a wonderful dancer if inclined toward the poetic. Snatched up in her embrace Luke tried not to laugh. Held as she is between the death of a friend and whispers of Joe Carmody sinking, Julianna's not able to laugh. Luke is happy, not least because his parents have accepted the marriage. It happened in the Nelson's snuggery, Aggie Simpkin asking how it felt to have a woman like Anna Dryden for daughter-in-law. Ma said she couldn't be happier. Julianna is likely on the end of opinions about him. Freddie Carrington wrote from Italy. *We are in the Borghese. Everyone else is with family sharing hugs and kisses. We share vintage champagne and bitter loathing. I heard about you and Ju-ju. I wish you well and hope not too many doors closed to you. Build more houses and make more money, Luke. You'll be amazed how many doors open to that.*

Daniel stands by the Wall watching. He hears the piano playing and sees them dancing. Julianna wears a gown of black velvet that makes her skin shimmer. She stands to one side smiling. The dog comes for a pat and Matty sits at the piano. It's a happy scene, a banner wrapped about the room would read, 'Peace on

Earth, Good Will to All Men.'

He is tempted to knock on the door and be part of the celebration. He has an excuse in Matty's toy soldier. Amulet, a blessing or curse, it weighs heavy in his pocket, a token of all that is lost. Then, handsome in a dark blue jacket, Luke Roberts comes into view. Callie has tried putting business his way. Some jobs are undertaken but the roof is refused; that the Boss is a modern-day Midas, everything he touches turning to gold, is not why it was refused. It is a matter of principle, and the principle being Julianna.

They dance together and passing the window are momentarily held in the glass as a page in an illuminated manuscript. Luke has his arm about her waist, his hand cradles hers. They keep space between them yet are welded together. One-two-three, one- two-three, Julianna's gown swirling, they convey an image of courtly love, *La Roman de la Rose*, yet their love is infinitely human. They have kissed as well as dreamed! They have touched and cried out! It shows in their faces. They are known to one another and no longer alone.

The toy-soldier left on the window sill Daniel walked away.

CHAPTER THIRTY

Beloved Lie

Freddie toyed with his hat. 'I think I'll go out.'

Evie yawned. 'Yes do. Go and have fun.'

'Fun? What kind of fun with everybody gone and none to call friend?'

'The fun you usually find in deep water.'

Freddie glared at her. 'I hate it when you are like this.'

Eve sighed, and dipping the brush washed the canvas. It's a bright day, the light in the gallery perfect. The maid has set up a tray of coffee and amaretto biscuits and for once Evie's head is not crashing. All it needs is Freddie to stop talking and go where he was always going to go.

'You and your nasty habit of pickin' up stray dogs and then kickin' them out, we've never had a more dreary start to the year!'

'Luke Roberts couldn't wait to be kicked out. He preferred his Norfolk kennel and a pretty little bitch called Ju-ju.'

'Yes, and I'm never goin' see either again.'

Evie shrugged. 'A night playing piquet with your shady friends, you'll find a new toy to amuse. How much did you lose last night?'

'Not overly much.'

'That's because Jamieson keeps an eye on you. Alone with the company you keep, you'd be minus your skin this morning never mind shirt.'

'You're a fine one to talk. Some of the creatures you've brought home, I wonder we're not dead in bed with our throats cut.'

'Goodness, you are in a Gothic mood! I should avoid St Peters today if I were you and look at some pretty Giotto paintings. You've been too long among the bruised and bloodied Caravaggio.'

'Ha-ha, very amusin'. Anyway I'm off.'

'Be careful! The Basilica is a magnet for others beside layabout artists. I know you're lonely but don't let loneliness lead you into danger.'

'I say, Evie, draw it mild, will you.' Freddie picked up his sketch book. 'I'm meetin' a couple of fellows, not keepin' a date with death.'

* * *

'*Oh, Io chiedo scusa*! I beg your pardon!' Dizzy from too much to drink last night he held onto the rail. He likes to come to the Basilica. The centre of the Holy Roman Catholic church, there's so much to look at he never feels he's wasting time. It's also a good place for meeting one's own. So far no one particular person stands out. Usually there's a sign, a look or a way of wearing clothes that helps a bumblebee recognise a flower. Last week it was Barnaby from Pasadena. They met over fifteenth-century illuminated scrawl. 'Can you read Latin?' says Barnaby. Freddie lied. 'Not a bit. Can you?'

They spent the day together. Come the evening there was no mention of illuminated scripts, only a back room and lips pulling. Barnaby goes back to Pasadena tomorrow but did say they'd meet to swap addresses. Now looking at his watch Freddie suspects the bumblebee has flown.

Chasing love is a preoccupation - love or sex, nowadays it's much the same. He should go back to the Villa but there is something tempting in the clandestine. It only stops being so when mistaking a wasp for a bee.

Monday they leave for England. Evie says we must show respect to the late Queen which includes wearing heavy mourning. Freddie never liked the old lady. He thought her a crosspatch whereas Bertie, the Prince of Wales, is ever smiling. Besides, black makes him pasty looking.

* * *

It is dark inside the Basilica, yet the genius of Michelangelo shines through. Carved in white marble, Mary, the epitome of grief, cradles her son. Knees spread, the folds of her gown heavy, she offers Him to the world. 'Look what you did to my boy.' Yes, thought Freddie, look what I did to mine!

They were wrong to winter here. Sex was the plan this time in Rome, sex and plenty of wine. So far he's indulged in both but without a hope of romance. Romance was Luke Roberts and a brief moment of heaven. Luke took one look at the Pieta and fled. 'I see my mother in this when our Jacky died.'

Freddie would have loved a brother. If he'd kept his distance he might have had one in Luke. He blames Evie. She wouldn't leave the man alone. An emotional nomad, she's always moving to the next fair-weather friend, who steals her jewels while whispering love poems in her ear.

It's likely she sees Freddie a millstone about her neck, and to be fair his life weighed against hers the scales would crash to the ground. Owen Passmore used to say the Maat weighing of the heart ceremony rendered even Solomon obsolete. Evie pushed Freddie to Cambridge. Sid saw it a waste of time, '*amo, amas, amat*, what has Latin to do life.'

Freddie is sick of England. Paris is where he's heading or New York. An apartment in Manhattan and a good atelier, he might yet be another John Singer Sargent. He had hopes of Julianna, that they might have a home together. Not Charlecourt! The family ghosts can rattle their bones along those corridors forever he won't be joining them!

* * *

'Is Jamieson back yet?' Evie enquired of the maid.

'No, Milady.'

'When he comes send him in please.'

Jamieson is gone to post the mail. Rome is aflutter with news of the Queen's death. Poor Bertie! Evie sent a letter of condolence. Later, when she's home in England, she'll send a more personal note. It's time they went home. Friday sennight Godfather Fitzwilliam weds Charlotte Walbrooke. It's a mistake, Hugh not gaining a wife so much as four walls and a ceiling. Charlotte won't make him happy. He'll have to hide his hair dye and quit his cabbage plot. A last resort, Evie sent a wire: *To Godfather Huggy-Bear Fitzwilliam. England expects every man to do his duty but not to forfeit his prize marrows.*

There are no such qualms about Ju-ju Dryden's forthcoming marriage. It's true she'll be erased from society diaries, but she won't care tucked up safe and sound in the Wolf's lair. Evie can't decide what she feels, and wonders if she met another like Ju-ju she might be content. The ability to love easily was denied her at birth. That she loves at all is nothing short of a miracle.

Yesterday Jamieson found a dog in a doorway. A pretty creature under the dirt it sits beside her now. She's named it Sidney and hopes it will stay. It won't hurt her. Nothing can hurt her! It's all been done before. Evie weeps and the dog crawls onto her lap, dog and bitch weeping together.

* * *

Freddie pretends to sketch the Pieta. A marvellous sculpture! It's as well a glass screen keeps people at bay or the Madonna would bear the pain of a million hands seeking comfort of her broken Son.

A fellow in a green muffler hovers. He too carries a sketch pad. Freddie would like to approach but is wary having heard the Carabineer pose as inverts, and if a fellow is caught he pays with his wallet *and* his arse.

The fellow with the muffler is smiling! Heart beating, Freddie kneels in a side chapel. There's the shuffling of shoes and then one pair of boots with metallic clasps alongside. Hands clasped in prayer and lashes on a smooth white cheek, the fellow kneels. Freddie drops his sketch pad.

It is picked up and handed it over. '*Mi..mille grazie!*' He stutters.

'You are welcome,' says the fellow.

'You speak English?'

'A little.' The fellow's eyes are cold.

Freddie shivered. 'It is cold in here.'

The lashes flicker. 'I know a place where it is warm. You like to go there?'

Freddie hesitates.

The fellow smiles. 'I am Paolo.'

'Freddie. How d'you do?'

'How do I do?' The lashes quiver. 'Come with me and find out.'

* * *

Freddie found out alright, the first kick sending him sprawling down the stairs. At first all was well, he, Paolo (if that was his name) took them on a tour. Born of the City he knew back street-churches few tourists would see, and dark places where martyrs died and where Leonardo da Vinci carved his name.

They went to a cafe. It was a good day, which made what followed more shocking. Two of Paolo's friends were waiting on the landing; that they'd done this before, waylaid some poor English fag, was in the insults accompanying every kick. Shocked, heartbroken, Freddie didn't argue. He's been here before and yet never with such venom. Flies ripped open and meat hanging out they wanted more than his money, they wanted his soul, and his velvet jacket, carefully parting the tails before taking turns with his benighted arse.

God knows why but they meant to mark him, the one with rotten teeth lining up a kick as Paolo supported Freddie's head. At the fifth or sixth kick he quit the scene. When in Rome do as the Romans do, that's what they say. Romans don't do this! They don't kick a man in the head and wipe shit on his face. Rome is beauty and white marble and Michelangelo.

He passed out of his body into the sky flying into blue blackness. The stars are beautiful, no need to stay with sadness. There was a moment of earth time where he saw Jamieson with fists swinging. Then Evie was screaming, except she was back at the Borghese, lamp-light highlighting her tears.

'Ah, Sis, don't cry.'

Freddie wanted to comfort her but couldn't stay. It's not his body, although the tearing of skin and bone does hurt, it is the pain in his heart, people and cruelty. It is Father and the way he was with little girls. It's Paolo and boys like Paolo. It is so many things. It is losing Luke and Ju-ju. It is his work, the painting he adores but is never quite good enough. It is Susan Dudley and her baby. It is today and tomorrow and every day. It is too much and the Honourable Frederick Erasmus Carrington sees no reason to stay.

* * *

'He is here, Senora.'

Black habit rustling, and white coif obliterating the stars, the Nun led the way. The call came an hour ago, the concierge battering the door: 'Come, senora! Your brother is hurt.' Evie was taken to the Orsepidale, Santo Spirito. Such a journey, the carriage driver singing Neapolitan love songs seeming to think Evie and accompanying police officer on some secret love tryst.

Jamieson was waiting. He crooked his finger. Evie knows that finger. It meant 'Say nothing.' Doctors were there with more policemen. There was a deal of shouting and much gesticulation, but other than Freddie found badly beaten near the Temple of Apula no one inclined to offer information.

Light fading and the oleander smelling so sweet, a Nun led through a garden which for some reason Evie associated with Gethsemane.

They approached a bed. 'He is here,' said the Nun.

Evie gazed down. 'No.' Hope caught her heart. 'That's not him.'

The Nun passed a sketch book. 'This is his book, Freddie Carrington.'

It was him, face swollen and eyes disappearing in bruised flesh!

She fell on her knees. 'Freddie, what have you done?'

'Madam!' Jamieson spoke. 'I must talk to the police.'

'Oh don't leave me here alone!'

'I won't be long. I need to smooth things out.'

Evie felt suddenly incredibly old. What is she to do? What can she do if Freddie dies! The Nun pushed her into a chair. 'Your Freddie walks with the Lord Jesus. Hold his hand that he may find his way back to you.'

'But look! Look at his face! Will he want to come back after this?'

'Yes, if he has love enough.'

'I love him.' Evie sobbed. 'I have always loved him.'

'Of course you love him. He is your son. Every mother loves her son.'

A lie of thirty years hovering on her lips Evie was silent.

The Nun held her gaze. 'Is he not your son?'

'Yes.' She sighed. 'He is my son.'

Bitter and beautiful, love a lock on her lips, Evie gazed down on her boy. Of course she is his mother. Who else would fight for him as she has fought?

Freddie was forced on her when she was a child, his father her father.

'Lying whore!' Face black with rage, he'd leant into her. 'I am Sir George Baines Carrington QC! How dare you suggest I am the father! This is the work of some filthy farmyard boy you were entertaining!'

Father was afraid the day the news broke and dangerous. Evie believed he would kill her. He warned her, 'breathe a word of your condition and you will be locked away and the child drowned.' Then Mother, who for years bore all in silence, chose to speak. 'Evelyn shall have the child. We shall raise it as our own.' Abuse followed, violence during the day and hissing at keyholes at night, '*Open the door, Evie, and let Papa in*'! It's what he used to say when raking at her buttocks, his saliva acid on her skin. Mother held firm. 'Once more at my daughter in this way and I shall do what I should've done years ago. I shall take a gun and put an end to my life. Try explaining that away.'

Evie and Mother were banished to the country with Nanny Goldsmith, Mother's nurse. The world rocked, servants turning their faces to the wall and Eve's belly ballooning. One day Father arrived with a birth certificate for Nanny to sign: 'My child born of Lady Carrington, sign and keep your pension.'

She signed. Nothing to be done then but make a vow: should the child be a girl then she and baby will go to the river and lie down never to rise.

Oh and how she ached to be loved as a daughter should be

loved. There was no love until Freddie was born. August '74 Evie returned to society via the Ambassador's Ball and a tubby banker from Rhode Island. Sidney spun her round the dance floor. 'You are one unhappy little lady. What's wrong with your life that you're so sad?' Then, he'd danced her out onto the terrace and onto his knee. 'I am a childless widower and rich as Croesus. I don't know what makes you weep but I am willing to give all to dry your tears.'

Sidney paid father a visit and took a cheque book with him. They were wed in Rhode Island. Evie will never tell Freddie of such brutality whereas Sidney worked it out. It was his habit of an evening to sit on the chaise, Miss Fancy, the Pomeranian, between them. He would take Eve's hand. She would pull away. One night they fought, Sidney shouting. 'Why did damage to your body cause the death of our child and why can't you bear to hold my hand?'

Years of humiliation were revealed, how when she was a girl Sir George would take her walking, her hand pushed through an opening in his trouser pocket. They'd walk together, he smiling at neighbours and lifting his hat, and all the while using her hand and no one in the world knowing but Evie.

Sidney returned to England on Freddie's seventh birthday, Nanny Goldsmith alerting them to danger. He went with Jamieson this time not a cheque book. Fearful of repercussions, Evie asked what he meant to do. Sidney shrugged. 'A rich man has many friends. The highborn live in mansions and wield power in parliament. The low live in alleys and carry clubs. Which d'you reckon most useful when dealing with a son-of-a-bitch like your father?'

* * *

Weary, Evie leaned down and kissed Freddie. Thirty years she has stood between him and danger. Every move was for him, every change of house, town and country, move after move, hurt after hurt, and all caused by one man. Looking back she thinks it ought not to have been left to Mother to threaten a gun. She should've done it. God knows she wanted to! Even now she dreams of taking one of his adored Purdey guns and shooting him *and* Mother, because however you view it Mother came too late!

There are those who know her secret, Stefan Adelman, God rest his soul, knew, as did John Singer Sargent, when in the jaws of Black Dog she cut her wrists. They swore not to tell on the condition she never again attempted suicide. 'You must not take your life,' said Stefan. 'It belongs to your son.'

Stefan went to his grave with a secret. Evie will do the same. Looking at her son so battered and hurt she wonders if it might be better if he did die. They say God is always looking for budding angels. Freddie is no angel but he doesn't deserve the cruelty of this world.

Doctors stitched cuts on Freddie's face, set a broken arm and bound his ribs. They said he was lucky to be alive and that unconscious was best, he is unaware of pain. A priest came holding out a hand for alms. He said Freddie shouldn't have been at the ruins, it was a bad place used by those outside the love of God. Jamieson told him to leave and 'take his miserable ass with him. There is no place or person the Lord did not love and a true Christian would know that.' Sidney knew what he was doing when he gave a home to the man. Evie knows nothing of Rueben Jamieson, that he adores Freddie is enough. Now, a squatting toad, he sits beside the bed, his glance never leaving Freddie's face. 'Is he in pain, do you think?' she asked.

'I hope not, madam.'

'His eyelids flicker. Do you suppose he's dreaming?'

* * *

Freddie dreams he is back in the Basilica gazing through plate glass. The Pieta is such a beautiful thing, clean and white, he yearns to break the glass, because somehow he knows if he were to touch Mary - even the hem of her robe – he is done with the pain of life forever. But he can't get started 'cos every time he climbs the rail Evie calls out, 'Freddie, please don't leave me,' and afraid she'll do silly things like cut her wrists he returns to the other side.

Evie thinks he doesn't know she's tried chopping her wrists and that every night she sips laudanum, the dose ever increasing. He knows about her wrists. There are other things he knows - in this liquid shifting state he knows that Evie and Sidney had a baby girl called Jenny who died. Freddie knows a horrible thing to do with little girls - so horrible he doesn't want to think about it but Nanny Goldsmith - who for some reason is in the dream with him - sits him on a stool behind a screen of pink-coated huntsman. 'Be a good boy.' She puts a finger to her lips. 'I'll come and fetch you when it's all over.'

'No, Nanny!' Freddie mumbles. 'I don't want to see it.'

He is alone in the room again. The door opens and Papa comes in leading a tiny girl as fair as an angel. Soon horrible noises come from behind the screen. Papa is whispering and the little girl weeps. Freddie sticks his fingers in his ears. 'Open the door!' Papa is shouting. 'Open the door and let Papa in!'

The little girl is so afraid! Why doesn't someone help her? Freddie would help but is afraid of what he might see. He thinks he knows the little girl, that she has hair the colour of his hair, and eyes the colour of his eyes.

They say that what the eyes don't see, the heart cannot grieve. It's a lie! Freddie never actually saw Papa hurt this little girl but she was hurt the same. It's why he's brought here time-after-time, George Carrington wants his son to know how he was conceived. Words couldn't do it - respectability had to be maintained. A fire-screen, and a lie, kept Freddie and his real mother apart.

'But damn you! No more!' The boy joined with the grown man and together they hurled the screen down smashing it to a thousand pieces.

'Ooh!' Freddie opened his eyes. 'Where am I?'

A Nun leaned over him. 'You are in hospital, Senor Carrington.'

'Oh, yes, that's right.' Freddie remembered. He'd been set upon, beaten by Paolo and his friends. Jamieson was asleep in a chair on the right side of the bed, Evie on the other side her cheek resting on her hand.

He was dreaming an ancient dream, a throw back to when he was a boy in Charlecourt. Always the same dream, Papa abusing servant girls, only this dream was different. He knew the little girl, saw her face.

'Oh!' He tries to move. He groans and Evie shifts in sleep, his pain becoming her pain, his grimace reflected in her face.

'Let me help you.' A Nun drew liquid into a syringe. 'You

were dreaming. Dreams can be helpful. They teach us things.'

'This one certainly taught me.'

'Was it a good learning?'

'I'm not sure. I learned a secret that hurt me to see it.'

'This will help.' The Nun shook the phial. 'Morphine eases pain and softens memories even to removing that we have no wish to keep.'

Freddie looked at Evie, the fatigue and care-worn face. So many years and so many nightmares! He knows now who suffered behind the smoke screen of a lie. He knows who started the lie; George Carrington started it, but it was his daughter that kept it. It was she who fought long and hard to keep the wretched screen in place. Not for her good! For Freddie! She didn't want him to share her pain. Now he knows why they both suffer the Black Dog and knowing will fight alongside her. He sees how his talent was born as well as his failures. He sees courage, how year-after-year, through good and bad, through laughter and tears, all was borne by this woman, his mother.

Evie is his mother! Evelyn Carrington is his mother! She brought him into a multi-coloured world of paint and poetry, and of music, and dear old Johnny Sargent, and all the shouting and screaming, and the being alive! Who cares from whose masculine loins he sprang! Look where he landed! Grace and beauty is his beginning! Not poor Lady Iphigenia's grey misery. And Oh Dear God he is so glad and so grateful!

'So, darling Mother,' he whispered, the name sweet on his lips. 'Because I love you, and because I plan to care for you, I will resurrect the damnable screen. I shall keep the beloved lie. Your secret now, Mother, is mine.'

The needle plunged home. 'Ouch!' He winced.

Evie opened her eyes.

A tear slid down Freddie's cheek. 'Hello, Sis.'

CHAPTER THIRTY-ONE

Shadow Man

Julia was clearing breakfast when the doorbell rang. It's been a busy week, letters and cards arriving. And flowers, so many, the back-parlour is a steamy hothouse. Later this morning caterers will ready the front parlour. Mrs Mac and Leah asked to arrange the wedding breakfast but Julia gave the work, and the worry, to an outside concern. She wants the maids to celebrate as friends not workers. Good and bad, faithful and fickle, they have been with her every step of the way - on the happiest day of her life she'll not be without them.

'You have a visitor, madam, Mr Greville Masson.'

'Thank you, Dorothy. Please show him in.'

Tall and sun beaten, and suddenly older, he ducked under the lintel. 'Good morning, Julianna. I hope I don't disturb you.'

'Not at all, Daniel! Dorothy, take Mr Masson's hat.'

'No don't bother! I shan't stay. I have business in town. I heard of your news and wanted to offer my good wishes.'

'Thank you.'

He hovered.

'You are well, Daniel?'

He shrugged. 'I could be better.'

'I understand you were delivering food over Christmas to refugee centres, and badly needed I imagine. A camp in winter, I would've thought you...!'

He cut across her. 'I made a mistake, a bad one. I didn't realise

431

I loved you the way I do.'

'Oh Daniel'

'It's alright!' He held up his hand. 'I'm not about to make a fool of myself, at least no bigger than already made. These things happen, stupid resentment and unanswered questions! We gamble with possibilities and lose the thing we wanted to keep. A man should be with his family at Christmas not fighting wars. I should've been with you and Matthew. I am sorry.'

'Thank you.'

'Staying away helped no one, not me and certainly not my mother. I am concerned for her. I see how she has deteriorated and fear for her sanity. I aim to get her away from Greenfields as soon as possible. The house is not good for her. It never was.'

'I am sorry.'

'Me too. I didn't want to come here. It was never my plan to stay, but then I met you, and while I didn't care for England and that darned house, I cared for you. I still care, most passionately, dearest Julianna, and while I know I shouldn't be talking this way... hardly the behaviour of a gentleman, I can't seem to stop. These are the words I should've said, words that filled my head day-after-day from morning til noon but that never got beyond my head. We all make mistakes. Mine was in believing I had time and love to waste.'

At the door he paused. 'One other thing, Callie has made some ridiculous plan regarding a meeting at the house this evening. She has invited one Madame Leonora, a so called medium to conduct a séance.'

'I did hear about that.'

'I can't get her to cancel. She says it is her birthday and she'll not give way.'

'I received an invitation in the morning post.'

'And do you plan to attend?'

'I can't. You see I am rather busy tomorrow and had thought to have this evening to myself, just me and Matty.'

He smiled bitterly. 'Of course you're busy! Tomorrow is your wedding day. I had hoped you might attend as she specially asked of you. I don't suppose you could spare an hour this evening? I'm pretty desperate.'

'Well yes, I could pop in for an hour.'

'I would be grateful.'

'Very well then.' She walked him to the door. 'Thank you for coming by.'

'Thank you for listening. The pity of it!' Daniel shook his head. 'Between us my mother and I have made a mess of things. My Strawberry Girl going one way and me another, this isn't how I had my life planned.'

'Things do change rather suddenly.'

'So they do. And when I said pity I wasn't referring to your wedding. I do most sincerely wish you well. There cannot be a more beautiful bride or a luckier groom. I just wish your wedding day could've been mine.'

* * *

'You are to stay and not to peep until we collect you,' said Mrs Mac.

Resigned, Julia gazed out of the window. As of tomorrow the maids are on a day's leave and will arrive *en masse* at the Lord Nelson courtesy of Nan and Albert. 'It's Luke's idea,' said Nan.

'He reckons they've looked after you and deserve a night away for a treat.'

Luke is so considerate. After much discussion of where to live he suggested the cottage. 'I'm likely to be away from Norfolk for at least two nights a week. I don't want you alone in a house you don't know. Stay put. Then if you've a mind we can go live on the moon.' Hands clasped about her waist he drew her close. 'Do you think you could be happy with me on the Moon?'

Julia thinks she could be happy in Hell if he were with her.

'Come now, madam! We're all done!' Eyes covered, the maids led her to the bedroom. 'You can look now.' A nightgown of pale ecru silk and matching peignoir lay displayed on the bed. 'Leah made it. She chose the material and did the cutting and sewing. We all embroidered a rose at the hem.'

The silk liquid in her hands, Julia gathered it up. 'Why, it's beautiful!'

'We thought it a pity you had to change your wedding dress for a darker colour,' said Dorothy. 'We wanted you to have something light and pretty.'

'All this heavy black,' Mrs Mac sniffed. 'It's quite unnecessary.'

Maggie chimed in. 'I heard the vicar's wife wore her old grey coat to market and was spat on and called unpatriotic.'

'Rubbish, Maggie!' said Mrs Mac. 'You heard no such thing.'

They fell into a quarrel. They are anxious about the future. Julia would like to reassure them but knows there will be changes. Last week she received a letter from Robert Scholtz, who offered a way out. '...*If you and Mr Roberts care to visit we would be happy to receive you. We have a nice place in Quincy and would make you comfortable should you choose to honour us with a visit.*'

434

When she told Luke he smiled. 'He said the same to me.'

'Would you consider it?'

'If you would! It's not as far as the moon and we have friends there.'

* * *

Ten o' clock Mrs Carmody was at the back door. Joe died on Sunday. Now Bertha comes every day and sits in the kitchen. 'I don't know what to do with myself. I don't know where to go or what to say because I've nothin' to say and no one to say it to. I miss his voice. I'm so used to him complainin' about this and that. Fifty years of marriage what else is there.'

Julia mourned with Bertha. His step revered, she loved Joe as a grandfather. So loyal! He braved the village to come to the opening of the Tea-Room. She misses him. Such friends are irreplaceable. The newspapers appear to have dropped the Adelman tragedy. And so they should, a post mortem revealing he died of a heart attack, and Karoline, it is believed taking her own life. Reunited with their son they rest in the family vault. A lawyer in Dresden has written declaring Matty a benefactor in Stefan's estate - Julia believes that, like her, Matty would sooner have the Bear.

Nan called to look at the change of wedding gown. Grey silk and chiffon, it hangs in the closet. 'Is this it?' she said, clearly unimpressed.

'I know it's not nearly as nice as the other but it is dark.'

'Albert wants to drape the Victory sign with black. I said we've a Queen to mourn and a handsome King to welcome. Ooh!' Nan stretched her toes. 'I'll never forget that day.'

'It was a day to remember.'

'You were in his company last year. I seem to recall you dined at Sandringham more than once. Are you likely to dine at such places now?'

'I imagine not.'

'Why is that?' Nan snapped. 'Is it because you're to wed an ordinary chap and not some tight corseted fellow who dies his hair and lisps when he talks?'

Julia let the moment pass. There's nothing she can say. She held the gown against her. 'Do you think it right for tomorrow?'

'It's not the brightest but it is elegant. What hat will you wear?' Julia brought the grey velvet cloche out of tissue. 'That's nice. Put it on!' Nan stepped back. 'I like the way the feathers curl about your cheek. It's a good hat, the sort Eve Carrington would wear. She's another you don't see these days.'

There was a brief, taut silence both ladies thinking their own thoughts.

'I've brought a gift.' Nan dug into her bag. 'I wanted you to have it now as there won't be time tomorrow. It's a photograph album. Time moves so fast, and folk always on the move, I thought a few pictures to be taken or like me you'll think your weddin' day never happened.'

* * *

Julia empties the closet. 'So what do you think? Is there room?'

Matty shrugged. 'A Wolf doesn't have clothes. He has fur.'

All week Julia has been rearranging the first floor. She moved the bed three times straining her shoulder trying to manoeuvre the chiffonier. 'You don't have to shove things around,' said Luke. 'I can do that when I'm here.'

She'd flapped her hands. 'I want things to be right.'

'Right?' He snatched her up and in a rare public show waltzed her from room-to-room. 'If I'm with you how can anything be wrong?'

Now, heart full to bursting, she makes room for him in the closet.

'Matty, you know that after tomorrow you may not refer to Mr Luke as Wolf.'

'But he's not my papa yet.'

'And when he is what will you call him then?'

'I shall call him my new papa.'

'Your new papa?'

'Yes. He said I could.'

She knelt before him. 'Matty, you are happy about us all being together?'

'I don't like Kaiser kept away. '

'He can come up the back stairs to your room but not to this. His fur makes a mess, and while I don't mind we don't know if your new papa will.'

'Mister Wolf won't mind. He sleeps with stars.'

'Even so, until we know how he feels keep Kaiser to your room. Now as I said I'm across the way this evening. I won't be long. Mrs Mac and Leah are out at a meeting but Dorothy will be here, and Maggie, so you're not to worry.'

'Are we going to Bostonia?'

'What?'

'Maggie says we're going to Bostonia, Mister Wolf is taking us.'

'Heavens alive!' Julia was furious. 'Dratted girl has been reading our mail. When did she say this?'

'Yesterday. She told the boot boy.'

'And the boot boy told Nanny Roberts! No wonder she was cross.'

'Is Bostonia far away?'

'Yes, it is.'

'Further than black crows and Susan?'

'Yes, and you'd never have to worry about crows again.' Julia smiled. 'Isn't it nice Mr Luke said to call him your new papa?'

'He didn't say.' Matty took off down the stairs. 'My papa in heaven said.'

* * *

Luke took a deep breath and walked into the public bar. A cry went up and pint pots were thumped on the counter. Albert dragged him close. 'You're a good lad, the best. I couldn't have wished for a better son whether or not.'

Albert has a kind of a break out now and then about Jacky, how his son died before he never really got to know him. In those days, struggling to pay bills, it was a busy life with no time to spare for anyone. 'Work hard and one day this will be yours!' It's a good philosophy, but you can't work all hours and know your children, as you can't always be there when they need you.

Everybody blamed anybody for Jacky's death. Albert carried it all and silently. This break out, maudlin hugging and skating close to the truth, is the result. 'You wanna drink lad?' He breathed Pipers Best into Luke's face. 'You must have a drink. It's a groom's duty to get drunk the night before the weddin'. It acts like a fog, stops him seein' what he's lettin' himself in for.'

Pints were pulled, jokes and ribald remarks tossed back and forth, men grinning as though Luke was a feeble-headed creature to be mocked. It went on so long he grew weary wanting tell them all to bugger off.

Julianna is at Greenfields this evening. He doesn't begrudge the old lady her birthday but he'd sooner Julianna wasn't going. It's the séance. The last effort caused such bother, why get involved again?

After last night's dream a chat with the dead is the last thing he wants. Italy and vines, it was the usual thing except there were no vines, there was mud and destruction. The dream started out alright, him aboard the cart and his lovely wife walking alongside. As always, he leaned down to kiss her, and then boom, without warning the dream became a nightmare. It was raining, hard rain that stings and bounces, and Luke stares through the rain at a river of mud sweeping down a mountainside to swallow a village whole.

They saw it happen, he and the men who left that morning to save the vines. The vines were never in danger - it was those left behind. On his knees weeping, he saw the far side of the mountain fall away, and as with Pompeii, a world disappearing, babies and beautiful wives drowned in mud.

He woke screaming. Even now he can't get away. It was a dream, he knows that. But it was so real, a tragedy played out before his eyes, a tragedy of huge proportion, or rather the memory of a life once lived and how that life, and the people in it in some God-given way have been offered to him again.

Now he sits in the Nelson with a pint of beer in his hand and feels the weight of the dream on his mind. About him men drink and laugh - and they've a right to! Tradition says the groom must be the butt of jokes and his bride referenced the ball-and-chain.

'What's the matter with you?' Nan sat beside him. 'You should be happy. You're gettin' wed tomorrow, or is that the cause of your long face?'

'I don't have a long face. This is my usual face.'

'Then God help Anna. Cheer up do! You're supposed to be havin' a good time.'

He swept the bar with his gaze. 'A good time?'

Nan took offence. 'We know the Nelson isn't the high-class company you're used to. These lads are behavin' like fools but they mean well.' She swept away. 'You're too high and mighty for your own good!'

Luke sipped his beer. The feeling of dread is to do with Matty: 'Keep an eye on him,' the thought when he woke this morning. So he is fearful and is looking but doesn't know what he is looking for. It's as though yesterday's father is anxious for the child of today.

* * *

Dorothy had her coat on.

Julia looked up. 'I thought you were staying in?'

'I am, madam. Reg is coming to drop a parcel off. I wondered if I might bring him to the kitchen for a cup of tea. It's a long ride from Lower Bakers.'

'You may do that, and you may use up the chicken left over from supper. Just don't let Maggie overdo it.'

'Thank you, madam.' Dorothy opened the door. 'Shall I walk with you up the Rise? They have cleared a path right the way up through the snow.'

'No need. Mrs Greville Masson has set fire to the world. All those lamps and candles, I imagine Greenfields visible from Mars.' Julia fastened her cape. 'If you would pop your head round Matty's door now and then?'

She set off. It was hard going even with the path cleared. Daniel did offer to collect her but she'd rather not. She'd rather not be going at all! Luke didn't want her there, his expression said it all. 'Go careful.' He'd bent his head, his eyes dark. 'You know what these things are like.'

Such eyes! Last night she tried describing the colour but couldn't find words. Like Freddie's painting, the *White Lady* and many shades of white, so Luke's eyes are many shades of blue. With Matty his eyes are the colour of cornflowers. When concerned or unhappy they tend toward basalt grey. When she is in his arms as the night of Fairy Common, and his body thrusting into hers, and he's telling his passion then his eyes are purple in shade.

Oh and she loves him! She loves his touch, his kisses, and his hunger for her. What woman would not want such a man?

Nan once said the lass that got him would rue the day. Julia will never rue the day. In church last Sunday they knelt side-by-side their hands together on the rail. It was a moment of reflection yet she could hear Luke's thoughts, so calm and true, and she thanked God for him as she thanked Him for Owen. That a woman should know love is a blessing, that she should be loved again is a miracle, that the new love should love her boy, is God's handiwork.

* * *

'Wolf, wolf, wolf!'

Matty lay in bed counting ticks of the clock. Kaiser is restless. Paws thud-thud, he paces the room. Mumma has gone up the hill to the Big House. She looked beautiful. Mumma is an angel, Mister Wolf says so. He and Mumma are getting married tomorrow. Matty won't be able to call him Wolf again so he is making up for it. 'Wolf, wolf, wolf.'

It's likely he should sleep and then, like Christmas, tomorrow will come quicker. Matty's never seen Father Christmas. Every year he thinks to see him but never does. He wakes and creeps down stairs to see the stockings hanging by the fire filled with presents. Now he lies awake for another visitor, but one not nearly as nice - he waits for the Shadow Man.

He calls him Shadow because that's all he ever sees. The first time was from the bedroom window, the man smoking a cigarette in the laundry room. Matty thinks a man in the pub and the one in the laundry room are the same; there was a fight, people shouting, and this man was kicked out of the pub, 'arse over tit, as Albert says. People laughed at the man's bloodied nose. The man hadn't a hanky so Matty gave his. 'Oy Matthew! Get back here!' Albert had shouted. 'You don't talk to Nat Sherwood. He's a thief and a bully-boy!'

Bad man is what Joe Carmody said when sweeping the laundry floor. 'Look at these fag ends!' Smoking is a grown-up thing. Matty found a cigarette end once and la-di-da'd it about the garden. It stank so he spat it out.

'Wolf, wolf, wolf!'

Fag ends are nasty. They can't be nice to smoke. Thinking this, and hoping to appease unknown gods, one day Matty stole a cigar from the silver box on the corner table. He laid it on the windowsill in the laundry room. A good job Joe Carmody didn't see. He'd have skinned Matty alive - Joe was always skinning people. He wanted to skin Callie, the old lady who steals plants from over the wall. She doesn't steal them anymore and so she still has her skin.

Joe is dead like Mr and Mrs Bear and Susan and Papa. Matty misses him and goes every day with Kaiser to the greenhouse to water plants.

The night before last Matty left another cigar. He and Kaiser kept watch at the window. Then the shadow slid over the wall and a match flared. On, off, on, off, a tiny circle of fire blinked in the darkness.

It was an SOS message!

Matty knows about Morse code, Mr Doodle is teaching him.

SOS . . . . - - - . . . . . is a message.

It means Save Our Souls. You send it when in distress, says Mr Doodle, like sailors when their boat is sinking. Matty doesn't know what a soul is but thinks the Shadow Man is in distress. Maybe he's lonely. Matty knows how it feels to be lonely. When Papa died he wanted to be with him. It's better now Mister Wolf is here but he wouldn't want anyone ever to feel lonely.

'Wolf, wolf, wolf!'

Papa used to say there are two ways of dealing with a bully, stand up to him or offer a peace pipe. Later tonight Matty will creep downstairs with another cigar and lay it by the Reckitts Blue Bag, *that keeps your linen whiter than white*! A cigar isn't a peace pipe but it's better than nothing.

CHAPTER THIRTY-TWO

Morse Code

Julia mistook the invitation thinking the meeting for eight when in fact, with more snow forecast and the need to leave early, it had been rescheduled for seven, consequently she arrived late and the séance ongoing.

'Oh you're finally here!' Callie swivelled. 'I thought you were never coming.'

'I'm sorry. I misread the invitation.'

'Never mind!' Callie swivelled back. 'Take a glass of wine and save apologies til later! We're onto something here and mustn't break concentration.'

A cup of mulled wine in her hand, Julia sat with Daniel on the sidelines.

'Absurd isn't it?' muttered Daniel. 'A dozen men and women chasing a glass tumbler about a table while asking questions of the air? It's bunkum! And we but gullible fools beguiled by an avaricious quack!'

'Does money change hands for this?'

'Naturally it does. Madame doesn't travel down from High-gate for the good of her health. She travels first class and demands a hefty fee. She calls it a donation. I call it fraud. It's a cheating thing along with human waste bottled as holy water and snake venom Virgin's Tears.'

It is different to the Long Melford sitting. There is no sense of mystery, more of a funfair sideshow, Madame Leonora heavily rouged and waving her hands about. It felt wrong. The letter E called out, a man leapt to his feet. 'Is that my wife, Emily? She died last year. I'm her husband, Major Patrick Saunders.' There was much excited conversation. Then Major Saunders was ordered to sit down again, it wasn't Emily the spirit sought, it was a man called Earnest.

'Shambles!' Daniel shuffled his feet. 'I've seen more order in a mutiny!'

'It doesn't appear to be working.'

'Depends what you mean by working. I'm not a total sceptic. I know there's more to life. In India I saw a peach stone dug into the ground and in the count of ten a peach tree growing. I've seen men walk on live coals and lie on a bed of knives and not dent to the skin.'

'And you think this along those lines?'

'I think it's about supply and demand. Someone asks a question and information is supplied. Saunders wanted to know of his wife. Now those at the table, the group mind, so to speak, are set on finding an answer.'

'From whom?'

'Better to say what rather than whom. These things tap into human emotion, the greater the need the more concentrate the energy. If it could be contained, the yearning to speak with the dead could move a mountain ne'er mind a tooth mug.'

'And yet you think it fake.'

'I doubt the spirits of the dead push that glass. I would hope no such phenomenon possible. I've seen men die and believe death deserves more than to be tattled before strangers.'

'People seek comfort.'

'There are better ways. I think those gone before talk to us by way of example. My father is the last person I'd seek to follow yet not so long ago I trod in his footsteps.' He shook his head. 'Anyway, that's enough of me. You've had prior experience. What do you make of it?'

'I don't know.' Julia closed her eyes and she heard a dog's tail swishing and a child singing. 'It is all so very odd.'

'What did you find when you sat before with this woman?'

'I wouldn't call it a happy experience. In fact it was quite shocking. Looking back I realise some of us were given hints of the future.'

'You've piqued my interest! Maybe I will sit in on the next round of absurdity. Who knows, I might yet be saved from a boring evening.'

Julia touched his hand. 'I wouldn't be too casual if I were you, Daniel. I heard things that night I wouldn't want to hear again.'

* * *

'Wolf, wolf, wolf!'

Matty and Kaiser are crouched on the bed peeping through the window. The Shadow Man is here! He's inside the greenhouse, his shadow through glass long and wet like a worm. Matty was hoping he wouldn't come. He couldn't leave a cigar! Dorothy and Maggie and Reg are in the kitchen. The door is open. They can see through into the parlour and the silver box and so he can't get it. Now there's no present for the Shadow Man, only fag ends.

Downstairs Maggie is messing with the piano banging it. She shouldn't do that especially as she's eating chicken. Mr Doodle says take care of the instrument and the instrument will take care of you. He says Matty has a good ear. Matty looks in the glass but can't see a difference.

'Wolf, wolf, wolf!'

Matty said his prayers earlier. 'Gentle Jesus, meek and mild, look upon a little child, pity my simplicity, suffer me to come to thee.' He loves Gentle Jesus and has a picture on the wall of Him carrying a Lamb. Matty likes the prayer but doesn't like the suffering bit. When Susan died the old lady over the Wall talked of suffering: 'Oh the suffering of it.' He told Oldie Hubbard. She said suffering doesn't mean hurt - it means to allow. That's alright. Now when he says the prayer Matty says 'allow me to come to thee.' It's much better.

Oh if only Joe was here! He'd put a stop to this! He'd get that broom and push the Shadow Man out the gate. But Joe can't be here. He's dead.

'Wolf, Wolf, Wolf!'

Maggie has gone out. Matty heard the door click and saw her running by the vegetable patch. In her red cape with hood pulled up, she looks like Lady Christmas. She's going to meet her sweetheart, the pot-boy, at the Big House. She'll get into trouble one day, says Oldie, and there'll be hell to pay.

'Wolf, Wolf, Wolf!'

Mister Wolf is out tonight at a Stag Do. Nanny Roberts said: 'Be careful at that Stag Do, Albert. It's a free bar but don't let every Tom, Dick, and Harry drink us dry. America or not, we've to get on with our lives.' Mumma and the Wolf are to go to Bostonia; Maggie read it in a letter. Matty is invited. It's a long way from black crows so he thinks he might go.

Kaiser won't be going. He's staying with the Seed Lady. Matty knows this because Tuesday after their piano lesson she came and stroked Kaiser. 'Such a good dog! I shall be happy to receive you.' Kaiser licked the Lady's hand and then Matty's cheek, saying 'don't cry.' Matty didn't cry but later when against Mumma's soft breast he did.

* * *

They are at the table now, twelve new sitters, Julia and Daniel among them. They have been sitting in virtual silence for a good half an hour. Glass tumbler and paper letters tidied away, they sit with hands linked. Julia is next to Squire Humphreys who is overweight and nervous, his hands moist with sweat.

He keeps asking 'is the spirit among us.'

Callie snaps at him. 'Be quiet! We are trying to concentrate.'

Madame Leonora sighs a great deal. Things are not going according to plan. 'Are you sure there's nothing?' says Callie. 'Ought we to go back to the glass? At least we had some communication with that.'

'I find myself blocked. Someone among us doesn't believe. While that person sits at the table it's doubtful any real contact can be made.'

Callie poked Daniel. 'That's you,' she hissed. 'You ought to leave. You're blocking the vibrations.'

'God forbid I should block vibrations!' Daniel pushed the chair back. 'Excuse me while I relieve you of the problem.'

'No!' said Madame. 'It's not you. It is a female who doubts.'

There was quick glance about the table, every lady suspected.

Julia hoped she'd be pointed out a Doubting Thomas and asked to leave. It's getting late and with things the way they are, late night trying of door-handles and broken glass, one must be wary.

'Yes, Mrs Dryden.' Madame looked up. 'One must.' She stared into nothing. 'So much noise tonight! The sound of anger and voices calling out.'

'What are these voices saying?' asked Squire Humphreys.

Madame leaned on her hand. 'People think I am a tap to be turned on and if I don't bring what they want they shout fake. They don't know how I suffer or how others suffer wanting to be heard.'

Daniel coughed. 'Ladies and gentleman, I think perhaps it's time to draw the meeting to an end. Madame is tired and needs to go home.'

'Don't interfere!' Callie banged on the table. 'I didn't bring people together and watch my good Madeira disappear down unappreciative throats to be disappointed. I want to know what went wrong all those years ago and until I get an answer I am staying and so is everyone else!'

Daniel would've spoken but Madame Leonora laid her hand on his arm.

'Hush, Danny Greville Masson. This poor fellow at my elbow doesn't need to die twice to be heard.'

'I beg your pardon?'

'Your newspaper friend? He thanks you for the rabbit's foot and the money. He says you're not to think of him anymore. He's in a place of comfort, a warm church, a blessing from the Lord, a sandwich and a jug of cider.'

'Good God!'

'What?' Callie rounded on Daniel. 'What did she say?'

Daniel shook his head.

'Tell me!' She tugged his arm. 'What did she say?'

Black Holes for eyes, Madame smiled. 'You were ever a noisy girl, Callie-Anne Greville. You could never keep your tongue still.'

'Oh!' Callie's hands flew to her mouth.

'Such noise!' Madame's head dropped. 'Why did you bring this? I'd sooner eat of a wooden plate than this costly perfection. I told you not to do it. But you had to buy it, to weigh me down among your possessions.'

'What is this?' said Squire Humphreys. 'Who is she talking to? Is this making sense to anybody because it surely isn't making sense to me?'

'Quiet!' Callie held up her hand. 'She's talking about the dinner service Henry gave her. It was supposed to be my wedding present! She came home to find it on her shelves. She took a hammer to it and smashed every piece.'

'Callie!' Julia couldn't help but speak. 'I thought that was you.'

'I know you did. It wasn't me. It was Justine. I saw through the spy glass and didn't lift a finger to stop her. Why would I when it should have been mine. But I beg you be silent! My life depends on it.'

'Oh do stop!' Madame gestured. 'Such a theatrical girl! Your life doesn't depend on yesterday's heartache! It depends on things that matter, on birds that sing and the scent of flowers. Now in your old age it depends on a warm quilt and a decent cup of coffee in the morning.'

'Tell me where I went wrong!' Callie was weeping, tears tracking the runnels in her cheeks. 'What did I do that you didn't love me?'

'I did love you. I still do. You didn't go wrong, you grew up. I gave you everything I could give. I was your tutor not your lover. Why didn't you settle for that instead of bringing the village to our door? One way or another, Missy, you robbed us of sleep and made a prison of our poor cottage for the living and the dead. It's time to let go, and leave us, and you, in peace.'

The table was in uproar, the sitters scattering. Callie was trembling. Daniel drew her into his arms. 'Come Mother. It's done now so let go of it.'

'Oh do let go!' Madame sighed. 'Then I too can go! The past needs us but we don't need it! If it should haunt you take a hammer and beat it until it is dead. It's what we did, Clarry and me. Killed it and put it with the dirty linen. You never loved me, Callie. You were a little girl playing games.'

'Justine!'

'It's over, Callie! Henry died and you moved away. You had a husband. Now you have a son. I could not have given you a love half as sweet. Cherish him and be at peace. The stars will fall. You'll see them streak across the sky. And when the Wall falls so shall I.'

* * *

Luke isn't feeling so good. Legs twitching and skin crawling as though an army of ants are breaking through, he has to get out. 'I'm going, Ma.'

Nan accompanied him to the door. 'So you're thinkin' of goin' to America?'

'Who told you about that?'

'Nobody told me, certainly not my son.'

'From whom did you hear?'

'Maggie Jeffers, the Town Crier, who else.'

'Oh, for Christ sake, Ma!'

'I know. Still it would've been nice to be told.'

'I'll tell you when there's anything worth telling. Right now all I can say is step aside or I'll be chucking up all over you.'

Out of the fug and smoke and beer fumes, the cold air hit him like a square fist. It cleared his head but the antsy feeling remained. It's been with him all day. Running about trying to fasten loose ends, he should have ate better. The business is good. He has three decent foremen on whom he can depend. They get jobs done with minimum fuss. Besides, this time of the year is quiet. It's all indoors and thanks to the Scholtz Hotel contract there's plenty of that.

Luke wrote to Daniel Masson declining their business. It's a conscience thing. Anyway, a new year, and a new job is promised. It's still in the negotiating stage but if it comes off it'll knock Bakers End sideways and concerns the Chelsea home of Lady Charlotte Walbrooke. So far he's only agreed to look at the plans, so much going on he needs to haul back a bit. Yesterday he only need think of himself, tomorrow he has a family.

* * *

It's cold and starting to snow. Luke planned to go to Fairy Common making sure his clothes for tomorrow will do. The coat is fine. He bought it in Savile Row, the chap there kitting him out in good black broadcloth. Other than that, he's asked no one what he should do or say tomorrow. At times like this he wishes Freddie nearby, as it is he will stand at the altar alone.

The best man for the job is a dead man. Jacky would be coming up twenty-three now. It's strange that he dreams of Italy but never of his brother. It's as though the link between them was severed that day. Doctor's said Jacky was unconscious before he drowned. A great gash in his head, he hit something diving in. 'If it's any consolation,' said one, 'he wouldn't have suffered.'

Poor sod! Luke went for him. 'How do you know he didn't suffer? How can you know anything?' That day he was a fool yelling. He's still yelling.

Midway to the Common, he changed direction, the scratching at his nerves becoming a roar. Betty is stabled at the cottage this week. If Luke was going to get drunk, which he wasn't it was best the old horse stays in the warm. Now, he changes direction thinking to see if she needs rubbing down. He won't knock on the cottage door. Julianna will be home now and you're not supposed to see the bride until the wedding. It's bad luck.

People ask if he's nervous. Until now he wasn't, as sure of his love for her as he is sure the sun rises. Now his stomach whirls, every hair on his head a bee's antennae an early warning system. Hands in his pockets he trudged across country. He hadn't gone far when he quickened his step, making a diversion through Wentworths' farm. Then, his hand on the gate, he heard it.

'Wolf, wolf, wolf!'

It came through snowflakes blown there by winter.

It brought him up sharp.

It came again. 'Wolf, wolf, wolf!'

It was like a dog barking but no dog.

It was Matty!
Matty is calling him.
Miles away but Luke hears him clear as a bell!
He ran.

CHAPTER THIRTY-THREE

A Soul Saved

Julia sits to put on her galoshes - Callie was in such distress, she stayed to see if she could help.

Daniel is coming down the stairs. 'What can I say to you after that?'

'I think it best we say nothing.'

'I agree. Talk about washing one's dirty linen in public!'

'Are you surprised by what you have heard?'

'Surprised? Hah! I used to think the Grevilles Massons a stoic kind of people. I see now we're creatures of passion, loving hard and clumsily, Callie's school-girl crush a case in point.'

'Is she much distressed?'

'She will recover. She's made of durable stock, all the Aunts living into their nineties. They bend rather than break.' He pushed his hands through his hair. 'Whether I shall do as well is debatable.'

'And Madame Leonora?'

'She's another in need of recuperation. Whatever it is she does, and speaking for myself the jury is out, it knocks her seven days from Sunday.'

'I don't think it helps any of us to go where we're not wanted.'

'No and should not be repeated.'

'I must get back.' Julia bent to her galoshes but shaky she couldn't manage.

Daniel knelt to help. 'I'll escort you down. You can't go

455

home alone.' They were thus when there was the sudden clatter of running feet and a shout.

'Madam! I say, madam!'

'Oh!' Julia started up out of the chair knocking Daniel backward.

'Madam!' Madame Leonora stood at the top of the stairs.

'For God's sake!' Daniel is on his feet. 'What is it now?'

'Madam!' It came again, a voice Julia knew. 'Hark to that noise!'

'Noise?' She gazed up the stairs to the figure standing back of the shadows.

'Listen!'

It was Kaiser howling. Julia fled, Joe Carmody's voice calling after: 'He's there! The nasty sod that hides in the wash-shed is after our little lad!'

* * *

'**Wolf! Wolf! Wolf!**'

The Shadow Man is inside the house! Maggie left the back door unlocked!

It happened as Dorothy's sweetheart was leaving. She was seeing Reg's cart down the lane to the main road. That's when the Man slipped inside.

Fur blown up like a Porcupine, Kaiser scratched at the door until there was nothing else for it, Matty must give the Man a cigar, and then, hopefully, he will go away. He put on boots and the woolly hat Oldie Hubbard knitted. Then, tying his dressing gown very, very tight - and trying not to cry - he knelt down.

'Now listen, Kaiser. We're going to play hide and seek. I'm to hide and you're to close your eyes and count to a hundred and then you're to look for me.'

Kaiser whined. He knew Matty was fibbing and that the real reason he was to stay behind was Matty's heart crying out, **You can't come! I can't let the Seed Lady have you! You must stay here and be safe!**

He locked Kaiser in the bedroom and crept downstairs. The parlour door was open. He went to the silver box, took the biggest cigar, and put it in his pocket.

'Is that for me?' the Shadow Man was hiding in the shadows.

Trembling, Matty nodded.

'What, just the one?'

Matty took another cigar.

'Nah,' the Shadow Man smiled. 'I reckon you can do better than that.'

'We mustn't!' Matty whispered. 'I'll get into trouble.'

'Gobble-gobble, you've got a funny voice, lad. You sound like a half-throttled turkey.' The Man took the glass shepherdess that stands on the bureau and the snuff box that once belonged to Mumma's papa. Then he gazed about as though planning to put the whole house into his pocket.

Matty held out the cigars. 'Here you are, Mister Shadow Man.'

'Shadow Man?' The Man laughed. 'That's me alright.'

'Please don't hurt my Mumma.'

'Where is your mother?'

Matty shook his head.

'She's out, ain't she, across the Rise. She don't know I'm here, nor does your maid out in the lane with her boyfriend. I'll tell you what.' The Man sat in a chair. 'I'll wait for them to come back. Think what a nice surprise that'll be.'

Matty put the cigars back. He knew no matter what he offered it wouldn't be enough. He wanted to scream but that hurts his throat, and as the Man says, he sounds like a turkey. People say his throat will get better. It won't. And anyway, he doesn't need to speak; the piano keys speak for him.

He can't scream but he can make a noise.

Closing his eyes, and clenching his fists, he put all the noise ever heard into the cigarette box - the bass notes of a piano, a train rattling into the station and a barrel of Pipers Best newly piped at the Nelson – and roaring, threw the box at the Man. He ran to the front door for Mumma in the Big House where all the lights were shining.

Kaiser began to howl and pound the bedroom door.

'Owoooo! Owoooo!' A scary sound, it rose up into the night sky.

Matty stopped running. He knew Mumma would hear Kaiser and come running down the Rise and the Shadow Man would be waiting to hurt her.

Matty loves his mother. She is his One and Only mother. He must do the noble thing and lead the Shadow away. He ran back through the house.

The Man almost got him! Red blood running down his face from the cigarette box, he staggered out of the parlour. 'Come here, you little sod!'

Matty ducked under his arm and ran out of the back door and didn't stop running, and as he ran he sent a message to the Wolf.

SOS ....---..... Save Our Souls!

* * *

Julia ran. 'Hold on, darling! Mummy's coming!'

The Rise never seemed so high nor the cottage so far. She tried the path but churned by carriages it was treacherous. Cape tearing and knees skinning, she fell. The untried snow was heavy and she had to struggle but at least she stayed upright. It was bitterly cold but she didn't feel it. All she saw was the cottage, all she heard was Kaiser.

'Daniel, look!' Matty was in the doorway, one moment a little boy in blue cap and woollen dressing-gown, and then gone, turning back into the house and danger. 'No! Not that way!' she screamed. 'Come to me!'

The kiddie was terrified and didn't know what he was doing! Daniel could see that. 'Go back to the house, Julianna!' He skidded by her. 'Tell Crosby to call the police! You may have intruders.'

'Intruders?'

'Matty's running from something!' Daniel kept going. It was pointless saying anything. He had thought to saddle a horse but the snow is heavy going and it would've meant unlocking the stables and there simply isn't time.

A figure appeared out of darkness. Bonnet askew and mouth open, the maid ran back down the lane. 'It's Dorothy,' panted Julia from behind him. 'Oh where has she been? She said she wasn't going out!'

Daniel ploughed on. What kind of night is this? Voices from hell and messages from the dead! His guts shrink thinking about it. Could it be real? Did the Pretoria News guy really speak through that wrinkled mouth or was it a trick? But then any idea of fraud is absurd. Only he knows what happened in Bloemfontein, how he washed blood off the rabbit's foot and sent it along with a hundred dollar bill to Jack's wife. No one but he knew!

But forget yesterday's mysteries! It's young Matty Dryden that matters. Daniel pushed open the door. 'Mathew! Where are you?'

'Matty!' Gown torn and wet with snow Julianna ran from room to room. 'If you are here hiding do come out! Mummy is here with Daniel!'

Upstairs the dog is battering the door and screaming.

'He must be shut up in Matty's room.'

'Wait!' Daniel shouted. 'Let me go up first.' He raced up the stairs and across the landing. The door was half off the hinges. 'Hold on!' he shouted. 'I'll let you out.' He got to the door, turned the key, and wham, it blasted open throwing him aside. Kaiser was down the stairs and gone. Daniel followed. He couldn't match the speed but the howling told him where to go. A terrible sound, a child weeping or wolf caught in a trap, who could tell!

* * *

Luke never ran so fast. Terror shifted him, muscles in his legs driven by memory. Three years ago, shaken out of bed by the Lord God shouting, Luke ran this way for the same child. If God is on guard again tonight He hasn't a hope of being heard above the noise of Ma bemoaning America and Albert pissed as a newt, and Julianna telling him to hurry, and rising above all of that Matty pleading, 'Mister Wolf, please come and get me!'

The thought of the child getting hurt drains the blood from his heart. It can't happen! Nothing must happen! They're to be married tomorrow! No one to give her away she is to come down the aisle on her own, and her little lad to carry the posy when needed. 'Can Kaiser walk with me?' he'd asked his mother. 'He is a good dog, and humble, and wouldn't misbehave.'

'Oh don't!' Momentarily he pulled up, not sure who he's begging only that again he offers his life for another. 'I'm begging you, not Matty! If you want a life take mine. If she loses her boy she'll die anyway. '

The woods were shrouded in darkness. It's been a bad year for animal life, a bitter wind and snow thick on the ground, those creatures that don't sleep through the winter have nothing to forage. It's the same with birds. Last Monday was so cold some fell midflight wings frozen. For some reason Luke associates Matty with a bird, the smallest, the wren. The kiddie is so alive, so here and now and so infinitely fragile, he must not die mid-flight!

* * *

'...wolf.....wolf....!'

The plan was to lead the Man away. Now, cursing and crashing through bushes the Man is so near, his breath melts the snow on the path.

Matty's chest hurts. He can hardly breathe. He is small, he was born small. Papa in Heaven said he was born before his time but not to worry because 'little is good.' Being little can be good! It helps hide him in places where only little things can go. But he is so cold and so tired he can neither run nor hide.

'Oy!' The Shadow Man reared out of nowhere. 'Come here, you little bugger, or I'll do you harm!'

Matty shrieked, dodged sideways, and scuffling on his hands and knees crawled inside the husk of a fallen tree.

'.......wolf...........wolf......!'

Dark eyes glowing and teeth sharp, the Wolf is coming, Matty can feel him pounding through the snow. But now he is more afraid. He thinks he may have brought the Wolf to harm as he might've brought Mumma. And, Oh he is so sad, because the Seed Lady told fibs! Being chased through darkness by a Shadow who wants to hurt people - there's no good purpose in that. Love is a big thing and so very heavy it is too much for a little boy to carry.

'Got yer!'

The Shadow Man grabbed Matty's foot and began to pull. Matty didn't struggle. He couldn't! So weary he couldn't do anything but be still and pray to Gentle Jesus, and close his eyes so not to see what is coming. 'I'm sorry,' he whispered. 'I meant to get it but couldn't. The box was in the parlour.'

* * *

Luke saw it happen but in slow motion as viewed through treacle. The moon rose flooding the world with light. That bastard Sherwood swung his fist at Matty. Then the dog arrived. Fur glistening, Kaiser hurtled out of the scrubland like some ancient heraldic dragon beast. Claws outstretched and jaws gaping, poetry in motion and justified anger, the dog launched into the air. Whump! He landed on Sherwood's back knocking him forward.

For a moment there was silence, so it seemed to Luke, though the dog savaging the man there must've been a racket. Matty was a curled up foetal shape, a frozen child, and a dead child for all Luke knew. Then he cried out and straight way the dog released Sherwood to go to his young Master.

'No!' Luke knew what would happen. 'Stay put Kaiser!'

Sherwood scrambled to his feet and snatching up a piece of wood ran at the dog. That's when Luke's mind turned to treacle. From then on all was slow and so damned painful it might have been happening the other side of the world.

Snarling, protective, the dog crouched over Matty. Sherwood swung the piece of wood. There was a terrible yelping and Kaiser lay still. Sherwood hung over Matty brandishing the wood. The dog wouldn't give up, and crawled forward inch-by-inch to lie across him. Sherwood raised the clump of wood.

Luke crashed through the trees. 'Get away you murderous swine!'

Sherwood ran.

Several things happened then. Daniel Masson arrived with Julianna. White and trembling, she fell on her knees cradling Matty in her arms.

'Is he alright?' asked Daniel Masson.

'I don't know,' said Luke.

'He doesn't seem to have any bones broken.'

'Get them home and call a doctor.'

'I imagine one is already on the way, Crosby will have sent.'

'Look to the dog.' Luke turned away.

'Where are you going?'

'Where d'you think.' Daniel Masson didn't try to stop him. He couldn't stop him. No one could have stopped him.

Luke strode on. There was no need to run. He knows where

Sherwood lives, a caravan by the quarry with the rest of the raggle-taggle mob.

The wood and the night heavy with time past and time present, he pushed through the snow. Three years ago he came this way for Matty. A decade before that he came, laughing and happy, a wild young fellow wanting to coax some bit of a girl into his arms - it was his dead brother he carried away.

Matty says there's good purpose in all things, the Seed Lady says so. Where that miserable shit Sherwood is concerned there is now a definite purpose. Luke never comes near the quarry. Whatever the season, he'll make a wide detour sooner than walk on tainted land. That he comes now suggests a Divine Purpose that has him undoing his collar and stuffing his tie in his pocket.

'I mean, it has to be the quarry, doesn't it, Jacky boy?' he muttered. 'Looks like I'm bound to do what I should've done years ago.'

Luke holds no anger in his heart, only cold determination. If he needed to stoke a fire he's only to see Matty lying in the snow and Julianna's face, her beauty drained away in fear. If that is not enough then there is Kaiser!

Sherwood threatened his family. There's no getting away with that!

* * *

The rat returning to its rat-hole, a trail of blood in the snow led down the gulley toward the slate workings. Briefly, it crossed Luke's mind to arm himself, to pick up a rock or a piece of wood. Rats run in packs. In going to the caravan site it's likely he'll take on more than one. Then so be it! In the end it comes down to the same thing, the need to defend those you love.

The quarry has been here for years, all that was good in the earth gouged out over centuries and tunnels beneath flooded with water. Everything and anything gets thrown in and very few come up to breathe as the Roberts family found to their sorrow. God knows how many animals have sunk below the scummy surface, and for that matter people. Every once in a while someone drowns. The village then is up in arms and Local Council hammers a warning sign into the ground, a skull leering.

It's a filthy disease-ridden pit and should be filled in and the memories with it.

The tinker's caravans are quiet, a thin curl of smoke rising from a damped down fire. This side of the quarry has no particular pathway. Steep and dangerous the steps are uncertain. Snow and ice heavy on the ground no one should attempt it, especially not at night but Sherwood is down there, and bloodsucking parasite that he is, he must be winkled out and squashed.

When the bastard came at him, the lump of wood in his fist wet with a dog's good blood, Luke was climbing down. Intent on keeping his footing he didn't anticipate an ambush. He should've for this is no Field of Honour.

Sherwood swiped the back of Luke's knees causing him to stumble. He fell, crashing through trees and bushes into the quarry taking Sherwood with him.

They hit the surface and were briefly held by a crust of ice. Ice cracked, the crust giving way, they sank through a layer of shit into freezing water.

Lodged against the quarry wall they fought, sinking by

degrees, cuts in the slate and roots of trees temporary foot and handholds. Luke managed to get free and began pulling back up the slate wall whereupon Sherwood hung about his neck, and scrambling, turned them out into deeper water.

Down they went, Siamese twins locked in misery. The water was thick and foul-tasting. It came to Luke then he might die in this awful place.

Boot-caps scraping Luke's shins, Sherwood held on. 'Help me!' Was the message in those clutching arms; 'I can't swim!' It was too dark to see anything but Luke knew it to be the case and felt terror emanating from the man.

Too bad, he thought. My brother drowned in this. Now you know how it feels.

The rat-gnawed carcase of a dog floated by. Ah, poor Kaiser, a brave dog, a valiant dog! What was it Joe Carmody was forever whistling, '*He who would true Valour see let him come hither, One here will constant be, come wind, come weather.*' Dear Joe, he was valiant in his own quiet way as was Kaiser. If Luke is to meet them on the Other Side maybe it won't be so bad.

Arms to his sides, he tried letting his body hang slack. Panic screamed fight! Get to the surface! Live and be happy with Anna and Matty! Every blood vessel busting, he wanted to fight but knew he must force Sherwood to let go.

But Sherwood guessed the plan and hooking his right fist about Luke's neck dragged him forward and began pounding his face. The same animal corpse floated by. Luke grabbed it and bringing it up between them jabbed the head - maggot holes for eyes - into that hated face. Sherwood pulled back in revulsion. There was a jolt, the sense of cloth ripping and of brief pain, a pointed object scraping Luke's chest, and then warmth against his skin.

Seeming to float backward Sherwood let go of Luke.

A shaft of moonlight split the water. Luke saw then that the chap was skewered to the quarry wall, a metal spike driven through his gut.

Luke is free to move and tries to swim but is tired. He kicked for the surface, he really tried, but was getting nowhere. Everything weighed him down, his clothes, boots, and the knowledge he'd killed a man.

I'm tired, he thought. My lungs...can't breathe... I just want to sleep.

Oh, Julianna, my own precious love, he thought, I am so sorry. I so wanted to love you and Matty but I don't think I can.

Then, out of the dirt and squalor, it seemed to him an angel came.

A figure made of moonlight swam toward him - an electric-eel - the water about him vibrating. A hand touched Luke's chest, a shock passing through his body, a thousand volts of energy. Then another angel came, a human angel, who dove into the water and grabbing Luke began to pull.

It was Daniel Masson who dragged him out of the quarry. It was his hands, blue with cold that turned him on his side and beat him. It was Daniel who yelled at him to breathe. Yet other hands touched Luke that night. Other arms held him. Another held him and kissing him whispered in his ear: 'Come on, brother mine, get movin'. It's your weddin' day! You don't want Mam and Dad cryin' again. You want to live and be happy.'

Whispering

They went ahead with the wedding; Luke would have it no other way. They were late arriving at the church. As usual, Bakers End news-reporter to the world, rumours of last night's events had spread, consequently the church was packed. When they appeared, Julia limping, her legs cut about, Matty pale in his sailor suit and white boutonniere, and Luke's eyes black and blue, the congregation gasped in unison. 'What a sorry looking lot,' one woman whispered. 'You'd think it a football match not a wedding.'

Julia, who had dispensed with a posy that she might hold Matty's hand, was inclined to agree. Yesterday her wedding gown was considered dark and dull. Today grey velvet is entirely appropriate, they are a sorry bunch, especially Luke and his black eyes. 'Sherwood wanted my eyes,' he tried joking. 'I wouldn't let him have them, not and miss seeing my beautiful wife.'

It was meant to be a joyful occasion, a choir singing and lots of happy faces. The choir was mute and the organ moped. Nan and Albert and the maids sat up front with Bertha Carmody, the rest were strangers. There was the odd face recognised - good faces, beloved and brave, like Daniel Masson, who sombre and elegant sat at the rear of the church. Callie was not with him but then Julia didn't expect her as she didn't expect Hugh Fitzwilliam who sat in heavy sealskin coat by the font waggling his fingers at Matty.

The vicar was sympathetically swift. 'God bless you both,' he said when pronouncing them man and wife, 'and keep you safe from other such villains.' At that point of the ceremony it is customary for the groom to kiss the bride. Luke did better. He reached down and lifting Matty up kissed them both, and then Matty still in his arms, they left the church.

A carriage took them to the cottage. There was a meal for those that wanted it but none felt like rejoicing, not after such a night and Kaiser lying cold and silent under a blanket in the back parlour, the knitted Lamb between his paws.

It appears the maids couldn't bear to be parted from the house, not even Maggie. One-by-one and in tears they came, 'did madam mind if they stayed home? They'd sooner help Matty get over his panic.'

Julia doubted Matty would ever get over it. She certainly wouldn't. Such a night! A hideous progression of mental and physical torture watching those she loved most in the world cruelly treated, who recovers from that!

Thank God for Daniel! It was he who jumped into the quarry and in saving Luke's life saved Julia. They'd brought him back propped between Daniel and Crosby, his clothes wet with blood and his face torn. 'Darling!' Adding bruises to bruises, she threw herself at him. 'My own precious darling! You went after him! How could you be so foolish?'

He hugged her. 'If this is what I am to hear when I do foolish things, you calling me precious, I'll stay a fool.' He smiled but his eyes were full of tears. Then Matty, sad little soul, crept downstairs to peep through the banister rails. Luke saw him. 'Come here, my own dear boy!' Sobbing, Matty leapt into his arms. For a moment the two stood together in silence recalling fearful things that Julia will never know because they will never tell.

They slept that night, what was left of it, with Matty between them. It was for their comfort and also to stop him continually creeping down to where Kaiser lay. 'The dog was dead when I got to him,' Daniel had said. 'It's as well. Had he lived I doubt he'd have walked. It was the last blow that did it though I wouldn't like to guess what broke first, the dog's back or his heart.'

The police came amid the wedding breakfast and stood in the back parlour, the constable taking notes and the sergeant heavy-handed with Dorothy.

'You say you were not aware of an intruder, Miss Manners.'

'No sir, not until I heard Kaiser'

'Kaiser? That would be the dog?'

'Yes sir. He started howling. That's when I came running.'

'Where were you when you heard?'

'Down at the bottom of the lane.'

'What were you doing there?'

Dorothy hung her head. 'I was saying goodnight to Reg.'

'And who might Reg be?'

'My sweetheart.'

'I see, bottom of the lane saying goodbye to your sweetheart and your mistress away and a thief rampaging around stealing goods and frightening a harmless little lad. Weren't you supposed to be here minding the shop?'

'I wasn't gone but a minute.'

'Ah well there you are. With chaps like Sherwood a minute is all it takes. And you saw and heard nothing before that to make you concerned?'

'No.'

'Thank you, Miss Manners. That'll be all for now. Perhaps

you'll send the other one in, what's her name, Margaret Jeffers.'

Dorothy hovered twisting her apron. 'Are me and Reg in trouble?'

'No, Dorothy, you are not!' Julia cut in. 'You made a mistake but it was an innocent mistake and for that you shan't be punished. Go and sort Maggie out. We are all upset, there's no need to labour the point.'

Dorothy fled in tears.

The sergeant frowned. 'You ought not to let her off so lightly, madam. Had she been here your lad wouldn't have been threatened nor your husband in danger of his life. People should take responsibility for their actions. If they did we wouldn't have one man on a slab and serious questions to ask of another.'

'What kind of questions?' Luke was behind Julia his hand on the chair.

'Well, for a start how did Nate Sherwood land up halfway down the quarry with a metal pole poking through his back?'

'I thought I'd answered that.'

'You said something about it, sir.'

'But not enough?'

'Enough for now I suppose. You say you fought, you struggled, and you both fell in the quarry and that at some point thought you'd drown.'

'Oh Luke!' Julia buried her face in her hands.

'It's alright.' He pressed her shoulder. 'It sounds worse than it was.'

'So you didn't think you were going to drown?'

'At one point Sherwood was pulling us both down. I tried not to struggle hoping he'd strike for the surface. Then there was that jolt and he let go.'

'That jolt was old mine workings, a piece of metal track sticking out the wall.'

'It was sharp. It jabbed me.'

'So I understand. Is that why your clothes were soaked with blood?'

'Yes but not my blood. I was only scratched.'

'Tell me about the jolt.'

Luke shrugged. 'I don't know what to say. A jolt is how I remember it, a kind of ricochet as though he'd run onto something or something run onto him.'

'It had to be one hell of a jolt to push a metal post through a body and out the other side. You sure you didn't give it a hand?'

'How could I have done that? I'm treading water. I'm drowning! There's nothing under my feet. If he was thrust onto a spike with force how did I get the purchase to do it? The only way I could have shoved him was if someone shoved me, and not just a man, a goddamn Goliath!'

'Yes well, that's understood.'

'Is it?'

'Yes of course, sir! Nobody is suggesting anything untoward.'

'Aren't they? Well let me suggest this.' Luke's hand tightened on Julia's shoulder. 'If I could have shoved him on whatever killed him I would've! And if I could've drowned him I would! That man brought terror to my family. He threatened harm to my boy, he hurt my wife, and he killed a bloody good dog! He deserved to die, and if you're looking to me for apology you'll get none. He's dead and I'm glad of it. Dead he can do no one else harm.'

Luke rang the bell. 'And on that note, gentlemen, I suggest

you put away your notebooks and share a glass of champagne with me and my wife because believe it or not this is our wedding day, and we, and I'm sure you, have better things to do than debate the death of a nobody.'

* * *

They buried Kaiser that evening as the last rays of the sun warmed the land. Luke said he would go out later in the week and get another dog but that Matty needed to grieve. Matty wanted to know what grieving meant.

'It means being sad,' said Julia. 'It means feeling what you are feeling and being grateful for Kaiser.'

Matty shook his head. He said sooner be ungrateful and have Kaiser alive.

Five o' clock they trooped out, Mrs Mac, Ben Faulkner, Nan and Albert, everyone. Luke carried Kaiser. 'Where d'you want him to lie?'

'I want him with Joe.'

'With Joe?'

'Joe is dead. If they're in one hole they can take care of one another.'

There followed a discussion 'What do you think, Mrs Carmody?'

Bertha wrung her hands. 'I don't rightly know. My Joe is to be laid down on Monday in St Mark's. I suppose we might drop the dog in secret like. I don't mind but I can't see the vicar agreein'.'

'Why don't we put him under the lavender?' said Luke. 'If you think about it, Matty, your bedroom overlooks the lavender, and if Joe is to come anywhere it would here by the greenhouse.' Matty nodded, though unhappy he saw the sense in it. Luke dug a plot and laid the dog in the ground, covered with his favourite blanket, a rubber bone and the knitted Lamb for company.

'Can we say a prayer, Mumma?' said Matty.

'Of course.'

'Can it be Gentle Jesus?'

They all stood and recited the prayer. Then he wanted a hymn.

'Can we sing *Away in a Manger*? Kaiser likes that.'

They sang all three verses and they wept.

* * *

Again, Matty slept between them. Restless, he tossed and turned. Julia took Luke's hand. 'Sorry,' she said. 'It's not the most romantic honeymoon.'

He brought her hand to his lips. 'Tush,' he said softly. 'A house full of maids with their hot little ears pressed to the wall, and us two separated by a wriggling fish, how can you not see the romance in that?'

Julia laughed, and then wept, and then laughed again. 'What a horrible day! I don't think I'll ever forget it.'

'I don't suppose you will.' He reached out wiping tears from her face and then wiped his own. 'Look at me,' he said. 'I'm in bed with the woman I love, and the kiddie I love, we're married and no need of looking back and I'm weeping.'

Julia huddled closer. 'I love your tears and that you love us enough to weep.'

He slid his arm under her head. 'It's a strange thing that when we are most happy we are most sad. It's been like this with me ever since we met. I'd think of you and like a fool I'd fill with tears.'

'Happy tears?'

'Not so much then but now yes.'

'Even with black eyes?'

'Especially with black eyes.'

'You know your bruises match the bruises on my knees.'

'Do they?'

'Yes, black and blue.'

'Alright then,' his breath was warm in her hair. 'When we've a minute to ourselves I'll kiss them better.'

'Will you?'

'Yes.'

'Promise?'

'Word of honour.'

* * *

Matty went back to his room complaining 'he couldn't sleep with Mumma and Papa talking and wanted his own bed and Kaiser and the kittens.' There was a horrible moment when he remembered, mouth trembling, but on he went, saying their bed is hard and they wriggle.

Softly and slowly and carefully - tender with bruises and smothering such sounds as may give rise to blushes the following morning - they made love then, his hands gentle with her knees but his mouth and tongue less so.

There were moments throughout the night when it wasn't easy to be quiet, when Julia had to hold onto the bed post so as not to scream. It was so very delicious and all so unexpected she wanted to ask: is this you, Mister Wolf, biting my breast? I always thought you a shy sort of man unwilling to kiss in public. Is this loving of your imagination? Or is it the result of former tutoring from a teacher accomplished in the dark arts, a woman - an artist perhaps expressive of colour and with a powerful imagination?

Not wanting to deny pleasure she remained quiet and submissive and blissful, the thought never becoming the word - which is as well because come the dawn her own exploration of her husband's wonderful body was surprisingly forthright. In the end she thought it best to remain dumb and accept the gift from wherever it was sprung.

* * *

She was woken by whispering coming from across the landing. Luke was asleep, his face toward the window, bruises dark stains about his eyes.

It was odd crossing the landing with no dog to greet her and no cold nose pushed into her hand. Matty was talking in his sleep. She knew he was asleep because although hoarse his words were easier to make out.

He was in conversation with someone discussing animals, Julia catching the words 'puppy dogs.' Then he began reciting nursery rhymes.

Oh the darling! Her heart rolled. He sounded happy and himself again! God bless him! Smiling, she leant against the door listening. First there was one rhyme and then another. Then he laughed at something that was said and he began to sing. That was when, suddenly cold, Julia went back to bed.

She would've tucked Matty in but others sang with him and a tail wagged, swish, swish, back and forth across the floor. They were best left to it.

'Oh where has my little dog gone?
Oh where, oh where, can he be?
With his ears cut short and his tail cut long,
Oh where, oh where is he.'

Buttercups

June 1902

They were doing the last of the packing when Luke found a red leather diary bottom of a tea chest. 'What's this, Anna?'

She came to the door, linen in her arms and hair tied in a knot. 'It's a diary.'

Luke leafed through. 'Whose diary?'

'Justine Newman's or rather Henry Lansdowne. I found it when we moved in. It's a chronicle of flower cuttings and seeds brought back to England, and presumably to Justine. It should stay here really. We don't want it.'

'Okay so what do I do with it, leave it on a shelf?'

Smiling, she rested the linen on her swollen stomach. 'You know you really mustn't spend so much time with Robert and Mamie Scholtz. All this "okay" and "yay" and drawling, you're beginning to sound like Buffalo Bill.'

'Does Buffalo Bill sound like that?'

'I imagine so.'

'What with a Yorkshire twang?'

'Oh it's a twang? I always thought it more a growl.'

'You're being a bit cheeky today, aren't you, Mrs Roberts?'

'No more than usual.'

'Well, enough is enough! You're coming with me.' He put the tea chest down and crossing the landing took her and the linen in his arms carrying her down the stairs and into the cart with

Ben Faulkner. 'Take Mrs Roberts to the Nelson, Ben, and don't take any argument. That's my son and heir she's carrying with that pile of linen and she needs to rest.'

There was a moment when she would've argued but seeing the sense she leaned down and kissed him - an odd moment, a reversal of a dream he used to have about Italy and mountains. He doesn't have that dream now or if he does he doesn't remember. In her seventh month and sick in the mornings she needs a bit of fussing. He's too much to do here to break away yet come the night he'll give all the fuss he can and be happy to do it. As things stand, Anna, the best beloved of Nan at the moment, she'll get plenty fuss at the Nelson.

That Mrs Roberts Senior blesses the ground under Anna's feet is because they stay in England sooner than move to Boston. They deliberated all of last year but in the end opted for England. One grandchild to smother and another on the way, Nan is over the moon and Anna the best daughter-in-law. Anna pregnant, he overloaded with work, Nan claiming she'd never see them again alive, and last but never least Matty, and his music, there was too much against it. It's likely they've good colleges in Boston but none with the influence of the Royal College of Music and none with such a patron.

The Big House is sold and the new incumbents, with stars in their eyes and visions of a line of carriages sweeping the Rise, want the cottage restored to a Gatehouse. 'It's only right, don't you agree, dear Mrs Roberts, the two should be reunited?' This from Augusta Simpkin, the new mistress of Highfields as they're calling it: 'One wouldn't want the wrong kind of person moving in.'

They came to the cottage that day, the two of them, in best

bib and tucker, Mr Mayor twirling his hat and Madame Mayoress simpering. 'Dear' Mrs Roberts was gracious and received them with a smile and a straight face. Anna showed her metal that morning and the outcome of a decent upbringing - Luke wasn't so well bred and took to the scullery laughing like a drain. The thought of those two living it large on the Rise was too funny.

'Disgustin'!' Nan wasn't in the least amused. 'I always knew him a thieving rascal. If they can afford to buy the Big House *and* the cottage think how much money he makes out of our pockets.' No question Gussy earns well as a lawyer but it's more likely Aggie's money left to her by a mother that made things possible - why else but a fat dowry would he marry her?

They have plenty nerve, that's for sure, especially Aggie who, before the telegram, couldn't bring herself to nod to either Luke or Anna. That piece of paper changed everything. It arrived the day they were wed, a knock on the door, 'Telegram for Mr and Mrs Luke Roberts!'

Mrs Mac was all of a twitter. 'Madam!' She came running in. 'It has the royal crest.' It did have a royal crest and was signed, 'for and on behalf of His Majesty, King Edward.' Though addressed to both, Luke passed it to Anna who read it, passed it back, and then asked Bertha Carmody how she would be getting home that evening and would she take wedding cake for her son.

The telegram went into Luke's pocket, the message a mystery to everyone else. The populous of Bakers End didn't need to see the content, they made it up as they went along, adding frills or taking away with the changing of the moon, so that by the beginning of this year not only did His Majesty send good wishes for their marriage and life, he sent an invitation to the Coronation.

Thus endorsed, Julia was yet again a person of note. The pendulum of public opinion continues to swing back and forth; she doesn't seem to mind. Augusta Simpkin does. 'Dear Mrs Roberts we heard a rumour you were planning to move. Does that mean the Tea-Shop is to close?' Again there were so many reasons why they let go of the N and N. Top of the list is Matty, following on his heels is the needs of a new brother or sister. 'As much as I love this,' Anna had said. 'I want to be able to enjoy both my children with a little more ease.' So the business was up for sale and within a week the Nanny Tea-shop business in American hands and the cottage to be a gatehouse.

* * *

The Greville Massons moved back to the States May of last year. If you pass Hatchards or any local bookshop you may well see Daniel Masson's handsome face on the cover on a new book, the best-seller, *The Life and Times of Daisy, Countess of Warwick.*' Other than the book is doing well, and Callie Greville Masson present at many of the book readings, very little is heard.

Dual weddings and a pregnancy resolved the issue of what to do with the maids. Leah went to Cambridge to manage the Nanny Two and is presently affianced to the greengrocer here in Bakers. Dorothy Manners, now Mrs Reginald Coates, serves behind the counter in her husband's bakery, and pretty she looks too. A new tea-shop, the Nanny Three, opens soon in Cardogan Street, Kensington; Robert Scholtz, primary mover behind the name, more such Nannies presently springing up along the East Coast of America. Mrs Mac was to be manager at Cardogan Street, yet lately wed, chooses to be with husband Ben and the Roberts in the new house in nearby Sloane Square.

'I don't mind helping out,' she says. 'It's only around the corner from the Square but the children must come first. Why would I give up care of Matty and the prospect of a new little soul to serve tea and a bun? And anyway I'm a partner in the Nanny business. Partners do not manage.'

* * *

So here they are packing the last bits before saying farewell to the Needed and Necessary. Julianna wept last night mostly out regret for past sadness. Then they got to talking of names. He said if the baby was a boy he was to be named Jacky. Anna said she didn't mind Jack but didn't want Jacky.

'Trust me,' he'd said, 'if he's baptised Jack he'll be known as Jacky.'

'Who says he's to be a he? What if he is a girl?'

'If he's a girl you shall name her.'

'I already know what she's to be called. Our daughter is to be Abigail Charlotte May Nanette Roberts.'

'That's heck of a mouthful. Why all of that?'

'To satisfy the women in our families.'

Luke didn't argue, if it keeps Anna happy he'll agree to anything except staying in Bakers. It was he who pushed to move. 'We ought to consider London. If Matty is to study at the Royal College we need to think about boarding. You can't be travelling up and down day-after-day.'

That did it. The thought of being separated from her lad

made the choice easy. Luke suspects that, like him, she feels the cottage holds on to what has gone before and that they'd all do better away.

With Mrs Greville Masson back in Philadelphia and the Big House having new owners you might think the connection between past and present broken; it abides, there are nights when the air positively buzzes and Matty is singing of stars and of dog's tails that wag. Invisible playmates don't seem to do him harm but now with Anna expecting they can offer a living playmate.

They plan to be settled in London by end of the month then it's all about waiting for the baby. His Majesty's Coronation is planned for August. It's not likely they'll get an invitation, but if they do the care and safety of Mrs Julianna Roberts and Master Jack Albert trumps even the crowning of His Royal Majesty King Edward the Seventh. If they can they'll join with others watching parades go by and they'll be glad along with everyone else because he is a fine man, and unlike many, doesn't forget a friend.

Next year when Anna and baby are able they'll holiday in Italy in the mountains and meet with new/old relatives. Ben Faulkner, the tutor cum odd-job man, who these days remains fairly sober, and Mrs Mac, the Good Fairy, accompany them everywhere. For a time they tried calling her Mrs Faulkner but it didn't work, especially with Matty referring to her as Mrs Doodle.

The Wolf has gone from the door never to be seen or heard of again. Silly but Luke misses it on Matty's lips though being called Papa makes up for it. Maggie Jeffers says there's power in a name and that she's thinking of changing hers to Simone. They still have the wretched girl and probably always will. She's going to Sloane Square though not to the kitchen, to the garden, where strangely she shows great skill, her fingers coaxing even the most jaded plant to life.

'Oh, you're not takin' her, are you?' Nan was scandalised when she heard. 'She's more trouble than a cartload of monkeys! If she hadn't left the door unlocked that scoundrel never would've got in.'

Luke would kick her out tomorrow but Anna, of the soft heart, says she feels responsible, and so what can you do.

They'll stay this last week at the Nelson and move Friday - Mrs Mac and accumulated dogs and cats and rabbits already in Sloane Square. That lady is their greatest friend, neither would be without her. It was she who phoned Luke last week telling of an exhibition at the new Tate Gallery. These days Freddie Carrington is the toast of the art world, particularly in New York, where along with John Singer Sargent the Scholtz' promote his work.

Mamie says the Carringtons have an apartment in Manhattan and spend a great deal of time there, brother and sister feted by American Society. When Luke mentioned the exhibition Anna said she wasn't up to it but that he should go. He won't be going. They'll doubtless be showing Freddie's most celebrated work, *Naked Man at the Window*. Once upon a time Luke didn't mind being laid bare before gawping strangers, now he has his children to consider.

Of course, that's just an excuse and he knows it so!

Luke went to the window and threw it open letting in the air. It's true he wouldn't want Matty to see that particular painting, Daddy with his private parts on display, but that's not why he'll stay away. In the past year or so he and Julianna have received several invitations to visit the Carringtons. Luke can't speak for Julianna but knows why he hesitates. That night on Fairy Common he learned he could be touched by a man and know pleasure, and while not inclined to repeat the experiment, prefers not to put it to the test. A man should be grateful for what he has and not flirt with temptation.

* * *

The red leather diary is on the widow-sill. Luke will find a better place for it. The people who lived here are long gone but their secrets oughtn't to be left open to prying eyes, especially those of a busybody like Agatha.

He sat on the sill and opening the diary leafed through. It was as Anna said comments about plants and seeds and how Henry Lansdowne acquired them.

For such a careless lover Henry had a particularly neat hand whereas those comments appended JN were open and flowing. Justine Newman was a clever woman, many of the notations made in the language appropriate to the country where plant or seed was found.

The Roberts are leaving much of the furniture behind. The piano, and the Meissen, are already transported to the Square, and the silhouettes, Luke wouldn't leave them behind. They will hang upon his study wall. A brief meeting and the giving of a silver sixpence, the lady in his heart forever.

He knows what to do with the diary. He'll bury it but not too close to the Wall because that is due to come down. Well done Aggie Simpkin! If that's the only good thing she does with her life it is enough. If anything can heal the wound between the Big House and cottage it is the bringing down of that wall.

* * *

Time is getting on. It's late, the night drawing on, and the sky a wonderful shade of cobalt blue. Much later and his beloved will be anxious. These days she can't bear them to be parted for long, nor for that matter can he. His heart beats better when next to hers.

The last of the chests aboard the cart he went back for his jacket and found the window had blown in and the diary on the floor, the binding split.

There was a piece of paper tucked in the back cover lining. It was a letter-heading of a firm of lawyers, Solomon Geddes & Son, Solicitors at Law, Surrey Street, Kings Lynn. There was a note scrawled on the back.

Unless you'd heard of the Newman Sisters, and the Will and the *'right of first refusal to the rightful stranger'*, the note would have no meaning. But if one understood Italian, and read between the lines, and wondered why with no particular breeze the diary should end up on the floor - and the note come to light on this, the day of leaving - then the 'rightful stranger' might think it an invitation to call at Geddes & Son to learn something to his advantage.

Then again it might be what it is, an old lady's thoughts meandering across time and space. As the note says, it's a matter of choice.

'A diary is like the earth in winter, it is filled with sleeping secrets. Some secrets should remain hidden for as with nettles they burn the hand in the pulling. Others secrets are like bulbs, they bring forth flowers to gladden the heart. In finding this diary, and compre-hending the word, La bella Italia, a secret is discovered. Knock on

Solomon's Door and another door will open.

As with all things it is a matter of choice. Things underground are often best left to their own devising, and sleeping dogs always sleep best undisturbed. The same could be said of knocking on doors, one never knows what is behind them. In the end one must decide which weighs heaviest, a silver sixpence or a bag of gold sovereigns. If the heart be light, and the purse none too thin, it might be best to let the secret sleep. In the end it is as we know - there is Purpose to all things and the Purpose is good.'

Luke pushed the note behind the lining. The doors locked, he dropped the keys through the letter box. Then he took a spade from the shed and buried the diary amid broken Meissen china and the skeleton of a beloved dog. The hole he dug might have taken Betty, his old horse, never mind a diary. But that's alright. He wants to be sure it will stay down for his life-time. And so what if an old lady was once so amused by a seven-year-old boy she thought to remember him in her Will? Why would he need a fortune when he has one already waiting in the Nelson her lovely face anxious to see him?

It's as August Simpkin said, 'if this right stranger was to step forward we wouldn't be able to buy the cottage, nor you, Dear Mrs Roberts, able to sell. It would hang in the balance and no doubt lead to all sorts of bother.'

* * *

The hole smoothed over he stood wiping his brow when the sky exploded.

'Oh my Lord!'

A shooting star sped across the horizon. First one and then another! Soon the sky was on fire with a meteor shower or some other celestial phenomenon.

On and on they flew these bolts of light. It was incredible, like Nature's Bonfire Night and a dozen Mattys with sparklers in their hands.

'Until the stars fall,' wasn't that the word to bring down the Wall?

Luke went to the cart and pulling the heaviest hammer took a swipe at it.

Nothing, not a dent! Whoever built this meant it to last. He pulled back and this time when he swung he thought of Old Joe Carmody and his hatred of the wall and the plants forever being whisked back and forth.

It was warm, the night on the edge of summer. Luke took off his shirt and swung again. This time there was movement along the top section and sand trickling. Bang, he hit it again, this time for Callie Masson and her disappointed hopes, and then again for Susan Dudley and her baby.

Soon there was a gap in the wall. A little more than a year ago Luke almost drowned. Someone or something got between him and Hell. It pleases Luke to think that it was his beloved brother, Jacky, who along with Daniel Masson helped haul him from the pit - one man alive in this world, the other ever alive in memory plus the maggot-ridden corpse of a dog.

When a thing like that happens, a second chance to live and love, it changes a man. He stops thinking of himself as alone. He knows he is loved and so is able to give love and receive – and such a love, a beautiful wife, a loving child, another on the way, good friends, and the whole of the world opening up before him. Now there is this, Luke Roberts a lone witness to the skies falling.

'Owoooo!'

He laid back his head and howled with the sheer wonder of being alive. He is grateful for the love given. At last, the Good Lord has sprung a trap – the Wolf is set free.

The End

Silent Music

Dodie Hamilton

Book One

Ricky

Camouflage

March 2005
The Grafton Theatre, Hereford.

'Blimey, Miss Ricky!' The doorman snatched the dog's leash. 'Cutting it a bit fine, aren't you!'

'The car broke down at the lights.' Ricky thrust the bag at him. 'There's her bowl and blanket. She can have one Doggobix but no more!'

'Okay I've got her! Go on, run!'

Skirts hiked and cello clutched to her chest, she ran, the doorman gazing up the stairs savouring the last sense of a lovely face and flashing stocking tops.

'I say, Miss Ricky!' he shouted - he always calls her Miss because, despite the red hair and ring through her nose, there's something old-fashioned about her. 'Watch out for Oily Webb and his slimy ways. Tell him to push off! He's no different than the rest of the lads.'

Two years that little cracker's been whizzing through the doors. Apart from Jenny Hughes, first flute, and fat Tommy Makepeace on tuba she never bothers with anyone. Some call her Ratty Tyler on account of her being unfriendly. She can be kind. Last year when Tommy Makepeace's dad was dying of cancer she went to the hospital and then to the funeral holding Mrs Makepeace's hand - you see it's not what Beauty says, it's what Beauty does.

The doorman settled the Greyhound under the desk. 'She is beautiful, ain't she, Patsy. All the blokes fancy her but she don't give them the time of day. She deserves someone with a bit of cash who can buy her a decent car instead of that rackety job. I mean, fancy it conking out, tonight of all nights.'

Tonight of all nights! Ricky raced upstairs. Until an hour ago everything was fine. The rehearsal went well and so she had time to go home and change. Then coming back BNR 275 stalled. A man offered a lift but Ricky never accepts lifts and so had to drag the cello, and Patsy, all the way here.

The changing room is chock-a-block. No time to change, she added her mess to the heap. No time either to change her Bikers for heels. Hopefully, the long skirts on her dress will hide them. She glanced in the mirror hoping her touch-me-not persona is glued on tight. When she played in Paris she had her own dressing room. Here in the Grafton everybody bundles in together. Climbing frames on the walls, and six-a-side football tramlines, is not the ideal setting for a symphony concert. A few years ago offered this as a venue she would've laughed but then the City Ensemble isn't the London Philharmonic, as she isn't the renowned cellist she'd hoped to be.

Legs pumping, she sped along the backdraught into the wings and knelt unlocking the cello case the skirts of her gown a pouched bluebell.

'Look what the tide's rolled in,' Jen Hughes, City Ensemble first flute, secretary, and general dog's body sauntered up.

'Don't ask!'

'I wasn't going to. It's the car. It's always the car.'

'It's a vintage TR4. There's bound to be the odd problem.'

'Odd!' Jen snorted. 'You should stick to the trike. You look bloody ridiculous riding that but at least it gets you here on time.'

'I couldn't ride in this.' Ricky shook out the skirts of her dress.

'Wow!' Jen whistled. 'That is gorgeous! Where did you get that?'

'The Animal Welfare shop.'

'What, the Charity shop in the High Street where the bag ladies hang out?'

'Are you likening me to a bag lady?'

'Yes.' Jen ruffled Ricky's hair. 'That or a demented Cockatoo.'

'Who looks like a demented Cockatoo?' Brian Clarke, first violin and leader of the Ensemble, pushed through the curtain.

Ricky shrugged. 'Apparently I do.'

'That's okay then. I like Cockatoos, especially the demented variety.' Brian squeezed Jenny's bum. 'And what are you doing out here, Mrs Hughes? Shouldn't you be on stage warming up?'

'I was waiting for you, Mr Clarke, to do exactly what you are doing.'

'Hussy!'

'Animal!'

'Oh please!' A new and apparently hot item, Jen and Brian are unable to keep their hands off one another. Ricky left them to it and began tuning in.

'Don't rush.' Brian yawned. 'We're to start with the Vaughan Williams instead of the Elgar. A sponsor's stuck in traffic and called asking to hold the Concerto. Naturally where money is concerned our esteemed conductor can hold anything, including his non-existent dick.'

Jen sniffed. 'The man is a moron.'

'Yes but a moron with money in his sights. Apparently, they're a racing syndicate over from Ireland. One of their party sat in on rehearsal and liked what he heard enough to buy a box for the performance.'

'Blimey!' scoffed Jen. 'They must be stuck for things to do.'

'Hey girlfriend,' Brian nudged her. 'We're not that bad!'

'We're not that good either. It's Ricky they come to hear not us.'

'Sad but true,' said Brian. 'I best get out there and organise the troops.'

'Bloody hell, Ricky!' Jen brushed her down. 'Look at all this fur! You've been at the dog pound again.'

'It's velvet. Things stick. And it's not a dog pound it's an animal shelter.'

'I don't care what it is. You can't keep baling them. You need to save your money for a better car.'

'I suppose.' Ricky shrugged and the shoulder-cuffs of her gown drooped revealing the curve of her breasts.

'Whoo!' Jen grinned. 'I wouldn't do that out front if I were you, not if you want to survive the front rows.'

'Front rows?'

'Yes! Your fan-club is here.'

'Oh no!'

'Oh yes, the Promenaders are here and all drooling at the thought of seeing you. The doorman told them to mind their manners. We're not holding our breath.' Jen nudged Ricky. 'Talking of drooling? Here comes Oily.'

'Ah Miss Tyler!' Smooth in white-tie-and-tails the musical director strolled into view. 'You are actually here. I imagine it was the car.'

'It was.'

'An uncertain beast.'

'These things happen.'

'And in your case with alarming frequency! Still...' His glance slid up and down her body, 'you're here now and as always so very beautiful. It should be a good concert. Let's hope your people behave.'

'They are not my people.'

'Possibly not, but they do follow you around. I've been reading about you on facebook. They have a page dedicated to Ravishing Ricky?'

'I don't do facebook.'

'Still without a computer? My word, you are determinedly alone. You should consider emergencies. What happens if I need to contact you?'

'If you want me, Mr Webb, I'm sure you'll find me.'

'But I do want you, Miss Tyler. We *all* want you. It's why we're here.' He tugged his tie. 'Anyway, let's hope your followers don't make a fuss.'

'If they do, it won't be Ricky's fault,' said Jen. 'Hank Tobin started this.'

'Harold Tobin is American and not expected to understand British eccentricities. Isn't it time you were on stage Miss Hughes?'

'I'm on my way.' Jen dropped a box of chocolates in the cello case. 'I came to offer Hank's customary pre-concert gift of atonement.'

'Thank you, but you needn't have bothered.' Ricky snapped. 'You can tell Hank Tobin it'll take more than a bar of Cadbury's chocolate to sweeten me up.'

'Tell him yourself,' said Jen. 'I'm not your messenger.'

* * *

The conductor hovered. 'So Miss Tyler, are you nervous about the Elgar?'

'No.'

'I understand you played the Concerto in Paris.'

'Yes.'

'And was it well received?'

'I believe so.'

'Before a knowledgeable audience?'

'Very.'

'Really?' Finger to lips, he stared. 'Mysterious lady, you have us all foxed.'

'There is no mystery. I prefer my own company.'

'Ah yes about that! A possible sponsor, a Doctor David Branagh, has asked if he might have a moment of your time after the concert.'

'I never stay after a concert.'

'Tonight is different. A soloist is required to mingle.'

'Sorry. You asked me to play. You said nothing about mingling.'

'What about the interval? I've arranged for wine and nibbles to be brought to the board room.'

'No.'

'Miss Tyler? Ricky! You have a full house tonight and a chance to show off your talent. There are VIPs in the box who, I hope, will offer a substantial grant. Surely you can give them a moment of your time?'

'The grant has nothing to do with me.'

'It's everything to do with you! It's you they plan to sponsor.'

'I don't want their money.'

'No but the Ensemble does! Concerts are expensive. We pay for the hire of music and rehearsal venue. Ticket prices don't cover it! I do what I can but can't do it all. Money earned tonight will pay for the next concert.'

'I understand that.'

'Then stay! It's not asking too much. Twenty minutes of your time is all. I mean, you come here, you're always late, sometimes you don't turn up at all, and when you do you bring your dog. Nobody complains. You have talent. Many of our players are not blessed with your musicianship but they give their all. I imagine they'd want you to do the same.'

'Alright.'

'You'll talk with the sponsor?'

'I said alright!'

* * *

Skirts folded about her knees Ricky sat in the wings. The orchestra is playing Vaughan Williams *Five Variants of Dives and Lazarus*. She'd like to be playing with them but must sit and wait. Maurice Webb asked if she was nervous. She's terrified. This venture on stage as a soloist - albeit an anonymous stage - is a first since Paris. Maurice Webb's entreaties, plus her own need to play, brought her to this point. The Elgar Cello Concerto in E-minor, opus 85, is sublime. She knows the work. She studied it for years. Mstislav

Rostropovich once held a Master-class at the Conservatoire. During the session he asked her to play the second movement and to stop when he said. She played all the way through. At the end he nodded. 'Yes,' he said, 'exactly like that.' It was the happiest day of her life. What followed was the worst.

This is her second year with the Ensemble. For amateurs they are pretty good. They have excellent musicians and a strong sense of commitment. If there is a weakness it's in Maurice Webb, the dentist with Simon Rattle dreams. Even so the Ensemble suits Ricky. Having found the world a dangerous place this demented cockatoo chooses to stay close to her cage.

A mirror hangs over the radiator. One glance and Ricky looks away. No wonder people avoid her. The mask, the scarlet hair, coloured contacts and pin through the nose, is a defence system so inbuilt she's not sure she could pull it down. Being Ricky is hard work. Last night, red dye dripping down her neck, she ached to be her natural self, but come the night and shadows, she knows blue eyes and blonde hair are infinitely more dangerous.

Hank Tobin, the first double-bass and giver of chocolate, reckons she's a Hermit Crab, a softer self hidden beneath a Harlequin shell. A fine one to talk, he played French horn with the Boston Symphony and now plays double-bass with Rent-a-Noise! What is that if not the need to hide?

The chocolate sits in the cello case. Gossip links their names, what Hat-did-with-Rat-on-the-Mat the talk of the dressing room. He is attractive, tall and rangy with bitter-mint green eyes. Jen is his foremost admirer. 'It's obvious he likes you. Why keep on about the sketch? Can't you take a joke?'

Ricky can take a joke. Hank Tobin is a gifted artist as well as a musician and sits among the orchestra sketching individual players. Last year it was Ricky's turn. It is a clever drawing, witty, a Punk Brunhilde surfing the clouds aboard a cello, Patsy, her Greyhound, in a cow-horn helmet running alongside.

It was funny, ha-ha! She laughed with the rest. Then it went on-line and the Promenaders arrived and laughter ceased.

Now she is scared and breathes deeply, trying to be calm. The dress helps, the weighty skirts and heavy blue velvet giving a sense of yesterday.

Abby, the manager of the Charity shop found it. Thursdays are Ricky's day to help out. In the back room among dog-eared books and sudden treasure she is safe. The gown is a Norman Hartnell creation, and designed when elegance was a byword and women wore elbow-length gloves.

A vegetarian, furs are anathema to Ricky as they are to Abby. 'I don't like them,' says Abby. 'A poor little fecker gave his life for this coat so I'm gonna get what I can for it!' Abby is a great support, the gown an example. A cellist must have room to manoeuvre. This is ideal, a tight bodice allowing the arms to be free and full skirts giving space for the cello. The cuffs are silk lined and grip the shoulders with the touch of a friend. So what if there is a whiff of moth-balls? It gives the sense of another age.

Last night Ricky sat in the kitchen reprising the final movement. Though raised in France she adores English music, Edward Elgar with drooping Walrus moustache her idol. Her father had a library of his work, a favourite recording of the Concerto with Jacqueline du Pres as soloist. Such genius! There was a time when Ricky dreamed of achieving similar expertise, but dreams fail, and as with the end of a rainbow, the vision retreats.

Soon it will be time to walk into the spotlight. Five years ago she stood in another spotlight, an ugly light stained with blood. Cameras flashed and reporters clamoured. It could happen again. She could walk onto the stage and be recognised and the whole damned hullaballoo starting up again.

Closing her eyes, she prayed to her Guardian Angel. 'Be with me tonight! I can't do this alone.' Then hands folded, and brow serene, Mamselle Veronique Talliere, formerly of the Conservatoire de Paris, waited for her cue.

Printed in Great Britain
by Amazon